Praise for Winona Sullivan's Sister Cecile mysteries

A SUDDEN DEATH AT THE NORFOLK CAFÉ
"The author has been a teacher and analyst for the CIA, and she has a devious mind. . . . The Boston scene, the teenager and the nun, and the dialogue are attractively written."
—*The Boston Globe*

"A smartly paced, alternately sweet and tough story that has all the moves of a gangbusting nun."
—*Kirkus Reviews*

DEAD SOUTH
"Solid prose, conniving characters, and an undercurrent of humor will leave readers eagerly awaiting Cecile's next adventure."
—*Library Journal*

"Equal doses of suspense and humor keep this tale of a kidnapped CIA agent hopping."
—*Mystery Lovers Bookshop*

By Winona Sullivan
Published by Ivy Books:

A SUDDEN DEATH AT THE NORFOLK CAFÉ
DEAD SOUTH
DEATH'S A BEACH

DEATH'S
A
BEACH

Winona Sullivan

IVY BOOKS • NEW YORK

An Ivy Book
Published by Ballantine Books
Copyright © 1998 by Winona Sullivan

All rights reserved under International and Pan-American Copyright Conventions. Published in the United States by Ballantine Books, a division of Random House, Inc., New York, and distributed in Canada by Random House of Canada Limited, Toronto.

http://www.randomhouse.com

Library of Congress Catalog Card Number: 97-094327

ISBN 0-8041-1568-0

Manufactured in the United States of America

First Edition: January 1998

10 9 8 7 6 5 4 3 2 1

This is dedicated to Edmund,
and to Ruth Cavin, my tough and wonderful teacher.

DEATH'S
A
BEACH

1

"Good night, Cecile," Leonie called to the nun.

"Good night, dear. Don't be late."

"I know. Ten-thirty."

"Be careful."

Of what? Leonie thought. She stepped out the door into the night, took a deep breath of warm air and felt a rush of freedom. She was out of there.

Leonie Drail was twelve years old with blond sun-streaked hair that hung in pale strands. Her eyes were clear blue like the water in Biscayne Bay on a sunny day, and she was gawky in a preteen way. Her father, Damien Drail, was a government agent currently on assignment, and Leonie was spending a few months living in Miami Beach with a close friend, Sister Cecile, a nun who headed a new retirement community there. Sister Cecile had been asked to keep Leonie out of trouble while daddy was chasing terrorists. In effect, the nun was Leonie's guardian.

Leonie was a good girl. She never caused any trouble for the nun.

That warm January night, Leonie went to her new friend Zoe Cabrall's house, reputedly to eat Red Baron pizza and watch a Stephen King video. It was a ten-minute walk.

Leonie drew a big bow on her lips and made a face in Zoe's bedroom mirror. "Whatcha think?"

"Cool. Pink and glossy. Mom's very expensive stuff. She'd kill if she saw us," Zoe giggled. "Know what I mean?"

1

"Right. Like I have a mother."

Leonie's mother had died when she was four. Cancer. But it was so long ago, Leonie barely remembered her.

"Sorry," said Zoe. "You have a nun. When's your dad getting back?"

Leonie shrugged. "Someday," she murmured, patting on some powder. "Too light."

"Does Sister Cecile wear lipstick?" Zoe asked.

Leonie giggled. "I saw some in Cecile's dresser drawer. She says it's sun screen but it looked like lipstick to me. Hey, I think my nose is too big. It's growing or something."

"Nuns are scandalous, my mom says. Like they wear real clothes and stuff these days. But your nun is okay, right? Does she wear a bra?"

"Of course," Leonie said, staring at her nose in the mirror. "I've looked in her dresser. Blue eye shadow or green?" Leonie ran her finger through Mrs. Cabrall's makeup. "How about both? 'Emphasize one feature to take away from another.'" she quoted from a fashion mag she had just read.

"Blend it. Watch this." Zoe darkened her lids, two toned.

"Okay, what about our hair?"

Eventually they settled into the family room with pizza and turned on the big-screen TV. Leonie felt very adult. She must look eighteen. She would show Sister Cecile when she got home. It was fun to shock the nun.

The girls ate and watched the movie. Then the telephone rang. They both jumped, pulled out from the darkest moment of the horror movie. It could be the Beach Beast on the phone, calling for a late-night assignation.

It was Zoe's boyfriend.

Zoe went to the next room with the portable telephone. She flopped down on the couch. "Raymond, I was *just* thinking about you. Whatcha doing?"

Leonie knew what was coming. Blah, blah, blah. Leonie groaned to herself. Raymond was a dork. He didn't even rate as a Beach Beast. Telephone conversations between Zoe and

Raymond usually lasted one or two hours. So she decided to go home, even though she was supposed to wait for a ride from Zoe's mom.

Leonie checked herself in the mirror as Zoe babbled on. The huge fake emerald earrings really did it. Her nose actually looked small beside them.

"Cool," Leonie said to herself. She gathered two large slices of pizza to eat on the way home. "See you later," Leonie said. "Call me tomorrow. Tell the dork hello."

Zoe waved triumphantly, one ear pressed to the telephone receiver. "Later . . ."

At ten minutes past nine it was dark. Leonie strolled down the Cabrall's walkway, leaving security behind with the low, well-locked, tile-roofed house of pink and white stucco.

Not far away, walking slowly down the beach close to the ocean, his gate unsteady, a tall, blond man spat into the water. He didn't care that his shoes were getting wet, he didn't care about much because as far as he figured it, life had ended. He was dead. One of the walking dead, he thought, and remembered days when he was a kid playing Dracula, playing vampire. He snarled, showing his teeth, then laughed. Not a cheerful laugh. It used to be fun pretending to have the kiss of death.

He lit a cigarette and inhaled deeply.

Strange thing, now that it was real, it wasn't so funny. Lately he'd been fighting the urge to get even, fighting it and losing, because life hadn't been fair to him. At least he would go down shooting. He felt the gun in his pocket. Maybe he could make a difference after all. Maybe he could do something constructive tonight. It might be fun. He began to hum.

Leonie looked back at Zoe's house, the pink and white colors visible even in the dark. It was a normal house. Unlike hers. She lived a weird life. Totally weird. Right now she lived in a place full of nuns and she wasn't even a Catholic, but she felt a warm glow for the nuns, just thinking about them.

3

Her lipstick was smeared. Pizza sauce was all over her shirt. "Piggy wiggy," she muttered and wiped her lips on her sleeve. She listened for the heavy breathing of the Beach Beast but all she heard was the rustle of wind through high palms.

She hopped along the sidewalk, doing a dance with a slice of pizza in each hand, suddenly glad she was alone and alive. There was excitement in the air tonight. She felt it, a magic sense of being on the edge. It was a night for risks with a steady wind off the ocean and the green parrots chuckling in the palms. Maybe she could sing opera at the waves or stand on her head and scream for marshmallows.

Nobody was in sight. This was the north end of Miami Beach, almost Surfside. Here there was only sand, houses, looming condos and small hotels. The beach itself was just a block and half out of the way and she wasn't expected home for an hour. She turned toward the beach.

Leonie walked to the ocean side of the island and went down an alley between the Boardwalk Hotel and a fenced-off tennis court. A path led to the water.

There it was. The ocean. Freedom. She didn't see anybody on the beach. It was just the way she liked it, a great expanse of sand and water. No people. All hers.

"Gweep, gweep!" Leonie called to some brown dowitchers pecking at sand. "Late snack time." She threw her pizza crust at the birds. Her laugh was met by the sound of the sea and the offshore breeze. The birds flew a few feet away and resumed probing for food with their long bills while Leonie Drail thought about her life.

Life. School was okay, she had a good friend, and the nun she had for a current guardian was neat. Considering everything, life wasn't too bad, she thought, and gave a very deep sigh. The huge hollow that had appeared in her heart with her father's latest assignment was not something one could fill with nuns, but the nuns did their best. She didn't even know when her dad would be back in the country, or even if he would be back. He had almost been killed not long

4

ago, and Leonie was still afraid for him. Her dad's job was dangerous.

When the man approached her, she thought it was her father, a dark, male shadow entering the edge of her thoughts. Her heart gave a painful jump. Only for an instant, because the impression didn't last. Daddy was in Cairo. Besides, this man was taller, blond, and his body was weaving.

"Stop, kid. What are you doing here?"

"Nothing." Leonie turned around and made a move back toward the muffled sounds from the Boardwalk Hotel. "I have to get Zoe," she said, and almost looked behind her as though her friend was beyond the dunes. The man was a drunk. She was suddenly scared. Terrified.

"Wait. I'll go with you. You shouldn't be alone."

He had a cultured voice, even Leonie could tell that, but it made him even more ominous.

"No." Leonie tried to run on the sand. It was impossible. Her feet sank, her legs worked twice as hard. Her heart pounded painfully. The balmy air became hot, suffocating.

He grabbed at her, catching her shirt. "I said wait."

"No. Let me go." She smelled sour breath. Beer, or wine, maybe.

"You're pretty. How much?" he asked. He caught her arm and pulled her to face him.

"What?" She didn't understand. "Let me go!"

His eyes were barely focused, his mouth twisted. She gave a quick chop to his wrist and he released her. She stumbled and fell back on the ground.

"You whores are all alike, playing games," he scoffed. "Come here."

She rose, eyes on him. "Let me leave or I'll scream," she said; her voice was a tiny whisper. She backpedaled in the sand.

That was when he shot the gun. It was crazy. A gun, just like that? The shot hit the ground. Sand kicked up, like in the movies. "Sheee," she whispered.

"Stay right there, don't move." He stepped closer, aiming

the gun at her chest. Then he lunged, jumped on her, crushed her down on the sand, knocking the breath out of her.

Leonie gasped for air. She couldn't breathe. His weight pressed her flat.

"Got you now."

She couldn't move.

2

THE man poked Leonie's chest with the gun, then tossed it aside on the sand. He pinned her shoulders down with both hands. His body crushed her, his stinking breath filled her nostrils. "Fun then dead. Got it? Dead, like me."

A drop of sweat rolled down his chin and onto her face. His fingers gripped her arms, making instant bruises.

"Why?" she gasped, totally limp. Her mind was starting to work. She had felt despair before. She had even wanted to die once, but not now. Not now. Talk. Make him talk. "Why?" she repeated. She tried to wiggle out from under him. She could barely move.

"Why, little hooker? Because I'm cleaning up Dade County. My last good deed."

"I'm not one of them." Leonie was trying to think. "I'm just a kid, dressed up, that's all." She knew that if she could move out from under him, even just a few inches, maybe she could get away and run. She had to. But he was too heavy. His wet eyes stared down at her. She knew what he saw, thick lipstick, iridescent blue and green eye shadow, rouge, huge, glassy earrings. She closed her eyes and shook her head. It was hard to think. "No, this isn't me. Please. Let me go."

He smeared her red lips with a heavy finger. "I know what you are," he slurred. His voice sounded odd, strangely inflected. He yanked on one of her earrings. She winced.

"Please," Leonie whimpered. Her mouth hurt where he had pressed too hard. Vomit rose in her throat. She was going to die.

"I'm going to kill you, kid, but first we party. You're dead anyway. I'll do you a favor."

Her eyes roved wildly, always coming back to his face, the big mouth, blond hair falling over a flat, sweaty brow. She would never forget that face for as long as she lived. And that might not be for long.

She turned her head to the side, looking away from him. She focused on the gun, tossed on a little hill of sand. It was just waiting to kill her, after everything else.

Maybe she could reach the gun. Daddy had taught her about guns. She could kill him! It was a chance. She had to get it.

One of her arms was free, splayed out on the sand. Her fingers wiggled slowly. Closer and closer. He didn't notice. His eyes were on her. She felt his hands yank and rip her shirt down the front. He was moving very slowly and deliberately as though he had all the time in the world.

Maybe he did, but it sure didn't seem like she did. Time was going to be up very soon.

Leonie's eyes focused on her attacker's arms, long blond hairs wet with sweat. The hairs looked like tiny snakes on his arms crawling down to his hands. Don't look at the gun. Don't look!

Her blind fingers reached for the gun. Strange whimpering sounds came from her mouth. She felt the gun stock, the barrel, the trigger. Her hands fumbled until she got her index finger on the trigger. Quick. She pulled the gun close to her chest. Aimed it fast. She had to kill him. Now. Just like the cowboys, the Masked Avenger, the Terminator.

The gun was aimed. Time stopped.

Nothing.

She couldn't shoot. It was pointed right at him and she couldn't do it.

7

She was going to die.

He saw the gun and his eyes opened wide in shock. With a sudden motion he wrenched it out of her hand. She let it go, easy. Too easy. It was all over. He had the gun.

One last chance. With every ounce of strength she possessed she gave a violent lurch. It wasn't enough to dislodge him, but he tilted off balance and his hands clutched at the gun for support. The gun was still aimed directly at his chest. His thick fingers pressed hard, looking for balance. The gun went off. A bullet, its sharp crack dulled by ocean waves thudding in the distance, entered his heart.

The man stared down at her wax features. He saw tears welling up in her pale blue eyes. That was the last thing he saw before his body toppled down at an angle, his torso off to her right, his legs still straddling her.

The gun landed on her chest, dropped from dead fingers. Leonie felt the cold weight smack her. She cricked her neck to see it, then picked it up, the dead man fallen half across her body, pinning her to the sand.

Flat on her back, Leonie held the weapon up and stared at it, a shadow gun thrown into sharp relief against the night sky. The gunshot still reverberated in her ears. Everything her father had ever taught her about firearms flashed through her mind in a split second. Dangerous. Deadly. Guns. They kill.

Like this one had.

Leonie was stuck under the man. She was sure he was dead, and for a flash she felt incredible exultation because she was very much alive. Then it turned to terror. She could see his eyes, blue orbs, wide open, fixed on the sky. His blood, seeping out beside her, soaked into the sand.

"Holy jeepers," Leonie gasped. Finally she pulled herself out from under him and stood up. She took long, shuddering breaths, conscious that her ears were ringing.

"What happened?" she muttered. "That guy. Dead." She shook all over, talking to herself. "Stop it, stop it."

Leonie talked to herself, words pouring out to nobody while

she rubbed a finger up and down the gun barrel, rubbing off a smudge of blood. Her eyes roamed the beach. No people. He was dead and somehow it was all her fault. She had killed him. Somehow.

She stared down at the body. The eyes were still open. His clothes: a suit, a blood-soaked white shirt, sandy, wet leather shoes, and there were those huge, hairy hands that had touched her. Bile rose in her throat.

"I didn't do it," she said again, talking to nobody. "I couldn't. Remember? Stupid jerk did it himself. I didn't kill that guy."

The sweat dried on her skin, the gun became glued to her hand. She drew the pistol closer and looked at it in the half-light of the warm January night. She felt the power in it, smelled the spent gunpowder and noticed the gun was shaking, or maybe it was her. Crickets whirred and the few mosquitoes in the brushy section of the beach hummed. The ringing in her ears faded and there was sound.

Leonie wanted to throw the gun into the ocean. Instead she dropped it. What was she going to do? What should she do? Maybe she should call someone. Was there a pay phone?

Was there something about her that had caused this? Did he know her?

He was tipped sideways and she saw the shape in his back pocket. Wallet shape. She pulled it out, fumbled, and opened it, looked at the face, looked at the dead man. Read the name in the dim light. Shook her head. "No." The face on the driver's license seemed to look at her. "Elliot Barclay," she read. Never heard of him. He had a lot of credit cards, and now his wallet had her fingerprints.

"Shit," she whispered and looked around her, spotting a plastic sandwich bag half-buried in a dune. She grabbed it, held the wallet with the plastic and rubbed it on her shirt to wipe off the prints. Latent prints! What if they connected it with her?

"Daddy, get home," she whispered. Why couldn't he be here?

She didn't want the wallet so she stuffed it back in a front pocket instead of where she found it because she didn't want to feel Elliot Barclay's still-warm backside again. She poked other pockets with her foot. It was essential that she know this man. He had died on her. He owed her, somehow. He had tried to rape her and she didn't even know what that meant. Well, she had an idea, but not really.

"What if a guy tries to do it?" Zoe had asked her earlier that night. "What do you think it's like?"

"It." She thought about rape, her body tightening inside, her features tensing as she struggled for control.

From his suit-coat pocket she pulled out a paper: a computer printout, numbers and names. She stuffed it in her dungaree-shorts pocket. Maybe she was going crazy.

Looking down, she realized there was blood on her shorts and T-shirt, and that her shirt was ripped halfway down her chest, exposing underdeveloped breasts. "He wanted 'it,' " she whispered again, but why had he wanted to kill her? And why had he died?

"Shit," Leonie sobbed. "Damn, damn Elliot Barclay." She cried, wiping tears on her ripped shirt.

Still weeping, she kicked sand in Elliot Barclay's face until it was covered. Then she took the plastic bag and reversed it around the gun, making a neat package. She didn't want to leave the gun on the beach, or even throw it in the ocean where some swimmer might find it. Someone else might get hurt. She would put it somewhere so the seagulls could poop on it. Forever.

But she couldn't move. Paralyzed, she just stood and sobbed.

3

LEONIE cried into the wind and no one heard her except a few evening birds. Time passed; the night air off the ocean blew cool and sweet, sweeping the panic from the child as she stared blankly at the waves rolling along the sand. She could feel layers of fear leaving her, one layer at a time until she could breathe again. But not even a hurricane could blow away the guilt.

Leonie Drail grabbed the edges of her shirt and drew them together to cover herself. She walked away from the corpse. The packaged gun was still in her hand. The expression on her face was calm under the tear stains, her eyes looked dead in the dim light, almost as dead as Elliot Barclay's. Nobody was anywhere. The killing had been just a bang in the night. Like she would have been, she thought. Another bang in the night.

She buried the gun. She found a place beside a sea grape tree and dug down with an old can, making a grave. There were a few old shells in the grave, a scrap of shiny paper, and the gun. She filled the hole again with sand, smoothed the sand with her foot, then tossed trash over it. Still no one on the beach. She was safe.

Twenty minutes later Leonie let herself into the front door of the Maria Concilia Retirement Community. It was ten-thirty on a Friday night. The whole world was room temperature, seventy-two degrees outside, seventy-two degrees inside, but she was freezing cold.

The old nuns would all be snoring in their rooms; Sister

Cecile would probably be in the common room reading a book, waiting up for her. Just like a mother. Just who Leonie didn't want to see right now. But she must.

Leonie took the back hall to her room, tiptoeing all the way. She had her own bathroom. She locked the door and began to scrub off all the makeup and the blood, even though her hands were shaking and her teeth rattled like hail on car windows. Her face was completely streaked with grime and tears. She cleaned herself thoroughly, making huge piles of bubbles, submerging her hands and arms into a filled sink trying to wash the man off. Then she held a cold washcloth to her eyes to get rid of the redness.

Finally satisfied, she put on some fresh shorts and a clean shirt. She took off her earrings and patted carefully at the blood on her ear. It hurt. She brushed her hair down over the injured ear. She wadded up her bloody clothes and stuffed them into her bottom dresser drawer. Finally she stopped shaking.

She walked into the common room nonchalantly, as though she had been home for hours. There was only one light on, the one beside Sister Cecile's chair. Thank goodness the nuns were always turning off lights. "Hi, Cecile." Her voice quaked on the edges, but Sister Cecile was deep in the Bible and didn't appear to notice.

"Leonie? Have a good time?" Sister Cecile put down her reading.

"Sure. Zoe got pizza. We watched a movie." Leonie didn't even try to smile. It wouldn't have worked. But the words were coming out okay, the rough edges of sound were softer than her raw nerves. She turned a little so her ear was away from the young nun. Leonie's eyes strayed to a discarded newspaper resting on the coffee table before her. She turned pale, then quickly looked at a blank window, forcing her eyes to notice reflections from the room.

Cecile looked at her ward carefully. Too carefully for Leonie's liking, so Leonie digressed, ignoring the sudden pounding of her heart, the overwhelming urge to burst into tears. She had to distract the nun.

"How come you're up so late? Couldn't you sleep?" Leonie asked. She wondered if her eyes were too puffy.

"Actually I was waiting up for you. I worry."

"I know," Leonie said. "Nowhere is safe."

"True," Cecile sighed. She stood up. "I'm always relieved when you get home. We should both go to bed now. Father Hanna is coming for an early mass tomorrow and I have some business to go over with him afterwards. Oh, and Sister Germaine left a piece of cake for you under the cake cover."

Cake. Leonie felt her stomach rise at the thought. No way could she eat a piece of cake. "Oh, good. I'll check it out. G'night, Cecile."

Somehow she came over to the nun and gave her a hug in the dim light. The hug was a little longer, a little tighter than usual. Leonie couldn't help it.

"G'night," Leonie repeated and headed for the kitchen. She heard Sister Cecile's "Good night, darling," and then the sound of a door closing. She was safe. Tears started sliding down Leonie's face all over again. Would she ever be safe again?

In the kitchen, Leonie flipped on the light and blinked to stop the tears. She waded through the huge space. "Cake, cake, cake. I have to eat cake."

It was a giant kitchen, kept intact when Sister Cecile's religious order had bought the old motel for a retirement home for elderly nuns. Leonie knew how Sister Cecile had arranged for the purchase of the motel, and now, only months later, the young nun was actually running the home, trying to make it work, filling the place with old nuns and a few paying guests.

And taking care of her, temporarily, Leonie thought, staring blindly up at the stainless-steel pots and pans hanging over a central island. She had grown used to the kitchen, the huge refrigerator and freezer always humming on one side of the room like two friends talking, two huge stoves winking pilot-light messages on the other. There was a major air vent over each stove and a ceiling fan at either end, as well as air-conditioning ducts that continuously blew out cool air. The room was alive,

13

and generally a comforting place to be. Tonight it was cold. Leonie was freezing, and she had to deal with a piece of cake.

The cake was enthroned in the middle of the long central table, covered with a huge glass cake lid. Sister Germaine, their incredible French cook, spoiled Leonie, and Leonie knew that the cake would be something fabulous. She lifted the cake lid.

Rich chocolate fudge was piled over a double chocolate cake, three layers, all perfectly arranged. Leonie felt like throwing up. She took a spoon from the silverware drawer, sat down at the table and mushed the cake on the plate. The spoon rattled on the china. Her hands were shaking again. Leonie rubbed a small piece of chocolate on the edge of her mouth just in case she ran into someone. Finally she took the cake and scraped it into the trash. The dish went in the sink where she rinsed it lightly and left it for Sister Germaine to see the evidence, a plate with chocolate smears on it.

Leonie returned to the common room. The place was lively during the day. Now a vast, empty space spread out before her, zebra stripes on the old Dade County pine floors were cast by lights against palms outside the windows. Cecile had gone to bed.

Leonie went to the coffee table and flipped on the table lamp. She picked up the newspaper. There was a photograph of a man on the front page.

Him.

She read the article.

It was about Elliot Barclay, executive vice president of the Royal Leaf Bank of Canada, its American branch located here in Miami. He was attending a major conference at the Miami Beach Convention Center. "Representing over $265 million in assets, Barclay is expected to recommend further investment in several Dade County development projects," Leonie read. " 'Investments here will be sort of stepchildren.' Barclay explained at the convention Thursday night. 'We expect to engender a good amount of local initiative in the projects. Hand in hand in North America. I'm particularly interested in the welfare of children. Pediatric centers will be our primary local investment as your health care system expands.' "

"Oh, right," Leonie muttered. That man was very interested in children. Not that she was a child. She was almost a teenager. Apparently that had been the problem tonight. She bit her lip as a hiccup bubbled up from within her chest; it was almost a sob. She'd like to tell them all what this man was really like. Bad. And dead. And he deserved to be.

"Elliot Barclay," she whispered as she tossed the newspaper back on the table. Elliot Barclay, the banker, was dead.

Finally Leonie went to her room and sat down on her bed and wept. Not for the man she couldn't kill, but for her father, who just wasn't there when she needed him.

4

"HE's dead." A loud sob came over the telephone. Desk Sergeant Peele held the receiver back and rubbed his ear.

"What? Who is this?"

"It's me. Amy." A howl ripped through the policeman's brain. It was his daughter, his beloved, only daughter.

"Who's dead? God, Amy, what's wrong?"

"Elliot's dead. They killed him, Daddy. You've got to get him. Get him! The bastard that killed my Elliot."

"Elliot? Elliot Barclay?" The policeman was aware of the body found on the beach. He even had heard the victim's name, but Elliot Barclay had only been a name mentioned by his daughter that had never actually stuck in his mind. He hadn't connected it to the latest local death. Of course he remembered now.

15

"I loved him, Daddy. I did."

Reggie Peele understood everything at once. His daughter was an important woman. She had loved an important man. The facts cut like razors into his heart. Elliot Barclay was dead.

"Amy, I'll fix it."

"Kill him. Make the killer suffer." Amy stopped sobbing.

"I will, Amy. My baby, my sweetheart." Desk Officer Reggie Peele made soothing sounds into the telephone. "I'll do it."

"Find his killer," Amy sobbed. "I *want* the killer."

"You'll have him," her father vowed. "I'll get him for you."

"Promise?" She sounded better all ready. "Kill him for me. Make him suffer."

"I will. I promise. I'll find out everything. I'll look into it right now."

"I can't stand this, Daddy."

"I'll get right on it. Don't you worry."

The policeman hung up. He rested his head in his hands and thought. Damn, but this was a killer situation. In more ways than one. One of the detectives walked in, and the old policeman turned to address him. "Ruiz, what do we have on that Barclay death?"

Leonie Drail's current guardian, Sister Cecile, had spent her entire life being a female. The waves of feminist thought, of antifeminism, of studies, pronouncements, psychologists proclaiming that women were absolutely equal to men, had flowed over her like water, slowly wearing paths into her psyche. Of course she had grown up thinking men ruled the world, having been born at a time when men actually did. It had been said that men were smarter than women, stronger. Everything, in fact, except more intuitive. Now, however, Sister Cecile knew the truth. She had decided to stop playing dumb for the world. Today, in fact, she felt new resolve. But the real problem she had now was not exactly related to feminism; it was motherhood. Motherhood had arrived suddenly, like a bomb, only a few months ago. And Leonie was not a baby.

Temporary though this situation was, Cecile took it seriously. Damien would come back and reclaim his daughter all too soon. But for now Leonie was hers, and Cecile loved the girl like a daughter. More, in fact. How could a mother love a child more than she loved Leonie? How could she stand so much love without bursting? It interfered with her life, with her thoughts, even with her praying. Was real motherhood that devastating and wonderful?

"Something's bothering Leonie," Cecile said.

"How do you know?" Sister Raphael was at the computer, loading in columns of figures as she graphed profits and losses for the month. The retirement community had only been open six weeks but things were looking good. A disorderly pile of papers was stacked to the old nun's right, a cup of herbal tea was in her hand. "Municipal bonds, no," she muttered, and set the cup down on the table. She made some marks on a paper beside the keyboard, then punched some keys, her liver-spotted hands flying.

Sister Raphael was in her seventies, a retired mathematics professor from Boston College. She kept the American branch of the Order of Our Lady of Good Counsel solvent when she wasn't knitting booties for grandnieces and -nephews.

"She was only on the telephone for five minutes," Cecile replied, making herself comfortable on the office chair. "I heard her say something like she had to do her homework. And when Sister Moira asked her how old she was last night at supper, she said she was twelve. Leonie always tells people she's thirteen. Why suddenly twelve? Something's the matter. I saw it in her eyes when I asked her about school. She was evasive, almost sullen. Like a teenager."

Sister Cecile stood up and paced.

"Leonie is twelve," Raphael said.

"I know. Usually she doesn't admit to that."

"Well, her best friend here, Zoe, has a boyfriend," Raphael noted and wrote down, "Deutsch-Südamerikaanishes, invest!"

"So what. Leonie had a boyfriend last week. These things come and go at that age."

"This is a very difficult age." Raphael argued. "Zoe talks to

17

Raymond for hours. Literally hours. Leonie told me all about him. He has pimples. Zoe probably had to take his call so Leonie hung up. And not being quite as interested in boys as her friend Zoe, maybe Leonie feels twelve."

"No," Cecile said. "She feel thirteen. I asked her. Anyway, Leonie went out to the common room and read the newspaper. She's been out there every night this week. Reading the newspaper. No telling what she'll find."

"Probably reading the comics. I love Dilbert. Maybe she's discovered Dilbert?" Raphael asked.

"No, it's not the comics. I very casually wandered behind her when she was doing it, and it was the news. I mean, what on earth would inspire her to read that? It's just not like her."

"I wouldn't worry. It might just be a sign that she's growing up, Cecile. Starting to be aware of the world around her. It's not a nice world, and with Damien on the other side of the globe, Leonie is stuck living with a bunch of nuns. We do tend to be rather insular. It's got to be hard for her. Maybe she's worried about her father and she's looking for news of that area."

"Damien does love her. He tries to be a good father. The man is doing a difficult job for his country and Leonie is aware of that," Cecile worried. "To have your father almost blown up by terrorists. It has to be wearing."

"She's surrounded by love here," Raphael pointed out.

"True. We love her. Sister Germaine loves her," Cecile muttered. She sat down again.

"We all love her. But suddenly she's an adolescent being raised by nuns. At least temporarily. It's like something out of the nineteenth century," Raphael pointed out. "Or perhaps the seventeenth century." The old nun nodded as she spoke, then ran her fingers over the computer keys to bring up another file. Strings of stock listings appeared on the screen. "You're doing fine with her, Cecile. Leonie misses her dad; maybe she even still misses her mother after all these years, but she's fine here. More girls should be brought up in the convent, the *vita consecrata*. She's fine."

"I agree. So what is it? I mean, it's more than just a newspaper. Something is seriously wrong. I can feel it. We have to find out. I have instincts." Sister Cecile's hands fluttered as she spoke. She did have instincts, strange insights that appeared by magic each time she looked at Leonie's face and at the strange blank look that had appeared in the girl's eyes recently. This was a far cry from the businesslike person Sister Cecile portrayed to the outside world. Or her nun side that prayed late into the night, part of the "common life" of the sisters. She was learning about being a mother, even if it was only a temporary state.

"Maybe she has a social studies project? Maybe she needs a man in her life. She's used to being with Damien. She needs a father-type. Do we know any men? Do you?" Sister Raphael asked.

"Men? None in Miami. Paul, if he were here. He would be a wonderful father. I wish he'd marry."

"He wants to marry you," Raphael pointed out. "Boston lawyer, your best friend, he'll never give up."

"True. I wish he would. Meanwhile I'll have to find a man for Leonie. Definitely a father-type. Someone to take her to baseball games. Her father's due back in a month, but that's not a certainty. I'll find her a substitute."

"Perhaps." Raphael murmured, looking back at her computer screen. "Maybe you could interest her in one of your cases. Maybe she's just bored."

"I don't have a case right now. Not even a case in sight."

"Well, I'll just have to pray for one. An interesting case."

Sister Cecile stared at the older nun. "Please don't."

Sister Raphael smiled softly and nodded her old head. "Just a little prayer. Then we'll see."

5

SISTER Cecile was provincial head of the Sisters of Our Lady of Good Counsel, an order of nuns based in France. While Sister Raphael crunched numbers, Cecile worked on the community newsletter. It kept the nuns in touch with one another; with the order's branches in Boston's Dorchester, in several southern states, and now the new retirement home in Miami, Florida. Each location sent in news of its own work, each partaking in the wellspring of union with Christ that religious orders strived after. Sister Joan coordinated the news, but Cecile had her own small column where she kept all the nuns informed about the new retirement home.

"We expect to break even next month," she typed slowly. "Besides our retired sisters we now have several independent elderly here, who are looking for a safe and Catholic community."

"Safe in Miami . . . safe Miami is an oxymoron," Cecile remarked to Raphael as she typed. "Or are we all just morons?"

"Morons. But we do our best," Raphael said.

"So far, in our seventeen available suites we have six retired sisters, three women, and two octogenarian couples," Cecile wrote. "I'm not counting you as old, Raphael. And I'm not mentioning Leonie."

"Fine." Raphael kept working.

Cecile knew her friend wasn't even listening, but she continued contemplating her order. The Order of Our Lady of Good Counsel was originally formed to counsel the daughters

20

of the rich and aid them in spiritual and material difficulties like unplanned pregnancies, but today members of the order did many things. God's will was everywhere, their founder had said in 1859, and with this mandate, the sisters' work had grown to cover unusual roles. "Wherever the Spirit leads us," Mère Sulpicia said in the Generalate's annual newsletter from France. The second mandate had led Sister Cecile in the direction of being a private detective. It was a serious profession and filled much of her time when practical; nuns had to make money these days.

"I'm a mother, too," Cecile said as she put away the newsletter. "I have to deal with that."

Raphael ignored her.

"Now what," Cecile said when her telephone rang.

"Hello, Cecile. It's Paul."

Paul Dorys was Cecile's lawyer; he handled her multimillion-dollar trust fund which, according to her father's will, could not be spent on "religion of any kind." It troubled Cecile that she could not use the funds to help her order but she did try to be as charitable as possible by contributing to secular projects.

Paul was more than her financial advisor; she considered him a dear, good friend. It was his misfortune that he had fallen in love with her. They managed to cope with the situation with some light banter, but because she knew how he felt his calls always made Cecile uneasy. It was good, though, to hear his voice.

"Paul! How's Boston? How are you?"

"Good. Pining away for you as usual." Paul sighed audibly. "Why don't you come back home?"

Cecile laughed. "Don't be silly."

"I'm not being silly, as you well know. Do you have your license yet?"

Gun license? Private investigator's license? Paul knew what she was. She felt a charge of excitement at his words. Something must be up. "Yes. Now I'm a legal private investigator in Florida. And I took your advice. I got a gun. But I don't like it,

Paul. Nuns shouldn't carry guns. I pray I'll never have to use it. In fact I've locked it in the convent safe."

"Good place. Actually I meant a marriage license. You and me. How about this weekend?"

She played it lightly. "I'm afraid I'm busy, Paul. There's a meeting with the chamber of commerce coming up then. Older people stuff for our community. Buying power, discounts, all that. And praying. We do a lot of that. I'm still a nun."

"Darn," Paul said. "Listen, I have a case for you. Something very big. Something very discreet."

"Tell me." The chill she had anticipated became a reality. Paul rarely called *just* to propose. This was business.

"An international banker was shot. Not far from you, actually. You may have heard the name. Elliot Barclay?"

Sister Cecile closed her eyes for the barest fraction of a second, recalling the recent news. "Yes," she said. "It wasn't far from here. It's frightening. What about this man?"

"Rumor has it Elliot Barclay's was not a tourist killing. He was a banker with some very big accounts; he had a half a dozen names of investors lined up for his corporations, and another bank wanted the business. Plus he was in a strange little group of international investors located in Miami calling themselves the Benthamite Consortium. Strictly confidential, this group."

"You're saying this man had enemies?"

"Big enemies. The Miami international banking industry as a whole doesn't believe Barclay died from a random act of violence, but the local authorities do. The police are busy chasing all the drug dealers in Miami Beach, local gang members, and such. Barclay was shot with an eight-millimeter bullet. A prostitute was shot the preceding night with exactly the same type bullet, and ballistics say it was from the same gun. Not too common for the streets, and not a clue about the gun. Still, the cops blame a street gang."

"That's normal around here," Cecile said. "There are ninety-four known street gangs in Dade County. Some of them are all female. Some may even carry eight-millimeter guns. What's the problem?"

"The prostitute killing makes it look like local toughs. However the Benthamite Consortium that I mentioned got together a few days ago when it seemed the police were making no headway on the case. The consortium would like this death investigated their way and decided to hire a private detective to look into it. They're looking for someone of complete incorruptibility. They put a search out all over the country. Couldn't find anyone to trust in Miami. Miami verges on Third World, as you must know by now. They figure they might be actually hiring the killer to investigate the killing if they went local."

"Yes," Cecile agreed. "They might. Gun-for-hire is a fad here these days. But we do have good people here, really. Miami is not primitive."

"You say. Anyway, I know someone high up in banking here in Boston," Paul continued. "That someone knew about you and about our connection, so I put out your résumé with some recommendations, and they went for it. You can have the job, if you pass the interview. Are you willing to investigate Elliot Barclay's death?"

Sister Cecile was quiet for a moment. She didn't know Miami that well yet; it had only been four months since she had left Boston, two months since she had gotten a Florida driver's license, one month since her investigator's license had come through. Her connections were reliable, but few.

"Of course I'm willing. How much?" She looked down at the depressing gray cement floor in her office. She wanted parquet floors in all the rooms for the old sisters. Tile and stone were hard on arthritic feet. They were running short on funds for renovations. She needed this job.

"Three-fifty a day plus expenses. I upped your rates."

"Did they flinch?"

"Hardly. These men are major money. I should have doubled your price."

23

"You're a dear, Paul. How do we handle it? Who do I see?" Cecile picked up a pencil and a scrap of paper to write on.

"The Benthamite Consortium's new capo. Man named Manuel Beaumont at the French Banque du Paix." Paul read off the number to call. "Tell him you were sent by Ms. Marcia Munnari. Got that?"

She repeated the names, number, and bank. "Got it. Thanks, Paul."

"Sure. Be careful. This consortium, it's odd. Another member died a year or so ago. Accidental death, if there is such a thing."

"I'm very careful, Paul. And I pray."

"I'm beginning to think it works. Now if only there were a God . . ."

"There is, Paul. You'll see."

"Bye, Cecile."

Cecile hung up happily. A case meant money for the convent. Sister Raphael's prayers must have been answered already, she thought. And this might be the very case to intrigue Leonie. Something to take the child away from her problems. Just the thing. A local murder! Elliot Barclay.

Sister Raphael looked up from her computer. "Well?"

"Maybe a job."

"Money?"

"Yes. Good money."

"Good money? Is that another oxymoron?" Raphael asked.

"I hope not," Cecile said. "I sincerely hope not."

6

LEONIE Drail had a compulsion to go back to the place where Elliot Barclay had died. She walked by the sea grape tree and the sandy path after school for five days in a row. It wasn't far out of the way from her usual route from school to home. She just had to cross the street and go up to the beach along the path beside the old Boardwalk Hotel. She walked slowly, looked at the sea grape tree, scuffed the sand, and wondered if the gun was still there. Then she would go up across the small wooden walkway over the dunes and down to the ocean, bypassing the area in the sand where she had left the body.

She hadn't told anyone what had happened, not even Zoe. The death was a horrible weight on her mind. She cried every night and when Sister Cecile asked her if there was some problem with her eyes, that they seemed puffy, Leonie told her she had allergies. "I had them in Washington every spring," she affirmed.

She knew she should tell the nun everything, but like many victims of rape, or near-rape in this case, Leonie blamed herself. Cecile would probably say it was all her fault for wearing makeup, for going out on the beach at night. Well, it *was* her fault, Leonie was certain about that. She should never have gone out on the beach. Sister Cecile would kill her if she knew. And now that horrible man was dead.

Leonie knew about death. Death was very tough, but she knew how to deal with it. Her mom was dead. This guy was very different from her mom. He had deserved to die. He would have killed her. He had told her that much. It had been his own fault that he was dead. Really.

Today Leonie felt like facing it. She walked right beside the place where she had left the body, then she went down to the ocean and stood looking out at the warm sea. Water temperature was seventy-three degrees; she had heard it on the news last night. She could just walk right in; it was like a cool bath. She could keep going forever. She loved the ocean. Florida people didn't realize that you could still swim in late January, that the ocean was always welcoming. Even on a cool day like today, the water looked very inviting.

She tossed her schoolbag and shoes behind her on the beach and walked out into the clear aqua water. It felt wonderful. She was on her way out to Cuba, or maybe Bimini. Whatever. She would really like to keep going forever, she thought.

The girl walked through the slowly deepening ocean, gasping as it rose over her stomach, balancing by holding her arms out to either side, running her hands along the gradually rising surface of the water. For some reason she thought of Sister Germaine. Sometimes Leonie hung out in the kitchen and helped cook with Germaine, and while she worked they talked. Germaine was really okay. Very okay. They had great talks.

She didn't really notice as the sand beneath her feet dropped lower and the water rose higher.

Sister Raphael was wonderful, too, like a grandmother who read comic books, played on the computer and knit fuzzy things. Leonie's eyes were half-closed and the soft wind blew against her cheeks. It felt good on her tear-weary eyes. And Sister Cecile was definitely her new mother. She loved Sister Cecile a lot and they usually talked every night before she went to bed. Maybe she should tell Cecile absolutely everything. Maybe the nun actually would understand.

"Blub."

Leonie took in a mouthful of water. She had gone right up to her neck without thinking, and a wave had come up. She tipped to the left. Suddenly a strong hand grabbed her, a muscular arm wrapped around her, bearing her up.

26

"Hang on, you'll be fine. I got you," a voice said.

Leonie felt herself being lifted by the strongest arms she had ever felt. A bear, she thought. A huge bear. For some reason she wasn't afraid. It wasn't like the other night. Up in the air, over the water and out, water streaming down her face, hair in her eyes. The bear carried her out of the sea and onto the beach, talking all the while. "I got you. Don't worry kid, you're going to be just fine. Right up on the sand here."

She was finally plopped down on the hard, wet beach where the waves came and went and tiny shells collected in little ridges. She turned and faced a huge, fully dressed, very wet policeman. They stared at each other for half a minute while Leonie blinked seawater from her eyes.

"Were you committing suicide?" he asked.

"Uh, no. I mean, it sounds silly, but I forgot where I was for a minute." Leonie was totally embarrassed. How dumb could you get. And this guy would think she was some dodo-type Kevorkian kid. She shuddered at the thought. "I got some living to do," she said, chin up, eyes straight at his, because he had scrunched down to meet her, putting his face at her own level.

He took a hammy hand and pushed her straggly hair off her face.

"I can see that. Feel better now?"

"I feel silly." She would never have said that to anyone, but this ham-handed man looked amazingly nice with his black hair slicked back by water, his tan skin, water dripping off his wide chin. He was a cop, too. He had on a uniform. Suddenly she shook convulsively.

"Cold?"

"No."

"What's on your mind?"

She almost blurted it out. I was right here when a man died. Right under him. Arrest me, officer.

"Nothing," she said.

"What's your name?"

"Leonie Drail."

27

"You shouldn't walk out here alone, Leonie Drail."

"It's daytime." She looked back at the beach. There were a few walkers, a few loners jogging. In the distance there was even a family with kids. It was a perfect Florida day. It looked great. She shrugged. She tried to look happy, but she didn't.

"Man was killed here last week," the policeman said.

"I know."

"So, it's dangerous."

"That was nine thirty-five at night. I wouldn't be out here then. I'm not dumb. Everyone knows what the dealers do over there." She pointed at the public toilets just behind some attractive bushes and surrounded by leaning coconut palms. "People do more than go to the bathroom in those places," she added. She was talking big. Ordinarily she wouldn't have said something like that to anyone, but Leonie actually liked cops. Her father was an almost-cop. He was a government agent, and that was even better than being a cop. If only she could talk to her father.

"Smart kid," he said, but he was frowning. This kid had just said something very odd and he was filing it away to think about later. "My name is Detective Cypress. Jim Cypress. Call me Jim." Then he added, because she was just a kid, "I'm a Miccosukee."

"No kidding. This your beat?" Leonie moved back and forth on the sand, making dents with her bare feet. She was dripping wet and had had enough of the conversation. It was time to leave. She glanced over to see if her schoolbag and shoes were still where she had dropped them.

"More or less. I'm looking into the murder."

"How come you're wearing a uniform? I thought detectives wore plain clothes."

"They do. I'm disguised as a cop."

"Bad disguise. Nobody talks to cops. Besides, you're all wet." Leonie was being flippant. She didn't want to be, but she was nervous and it came out that way.

"I was saving you from drowning. You're wet, too."

Leonie laughed. Suddenly she looked beautiful. Twelve years old, almost a woman, she had no idea how she looked to the police detective. She had perfect teeth, the beginnings of a womanly figure made clear by the wet white school-uniform blouse and short plaid skirt that clung to her thin body. Her sun-bleached hair was already starting to dry with long wisps blowing back from her face, and her nose was definitely not too big.

"So, you'd better go home and change," she said before he could, and she turned to walk back toward the boardwalk and the place on the beach where she had left her bag and shoes. Leonie plastered a smile on her face. He would never guess what was going on inside her. She hoped.

"What will you tell your mom?" Jim Cypress asked, coming along next to her.

Leonie shook her head. "No mom. Sister Cecile."

"You live with your sister?"

Leonie shook her head. She didn't want to explain. "Sister, Sister, Sister," she said. It was a hazy way of saying she was living with a whole convent full of nuns. "I gotta go. See you 'round." She picked up her backpack and shoes from the sand and kept walking until she was at the long, coral rock wall that separated the beach from the parking area. She hopped up on the wall, an awkward motion that half tipped her over. She dusted the sand off her feet so she could put on her shoes.

From where he stood and dripped seawater Jim Cypress watched her, then he came over and sat beside her. She edged away with a jerk and put a sneaker on. She tied it very slowly, concentrating on each loop.

"Heard anything about the murder?" he asked.

"Elliot Barclay?" Her voice came out cold. "No. The kids at school talked about it last week. Not this week. It's old."

"They don't know anything? No gang's bragging?"

"No, none of that." She sounded very positive.

"No kid saw anything?"

"How should I know?"

29

"Kids talk."

"Not to cops, they don't," Leonie said firmly. She put on the second sneaker and fumbled with the lace. Sometimes her fingers couldn't do anything.

"How about you? Do you talk to cops?"

Leonie didn't like this conversation. It was making her very nervous. She picked up her backpack and slung it over her shoulders. Her shoe was still untied. She shook her head and made a face. One trick she had learned from her father was that when you didn't want to answer questions you asked them yourself, so she did. "What was that Elliot Barclay doing out here that night?" she asked. "What business did he have out here? Wasn't he staying at one of the fancy places back that way? He was just asking for it. Everyone knows that."

Leonie gestured toward the Fontainebleau Hilton, the Doral, the Eden Roc and all the other towering buildings that stuck up like the Rocky Mountains on the way to the art deco district. "He was such a fancy banker, why was he slumming it down here at this end of the beach?"

"Good question," Jim nodded.

"Was he looking for a hit? Drugs?"

"Not that we can figure."

"Well, I think he was up to no good." Leonie stood facing the policeman. "I think he was up to something dirty." She was very positive. Her blue eyes gleamed small sparks of fire.

Jim blinked. "You just may be right."

"I am. I got to go." She turned and walked away, shoelace dragging.

"Wait. Where do you live?"

"With nuns," Leonie said, tossing the words behind her as she went into a jog. "At Maria Concilia Community."

She kept jogging. The policeman didn't follow, she knew because she looked back and saw his dark shadow watching from the wall. Then she tried to think of nothing but street sounds all the way home. It was hard. The reality was that she had been too close to death, she had almost drowned herself. It had been quite a drop-off where the shallows ended and everybody knew about the riptides off Miami Beach. The policeman had grabbed her just in time.

Maybe she was going crazy. She really had to talk to someone badly.

Her shoelace would never be the same.

SISTER Cecile got up early and went to Mass at St. Patrick's Church. Sister Germaine always drove a load of nuns there in the community van for the eight-thirty mass, but today Cecile went to the seven. Sometimes her job encroached on her praying time, but the end result was that she still prayed, only earlier in the morning. She got less sleep when she had a job. Today, for example, she had an appointment with Manuel Beaumont, the president of le Banque du Paix. His office was high above le Banque du Paix's Miami headquarters downtown.

Sister Cecile arrived promptly at the correct address, went up in an exclusive elevator and stood in the upstairs lobby of a huge office looking at artwork bearing recognizable names: Picasso, Dalí, Miró, the renowned masters whose pieces could still be found in a shrinking market. This bank had money on the walls.

Eventually a secretary led Cecile to an office with more art, mahogany trappings, soft chairs. Manuel Beaumont rose when she entered. The secretary left.

Manuel Beaumont was a dark man of medium height, large nose and brown eyes. He wore wire-framed glasses and had long hair held back in a ponytail, an affectation that made him look more like a drug dealer than a banker. His suit was classic gray banker style. He reeked of wealth and charm. It was déjà vu. Sister Cecile had seen him before in a thousand places before she had become a nun. Or maybe it was just men like him. She had never cared much for money or what it did to people. They all became alike: little rich men in impeccable clothes who drank costly wines. She forced a smile, knowing that she appeared to be as affluent as he.

Her mode of dress was a deliberate deceit. She wore what she referred to as her successful detective disguise: upscale, expensive clothing from one of the South Beach boutiques. She had even applied a fifteen-dollar lipstick. Her soft brown curls had taken on red-gold highlights from the Florida sun and her huge leather case spoke bucks. It was one of the ways she could use her millions of dollars. Her professional life was clearly not the "religion of any sort, kind or manner" that had been carefully forbidden by her father's will, and her detective fees could go to the convent.

Money was a game she could play. Taking her vow of poverty quite seriously, she regarded money solely as a game. Nothing more. Money could always make money. Manuel Beaumont would never know how she really felt about money.

She introduced herself.

They sat in plush chairs overlooking Biscayne Bay and talked, beginning slowly by sipping tea and gurgling polite words at each other.

Finally, "We have great interest in seeing that his killer is brought to order," Manuel Beaumont said in his attractive French accent. His eyes never strayed from her fifteen-dollar-lipsticked lips, except now and then to meet her serious gray eyes, or rake over her elegant self.

"You see," he honked, "Barclay was one of our small group. Initially there were seven of us, now five. We have lost too many." He looked appropriately sad. "We would meet and play little games. Card games. Strict, confidential afternoons, you understand. Very civilized. And of course we would discuss business. We are, we were, philosophically compatible."

"A compatible group." Sister Cecile nodded and sipped tea. She dutifully ignored the sticky buns covered with thin almond slivers because it was Wednesday and the order fasted on Wednesdays. Bread and water all day. Tea to be social was okay, she had decided, but she would not rationalize the buns into bread. It was a matter of sacrifice, something her order asked of its members.

"Yes. We met last week as usual and Elliot was tragically missing. We discussed it and decided to take matters into our own hands. The police? Foof! So many dead in this town, Elliot is not important to them. Last year they regarded Cosima's death as a hit-and-run. And now the police are digging under garbage cans looking for a local scumbag killer when we are all quite certain Elliot was killed by one of our enemies. This was *not* a random killing, Ms. Buddenbrooks. We want the killer. If you find him and have no proof, but proof enough for us, we will take care of it. Keep your findings confidential. If you can." He looked vaguely skeptical after that deluge of words.

"I do have legal obligations when I find the killer. You know that." She was careful to say "when" rather than "if."

"We, in the Benthamite Consortium, are from several countries. We all understand the law. We also understand politics in Miami."

He smiled. His teeth were white against olive skin, his lips full. Cecile was surprised to find him attractive. She could see he was a brilliant sort but too smart in his own world to recognize the importance of other people's worlds. "Your banks compete?"

"Of course. But we don't kill."

"Ordinarily." Cecile was serious. "But what if one of your own did kill him?" she asked.

"All things are possible. In our group we have agreed that to do what is most useful is best. Utilitarian ethics are acceptable in the financial world. What produces benefit to many is good;

contrarily, what diminishes happiness is bad and must be eliminated. Benthamite philosophy, loosely called Utilitarianism. Useful equals good. Our group calls this the principle of utility, and it tells us we cannot have a murderer in our midst. If one of us is, you must expose him."

"Utilitarianism," Cecile murmured. She had heard of worse philosophies, but not much worse. Cultural hedonism, she thought, but not her problem. All she had to do was find the killer, not rationalize the killing. "And this Cosima you mentioned? Another death? You want me to investigate two deaths?"

"Cosima Benedict was the only female member of the consortium. Beautiful woman, family descended directly from the de' Medicis. Last year she was struck by a car as she crossed Indian Mound Road in Coral Gables. It's down as accidental death."

"It wasn't?"

"No proof either way." Manuel dusted his hands together. "She was very close to Elliot. Coincidence? I think not. Not now."

"You think the same killer?"

Manuel nodded. "We all agree it's likely. It makes this more urgent. You understand? However, we already had her death investigated and came up with nothing, so concentrate on Elliot, if you would."

"Absolutely. But there have been two deaths." Cecile was silent for a moment. "I'll keep this in mind. Meanwhile, I have a regular contract for my services." She handed him a prepared paper reflecting her new rates. "I will expect payment weekly. Monday mornings will do. I submit written reports as well. From you I will expect full disclosure of whatever you might know, of any wrongdoing by this man, enemies, whatever may be relevant to this case. All records will remain extremely confidential. You can call me at any time for an update."

He nodded.

"About Elliot Barclay. I need background. What can you tell me? Loosely."

"Elliot was in and out of town. He handled the South American sector of the Royal Leaf Bank of Canada. The Leaf liked him to come back to Toronto regularly. He keeps a condo near South Beach. There is a friend staying there now. After Cosima died, Nica moved in."

"How often was he in town?"

"Alternating six month periods with trips in between to Toronto. This is the end of January. He was expected to stay here right through March and establish a new edge corporation. We were all interested. It would originate here with Canadian facilities and a connection in Argentina, a connection that is already secure. Argentina's potential is tremendous. A ripe market for a new edge in spite of their unconscionable inflation problems." He laughed. "You know what the South Americans like about this country?"

"No," Cecile shook her head.

"They think it's stable." He chuckled. "Well, in some respects they're absolutely correct. And the new edge will reflect that stability."

Sister Cecile nodded. She had already learned from Sister Raphael what an edge corporation was, a corporation that may be owned by a domestic or foreign bank that primarily finances foreign trade. Miami was awash with them. "They have a great deal more confidentiality than normal banks, don't they?" she asked.

"Oh, yes. And they take risks that regular banks don't." He laughed deprecatingly. "And they move very quickly. International trade needs them. Miami loves them. Cosima was a lawyer well versed in international law and an expert on edges. We still miss her expertise. Elliot Barclay was a pure money man. But how an edge works? Say you want to get a load of stylish clothing from Honduras, you need ready money, you go to an edge. They give you the short-term loan the next day. You get the clothes, toss them in the free zone here in town and ship them out in new packages quickly. The money is returned to the corporation in weeks rather than years."

35

"Miami's a center for this?"

"About half the banks in the city finance international trade," he agreed. "Big money. People invest in these edge corporations because the interest rates are higher."

"And risky," Cecile murmured. "Could Elliot Barclay have been involved in something speculative with an edge?"

"Possibly," Manuel Beaumont agreed. He shrugged. "The edge corporations are an oddity. Owned primarily by foreign banks, but incorporated solely in this country. Strange little creatures. Maybe an edge bit him."

Manuel laughed lightly at his joke then took a large mouthful of a sticky bun.

Cecile chuckled politely. The bun looked delicious even as pieces dropped on Manuel's suit. "I need somewhere to start. Lists of people he knew, possibly enemies, friends. I need access to his office, to all his records and to his apartment." She saw a crumb on the edge of Manuel's lip. She almost reached across the table to wipe it away. He was not the type to wear his crumbs on his face or almonds on his shirt. He was more disturbed by this murder than he let on. Or was it murders?

"We anticipated what you would need," he said, and handed her a large manila envelope. "Confidential material. You'll find everything here including the police report and keys. Each member of our group is named. We each expect to meet with you. Perhaps it is one of us after all," he said. "By the way, the police report came to us with some difficulty, you understand. You should not have it."

She smiled and inserted the envelope into her purse.

Manuel went on. "I suggest looking at his apartment. Call Nica first, she'll be there. His friend."

"Fine. Now what about the dead prostitute. I heard that the bullets were the same."

Manuel shrugged. "Something more for you to discover. We don't care about the prostitute."

"It may be related. Meanwhile, my first report will be in

36

your office on Monday. And you do know," she said finally, "that I am a nun?"

"A nun?" Manuel stood up. "You're a nun, *une religieuse*?"

"Oui." She smiled, "I mean, yes."

He looked at her hard. "These days you are different. You nuns. Does this change things? You don't investigate murders?"

"Yes, I do investigate murders."

"You came very highly recommended." He cleared his throat. "Very highly. That is what matters." He walked over to the window, a half wall made of glass that opened to Miami's great buildings lining Brickell Avenue.

Manuel spoke clearly, but his back was to her so she couldn't see his eyes. "Besides, we already knew you were a nun. You've been investigated. One more thing. Elliot had some numbers in his possession. See if you can find them. This is very important, you understand. A paper with names and numbers."

Sister Cecile folded her hands in her lap. "Numbers," she said. "I'll definitely find the numbers."

"Excellent."

Ten minutes later Sister Cecile was out on the street. Among other things, she carried a paper authorizing her to enter Elliot Barclay's banking domain.

She walked rapidly. The infernal heat and brightness were a blessed relief from the Frenchman's heavily slanted cynicism. She gulped the hot, city air and turned in the direction of Elliot Barclay's bank, the Royal Leaf Bank of Canada. It was only half a block away, down on Brickell Avenue. No reason to delay. She would start there.

8

"No, you may not go through Mr. Barclay's office effects," the woman said. She had black pigtails, white skin, red lipstick. Tall and thin, her desk plate read AMY PEELE.

"I have a letter from the bank president. I'm authorized." Sister Cecile pulled out a paper from the huge envelope Manuel had given her and handed it to the woman.

"If you would wait right here, I'll check on this," Ms. Peele informed her stiffly.

An hour later Sister Cecile was finally allowed to use her key to Elliot Barclay's office.

Amy Peele sniffed. Her black pigtails switched from side to side. "I will go in with you."

"My authorization came from the chairman of the board of the Royal Leaf Bank of Canada, Terrence Canby, as you must have discovered after all this time." Sister Cecile waved the paper she had produced from her packet. Why was this woman being so obtuse? "I have everything here to guarantee me entry anywhere. Alone. Truly, Ms. Peele."

"There are personal items in that room," Amy Peele insisted. She was a possible thirty-five, her long face was mutinous, not quite pretty. Her pigtails looked as though she had chewed on them recently. "I remained while the police were there. I will remain with you. I am reorganizing all of Mr. Barclay's work. I am responsible for that office."

"But I am not the police." Sister Cecile smiled, nodded, and pushed past Ms. Peele. She slammed the office door behind her, then locked it with the inside dead bolt. She listened for a moment to a thumping noise on the door and felt a brief flash of remorse at the woman's anger.

She turned to look at the dead man's office.

The room didn't say much about the man. Dull corporate art, Danish modern furniture, glassy tabletops. Not even a fake plant. There was a photograph, face-down on Barclay's desk. Cecile righted it and looked. Elliot Barclay himself, wearing low-hung purple swimming trunks; he had an arm casually draped about a dark-haired woman who wore only a few black strings. Sister Cecile stared. Cosima or the new one? What was her name? Nica. Elliot was hardly dressed at all, thick arms flexed to show inflated pectoral muscles. He had a gleaming swatch of blond hair, puffy, faded blue eyes. He was probably considered attractive by South Beach standards. Sister Cecile shuddered. She didn't like the odd light in the man's eyes. She looked again at the woman, quite lovely; slim, elegant, black hair, red lipstick, Amy Peele's makeup job, but this woman was beautiful.

She checked the desk: charts, reports, several expensive pens. Amy Peele had probably scooped out everything of importance. In a drawer Cecile found a VCR tape of *Key Largo* from Blockbuster, probably overdue. She sat at the desk for a moment and pretended she was Elliot Barclay. She sniffed the air and smelled nothing but crisp air-conditioned air.

She found a small closet. Nothing but a collection of umbrellas, two raincoats, some rubber boots. A Canadian closet, Cecile thought, and looked in the raincoat pockets. Nothing. She compressed the coat's cloth with her hands and suddenly felt something hard in the lining. She reached down into a pocket, found a way through a hole and retrieved a square of what felt like cardboard. A computer disk? Yes. "Eureka," she murmured.

She stuffed the disk in her purse for Sister Raphael to deal with later. She tossed the tape of *Key Largo* into her bag with the consideration that she could watch it some night and get a flavor of the way things used to be. She would return it to the video store later.

Finally Sister Cecile turned on the office computer. Blips then a list of files. She called up one after another. Nothing mysterious, no passwords, or clandestine files filled with pornography. Aside from the usual networks and a computer game involving bowling balls and woodchucks, there was little of interest. Certainly the police must have gone through everything here already. She left the machine on to the woodchuck game and went to the office door. She opened it and called, "Ms. Peele! Could you help me, please?"

Amy Peele appeared instantly, her cheeks splotched with pink circles of anger. She looked bereft, Cecile realized and felt a touch of compassion. The woman must have been fond of her boss. Nothing abnormal about that. Cecile's compassion turned to guilt.

"I'm terribly sorry I shut you out, but it's my job. It's difficult to investigate with someone looking over your shoulder. I didn't mean to offend you, but really, I needed to get a feel for the man. Breathe the air, sit in the chair. It's the way I work. There didn't seem to be any other way. Please accept my apologies."

Sister Cecile put on her most amiable face and it apparently worked because Amy's features softened slightly. "Apology accepted." Amy put out her hand and they shook.

"I feel involved," Amy admitted. "I do want to discover the truth. Desperately. Please keep me informed." She held out her card and Sister Cecile stuffed it in her purse.

"I'll let you know," Cecile said graciously. "There isn't much of a personal nature here, is there?"

"No." Amy saw the woodchuck game and softened even more. "He loved that game. Big woodchucks chasing little woodchucks, little ones running after big ones. He asked me to play it with him sometimes. And those clever bowling balls."

She noticed the righted photograph and looked away, her hands groping up for the pigtails. "I intend to see to the bottom of this death myself, you know," she said in a small voice. "I did know the man. I worked with him. I want to see the killer brought to justice, personally." Her well-modulated voice rose to a childish pitch.

"I understand," Sister Cecile said. "And if you could help me, we can discover who and why."

"Certainly." Amy Peele stood up very straight and tucked her chin in. "You have my card."

"Is there anything on the computer of an unusual nature?" Cecile asked. She didn't want to pursue woodchucks, nor this woman's fixation with the victim.

"No. I'm trying to carry on with his projects. Of course the newest edge corporation is in total chaos now. We can't find the list of potential investors. There's nothing on it in the computer. There has to be a list somewhere. You didn't see a list?" she asked hopefully, the small chin untucking a little bit.

"List? No. There was a lot of material in the drawers, but I expect you've been through that. The photograph is of Elliot?"

"That's Elliot," Amy Peele said.

"Handsome man."

"Very big man."

"Clearly. And the woman?"

"Oh, some girlfriend. I don't know." Amy Peele turned her back to straighten the desk chair.

"Really, I'm sorry I had to burst through." Sister Cecile studied Amy Peele carefully. The woman's exterior was professional, the dove-gray suit, the peach blouse, the severe expression, restrained pigtails. She looked like a nun was supposed to look, Cecile thought suddenly. But Amy Peele wasn't the nun here. She was. She would have to keep that fact firmly in mind.

"Thank you, Ms. Peele. I'll be in touch."

Cecile sped down in the elevator and headed out into the stark Florida sunshine. The street was wide and hot like a blacktop oven. Heat blasted off the buildings.

The sunlight was blinding. Cecile squinted and delved for sunglasses in her bag.

Suddenly a heavy man slammed into her and grabbed her

around the waist. She moved automatically. Her right hand tightened around the leather bag, her left arm rose and jabbed out, fingers angled to do the most harm. Her knee flew up and she heard a satisfactory grunt and curse as she hit crotch. The arms let go. She let out a wild whoop. Noise, a woman's best defense. She whooped again, flopping back onto the hard pavement as her attacker gave a final, angry lunge to get her bag. She hung on to it for dear life.

Seconds later, when she was able to focus on the fleeing male figure, she made out the thick outline of an older man in a baseball cap. The bright sun created a shadow figure, a fast-moving, thick silhouette that vanished around a corner.

She still had a stranglehold on her bag. The sunglasses had flown from her hand and lay several yards away. She sat up, shaking as the reaction set in.

"Hookay, lady?"

She took a hand and felt herself pulled up by a smiling Hispanic. "Fine," she managed, patting herself. "What did he look like? Who saw his face?" she asked, waiting for an answer. She was surrounded by a cluster of earnest, everyday people.

All eyes were blank. Nobody had seen a thing. In fact, suddenly even her sunglasses were gone. She could have sworn she had just seen them several feet away on the sidewalk. "Nothing? Nobody?" She shook her head and exhaled. Random thug, or was she already enmeshed in the murder? Random, she told herself. It had to be random. She patted her leather bag and smiled at the people still there. "No harm done," she said, and walked away.

9

It was five o'clock in the afternoon. A vase of fresh-cut pink and yellow gladioli stood on the Queen Anne console. Funereal but elegant, Amy Peele thought. Very appropriate. Her incisive mind was back in working order after her confrontation with Cecile the day before. She had lost control for a moment. That couldn't be allowed to happen again.

The flowers were precisely placed in anticipation of this meeting of the Benthamite Consortium held in the executive quarters of the Royal Leaf Bank of Canada.

The men arrived, one at a time, nodding, speaking little. Amy greeted each one, then she brought out a tray of freshly baked, crusty French bread and a huge crystal bowl of beluga caviar along with silverware and small crystal plates for each person. She placed the food on the oval mahogany table and left. She was responsible for them meeting here, discreetly planting the seed and promising that it would be a very private place; a meeting in honor of Elliot. Of course they had already met, but that was before that expensively dressed woman appeared on the scene, hired by one of their own. That woman was a private investigator? How could they have hired such a creature?

The men barely noticed Amy Peele. Amy knew exactly what they thought. They didn't believe she was of the caliber of Cosima Benedict, damn her. Amy recalled Cosima with a tiny surge of triumph, because Cosima was dead. They would learn, these men, who really kept things together, who always had. She had been the mind behind Elliot. They would all

43

learn to depend on her as he had. She would offer suggestions, maybe even be Elliot for them. But first she would listen.

The men sat around the table on tall-back Queen Anne chairs and helped themselves to the caviar while a white-jacketed Hispanic youth brought them drinks, then quietly vanished.

Manuel Beaumont spoke softly. "The emergency meeting of the Benthamites has been called to report that the private investigator has been found satisfactory and hired." He paused significantly and looked, in turn, at each of the four other men. "She appears to understand our philosophy. Perhaps too well."

A fifty-three-year-old, blond man, vice president of the Erste Gesamtdeutsche Bank, or Vista Bank of Florida, as it was known in America, tapped the table briefly and shifted his glasses up on his nose. "You have given her our names, then?" He was Ross Olhm. His family held controlling interest in a number of German manufacturing firms. He was in this for pocket money and the thrill.

Manuel Beaumont grunted yes.

"We agree then, one of us must have killed him?" Ross asked. "And dear Cosima? We have come to that same conclusion? Someone is killing us?"

Beaumont scooped up a knifeful of caviar and spread it on a chunk of bread. He spoke deliberately, pushing the shiny black eggs into position. "It had to be one of us. Elliot Barclay was our leader. We must, I stress, *must,* find his killer." He paused, taking each man into his velvet gaze. "Operation Deontology must be completed as planned. Whoever you are, you who killed him will be found." He took a bite from his bread, oblivious to the crumbs dropping. "Meanwhile, whoever you are, we will continue as we must. And when our independent investigator uncovers you, you will die. We have agreed. Correct? It is useful to have the killer die."

The other men all nodded, each acting as if it was someone other than himself who had done the foul deed and killed their leader.

It was a strange group—men from different countries, men

44

of power whose sole reason for forming this group was for more power. They lacked trust, the bottom line of morality. Trust, perhaps, was not useful. Their philosophy precluded it.

"We have two masters," Claudio Almeida summed up finally, "pain and pleasure. It is for them alone to point out what we ought to do, to determine what we shall do. Meanwhile we shall continue the plan to control. And in line with our philosophy, brothers, don't forget what's important. The names. Whatever happened to Elliot, we need the list of names. Our next project depends on it."

"Here, here," the Texan, Barcus Dumplig called. The only American member of the group drawled his way into the conversation. Barcus Dumplig was from eastern Texas, owner of mining and oil reserves throughout the world as well as being a major shareholder in a number of unnamed corporations. It was said that if he whispered to the right man, the president himself would jump. Barcus Dumplig was the perfect example of how hedonistic calculus, the Benthamite philosophy, worked well in business. He didn't care whom he squashed. He spoke in a mucky twang. "Murder's gotta end. So this lady's good? She's gonna find who dunnit? She's gonna find the list? I mean, fellas, we can live without Elliot. Can't live without the list."

"The lady's competent," Manuel nodded. "Very."

"I would like to meet this investigator," Aristippus Tselementes said. He was heavily into shipping and very Greek. He ran tapering fingers through his shoulder-length hair and tilted his chair back an inch. "You are sure she is the best? Honest? One not to be tampered with? And clever?"

"You would like to buy her, Aristippus? You would love her; she is *très chic*. Very beautiful," Manuel Beaumont laughed quietly. "But she is already rich. Not as rich as you, and she is also a nun. One does not touch this nun, they tell me. I have checked."

"Really?" Aristippus closed his eyes, then opened them slowly.

45

"A nun? Gawd awmighty," Barcus Dumplig hooted. "What the hell kind of stunt you pulling on us, Manuel. A nun?"

"Integrity." Manuel Beaumont beamed. "As your new leader I have hired integrity. Sister Cecile Buddenbrooks has it."

Behind the door in a small kitchen, Amy Peele sat with her ear pressed to a tiny receiver. The microphone in the vase of flowers was very good. "Integrity?" she whispered to herself. She covered her lips to keep from laughing aloud as she recalled Cecile pushing her aside and locking her out of Elliot's office. That person was a nun? Well, if the nun was as great as these men thought, each and every one of them was doomed. And maybe the nun would succeed, Amy thought with a grimace.

Her own two attempts to catch the nun had failed. The first, of course, to keep her out of dear Elliot's office, the second, the aborted attack by her father, a wasted attempt to retrieve all the papers the nun had been given by Manuel Beaumont. Poor Daddy had suffered from that nun. She had kneed Daddy much too hard. The nun would be made to pay for that. But first, maybe the nun would find Elliot's killer.

Amy Peele scribbled down some notes on a yellow legal pad. The first page was titled: Things to tell Daddy about the case. The second page: Ideas on death. How to kill the killer, and get even with the nun for hurting you. Amy Peele had a childlike tendency to write down her thoughts simplistically. Her handwriting resembled that of a schoolgirl's. Her brain was more like the computers she used. Somewhere in her intellectual development she hadn't quite grown up, but few people were aware of this. People considered her a very brilliant woman.

And she was.

10

THE ocean waters pounded on the beach. Gulls and small black birds flew along the shoreline for as far as Cecile could see. She walked slowly, covering the area where Elliot Barclay had died. Late afternoon, there were people here now, a few in the water, most just walking along the hard packed sand by the waterline, as she was. Other souls were splayed out like chickens on the grill basted with PABA.

Cecile had gone through the packet Manuel Beaumont had given her. She knew everything the police knew, and she knew who was in the Benthamite Consortium. She sorted things out as she walked. She had lost a day to convent business. The paperwork in running the retirement community was mind boggling. Permits, registrations, forms. And she had to solve a murder, too? But what she really wanted to do was spend time with Leonie. The child was paramount in Cecile's list of priorities. The nun wanted to take the child somewhere, a trip to the Everglades, a trip to Monkey Jungle maybe, anything to pull the girl out of the funk she was in. Maybe she should talk to Sister Raphael about this again.

Sister Cecile prayed. She pulled out her old black rosary beads and walked along the sand, a woman dressed in an expensive blue suit from the Jordan Marsh department store in Boston, she carried her shoes in one hand, her beads in the other. The sun hit her from the side, throwing half her oval face into stark relief, her body into silhouette. A few male heads turned to look because she was a good-looking woman. She noticed them, but it was as though they were from another world. It could have been different. She liked men. But she had chosen this. She prayed.

Back in the community, nothing stood still. While Sister Cecile prayed, other nuns were praying, too. Among those busy souls was Sister Germaine, daughter of a five-star French chef, and a master chef in her own right. In Boston she had cooked for the convent, and two days a week cooked in soup kitchens. Sister Germaine was the heart and soul of wherever she was, because she was the cook. She knew what everyone ate in the Maria Concilia Retirement Community, and how much, and she knew about special diets. People's minds were reflected in their stomachs.

She was in the small chapel that afternoon, praying specifically for Leonie. It was her secret, she thought. Leonie was troubled. Germaine had known it for a week.

The cook was certain she was the very first nun to know that Leonie Drail was in trouble. Ever since she had discovered the chocolate cake discarded in the kitchen trash, the very same large piece she had left for Leonie the night before, and had seen how carefully Leonie left the plate in the sink as evidence that she ate it, the French cook knew there was a problem. She just wasn't sure what it was. But she would find out. Not only a cook, Sister Germaine was a food detective.

The afternoon that Leonie had arrived home from school all wet, Sister Germaine saw her run to her room. Sister Germaine planted herself down the hallway, then stood and waited a full half hour before she saw Leonie emerge from her room, dry and neat. All great chefs had patience. It was the secret to fine cooking.

"Ah, Leonie, I need some help. Got some moments?" Sister Germaine asked, stepping out of the shadows.

"You're supposed to say, 'Do you have a moment,' " Leonie corrected with a grin. No one, it seemed, had ever taught the French nun the elements of American clichés and Leonie had taken up the task. Sister Germaine appreciated this and repeated dutifully, "Do you have a moment?"

"That's better."

"Well, do you have one?"

"Yes."

Leonie followed Germaine to the kitchen where a huge pile of carrots waited. "Wash and feed through the food processor. Someone donated twenty pounds of carrots and I will blanch and freeze them. Then we toss carrots in the supper sometime. Eh?"

"Eh," Leonie agreed and washed some carrots.

"You went swimming today?" Germaine asked five minutes later.

"You saw me wet?" Leonie was trimming off carrot ends and almost chopped off a finger.

"You looked wet."

"I walked along the ocean after school and it looked so great." Leonie's words came out almost naturally but too fast. She scooped up more carrots to feed in the slot of the food processor, moving a little faster than she should have.

"You jumped right in," Germaine completed for her.

"Yes. Yes, I did."

Five more minutes of silence passed, the only sounds were the whacking of sharp blades as they sliced carrots and chopped off blemishes. Sister Germaine tossed a large pile of cut carrots in the pot to blanch. "Boil for two minutes," she murmured. "Cool, freeze suddenly."

"Quickly. I don't think people say 'freeze suddenly,' " Leonie said, then went on. "Germaine, my father kills people sometimes. At least once."

"I didn't know that."

"When he was threatened. Self-defense. He said it was okay."

"But he doesn't like to kill people."

"No. He doesn't like to."

"He is a good man, Leonie. He is like a policeman, a *flic* for the government, eh?"

"Yes."

"A *keuf*, maybe," Germaine said in a softer tone. "So, that was all right, I think. Death is unkind, but those policemen, the *flics*, they have a hard task, but they protect us."

"Protect," Leonie repeated. "Yes." She looked considerably happier than she had only moments ago.

Sister Germaine was beginning to understand. She would learn more about this tomorrow. She would pursue this another time. She was patient, very patient. Things rise, things settle. Later she would talk to Sister Raphael about it. Raphael would know what to do.

Leonie thought about Sister Germaine's words for the next few days. Maybe she wasn't guilty after all. Maybe she should never tell anyone, ever, and it would just go away.

It was evening and she was doing homework, trying to concentrate on a page of pre-algebra problems. Lately she had trouble concentrating and tonight she ended up chewing on her eraser, staring at the wall. She was in the seventh grade of a small Catholic school nearby. While not a Catholic herself, Leonie and her father had agreed she should go to this school because of its proximity, and the fact that it was a good school. Meanwhile she had to do homework.

She got up and went into the bathroom. The school uniform that had accompanied her into the ocean the other day was still damp, hanging in her shower. Things dried slowly in the soggy Florida climate. She knew that the plaid skirt could take weeks to dry and grow fuzzy orange mold. Luckily she had a spare. And she hadn't really told Sister Germaine anything during their talk.

Everyone knew it was all right to kill in self-defense, and Sister Germaine had confirmed that quite clearly, Leonie thought as she stared at the school uniform. Why did it feel like her fault?

She returned to her desk and sat down. One last word problem. Of course she hadn't actually killed the man herself. It had just sort of happened. But she had been so close! And he would have killed her. And more. She had the ripped, bloody shirt in her drawer, the stained shorts, saving the evidence for

God knows what. She knew where she had buried the gun that he had threatened her with, the gun with her fingerprints all over it. Wrapped in plastic, saved for posterity. She knew everything. Fine. Forget it, she told herself.

She finished the problem then slammed the book closed. Why did she feel so guilty? Why couldn't she bring herself to tell Cecile? She really had to, and then everything would be fine.

"Just fine," she muttered aloud, but deep inside her she knew it wasn't true and that she was guilty. Now what was she going to do? "My entire life," she mused aloud as she stuffed the completed homework into her book. "It's always going to be there."

Maybe she should tell Sister Cecile everything. Or maybe she should wait for her father to get back. But that could be months.

Sister Cecile was in the hallway outside Leonie's room and heard a few words. She knocked cautiously on Leonie's door.

"Come in."

"Busy?" Cecile saw the math book on Leonie's desk.

"I just finished." Leonie patted the book.

"I thought I heard you talking to yourself."

"I was wondering if the work was okay. I just finished." Leonie made a small face at the book. "Math's tricky."

"Want me to go over it with you?"

"I don't know. Can you do this stuff?"

"Maybe. Let's see."

Five minutes later it was determined that Sister Cecile could still do simple algebraic word problems, but not as well as she used to. "I forget," she apologized. "These concepts are complicated."

Leonie nodded. "I know. Life is very complicated sometimes. I used to think it was simple."

"You must be growing up."

"Yeah."

They sat quietly for a while, Leonie flopped on the bed, Sister Cecile spread out on Leonie's big overstuffed chair. The nun finally broke the silence. "I guess living with a bunch of sisters must be tough."

"I like it." This was the time to tell everything, Leonie thought. Right now.

"You need a man in your life. Like a father. You're used to talking to your father and he's out of communication now. You have enough mothers here, mothers, grandmothers. Lots of us. I'll have to introduce you to some other adults. Like men. You don't have any men in your life. We're not bad sorts, us grown-ups."

"Some of you," Leonie admitted. She knew she was looking much too serious, and the conversation was taking an off turn. Man in her life? One had just died on top of her, for goodness sake, another one had hauled her out of the ocean. Did she need a man? She would tell Cecile as soon as the nun finished babbling about men. Sure.

"I'm working with a lot of men on a new case," Cecile said, fumbling her words. "I'm investigating the death of that man who was killed, Elliot Barclay. Know who that is?"

Leonie's jaw dropped infinitesimally. Could Sister Cecile possibly know? No way. "No kidding," she said.

"I thought you could help me."

"Me?" Leonie gulped. This was not what she had in mind at all. How on earth could she tell Cecile she was the solution to the nun's latest case? She was doomed. How could she tell now?

Cecile went on, seemingly oblivious to Leonie's figure suddenly rigid on the bed.

"Some bankers in town think he was murdered by one of their own, that it wasn't just another tourist killing. The bankers hired me. The police don't even know I'm on the case. They don't like private detectives on their murder cases, so outwardly I'll just be checking into his life. Seeing who this man, Elliot Barclay, really was. I'll be sure to uncover motives, if any exist. If someone really wanted this particular man dead, I'll find the killer."

52

Leonie felt cold, like after the death. She forced herself to move a little. Act natural. "Maybe he killed himself?" she asked cautiously.

"There was no gun. The wallet was gone and the gun was missing," Sister Cecile said. "Maybe you can help me. We can talk over the facts of the case, get ideas, come to conclusions. I got a copy of the police report. Not that I was supposed to, but Paul faxed it from Boston. There was someone in Miami who faxed it to him. And the people who hired me had a copy, too. I guess it's common knowledge. Police reports tend to get passed around."

"I get it. Undercover stuff." Leonie said. Hollow words, but Cecile didn't seem to notice. And the wallet was missing? Someone must have been there after her and copped the money.

"I think I'd like to know about his life," Leonie murmured, her mind racing. "Find out if he had a girlfriend, stuff like that." See if he deserved to die, Leonie almost added, but didn't.

"Apparently he did have a girlfriend."

"Really?" Leonie was surprised. "No wife, no kids. That's good."

"Why is that good?"

"He's dead." It was a small consolation.

"True. He was an executive vice president of a Canadian bank; he lived part-time in Miami, part-time in Toronto. He was setting up a new edge corporation, something about international trade."

"I think you should look in his personal life," Leonie said. "Maybe he deserved to die. I mean, maybe he was out causing trouble." Maybe you can tell me I did a good thing, she thought, but her mind was going numb. She tried to think of what Sister Germaine had told her about killing in self-defense.

"Nobody deserves to die," Cecile said. "He was a respectable business man."

"You think. What if he had done something bad and he should have died."

"People shouldn't be shot."

53

"What about war?"

Cecile frowned. "War?"

"Well, my dad's killed people. At least one person, someone who tried to kill him. That's war."

"Yes, but your father doesn't want to kill. Sometimes he has to."

Leonie nodded. That was exactly what Sister Germaine had said. "We'll have to investigate carefully, then. If you're right, maybe there was a reason he died." She looked at her guardian cautiously. This was going to be very tough. She was going to have to tell Sister Cecile. She really would. Maybe tomorrow.

She watched Sister Cecile pat her blue skirt down over her knees. When Cecile wasn't working as a detective she wore the modified habit of their order, a white or blue skirt, white blouse, gold cross, and small veil. The skirt patting went along with the nun identity. Leonie recognized it. Cecile was acting like a nun. Could she ever tell a nun what happened?

"Cecile," Leonie asked without warning, "when a man wants you, is it your fault or his?"

Leonie saw the shock in Cecile's eyes. Darn, but Cecile was going to read something into the question, Leonie thought. "Zoe asked me what I thought," she said quickly, "and we argued about it. And boys have said things to us. So whose fault?" Leonie really had to know this one. Her guilt all hinged on it.

Cecile took a long time to come up with an answer.

"I would say it's the fault of the aggressor. Whoever that may be. And whether it's a fault at all really depends on the situation. I mean, desire isn't really a fault, is it? God gave us desire. What we do with our desire is something else entirely. That's where right and wrong come into the picture. With our choices." Cecile frowned, looking uncertain. "Does that make sense?"

It did, actually, Leonie thought as she pictured herself walking down the beach, doing nothing, just walking. She hadn't provoked the attack. He had been the aggressor. She had just wanted to go home. "It makes sense. But it's complicated. I mean situations are complicated."

"And that's just the beginning," Cecile smiled. She patted her skirt down again. Leonie could see the nun was off in another world now, not a world of trouble, but one of love.

"Did anyone ever want you?" Leonie asked.

"Me?" Cecile nodded. "Yes."

"But you're a nun."

"I wasn't always."

"Tell me. What did you do?"

Sister Cecile didn't say anything, she just looked enigmatic. "I can't really say, now," Cecile said.

Five minutes later the soft bells announcing compline rang, and Sister Cecile left, ending the discussion with a hug. It was time for the nuns' evening prayers. Leonie flopped down on her bed and tried to let all the words that she had just heard settle in her mind. If they would ever settle.

11

SISTER Cecile felt guilty, too, as she hurried to compline. She just hadn't wanted to pursue sex-talk with Leonie at that time. In fact she didn't quite know what to say to an almost teenager about sex. It was not something a nun knew much about. But it might explain Leonie's odd behavior.

Being a mother was too hard.

Cecile loved compline, the evening communal prayers of the nuns. Here they joined together in what the pope himself referred to as the "common life," a powerful countercultural antidote to the ills of the world, a redress to the consumerism and narcissism of the late twentieth century. It was a relief to gather with the community in the small chapel and listen to readings from the Bible, and to pray. The nuns took turns doing the reading, the prayers were said together.

Sister Cecile stayed on afterward, adding some private prayers of her own. Mothers must spend a lot of time praying, she thought later as she finally signed off with God and left the chapel.

A glance at the refectory clock as Cecile passed by showed it was nine-thirty already. Almost bedtime after a long day, and Sister Cecile still hadn't told anyone about the attack on her that had occurred after her visit to the Royal Leaf Bank. Maybe she should tell Raphael? Or maybe just forget it. It could have been a typical smash-and-grab scene, the kind of thing that happens all the time. Cecile put it out of her mind. After all, nothing had come of it.

Maybe Raphael would have some advice for her about Leonie, she thought. The hint of sex in Leonie's message worried her. Children had sex. She had heard that they did. But not Leonie! Please, God, not yet.

She decided to drop the computer disk off with Sister Raphael. She knocked lightly on the old nun's door.

"Come in." Raphael was on the verge of going to bed, but still puttering around.

Cecile came in and held up the disk. "I've told you all about my new case; this is what I found. It was in Elliot Barclay's raincoat pocket."

She handed Raphael the disk then plopped down on the chair. Raphael's bedroom was large and comfortable, most unlike the drafty cubicles where they had lived in the Dorchester, Massachusetts convent. The rooms in the converted motel in Miami had been built for couples and for the most part now housed singles. For many of the inhabitants it smacked of over-generous space.

"Should I go check it now?" Raphael asked. She held the disk up with her old hands and turned it. "Hope it's compatible with our system."

"No, it's late. Go to bed. Do it when you get a chance." Sister Cecile looked around the room, her face still reflecting the worries she had brought with her. Sister Raphael just might have the answer, she thought. Sister Raphael knew everything.

"Do you think Leonie's into sex?" Sister Cecile asked. The question popped out of its own accord, startling both the nuns.

"Sex. Leonie? Oh, I don't think so. I'll ask her." Sister Raphael said as she walked over to her small bookshelf. She put the disk on top of a row of books. She didn't appear concerned.

"Ask? You can't actually ask her about sex."

"Why not?"

"Well, she might be afraid to say. We don't want to push her into a lie."

"I don't think she would. Did you ever talk to her about sex?" Raphael asked.

"Well, I assume she knows."

"Hmm," the older nun murmured. "Do you?"

"Well, I know." Sister Cecile said. "Sort of."

"Maybe you should talk with her," Raphael suggested.

"Me? Maybe her father already told her everything. What about you? Do you know about sex, Sister Raphael?"

Cecile hadn't addressed Sister Raphael as "Sister" in years, not since the younger nun had come back to the Boston convent as a newly professed religious.

Raphael must have noticed because she spoke reassuringly. "I think I could speak with her. Leonie is twelve years old, and she must know about reproduction. That's not exactly sex these days, but I'll deal with it, Cecile. If she wants to know, she should find out the right way. The fact that she's asked you is critical. We have to act now. And I'll look at the computer disk, too. Don't worry."

The younger nun got up from the chair. "Thank you, Raphael." She let out a long sigh. "I don't know what I'd do without you. All these important things."

"Goodnight, Cecile."

Sister Raphael couldn't sleep. Her friend, Sister Cecile, was deeply worried, Raphael could see that. Sister Raphael said an entire rosary, then she tossed and turned for a long time. Finally the old nun got up out of bed and put on her everyday clothes. It was midnight. It was much too late to go stumbling around the convent like a senile old nun in a nightgown. Sister Raphael was quite aware of appearances. On the other hand, there was nobody awake in the convent to see her. There were times to act, and this was one of them. Senile or not.

She picked up the computer disk and tiptoed out to her office, still barefoot.

Moments later she had the machine humming and brought up the program. "Well," she said out loud and punched some keys. She heard a strange bleeping noise. She pushed more keys, studied the results, hit some more keys and heard a discordant crash, then a siren. Small woodchucks wandered around her screen escaping bowling balls.

Sister Raphael played "Woodchucks and Bowling Balls." It took her about five minutes to get into the game. She finally hit a woodchuck. A large "SPLAT" appeared on the screen. Computerized blood dripped across the picture. "Disgusting," Raphael said and turned off the computer. There were some games she secretly enjoyed, computer games mailed to her surreptitiously by her nephew in Massachusetts. But not this.

She put the disk away, turned out the lights, and left the office. From there the old nun went directly into the small chapel near the front of the retirement home. She said a few more prayers, but she was still not tired. Sometimes Raphael just couldn't sleep.

It was very late when Sister Raphael drifted out the front door of the Maria Concilia Retirement Community and onto the small, screened walkway that bordered the street. The area was heavily fenced, with the grassy edge planted over with wide palms that were thrown into relief by lights aimed at the building. At the end of the little walkway was an outdoor sitting area; a small garden with a dysfunctional fountain. Old stone benches in need of repair waited for a donor to supply quality cement and stones. Crickets and colossal cockroaches dwelled under rotting ferns.

Raphael took a deep breath, inhaling the sweet scent of a Miami night. She looked carefully at the heavily locked and screened wrought-iron gate that opened up to the main street, a street often inhabited by unsavory characters after dark.

There were noises everywhere, the bugs, the night birds, and a soft sound from beyond the gate, a breath of air, or a person breathing, a scrape of a foot against an old cement sidewalk. It seemed safe. Sister Raphael had a thought that she might be stepping on squishy night bugs, barefoot. She sat down quickly on one of the crooked stone benches and looked around. She heard sounds. Then she saw a shadow. A huge man, looming like a behemoth in the dark, was staring in. How could she have missed him!

Her heart pounded. The metal door lock was flimsy. The mesh that covered the blank spaces was weak. Sister Raphael looked at the distance she had to go to get back inside, still barefoot. Too far. She sat up straight. "Are you looking for someone?" she exhaled shallowly. She was stuck to the stone like glue.

"You're a nun? A sister?" She could feel black eyes on her as he spoke. A dark, thick voice.

"Yes."

"Do you have a little girl living here?"

Raphael gulped. "Who are you?" she asked, trying to see in the shadow.

"I'm a policeman. Jim Cypress's my name."

"Who?" Raphael asked.

"Jim Cypress."

"Like the tree?"

"Right."

"Cypress?" Raphael frowned.

"Miccosukee. That's a Miccosukee name. Indian. Native

American. Whatever. I met a little girl the other day. I think she lives here."

"You're police? Why? Did she do something?"

"She walked into the ocean."

"Leonie did what?" Sister Raphael stood up too fast. It hurt. That and sex, too? She lurched to the gate. "Do you have identification?" She stared through the mesh and through the dark at the Indian policeman. The Miccosukee were the tribe of the Seminoles who had never given up. In fact they had been legally at war with the federal government up until very recently. Maybe they still were. It was a very persistent tribe, and this man looked very persistent, even in the dark.

Jim reached into his pocket and pulled out a badge. He pressed it through a small opening in the gate. She stared at it in the gloom. "More," Raphael demanded. "A picture ID. And why are you here now? It's the middle of the night!"

Jim groped in his pocket and pulled out his picture ID. Sister Raphael read it slowly through the mesh of the gate.

"Sorry it's late," he said as she read. "I was checking around the neighborhood. I have a case in the area and saw movement in here so I thought I'd take a look. The girl has been on my mind."

It was a reasonable explanation. The ID looked good. Raphael decided to open the gate. Carefully she turned a series of locks and let Jim into the small sitting space. He walked in, smiling faintly. It occurred to Raphael that he was suddenly thrilled to be enjoying the forbidden pleasure of a secret nun garden.

"It's the middle of the night," she repeated, still conscious of darkness and street noises.

"I was worried." His eyes turned down to the ground beside her in a typical Miccosukee manner.

"All right, I think we'd better talk," Sister Raphael said. "About Leonie."

She watched as he lowered his great weight gingerly onto a carved bench. She sat down opposite him. She studied the man. Possibly six feet tall, he had the build of a weight lifter with thick arms straining the white, short-sleeve shirt he wore. He was handsome, she decided, with a wide mouth that looked as though it could split into a huge grin. His hair was dark and long, although it was hard to see in the dim light. He wore well-fitted dungarees and brown leather boots. Finally his eyes lifted from the ground and met hers.

"Tell me about Leonie?" he asked. "This is the girl who lives here? Isn't this a convent?"

"Retirement community," Raphael said. "Leonie lives here with us at the moment. She belongs to Sister Cecile; that is, Cecile is her guardian. Leonie's father is out of the country for a few months, so Cecile is currently in charge. You said Leonie walked into the ocean? I want to know about this. I can't believe she walked into the ocean. She told Germaine she went for a swim."

Jim nodded. "The other afternoon. It wasn't exactly a swim. More like a walk. She claimed she didn't notice it was getting deep. I followed her in, when I saw her heading farther out. Sort of strange, I thought at the time. She really didn't seem to know what she was doing. Luckily I was there and pulled her out. Could she be suicidal?"

Sister Raphael didn't speak for a moment. She put her hands together, twisted them and rubbed her wrists. "I thought she was happy here." Raphael sounded fierce in her concern. "She told Sister Germaine she went swimming with her clothes on. We've been worried, Germaine and I. We didn't tell Sister Cecile. But, no, I don't think she's suicidal. I think, perhaps she was telling you the truth. That she just walked in."

"This Sister Cecile, who is she?"

"She's the head of the retirement community at the moment. I help." Sister Raphael sat up straight. "I'm not as old as I look. I do the books."

"I see," Jim said. "You say your Sister Cecile doesn't know that Leonie came home wet?"

"No, she has enough worries. We didn't want to tell her. It

61

didn't seem a crime. We thought maybe she was just swimming. Children don't mind going in the water with their clothes on. I can remember doing it myself."

"This Sister Cecile, she's too busy for her own ward?"

"Not at all. It's just, well, it's as though Leonie has lots of mothers here. No father at the moment, but lots of mothers."

"Right," he said dryly. He didn't look as though he believed her much less understood what she was talking about. Raphael was horribly aware that she must resemble nothing more than an old nun quivering in agitation. She glanced down at her bare feet, moving them back into the shadows.

He continued to talk. "Could you tell me, do you folks delight in the gory details of the news?" He stared at her.

"Why?"

"Leonie knew a lot about the Elliot Barclay murder. More than the police have let out."

"I don't understand."

"She spouted the time of death as though it were common knowledge. As a matter of fact we have an estimate, but she appeared to hit it to the minute. This hasn't come up in the community? You don't recall the Barclay murder being discussed?"

Sister Raphael's head was spinning. Had Cecile discussed the case with Leonie? Had Cecile read the police report, and perhaps let something slip? Possibly she had. "I would imagine it was just a guess," Raphael said. "The story has been on the news and in the papers. Maybe she read it? Leonie's been reading the papers lately. We think she might have a social studies project."

"She couldn't have read the time of death."

"She probably just made the time up."

"I wouldn't assume that. There are no coincidences in police work."

"That's exactly what Cecile always says," Raphael admitted. "However, in this case I don't see how it can be anything but coincidence." She could hear her voice still quivering and didn't like the sound of it.

62

"More likely the girl witnessed the murder."

"Witnessed the murder? Leonie? Oh, no. She would have told us. Believe me, the child isn't afraid to talk to us."

"Just how old is she?"

"Twelve."

Jim Cypress stared at the dark tree above Sister Raphael. "Twelve-year-olds don't tell anybody anything."

"Oh." Raphael nodded dumbly. Of course. She had forgotten. He was absolutely right.

"Perhaps I should speak about this to Sister Cecile." His lip twisted as he said the name.

"Why? I mean, we really are competent here. You'd be surprised at how well things are going."

Jim made a sound almost like a laugh.

"Really," the old nun said. "But you may talk to Sister Cecile if you must. I can make you an appointment. I don't know her schedule offhand." Sister Raphael's words came out like earnest drops of night dew.

Jim Cypress nodded. "I want to know how Leonie knew the time of death. If she's a witness, it's important we talk to her as soon as possible, and to do that officially, I need to have that nun's cooperation."

"That nun," Sister Raphael murmured to herself. What an interesting way to speak of Sister Cecile. "I'll speak to that nun first thing," she agreed.

"I want to know where Leonie was when Elliot Barclay was killed."

Raphael nodded. "Maybe you can tell me something. I read in the paper that the same gun that killed this man was used to kill a prostitute the previous night. Is there a connection between the two deaths?"

"You really do read the sensational news."

"I read everything, and they only publish stuff like that. I yearn for good news. I dwell on the comic section because everything else is bad news."

Jim Cypress apparently liked what he heard because he

gave a satisfied rumble. "We don't know what the connection could be." He glanced at his watch. "It's late."

"I know. I'll call you in the morning with an appointment time. But, Detective Cypress, tell me about yourself. What shall I tell Sister Cecile? With whom is she meeting."

"Police Detective Cypress, only Miccosukee cop on South Beach. That's all."

"Miccosukee," Raphael repeated.

"Seminole."

"And a very competent one, I imagine." Raphael was satisfied. She had always admired Native Americans. She rose slowly from the cold bench. "I'll arrange a meeting and call you. Come to the gate so I can lock it, please."

"Leave a message if I'm not there." He handed her a card with his name and the station-house number on it.

Sister Raphael liked that. He was a real professional. How interesting, she thought as she locked the gate, that this man and Sister Cecile were working on the same case. "I'll call tomorrow. Don't you worry about a thing."

12

IT was very late when Jim stopped at his station house to check for messages before signing off for the night. He informed the desk officer, Reggie Peele, that he would be expecting a message in the morning. "I may have a witness to the killing," he said. He wouldn't have even mentioned it but he was tired and it was late and Reggie was an old-time Florida workhorse in the department, ready to retire. Not a particularly pleasant man, but Reggie Peele had been around the block.

"Things are starting to crack open?" Reggie asked.

"Yeah, I found a kid. Might know something."

"Great work. See you later, Jim."

Sister Cecile had an appointment with Nica Rabelais at Elliot Barclay's apartment for eleven o'clock the next morning. She missed seeing Sister Raphael, who slept in, and that was not surprising, since Sister Raphael hadn't gotten to bed until 2 A.M.

Sister Cecile left the convent early, dressed for business in a six-hundred-dollar off-white linen suit from Burdines department store, a large canvas purse filled with a copy of *The Autobiography of St. Thérèse of Lisieux*, and her credit card. She needed a car for the case and had allowed herself time to pick one up, something that would impress the Benthamites enough to trust her. Money, she thought disconsolately, even bought trust.

A small Cadillac would be nice, she thought, as her cab pulled up in front of Distinctive Vehicles of the Beach. Or perhaps one of those old Bugattis.

The saleswoman talked her into purchasing an old classic 1967 Jaguar, a shiny black Mark II. It only took a half hour to complete the paper work, because, as usual, money talked.

Cecile had been told, no, ordered, by her mother superior to use her money in any way that did not offend God. So when the case was done she would donate the car to a charity.

How could an old Jaguar offend God, Cecile questioned as she pulled out quickly onto the road, relishing the feel of the gears. The car was speedy and small, perfect to maneuver among the impossible traffic and miniature parking spaces she was bound to come up against. She drove directly to her appointment with Nica Rabelais, the woman who lived in Elliot Barclay's apartment. It was located in a new condo complex on South Beach replete with coral-rock walls and a natty doorman.

Nica Rabelais must have been waiting. The door popped open quickly and she was there, pale-faced, wearing a red silk blouse and dungarees. She had medium-length black hair and deep blue eyes: a startling combination of primary colors. And, yes, she was the lovely woman dressed in strings in the photograph on Elliot's desk, but she looked terribly thin and terribly ill.

"I'm Nica," she said and held out a languid hand.

Sister Cecile introduced herself as Cecile Buddenbrooks, not as Sister Cecile.

Nica offered coffee and soon after, they were sitting in Elliot's living room, a huge space decorated in black and white ultra-modern. Nica splashed back against a white leather chair as though she were designed for it. Cecile chose a black chair so she wouldn't become invisible in her beige colors. Above them a huge white ceiling fan turned slowly. Frigid air-conditioning made the place feel like the Dorchester convent in January. Cecile felt the chill and repressed a shiver. People like the contradictory sensation of freezing in Miami, she had discovered.

"They've told me to offer all cooperation," Nica said, dragging her words out with effort. Her hands shook on the coffee cup. "I don't know what to tell you. I live here, I took care of Elliot. I'm an actress, so I go to castings now and then. I do the Beach scene, make connections, that's my thing. I work now and then doing parts in local films. I figure it's easier to get work here than in Hollywood, less competition. Or maybe I'll just marry rich. I've taken this week off. Flu, maybe, or do you suppose I'm actually in mourning?" Her voice held tiny tremors at the edge of each word.

She draped a leg up over the chair arm and cradled her coffee in her hand. She seemed very up-front, Cecile thought, but definitely not at her best. On close look her pale skin had a greenish tint, her hair owed its springy health to paste and glue, and her startling blue eyes were red around the edges.

Cecile spoke gently. "How did you meet Elliot?"

"One of those late nights. He brought me home. I stayed on."

"Can you tell me about him? What kind of a person?" Sister Cecile remembered Leonie's words. "Did he deserve to be killed?" she asked.

Nica's mouth opened just enough for the words to come out. "Now, that's a good question. Seems to be what the jury's looking for these days, isn't it. If he really deserved to die, it's okay, isn't it?"

Cecile didn't answer that, surprised that Nica actually sounded cynical. She watched the other woman, and waited.

Nica sipped her coffee and appeared to think.

"If he deserved to die," Nica ruminated, "it was probably no more than any other man on the prowl. There's a type of person comes here looking for a real slice of the night pie. Gay, straight, doesn't matter too much. You look for what you want. But there are normals, people who just live here because they like the decor. Generation-X types, modern youth. Elliot was more of the old-school macho pig-man type. You know? And there are old folks. Lots of them here, too."

"Um," Cecile said. Nica was rambling. "You must miss him."

Nica frowned suddenly. She stood up to walk around the room. "No. I was going to move out. Had it all planned, but when he died his family asked me to stay on, keep an eye on things until the will gets settled among his relatives in Toronto. There's an ex-wife who claims a share for the kids, some brothers. I have free rent for a month or two. My good luck." She ran a hand along the edge of the black leather couch, her red fingernails making a startling contrast.

"Why were you moving out?"

"Like I said, he had a pig streak." She made a suggestive movement with her shoulders that was not quite lost on Cecile's nun sensibilities. "And he used to roam. He'd vanish for a night, off and on. That didn't bother me, but these days it isn't safe, you know? I'm monogamous myself. Most of the time. One at a time. I have my ethics."

Nica wandered over to a glass-topped coffee table and picked up a magazine. She waved it at Cecile. "And there was this kind of stuff. He got crazy about a month ago. Couple times a week he'd bring home crappy magazines. Kinky. I keep this one in his memory."

She tossed it into Cecile's lap and the nun looked down, then up quickly, letting the periodical slide to the floor where she gave it a shove with her foot to move it from her immediate vision. It wasn't the leather and chains, but what was behind them that bothered the nun.

"And then he roamed a little more. Getting weird. I told him I'd be leaving; he didn't seem to care. But he went first."

"You didn't love him?"

"Love?" Nica sounded surprised. "More coffee?"

"I'm fine, thanks."

The black-haired woman returned to her chair and sank into it as though exhausted. "Love? He wanted a girl on the arm and . . . ," she nodded toward the bedroom. "I wanted a place to stay. He worked at the bank all day; I slept in, went out, strolled the beach. South Beach. We were convenient for each other. Nice life while it lasts. It's not unusual, you understand."

"It's too bad. No love at the end," Cecile said.

Nica smiled sadly. "Real love is waiting. This was a temporary state. No big deal. A marriage of convenience without the vows."

"Vows," Cecile repeated, thinking of her own. Poverty, chastity, and obedience. Apparently the concept of vows was foreign to Nica. "You must know some of his friends," Cecile said.

"Some."

"He belonged to a consortium. A group of like-minded men. Did you know any of them?"

"Manny Beaumont, Olhm, some crazy Texan," she said. "Some other guys. Representatives of the universe, from what Elliot used to say. Germany, France, Canada, Greece, all tied up. A woman who got killed, Cosima something, maybe more. Who knows? Before my time. These men, these swine-men thought they could run the world. But they weren't exactly friends."

Cecile grew thoughtful. "Did they ever meet here?"

"They met on Fridays, and they rotated restaurants. I called it Miami's floating crap game because it was all crap."

"Why do you say that?"

"They asked me to get girls once. What did they think I was, a pimp?"

"Of course not. What happened?"

"I got girls. I charged for the references." She gave a little laugh.

Sister Cecile stared at the young woman. This was the new age, she thought with a touch of awe that such an incredible lack of self-awareness could exist in what was the remnants of the "me generation."

"I expect the police have gone through this place?" she asked.

"Thoroughly. So did Manny Beaumont." Nica switched her legs from one side of the chair to the other. Then she tipped her coffee cup up a half inch above her open mouth and let it run in like a waterfall. A small amount missed and ran down her cheek. Nica wiped it with the back of her hand. She was definitely unsteady. "Nothing here, as far as finding anything. Of course the cops were just going through the motions. They think it was a street punk killed Elliot. Lot of street gangs in Dade. But they have a stamp to their work and Manny is not convinced it was gang style, as you know. You may also not know that statistics of gangs are vastly inflated because they get more money to fight them if there are more of them. Understand? And cops like money, task forces, stuff like that."

Cecile nodded. "Nobody found anything?"

Nica smiled. "No."

"What did they miss?"

"Nothing."

"Mind if I look around? I always feel that people miss the most obvious places, don't you?"

"Be my guest."

Cecile started with the couch cushions. "Maybe something fell back here," she said. Under the cushions she found dust balls and three dollars and ten cents in quarters and dimes. She put the money on the coffee table.

"Keep it," Nica said. "Couch money is finders keepers."

69

Cecile nodded and stuffed it in her suit pocket. She could put it in the community restoration fund. Every little bit helped.

After twenty minutes of poking through Elliot's personal objects, Sister Cecile decided to get to the nitty-gritty of things even while Nica stood three feet from her at all times and watched. Up close Nica had bad breath.

Cecile dug under the mattress, into the toilet tanks, behind picture frames, and in the tea canister. She lifted loose rug edges, peered under table lamps, and flipped inside books. Nothing. It was a bust.

"See?" Nica said when Cecile was done.

"Thanks, Nica, it was good of you." Cecile stood by the door, ready to go.

"Sure. I told you, nothing here." She patted her motionless hair and walked to the phone. "I'm going to an appointment with a doctor. Got to get something for this flu."

"Good luck. I may be back."

"Any time."

13

LEONIE met Jim Cypress again that afternoon. She had taken her usual path home from school, skirting along Collins Avenue. This time she stayed on the sidewalk. No more looking at the place where the body had been. It was a dead giveaway. Besides, she was going to tell all. Soon.

This time she saw the policeman first. He appeared from a distance over the shimmering heat of the hot afternoon. He seemed to be walking in a mirage of water on the cracked, dry, cement sidewalk. A sudden January heat wave had put temperatures up in the eighties, but everyone said things were going to change. It was going to get cold. That meant sixty degrees, forty at night. Meanwhile Leonie was enjoying the heat. Her eyes were half-closed from the sun's glare as she watched Jim. She knew exactly who it was even though he was obviously pretending to be a tourist. He had a big, bulky shape. Solid. He was wearing knee-length shorts and a plaid shirt and big black sunglasses. He even had on a safari hat. He passed by the path through the alley that went up to the beach where Elliot had died.

Leonie didn't want to walk past him, but she couldn't do much about it, so she came up to him as though she didn't care. She even remembered his name. Jim Cypress. She could play it really cool.

"Hi, Jim. Nice hat."

"Hi, kid. How's school?"

Leonie swung her book bag and grinned. "Okay."

"Going swimming today?"

"Yeah, sure. You, too?"

They both laughed.

"Actually I was thinking about it," Jim admitted. "It's hot enough, and maybe I'll run into someone on the beach who saw something."

Leonie nodded. "Maybe."

"Someone must have seen something."

"Sure. Why not," Leonie said. She wondered if her words sounded stiff. But they were walking slowly, her book bag was swinging to a slow beat, everything was normal. She was cool. Nothing had changed except the guilt that nibbled along the edges of her mind.

"Maybe you can work on the case with me," Jim continued. "Like, ask your friends if anyone saw anything that night. Find out where everyone was. Stuff like that. You could be a detective."

"Neat idea," Leonie said. She couldn't keep the grin off her face. This was exactly the approach that Sister Cecile used. These two should get together. She almost said something but remembered just in time that Cecile wasn't supposed to tell the police she was on this case.

"Try it. Ever do any detective work?"

"Lots," Leonie said. "My dad is an investigator."

"That so?"

"Secret stuff," Leonie said solemnly. "He's great. He talks things over with me sometimes, and I help Sister Cecile. I saved her life twice, but I never told her."

"Really? Why not?"

"She didn't know I was there either time. And then, the last time, Sister Raphael and I saved her together."

"Sister Cecile? Who is she?" He sounded totally innocent of any knowledge of this person.

"Oh, she's in charge for now."

"She doesn't sound very competent."

"Well, she is. She prays a lot, and says it helps, but all along it's me who's helping. But she's cool."

"You should tell her you helped."

"Well, I wasn't supposed to be in those places."

"So, you usually go where you aren't supposed to?"

Leonie shrugged. "Not always." Her eyes went out to the ocean and she frowned.

"Where were you when Barclay was killed?"

Leonie was ready for that, had expected it somehow. "What night was that?" she asked, breathing very carefully.

"A week ago Friday."

"Friday? Friday. I must have been at Zoe's." She was quiet a moment. "Definitely Zoe's. We had Red Baron pizza. And we watched a video."

"No kidding."

"Yeah. Zoe's my best friend."

"Where does she live?"

"Down that way." Leonie gestured back in the direction from which they had come.

"Where do you live?"

"Down there, two blocks from the beach. I gotta turn off

right here." She stopped and looked up at the huge man. "You haven't found the killer yet?" she asked. "No clues?"

"Nothing we can pinpoint," Jim said. He sounded worried. "Ask your friends at school. Maybe somebody saw something. Ask around."

Leonie didn't want to do that. It would be stupid, but she was afraid to say so. Besides, she liked Jim. She even liked the two lines that appeared between his eyes when he looked serious. "I will," she agreed.

"Meet me along here tomorrow? Tell me what you find out? I pay with ice cream. A 'super cone' if you get something."

"Super cone?" Leonie grinned. Cecile was always telling her not to eat so much sugar, and had practically forbidden her to buy candy bars and street food. But this would be different, she wouldn't have to buy it, even. And then there was the fact that she would be working on the same case with Cecile. If she didn't have a problem with that, a major problem, she might actually enjoy this. "Deal," she said. "Bye, Jim."

Jim Cypress watched Leonie bounce down the side street, heading to her home. It was hard for him to believe that the girl actually lived in the Maria Concilia Retirement Community. She seemed perfectly normal. A very likeable, very smart kid, but nervous. Something was on her mind. It didn't take an expert to see that. It was going to take time to find out what the kid knew.

He headed for a nearby telephone booth to call his station house. The old nun was supposed to have made an appointment with this Sister Cecile person, but when he had called the police-desk office earlier, there had been no message. He called his office again.

"Cypress here. Any messages?"

He listened for a moment, his eyes straying down the street. He saw a familiar car drive past, a blue Taurus with heavily tinted windows. He squinted in the glaring sunlight trying to see inside as the car turned down the way Leonie had gone, but he couldn't make out the figure inside. Definitely a familiar car. It couldn't be Reggie Peele. He wouldn't be down at this end of town, although the older man did have a car like that.

Jim turned to the telephone. Finally a voice came back on the line, and he forgot about the car that looked like Reggie's. "Appointment for ten o'clock tomorrow morning? Great. Thanks."

Tomorrow morning he would meet the nun. That was going to be interesting. He was beginning to feel very protective of little Leonie Drail. Every instinct told him that this kid knew something. The trick was to find out what.

He turned to stroll back to his white Mitsubishi. Two minutes later he was moving down Collins Avenue heading south, air-conditioning unit blasting against the stifling heat buildup in the car.

First he would stop for some food for supper. It was his early night and he was done for the day. There was a major grocery store up ahead, and he was going to buy himself and his wife a Red Baron pizza for supper, just like the one Leonie had mentioned. Power of suggestion, maybe, but it sounded good.

He wasn't sure how his wife, Stephanie, felt about frozen pizza because they had only been married six months and were still in the home-cooked meal stage. It was tough on them both. Time for some fast food, he thought. Maybe if he picked up a good video, a bottle of Beaujolais Villages and some deli salad to go with the pizza, she'd go for it. They could pretend they were kids.

He grinned at the thought. He had a great wife who had a good job at Elrigh Chemical. Marrying Stephanie had been a serious break from his Miccosukee background, but his mother had already left the tribe when she had taken him out of the Miccosukee area as a child and run off with a Cuban businessman. It hadn't lasted. His mom was back on tribal lands. But he wasn't.

For all his high-flown detective status, Jim Cypress was

still just the Miccosukee with the Mitsubishi to the people on the Miami Beach force. He had a lot to prove. And he had a great need to do everything exactly right. Sometimes it was hard because it conflicted with his Miccosukee heritage. Honor, silence, loyalty: such virtues were sometimes just not all-American.

14

SISTER Raphael told Sister Cecile all about Leonie's walking into the ocean as soon as the younger nun returned from seeing Nica. "He wants to talk with you, this policeman," Raphael said. The old nun looked nervous; there was sweat on her chin. "Because you're her guardian."

"About what, exactly?" Sister Cecile asked.

"Well, it looked like Leonie was heading out to Key West but she forgot the boat."

"Nonsense. She's alone with a bunch of nuns, her dad's out of the country for a few months. New school, new friends. She's a little stressed, but twelve-year-olds get that way. I remember. I went swimming with my clothes on a few times."

"Maybe she thought she was Christ and this was the Sea of Galilee."

"Stop trying to be funny." Cecile knew it was a nervous reaction, Raphael's dim attempt at humor.

"Sorry," Raphael said, wiping her chin. "Anyway, I like this policeman. He was genuinely concerned, and he also thought Leonie might know something about the murder of Elliot Barclay. Kids see things."

"She would have told me if she knew anything," Cecile

said. "I've already asked her to help on the case, thinking maybe it would make her feel needed. She has amazing insights. I thought she would like to help. But I don't think she's disturbed, and I don't think she knows anything about the case."

"But this is a murder, Cecile, and she's a child. Maybe she's under stress. Maybe because of her father being injured, and then going back to work so soon. A death in the neighborhood could be very frightening for her. Imagine just walking into the ocean."

"Personally, I would love to walk into the ocean," Cecile said. "It's such an amazing color, so cool this time of year. I think she's acting normal. I wish I could get away with it."

"With acting normal?"

"We do have the convent pool," Cecile pointed out, ignoring Raphael's remark. "I swim every day."

"Chlorine. Do you know what that does to people with gray hair? Imagine a nun with green hair." Raphael patted her head. It was showing traces of a green tint. "Like mine. Not that I'm vain. I'm thinking dignity. Anyway, I told him I would schedule an appointment with you." Sister Raphael became serious. "May I?"

"Go ahead. I have nothing planned until one in the afternoon tomorrow."

"Fine. I already scheduled the appointment for ten o'clock tomorrow morning. I checked your calendar. Now, don't worry, Cecile. It will be fine."

Sister Cecile took a huge breath. Raphael was running her life again. She shook off the feeling that things were suddenly out of control. "I'm not worried," Cecile said. "Not at all."

Sister Cecile spent a bad night. She was not particularly happy about this entire situation. A policeman? What could she say? It didn't seem right, somehow, that her motherhood should be questioned. Might she be considered an unsuitable guardian? Would they call Leonie's father, wherever he was, and report that the woman he had put in charge of his daughter was doing a bad job? Maybe they would call HRS, the dreaded state welfare department that took children away from unfit mothers and placed them in homes for pay. She was worried, for the most part, because Sister Raphael was. And Raphael only worried when there was something to worry about.

She had no doubts she could convince the officer that Leonie Drail was having an excellent sojourn in the community. Religious, she could point out, did even adopt children. It wasn't unheard of. Leonie would testify that living in a convent was just fine, thank you. But what about the rest of it? What was going on with Leonie, anyway?

"Leonie was walking into the ocean?" Sister Cecile said it out loud later in her empty office. It was almost time for the appointment and she was nervously pacing the floor. She was dressed in the semihabit of her order. The gold cross around her neck gleamed with the morning light that slanted through the window. Her small veil perched on top of freshly washed curls and there was not a hair out of place.

The buzzer rang promptly at ten o'clock. Moments later Sister Louisa escorted a huge man into her presence, a tan-complexioned man who held out a thick hand and shook hers when they were introduced. Then Sister Louisa vanished, leaving the nun and the police detective alone in the office, staring at each other.

For a frozen moment they stood, silent, assessing, studying each other. Cecile's words burst out first.

"I was terribly distressed when Raphael told me about the incident in the ocean. I'm grateful you were there to help Leonie." Cecile's Connecticut accent came out thickly. It was an emotional moment. Her own integrity was hanging in the balance.

Cecile was still standing as she spoke. The police detective was very tall and her gray eyes were forced to look up to meet Jim Cypress's dark gaze. Then she looked away, finding her chair behind the old motel desk, her hands groping along the top of the chair as though she were blind. She maneuvered into it carefully. "Please, have a seat."

Jim sat in the red, faux-leather chair that had come with the motel. Then, in a slow, Florida drawl he recounted what he had told Sister Raphael in the garden. "I had to follow up on it," he said finally. "In good conscience, I couldn't let it rest."

"No. You were right coming here. Leonie means everything to me. I love her dearly; we all do. The nature of her father's work means he is incommunicado for long periods, and other than Damien, she has no immediate relatives. We became close a while back; it seemed right that she stay with us. Everyone was happy about the arrangement. Leonie is very bright, by the way. Very up on things."

Sister Cecile stacked a pile of receipts on the desk. She knew she was babbling. It had always been hard for her to explain her emotions.

She looked up suddenly. "I love her." She stopped, her voice stuck in her throat for a moment, then went on, "Like a mother. It's so hard to believe. Was she disturbed? Do you think she was suicidal?"

Jim pursed his lips. The usual Miccosukee custom of looking away from the person one was speaking with was an advantage in some ways. Sister Cecile didn't realize what it was, that he was listening to every shade of her voice and that each shade gave a clue to what the speaker really meant. But she saw understanding in his eyes when he looked up, and she knew he had read something she didn't want him to know, that she was worried. Seriously worried.

"Suicidal? No. She actually seemed surprised at what she had done. Her explanation was that she was just walking into the water and a wave came along. I'd seen her from the shore and she was walking straight out. I just reached her when the wave hit. She probably would have been okay without me. She said she can swim. Is that true?"

Cecile nodded. "She's a good swimmer. It could have been stress."

"Matter of fact, I think she's fine," Jim said. "She was more embarrassed than anything."

"She would be. She sees herself as very tough, but, of course, she's a child. She's very vulnerable. And her father being away . . . he had a serious accident not that long ago. It was a hard few weeks for us all, but he's fine. Still, it could have left her with a lot of fears." Suddenly Sister Cecile stopped. "Oh. Here's another possibility." She paused, unsure how to express her thoughts.

"Yes?"

"Sex. She asked me the other night about desire. What it's all about, you know? Did you talk to her about what was on her mind? Did she ask you anything?"

Sister Cecile watched as a grin came and went in record time on the detective's dusky face. He was a good-looking man.

"No, she didn't ask about that," he said. Then he looked away to better hear her reply to his next question. "Have you explained everything about sex to her? Has her father?"

"I hadn't actually thought about it." Cecile's voice sounded dry, crackling. "She's almost a teenager. She probably knows the mechanics, although not firsthand." This was hard going, but she pushed on. "I only became her guardian a few months ago, kind of an adjunct to her father while he's away, and she's not Catholic."

"Interesting. Is sex different for Catholics?" He stopped suddenly and stared at her small veil settled on top of brown curls, then down to her gold cross gleaming against a white blouse. "Uh, sorry. But you're her mother-figure. Have you told her what to expect? It's a tough world out there. There are prostitutes her age. Twelve-year-old prostitutes. Kids doing tricks on the beach. It's baby town. Maybe you haven't noticed?"

"Yes. Of course I have. Leonie probably knows more than I do, because kids talk, you're right." She smiled. "But maybe not. I will speak with her about it all."

"Soon. Maybe you should have a married person do it."

"Maybe." She wasn't going to tell him anything, Cecile

thought suddenly. He was clearly trying to discover if nuns had sex lives. "Most parents don't tell their children anything, anyway," she said, "so I don't think you can fault me for my lifestyle, or even make a fair connection between that and my telling Leonie anything about the business of procreation."

Jim chuckled. "You're right, but you're the one who brought it up. There's one more thing. I'd like to ask your permission to speak with her again about the night the man was murdered here on the beach. I think she may have been a witness."

"Leonie?" Sister Cecile's voice actually squeaked.

"Where was she that night?"

"Was it Friday? A week ago Friday?" Sister Cecile knew very well when it had been. Of course it was that Friday.

"Yes."

Cecile took her time. "Friday," she murmured, giving a nunlike illusion of fingering her beads. "Weekend. Probably at her friend's house. Zoe Cabrall. They usually hang out, eat calzone or whatever. She always gets a ride home, though. Now, that night," she paused again, "she must have come in about ten. Zoe's mother was to drop her off, and she was in on time. I heard her come in, then a few minutes later she came out to say good night like she always does. I can't imagine Leonie witnessed anything."

"You're sure?"

"Quite." Sister Cecile's heart thumped. Was she so sure? Was Leonie really hiding something from her? Had she been out with a boy, possibly having sex? Leonie had been rather subdued that night. Was that the reason? "I'll ask her about that Friday," Cecile said finally. "And you may, if you wish."

"Excellent. Meanwhile, I've asked Leonie to question her friends at school to see if they noticed anything that night. But I want to clear this with you. Because of her situation, maybe it will give her something to think about. Kids do see things. I ran into her yesterday, coming home from school and mentioned she do this. Then I realized I should have asked you first."

80

"You want to involve her in a murder case?" Cecile tried very hard to look scandalized.

Jim turned purple at her implication. His eyes roamed the office, floating from one thing to another while he struggled to form words. Cecile thought he might be angry. She had no clue how tough it was for the Miccosukee sometimes, a people more used to silent observation than big speeches. She saw his eyes focus on her private investigator's license, framed and hanging between copies of some Fantin-Latour roses and Carlo Crivelli's *Virgin and Child*.

"What's that?" He pointed at the wall.

"Crivelli's *Virgin and Child*? I thought it was very art deco, Miami Beach style. Venetian school, actually."

"No. The license. You're a private investigator?"

"That? Yes."

Jim rose and went over to the framed license and studied it. "This is new. Any cases yet?"

Sister Cecile nodded. "Yes. I was lucky. A connection from Boston."

"Odd. But that explains something Leonie said. She's helped you before?"

"More or less."

"So asking her to help me wouldn't be too much of a jolt?"

Suddenly he grinned down at her, throwing Cecile into a near state of shock. It was as if he had seen right through her, knew, somehow, that she had already asked Leonie to help her with the very same case. Impossible.

"She might enjoy it," Cecile agreed. "It might do her good to have a male figure in her life, as a friend. You would be careful? She's, well, she's like my own child in many ways. If she were hurt . . . I'd have a great deal of difficulty dealing with such a prospect."

"Trials of parenthood."

"Are you a parent?"

"Eventually. Not yet. Six months married."

"Congratulations."

Jim nodded. He was still standing. "I should be off. I'll keep an eye on her. She's a good kid."

"Thank you."

"I actually said 'thank you' when he left," Cecile breathed to Sister Raphael, who had returned from a walk bearing a bag of mangos and a coconut. "He wants Leonie to work on the Barclay murder with him. Can you believe such a thing?"

"Perish the thought," Raphael burbled back. "He did seem like a nice man, though. He's a Miccosukee. Very proud tribe. They've never been conquered, you know. He was very concerned about Leonie."

"Lord deliver us from concerned Miccosukee policemen," Cecile said softly. It sounded like the beginning of a litany.

"And from the malice and snares of the devil," Sister Raphael completed.

15

REGGIE Peele hated blacks. He hated the Miccosukee as an offshoot, because they were just as bad and probably all had black blood running through their veins. He hated homosexuals, he hated Jews, he hated Irish Catholics. He also hated Cubans, Italians, Greeks, and Russians, as well as all Southern Baptists. As a policeman he had managed to do a lot to keep these subversive people under control, but they kept springing up everywhere. Particularly the Southern Baptists, who rarely did anything that they could be arrested for. And Reggie Peele hated Jim Cypress. Few realized how pervasive Reggie's hatred was, and that his arrest record was highest among these hated groups.

When his daughter, Amy Peele, had fallen in love with Elliot Barclay, a man of respectable English descent, Reggie had been informed in vague terms by Amy that she worked with a wonderful man. Reggie had felt it was only a matter of time before the banker would succumb to his daughter's charms. They would have been a perfect match: money and good blood. Of course at the time Cosima Benedict was alive; Amy had mentioned Cosima in passing. It had been a convenience when Cosima died. Cleared the path for his daughter. He never questioned that Cosima's death had been anything but accidental. Besides, the death had happened in Coral Gables, not his jurisdiction.

Reggie hadn't asked Amy about what happened next between herself and Elliot. But one day Amy mentioned Nica Rabelais. "Bitchy prostitute moved in with Elliot. Another diversion, like Cosima," Amy spat. "Elliot relies on me more every day. He won't marry the bitch. He wants a woman. A lady. He counts on me."

Later, when Amy had told him that Nica Rabelais, the live-in lover of Elliot Barclay, was planning on moving out, Reggie had rejoiced and put on hold his simmering plan to arrest Nica for prostitution.

But then Elliot Barclay was murdered. Amy was truly devastated. Reggie, dedicated father to the core, felt tremendous anger, a father's anger that someone had hurt his little girl. "I will find the killer," he vowed to his daughter again, during one of their phone chats. "Your pain will be avenged, Amy. I'm working on it. The Miccosukee has the case. I watch every move he makes. Indian's on the case day and night. Soon as I get a hint of who the killer is, he's dead meat."

"Daddy, it hurts so much," Amy whimpered.

"Cypress is doing my legwork, damned Miccosukee. But he has a good arrest record. I've been following him in the Taurus. Everyone has a Taurus so he doesn't know. Smart Indian ain't so smart."

"Tinted windows," Amy mused. "Nobody can see it's you. What have you found out?"

"Not much, but I will. I always do."

Reggie Peele knew about Sister Cecile's investigation, too. Amy had called him from her office when Cecile had first arrived. "The investigator is in Elliot's office, cleaning it out," she screeched over the telephone. "She locked me out, the witch! What should I do?"

That was what had brought on the abortive attempt by Reggie to attack the nun and rob her of her large purse. It didn't work, and the end result of his failed attack on Sister Cecile was that he now hated her, too, with deadly passion. Another person to get even with in the future. Reggie's list of resentments grew with each new person he met.

Reggie was a detective, but an alleged job-related injury resulting from moving seven bales of marijuana from a bust location to the evidence room had reputedly strained his back beyond repair. He worked the desk now, at detective pay, and he figured he could run this whole thing from his seat.

"You say you got a witness?" Reggie asked Jim Cypress. It was lunch break in the station house. Jim had just returned from his talk with Sister Cecile.

"Maybe. It's just a kid. I got permission to speak with her," Jim said. He was munching a piece of leftover pizza from the night before.

"No kidding." Reggie Peele smiled, showing withered old teeth. He had the Englishman's habit of sucking his tea through a sugar cube and it had done bad things to his pearly whites. "What's her name?"

"Leonie Drail. She's a nice kid. I'd like a kid like her. Cute little blond," Jim said.

"Not likely you'll have a blond," Reggie said.

"Hell, Stephanie's as blond as they come."

"No kidding." Reggie was thoughtful, hiding his sense of apartheid that such a marriage could be contracted, much less result in a mixed-blood child.

Jim arched his back and stretched. "We're trying for a kid."

Reggie hid his disgust by reverting to the original topic. "So, this witness, she's a real witness?"

"Maybe."

"Where's she live?"

"With a bunch of nuns in that new retirement community."

"The Maria Concilia Retirement Community?" Reggie asked.

"Weird bunch. Old nuns."

"That's the place. The head nun is the kid's guardian. Unusual, but okay, I guess. She's cool."

"How will you approach it? We're talking very touchy stuff here. Kids."

"I figure I'll get the kid's confidence, then she'll tell me who did it. Simple."

"You figure one of the kid's friends for it?" Reggie asked. He opened his lunch as he spoke, a foot-long sub with extra ham, delivered from the sub shop across the street. He ordered the same thing every day. He opened a small container of cucumber salad dressing and poured it on, hiding his excitement at the information he was getting.

"Maybe. Something like that, or she would have said. The kid's got something on her mind, in any case. Meanwhile I've got a call on a break-in down Lincoln Road. Someone's talking." Jim munched on a pizza crust. "So I gotta run."

"I'll give you a hand with your reports if you get behind. That Barclay case has got to be a priority. Big name banker, the Canadians don't like it when a national gets killed. Lot of tourist money there." Reggie tried to make his offer sound casual by running his words through dripping bites of sub.

"I'm caught up. But there's something I want to look into that hasn't come in yet. If you could give a call to the lab for me and see what they have on Elliot Barclay's shirt. Full lab report. That would be a help. And I have a sample of something I want tested." Jim pulled out a small manila envelope from his front pocket and tossed it on Reggie's desk. "I need to know if there was any of this on the murder victim's shirt. Check this into the lab for me."

Reggie was nonchalant. "Glad to."

When Jim left a few minutes later, on his way to Lincoln Road, Reggie observed him carefully, hoping Jim would suspect nothing from his offer to help. Reggie was quite aware of his own reputation as an unsympathetic bastard who always put in a full day's work and not much else. He would have to be careful.

After Jim left, Reggie called down to the lab and asked for the Barclay case analysis to be sent to his desk immediately. "Priority," he said. "And I'll be dropping something off later from Jim Cypress." Reggie tapped the envelope on his desk.

"Sure, shirt results by four this afternoon. You've got it," the technician said.

"And the victim's blood type, too," Reggie added. "I need a duplicate on that." Maybe there was someone else's blood on the shirt. Maybe that's what this was all about, Reggie thought. He was determined to get to the bottom of this for Amy's sake. If the suspect's blood type matched what was on the shirt, that would clinch it. DNA results would come later, if necessary. But for now, he had serious plans to take care of the murderer himself. He wasn't exactly sure what he wanted to do, but revenge for Amy was the real priority.

Ten minutes later, Reggie called Amy and told her about the possibility of a witness. Amy had a brilliant suggestion. "Follow that girl that the Miccosukee knows, Daddy," she whispered into the telephone. "If she saw the killer, she may go back to him. You have to make her tell. Maybe it's one of the consortium. Talk to her, threaten her!" Amy Peele sounded almost hysterical, her voice quivering over the line, wrenching at her father's heart.

"I will, precious, I will."

After he hung up, Reggie Peele looked at the old round wall clock. Time to make a few phone calls. "Is there a Leonie Drail registered at your school? Twelve years old, female. This is the police station. Someone turned in a kid's wallet, name, age, and money, no address. . . . No? Thanks. Any other schools in the district?"

Ten minutes later Reggie knew Leonie went to St. Patrick's

School, what time the school let out for the day and had a complete description of the child. It was the one he had seen talking to Cypress the other day.

This was a piece of cake. He realized he had time to run by Leonie, casually, as she left school, see who she hung out with, and make it back to his desk before the lab report on Elliot Barclay's shirt arrived.

"Officer Peoples, could you take the desk for a few hours. I've got to see the chiropractor. The pain's getting bad. A quick adjustment. I'll be back before four."

"Sure, Reggie. No problem."

Reggie hobbled out of the office, leaving the icy air-conditioned world for the sweltering subtropical sun. His fair English skin had long ago turned a permanent red, his nose and cheeks a mass of broken capillaries and precancerous lesions. On the other hand, the Lord had blessed Reggie Peele with a full head of white hair. It was his pride and joy and he had coiffed it into great fluffy tufts that tended to lose their spring in the South Florida humidity. He didn't look like an evil old man.

The moment he stepped off the sidewalk and into the parking area, his bent posture disappeared and he walked swiftly. There was no time to lose. The grammar school got out at two-thirty and he was going to be there when Leonie emerged. He knew exactly who she was now, having followed her the other day when he had been scouting after Jim. The Miccosukee was so clueless, he thought. Reggie laughed out loud. He gunned the Taurus out onto Washington Avenue, and headed north on Miami Beach.

16

SISTER Cecile was rushing to make her one o'clock appointment that afternoon. Leonie would be fine, she thought as she drove the old Jaguar across the causeway. She would talk to her ward later, after school.

Biscayne Bay gleamed with extraordinary beauty, but for once Sister Cecile didn't see it. She had things on her mind. She was going to meet with every member of the consortium that had hired her. This was number one. "Method and order," she mumbled to herself as she drove. "Method and order."

She was momentarily distracted by her own thoughts. It was too much of a coincidence that she was working on the same case as the policeman who had met Leonie. Sister Cecile didn't believe in coincidences and she didn't believe that this was one, but for the life of her she couldn't understand what the unifying factor was in this business. There had to be one common element. What was it?

She met with Aristippus Tselementes at the Brickell Club. It was a perfect place to meet people connected with downtown business. It was right there, located on the twenty-seventh floor of the Capitol Bank Building in the heart of Miami's business district.

She met the shipping magnate in the small lobby; they were quickly seated in the dining area. "Nice of you to take the time," she smiled at the man. She unfolded her napkin and looked around.

"Incredible," she murmured. The view was breathtaking

and she found herself speechless at the bay's blue beauty. Hit by a huge Florida sun, rainbow colors bounced heavenward from the glistening cruise ships. The water was the color of her mother's eyes. It was one of those moments when she paused for a tiny prayer of thanksgiving for the beauty of her world. Then the menu arrived; food to compete with the view.

Such competition didn't go down well at all with the long-haired Greek who had been expecting her immediate and full concentration. He hummed, tapped his water glass and cleared his throat. Finally it occurred to Cecile that he was demanding attention.

She turned to him. "I've been anxious to meet you, sir. It's a serious case and I need insights." She kept her face grave, no smiles, no hint that in spite of being a nun, she was a woman and he was a man. But it always came down to that sooner or later, anyway.

It came sooner. He smiled broadly. Nice teeth, full lips, wolfish grin, a face that normally got its own way.

"Manuel told us about you."

She nodded, giving him the full attention he demanded.

"They tell me you are incorruptible?" He looked pointedly at her expensive clothes, perfect face and the large gold cross. "And brilliant. What would you like for lunch?" Apparently he liked to dazzle with non sequiturs.

Cecile almost said, "I'll have something corruptible," but instead rattled off her request, "Evian water and the red snapper in lemon and cream with radicchio leaves."

For himself, Aristippus ordered a gin and tonic, then salmon scallops with caviar. They chatted about Greece for a while; Cecile had traveled extensively in her youth and spent a month on Hydra. The talk lasted through appetizers of creamed asparagus tips with prosciutto. She hesitated to get down to business too soon; the man across from her seemed determined to make some sort of impact on her, and she decided to let him, briefly.

Eventually she asked, "Why, exactly, are you personally interested in bringing the murderer of Elliot Barclay to justice, Aristippus?"

"Please, call me Ippi," he said, his oily voice sliding across the table. He put his hand on hers as he spoke.

"Yes, Ippi," she said and slipped her hand back to her bread plate for a crust of pumpernickel to bathe in the leftover asparagus sauce. "What is your personal concern, Ippi?"

The Greek looked crestfallen, an obvious act, and then he laughed and went into a monologue. "Money, of course. I can see it drifting away with Barclay's demise. He was a hoodlum, a very classy hoodlum, hung out on South Beach a lot, a regular at Liquid, that glam-o-rama club on the corner of Washington and Espanolia. And he slummed. But he was all manner of brains. We had a deal set up, our group, and it looked promising. I'm thinking of getting out altogether now. Beaumont isn't as good."

"What was the deal?" Cecile put down the pumpernickel and took a delicate bite of snapper with the right amount of dill. It had just arrived.

"Confidential?"

"Oh, very. Regard me as your confessor."

He met her clear, gray eyes. "Not likely."

"What were you up to with Mr. Barclay?"

"Overloading an edge corporation." He shrugged and smiled. "Then pulling out the rug. Standard procedure for the S and Ls. Our philosophy is 'the greatest good for the greatest people,' but we consider ourselves much more valuable than our investors, so we fill in the blank with ourselves as the greatest people."

"Is this legal?"

"Bankruptcy isn't illegal. The American government doesn't insure foreign banks, so they take no loss. Nobody is particularly unhappy except possibly some cocaine lords who invested in the first place, and they deserve to lose. Besides, there will be no actual bankruptcy and no one will really sacrifice anything. The investors would be compensated by long-term bonds and some Asia-based mutual funds: high risk, big returns. No reason to kill. You see, I'm being very up-front with you."

90

"I think I'm beginning to understand," Cecile nodded. "A scam."

"Not at all. Should bankruptcy befall our corporation, it would be legitimately connected to risky provinces. You understand that the greater the risk the more money one can make. It's axiomatic in banking. Besides, there may never be a bankruptcy, just a thin line."

"I understand that. You have a legal obligation to safeguard your depositor's investments; that's also axiomatic. It's still not ethical to stiff a crook."

He laughed again. She was totally aware of his eyes on her. She couldn't move without him looking at even a simple twitch as if it were an erotic gesture. From wherever, his dark eyes would return to her lips until she felt obligated to pat them with a napkin in case there was cream sauce somewhere.

She tried to floor him with her grasp of business concepts. Maybe that would distract him, she thought, so she talked about debentures and selling short and municipal bonds, words that matched her expensive clothes. Maybe she had done this all wrong. Instead of the light blue linen designer suit that had set her back several thousand she should have worn her polyester off-the-rack white skirt and a cotton blouse.

Sister Cecile didn't know how the blue suit picked up the blue in her hazy gray eyes, but after a while she realized that he was staring into them with no concept of what she had said.

"Eh," he said after she had finished with a long, financial sentence that switched midstream to the murder.

"Well?" she asked. "Tell me about motive."

He thought a moment, replaying her last words in his mind before he answered. "Elliot Barclay had a list that differentiated the types of investors and spelled out our game plan. We can't find this material. It's invaluable, but is it worth killing for?" He shrugged. "No, the only people who might want him dead are in the consortium. Fewer members, more profit. A minor motive, but real."

She smiled. "I understand. Still, I question that motive.

What about Cosima Benedict? She was killed too. Do you see a connection? What do you think?"

His eyes half closed. "Cosima. Odd, but I still believe she was murdered. A car hit her as she left a friend's place in Coral Gables. Late night. Someone had called her, perhaps? She was alone and Cosima rarely traveled alone. Usually Elliot escorted her. He was devastated. Said he couldn't understand what she was doing out then." He looked at Cecile again and shrugged. "Murder, yes. But we've never found a motive. Nowhere. Cosima was more useful than troublesome. But, Elliot was different. Perhaps there was a motive for his killing."

"Elliot himself, money, a list of names and numbers. That's it?"

Aristippus nodded. "Minor motives."

"All right, let's look for another motive. Tell me about Elliot Barclay. You say he liked to slum. He was found in an underpopulated section of Miami Beach, a good mile from the cool section. He was shot with a gun that had been used to kill a prostitute, but the gun can't be found. My first thought was that he was killed in the same place and at the same time as the prostitute, but the police report says he was killed on the spot where they found the body, and it occurred the night after the prostitute died. He was found in a deserted place on the sand. Time of death is set around nine-thirty, ten o'clock. That's early by beach-life standards. That's the first puzzle I want to solve. Why there? Why then? Now, you people don't think his was a random death. But my question is simple: why the beach? More specifically, why that part of the beach?"

"Excellent question. Perhaps a clandestine meeting?"

"Did you kill him, Ippi?"

"No." Aristippus looked modest. "We all feel it was one of us, but none of us will admit to it. Silly of us."

She stared at Ippi Tselementes thoughtfully. "Do you know Nica Rabelais?"

He seemed to choke, briefly. "Nica? We all do. I don't care for that type, though. You clever, northern-style women, now, you appeal to me. She is too brittle for me."

Cecile chewed her last bite of fish as he spoke. She didn't quite believe him. Nica was beautiful, no man would turn her down. Plus the fact that she was a prime opportunist. "No jealousy, then." Cecile took a sip of the white wine he had ordered. "Have you seen her since the death?"

"Barcus did. Barcus Dumplig, the Texan? Very mouthy sort. He was over there last night and found out some rather disturbing news. Matter of fact, he called me about it."

"What was that?"

"Nica is HIV positive. She has one of those AIDS-related pneumonias."

Cecile felt a lurch in her stomach. "Oh." She couldn't speak for a moment. Nica? But it had only been a cold. Impossible!

"That's tragic. The poor thing. The poor, dear woman." Cecile looked away, shocked. "She was sick when I saw her. She was going to the doctor." Cecile spoke automatically as she tried to comprehend the terrible news.

"I was shocked, too," Ippi said. "AIDS. Funny thing about it. You think with enough money it won't come your way, but it will. It or something else."

Sister Cecile was still stricken. Nica? She'd had a cold. A bad cold. The disease took on a face. It became real. It became a motive. Cecile shook her head.

"Well, it is difficult," Aristippus Tselementes said. "Barcus wondered if I'd had relations. Thought I might need testing. Not that I'd want to know if I had it. Barcus is in a panic, himself. Even with protection. You understand one can be careless." He tossed his hair back like a woman would.

Sister Cecile stared at the man across the table who so casually talked about relations and didn't mean his relatives. He meant sex, and ultimately, death. The absurdities of the English language. "Nica," she said tentatively. "So pretty. Dear God have mercy on her." Her mind raced at the implications. "What about Elliot?"

Ippi attempted to smile. "It's only sordid when your friends don't have it, isn't it? It's moot whether Elliot was HIV positive now, but it does give cause for thought. It's possible that

93

he faced a shortened life span. Maybe he didn't even know. That's irony."

"He could have given it to Nica."

"He probably did. Or maybe she gave it to him? Elliot could have picked it up somewhere else. Maybe he didn't have it."

"Maybe he did," Cecile speculated. "I think it's important that I investigate his other side," Cecile said firmly. "This non-business side." She turned to the waiter as he removed her empty plate. "I'll have a decaffeinated with milk, please." She continued, "I need to become acquainted with this so-called seamy side. I'd like your help."

"Seamy side? You're asking me?" He chuckled. "You don't think I'm the killer then? You won't stop the investigation with me?" He had recovered too quickly from the mention of AIDS. Maybe he was in denial.

Cecile fingered the heavy gold cross around her neck and pushed her words out carefully. "You've clarified the motive. I appreciate that."

"*I* have no motive." He looked like a little boy with huge dark eyes. A specter of death still floated between them. He had forgotten, but she still saw it.

Cecile laughed carefully. "Really? This invaluable list of Elliot Barclay's might be worth having. We'll have to find it. Meanwhile, I want one of you to take me to Elliot's slumming areas. I need a guide, or at least some serious information about where to start."

"Barcus Dumplig would be your man. Not me. Give him a call."

"Barcus Dumplig?"

"Give him a call. He'd be delighted to show off some grunge."

Cecile walked slowly from the building to the parking garage; she tried to shake off the knowledge of Nica's disease but it lingered like a dark shadow. AIDS patients could live for years. Advances were being made. Maybe Nica would be fine.

94

She started up the car, turning out into traffic like a jack-rabbit out of a hole. It was a perfect day, perfect for driving her small Jaguar back to her office and making arrangements with Barcus Dumplig for a tour of the dark side.

17

REGGIE Peele was coming out of a Laundromat when Leonie left school with her best friend, Zoe Cabrall. People lingered in Laundromats, and the one near the parochial school was at just the right distance to keep an eye on things without drawing attention to himself.

Reggie almost missed her among the masses of plaid-skirted, white-bloused children, but Leonie and Zoe soon separated themselves from the hustle of parents and children, and walked in the anticipated direction. Reggie fell in behind. It was easy because the girls were walking slowly, their heads together. "You oughtta like Carlos," Zoe was saying. "I almost did. He's cool. Almost fourteen."

"Zits," Leonie said and shook her head. "Lip zits."

"Lip zits are nothing."

"Did you ever kiss him?" Leonie asked.

"Of course, dummy."

Leonie grimaced. "No way. I would never kiss a zit lipper."

"Check my mouth," Zoe pointed at her lips. "Perfect. No contagion, no zits."

"Think of all that puss," Leonie said and looked behind her to see if Carlos was behind them. There was no one but some younger kids, though, and an old man.

Reggie was convinced they were discussing the murder.

The blond girl looked very serious, her head bobbing back and forth. She kept looking around her as though she had already been spooked once. The other one had pointed to her lips. Reggie was convinced she had said, "My lips are sealed," or words to that effect. Clearly they were discussing something important.

Maybe I should just grab her and shake her down, Reggie thought. Then get rid of her. She had to be a Catholic, going to St. Patrick's, living with nuns. Catholics were no good. She was a disposable. Like the people he had read about in Columbia who were shot by the politicians' gangs. Homosexuals, homeless kids, nonbelievers. In Columbia such people were considered to be "disposable." They had the right idea in some of those countries, Reggie's thoughts continued. Entire classes of people were shot on the streets, eliminated by whatever drug-infested gangs were running things that week while the police looked the other way.

Reggie followed the girls until his back hurt so much he stopped the surveillance. Normally, Reggie's alleged back injury didn't bother him at all, but sometimes when he was pretending to limp it became real. It had happened today as he was trying to impress the desk officer at work by hobbling out, ostensibly to a chiropractor. It hit him like a jolt of electricity when he stepped up the pace to follow the girls. It was all the kids' fault.

"Damn," he muttered as another twinge of pain told him he might do well to return to headquarters. Leonie had suddenly burst into a jog.

Half an hour later Reggie Peele was back at the station house. Officer Henry Peoples looked up from the desk as the white-haired man hobbled up.

"Looks like the adjustment didn't help," Peoples said sympathetically and vacated his seat for Reggie. "Got some reports here for you. Lab stuff."

"Yeah, great, Henry, thanks. Yeah, the damn back gives a lot of grief. Thanks, buddy."

Reggie settled back into his desk chair and shuffled through the papers. The lab report on the victim's shirt was complete. Two types of blood, one B negative, the other AB positive. The latter was the match with the murder victim. And there was a note on tomato sauce. Perfect match on the shirt with ingredients in the sample Jim Cypress had sent in, a sample labeled Red Baron pizza sauce. Not important, Reggie decided. Who cared about pizza sauce. But the blood type was critical. The killer's blood is on the shirt, Reggie thought triumphantly.

The old policeman went on to a second report on the victim's blood. He read the clinical terms, then stopped. His face turned as white as his hair.

Elliot Barclay had been HIV positive.

"Shit," he whispered. "Triple shit." The man Amy loved had been a walking specter of doom. Reggie's hands shook as he reread the paper. His daughter had been saved from death by a killer! It was crazy. It changed everything. He had to call Amy. He punched the numbers, his old fingers trembling. Was it possible his daughter had sex with this man. Dare he ask?

A father's worst nightmare was threatening his genetic complacency. Things like this just never happened to people like him.

Sister Raphael met Leonie when she came home that day. The old nun was ready to talk to Leonie about sex, just as she had promised Sister Cecile, and she was determined to make the best of it. She followed Leonie into the kitchen.

"We had a huge fruit salad for lunch," Raphael said. "You should try some for a snack."

"Um," Leonie said. She opened the refrigerator door.

"It's in the big blue plastic container."

"Yeah, thanks."

"Maybe I'll have a snack, too," Raphael said.

"Sure. Here," Leonie handed the old nun the bowl of fruit salad. Then she pulled out a gallon jug of milk. "I'm going to make a fruit shake," she said. "Want one?"

"Please."

Five minutes later they were at the table drinking cool fruit shakes. Leonie looked fine, Raphael thought. Maybe this talk wasn't necessary. But she had promised Cecile. They couldn't afford to wait until Leonie's father returned; besides, Damien was a man. This was a woman thing.

"You walked into the ocean," the nun said abruptly. It wasn't what she had intended to say.

Leonie looked wary for a flash in time, then grinned. "I just felt like it."

"The policeman stopped by. Jim Cypress. He was a little concerned. I told him not to worry."

Leonie nodded. "Jim. He really is a cop then? It's okay to talk with him about stuff?"

"Yes."

"He told Cecile, didn't he? And she's upset, I bet."

"Sort of. I said maybe you were trying to walk on water."

"Did she laugh?"

"No. And then I suggested maybe you were going to Key West and forgot the boat."

"You should have said I was Moses, parting the Red Sea."

"Cecile wouldn't have laughed at that either. She's convinced you have a hidden problem."

"Oh." Leonie frowned and Raphael felt a strange shock run through her bones. Leonie looked guilty. Cecile was right.

"Well, we thought it might have to do with sex," Raphael said bravely.

"Oh. Sex?"

"Yes. We thought . . . well, we wondered. Uh. Well, we hoped that you understood about it." There, it was out.

"Like what?"

"Like, maybe somebody was making overtures and you didn't understand. Or something."

Leonie sat there. It felt like hours to Sister Raphael, who saw things pass over Leonie's face, hard to define things. Finally Leonie spoke.

"Sister Raphael, last year my dad told me about sex. I mean, he really did. He got me a book to read, and then he said watch out for it, like it was good but it was bad, you know? Like you were supposed to love someone and be grown-up."

"And be married," Raphael added firmly.

"Right." Leonie nodded. "And the school does AIDS awareness. They all do. But you know something, Raphael? The kids still do it."

Raphael felt her heart sink. "I know."

"How do you know?" Leonie asked.

"I read *Newsweek*."

They didn't talk for a moment, both taking long drinks. Leonie let the liquid roll back down the edge of her glass and swirled it around. "I think I won't do it," she said finally. "Until later."

"Much later. It mixes you up when you aren't ready. Besides, there's AIDS. A doctor friend of mine told me adolescents are getting it now. You can't believe kids when it comes to that, saying they don't have it, because they don't know. Those things, those rubber things? They don't always work. Have you ever seen a person with AIDS?"

Leonie nodded. "Everything's on the Beach."

"And the moral thing," Raphael said finally. "It's not right to do it when you aren't married."

"I knew you'd get to that." Leonie didn't exactly grin, but Raphael could see something there like she was going to call Zoe up and tell her everything.

"That's the bottom line, the moral thing," Raphael said and closed her eyes and wondered if Leonie understood, or wanted to understand, or even if she could understand. "If a person asks you, or tries to start something Leonie, please say no."

Leonie got a strange look in her eye, as though she were seeing things far beyond Sister Raphael's understanding. "Raphael, people are weird out there. Do you believe in angels? Like maybe to protect you from weird things?"

"Absolutely."

"Sister Cecile does, too. Maybe you guys are right." She took another drink and set down the empty glass. "I'm going to take a swim in the pool. Want to?"

"Later. Thanks anyway."

Sister Raphael watched as Leonie put her glass in the dishwasher and turned to nod a smile back before she left. Leonie was getting pretty. Almost thirteen, thin, but suddenly elegant, with an amazing grace of motion as though she had been studying how Sister Cecile carried herself and was mimicking it. Leonie had her head on straight when it came to sex, Raphael decided as she finished her fruit shake. But there was something else bothering Leonie.

It wasn't sex.

Sister Raphael got up from the table and took care of her dirty glass and the blender. Then she went for a walk around the retirement home to limber up her knees. Getting old was a bother, but she dealt with it. She walked out and along the sidewalk just as Sister Cecile pulled up in her black Jaguar and maneuvered into the small off-street parking area beside the retirement community.

Raphael spoke before Cecile was out of the car.

"Leonie knows about sex," she said.

"What!"

"Her father told her. She's going to wait, Cecile, it's okay. But there's something else bothering her."

"Are you sure?"

"Very."

"What?"

"I don't know."

Sister Cecile locked the shiny black car and frowned as she walked through the parking lot, Sister Raphael at her side. She did have an elegant walk, and an expression on her face much like the one Leonie had worn just a short while before. Sister Raphael was amazed. If Raphael hadn't known otherwise she would have said that Cecile looked very much like a brunette version of her ward, Leonie Drail.

"It's like having a poodle," Raphael murmured to herself. "You get one, you start looking like it. Or it looks like you, and maybe acts the same, too." It was a terrifying thought. Leonie? Sister Cecile?

18

LEONIE had put it off too long. She was sick inside and out. Nobody knew, either—that was the worst thing. When she was a kid, she had told her nanny everything. Nanny was a good woman who quit her post not long after her sister died. Then Nanny traveled west to take care of the sister's children. Some kind of loyalty, Leonie thought at the time. Deserted again.

And just what happened to all the confidences Nanny had heard from her? Did Nanny tell tales? Leonie-tales told to the sister's kids? Leonie got the creeps just thinking about it. Sister Cecile wouldn't tell anybody anything, she hoped. Maybe it would be like going to confession, whatever that was like. Anyway, she was going to tell the nun everything.

Leonie thought about sex and the conversation with Raphael. Of course her dad did his best with the sex thing. Leonie chuckled when she thought of Sister Raphael and the nun's worries. Well, as usual, Raphael was somewhat right. And as usual, Leonie was convinced that Sister Cecile had put her up to it. Cecile could read her like a book.

Leonie had a secret feeling, a feeling she rarely admitted even to herself, that her mother had been very much like Sister Cecile.

So she was going to Sister Cecile immediately.

At nine-thirty that night Leonie Drail knocked on the nun's bedroom door. Leonie had only been in there a few times and it was always an amazing experience because of what was in the room. She knocked timidly. No answer. Leonie stood for a moment then turned the doorknob and entered. The room was strange to her without the nun in it. Or maybe it wasn't strange at all; it was just empty.

Leonie looked around, her eyes scanning the room for personal effects. As usual, there was nothing. In the dim light coming through the half-curtained window she saw the lamp bolted to a dresser. Leonie knew it was a leftover from the building's motel days; at least it worked. She turned on the lamp and stared at the chair where she would wait for the nun. The solitary chair stood like an arthritic old man, straight-backed, stubborn hardwood, dented with age. It was not comfortable. Leonie didn't know it, but it was a piece of furniture Cecile had picked up at the Salvation Army thrift shop on Bird Road, along with the couch for the living room and several other vintage pieces.

Leonie focused on the bed, a narrow bed covered with a white, stringy spread. The bed itself looked stiff and uncomfortable. Leonie inspected the floor. It was covered with the same blue rug, spotted with mildew, that was there when the nuns moved in. Not a floor she would ever sit on. On the wall over the door was a crucifix.

That was it. Not even an alarm clock. How did the nun get up in the morning, or did she ever sleep?

Leonie sat on the wooden chair and waited. She would love to look in the closet and in the dresser, just to see what was there. She had done that once before, but tonight Cecile might appear at any time. Besides, Leonie told herself with a touch of new maturity, it was none of her business.

Maybe she had time for just a peek.

No. Leonie shifted on the chair. It was uncomfortable, but Cecile should be in soon, Leonie had seen her in the common room playing Old Maid with some of the ancient residents. Cecile did that frequently. Apparently she liked playing cards with the old nuns.

Ten minutes went by. Leonie had a watch, so she knew. It was a very long ten minutes and Leonie almost left. She stood up and paced, walked to the door, turned around and sat again.

Leonie stared at the doorknob. Finally it turned. Sister Cecile walked in, her face looking drawn and tired. Leonie rarely saw the nun looking like this, but the nun didn't know she had a visitor when she first entered. Then she saw Leonie and the face, the face of a tired angel, suddenly became the face of Sister Cecile, smiling, soft, and wary.

"Hi," Leonie said. "I came for a visit."

"I see."

"I've been waiting."

"Well, not long, I hope." Sister Cecile sat down on the edge of the bed and it barely seemed to give. Leonie suspected that Sister Cecile actually slept on a board, and not a mattress at all.

"You don't look very comfortable. How about you take the bed, I'll take the chair?" Cecile offered.

Leonie jumped up at the invitation. "Sure?"

Cecile grinned. "I know about that chair." She stood up and they changed places. Leonie sat carefully, just in case it *was* only a board. It wasn't, just an extra-firm mattress. That was a relief. It was hard to imagine anyone even remotely human sleeping on a board.

"How's school?" Cecile asked.

"Oh, the usual. That's not why I'm here." Leonie looked at Cecile and wondered if maybe she should just leave.

No.

She jumped right in. "Actually I wanted to tell you something about that night."

Cecile didn't say a word. She didn't say, "What night?" She just nodded as though she knew. "Okay."

"Well, we ate a lot of pizza, watched a scary movie and then what's-his-name called Zoe, and they got going on the telephone, so I figured I'd walk home. Zoe's mom wouldn't be along for another hour."

Leonie watched Cecile carefully, but the nun just sat on the hard chair, totally still.

"I figured I'd go down to the beach. I love the beach." She paused. Her voice was rattling, out of control. "I still do. Even now."

Cecile nodded, her gray eyes intense, her lips barely parted. It looked as though she wasn't breathing.

"Well, I saw him. Funny, I thought it was Dad for a minute, but no such luck. He came up. He thought I was a prostitute."

Cecile's mouth tensed.

"I had on a lot of makeup, put my hair up at Zoe's."

Understanding showed in Cecile's eyes. That and a growing fear. If she had talked just then, Leonie would have quit and run out, but Cecile still didn't speak.

Tears fell from Leonie's eyes, one right on her lap, then one after another they rolled down her cheeks. "He grabbed me. I tried to get away, but he had a gun. He shot it at my feet. He was so weird." Leonie shook her head, not believing it even after all this time. "He got me down on the sand, said he was going to clean up South Beach, have some fun, kill me." The last words came out with a big sob, rising in the still air of the room. Leonie pulled the words down with an effort. "He said that."

Cecile moved over to the bed and put an arm around the girl, giving her a hug. "Leonie, Leonie," she whispered.

"I picked up his gun from the sand. He had his hands all over me," Leonie said, rushing the words, determined to finish. "I had it aimed right at him; I was going to kill him." She felt Cecile's arm tighten around her, and she kept on. "I couldn't do it. Couldn't kill him. So he grabbed the gun." She let out a huge breath and shook all over. "He had it in his own hands, but it was still pointed at him, and it went off. He died right on top of me."

There was a long silence in the room while Leonie waited for the verdict, tears flowing, shoulders shaking with quiet sobs. "It was all my fault. Everything was my fault."

Finally Cecile spoke.

"Nothing was your fault." The words came out straight, sure, bullets of tranquility aimed for Leonie. "You did nothing wrong," Cecile said. "He died because he was trying to do wrong. He was a grown man, he was totally responsible. Do you understand that, Leonie?"

Leonie looked sideways at her friend, her mother, her very

104

own nun, and she saw tears. The nun's face was awash with tears. "I told myself that," the girl nodded. "But if I hadn't been there, done makeup and all that . . . I shouldn't have been on the beach."

"Not true. It's *your* beach."

"My beach." Leonie said the words slowly, miraculously understanding that it *was* hers. Her beach.

"He tried to hurt you on your beach. It's your face, you can wear makeup, you can pierce your nose, whatever. It's *your* face. It doesn't make you responsible for his actions."

"My face," Leonie said in wonder. It was dawning on her that maybe she wasn't guilty. But it was going to take a while. She let out a very deep shudder. "Still. I feel so awful."

"The man died," Cecile said, sniffling. "He died on top of you. Of course you feel awful. He was trying to hurt you. Only God knows what was truly in his mind when he died. Only God knows about him, Leonie. But we all know about you. It wasn't your fault, darling, and don't ever think it was. NOT YOUR FAULT." She said it in capital letters.

Leonie still didn't quite believe it. A big hiccup rocked her slender frame. "I didn't think anyone could love me," she said so quietly it was almost inaudible.

Cecile hugged her even more tightly until Leonie felt it, hard. It was hard enough to feel like love. And suddenly Leonie felt the love.

"I love you, Raphael loves you. We all love you. Your dad loves you. We're all your family." Tears were still running down Cecile's face. It made Leonie feel much better, just seeing those tears, someone else's tears for her pain.

"Okay," she managed.

"Should I get in touch with your dad?" Cecile asked. "I can, you know. Through the agency."

"He doesn't have to know," Leonie said. "He might . . . he might be disappointed."

"Leonie, he would probably kill Elliot Barclay himself if the man weren't already dead. Believe me, he wouldn't blame you. He *loves* you, and he also knows you. He's your father."

"Well, we can tell him later. Elliot Barclay was a turd." Saying the name like that made Leonie feel better. "Turd," Leonie repeated and let out a tiny, almost hysterical giggle.

"Triple turd," Cecile agreed.

They both laughed through tears. There didn't seem to be much more to say, triple turd said it so well. But they continued to talk for another fifteen minutes. Finally Cecile suggested a raid on the freezer. "Nobody will be up. There was a sale on that special ice-cream cake dessert. We could go split an entire one between us and celebrate that you're free of this."

"Sister Germaine will be mad," Leonie pointed out. "She counts everything."

"I'll tell her tomorrow that it went for a higher good," Cecile assured the girl. "Besides, I'm the boss here."

"Let's go."

They ate by the light of the pool patio fixture shining in through the window, neither wanting to subject herself to the glaring florescent lights in the kitchen. They consumed the entire cake. Every so often another tear would emerge and Leonie would wipe it off.

"What about Jim Cypress?" Leonie asked. "Should I tell him?"

"One of us should," Cecile said.

A long silence followed.

"Okay, I'll think about it. It's late," Leonie finally said, squinting at the huge wall clock in the gloom.

"Can you sleep?" Cecile asked.

Leonie nodded. "I think so."

"Good. Let's clean up and go to bed."

Quietly they loaded their plates into the massive dishwasher, mopped the table, tossed the empty cake box in the trash. For just a flash, Leonie felt so good she wanted to sing, but instead something Sister Cecile had said earlier came back in a sudden flash. It was worth pursuing.

"Did you actually say something about getting my nose pierced," Leonie asked as they walked through the kitchen door.

"Did I say that?"

"I heard you. What do you think?"

"I'm calling your father, first thing!"

They both burst into laughter.

19

NICA Rabelais returned to her apartment that same evening and undressed for a shower. After that she planned to take a little nap, then she would go out. She was a beach person; for beach people the night didn't begin until after midnight, and it lasted until dawn.

Tonight she would do it with a vengeance. She knew she was sick now. She knew the whole story. The doctor she had seen at the clinic had warned her to take it easy because her pneumonia was bound to get much worse if she didn't rest. She could die very soon in that case, or face endless hospitalization. But with good care she could live for a long time. She stood in front of the full-length mirror in the bedroom and stared at her naked figure. Still looked good. None of those ugly sores yet. What a shame it all had to end with ugly. She ran over the conversation she had had with her doctor.

"How long, exactly?" Nica had asked.

Doctor Phipps had smiled and looked knowledgeable. "Quality time?" she had said. "Years. New drugs are being developed all the time. It's hard to say actually, but healthy habits will make your time much more pleasant."

"For who," Nica had murmured and slipped off the examination table, her eyes on the doctor's box of rubber gloves, popping up out of a dispenser box like Kleenex, or condoms for Martians with pentagonal sex organs.

Now she was home, staring at a regular box of pop-up tissues on her bed stand. She took a long shower, but she still felt dirty. So what. Tonight she was heading out to Liquid for some quality time just like the doc suggested. It was the place to go these days, but like everywhere else on the Beach it would probably fade out this year and something else would be cool. It passed through her mind that Liquid's popularity would probably last longer than she did.

She shrugged. First a little nap, then the new dress, some makeup. She still had a life. Maybe a brief life, but it wasn't over yet.

The telephone rang.

"Yeah?" She listened for a moment as the caller talked.

"Sure, I remember you," Nica said, and she flopped back on the bed. It was hard to stand up sometimes. She got dizzy. She settled back and listened intently to the speaker. Then she talked some more.

"Did I know? Sure, I knew he had it. He was freaked out about it. He got strange. AIDS does that. He knew he had it, definitely. I didn't, though. Big shitting surprise."

She listened again.

"How the hell do I know? One of us gave it to the other one, or maybe we both had it to start with. It's too late to worry about that, don't you think?" Nica didn't even sound angry.

Nica closed her eyes and listened. "Come over. Sure. We can talk about it. In a couple of hours. About eight o'clock, okay? Doorman's off then. Just ring the buzzer, I'll let you up."

Nica hung up, shaking her head. People were crazy, she thought. Who cared when you died. Have some fun, burn out. "Out, brief candle," she said aloud and wondered where she had heard the expression.

Nica Rabelais died that night. She was shot from behind, pumped full of Federal 123-grain FMJ load, the upper limit to bullet weight for a 9mm. The body was reported the following morning at ten o'clock by Claudia Gonzalez of the Upright Cleaning Service. Ballistics assumed it was a man's load, coming from a heavy gun. It certainly wasn't the type of bullet that had killed Nica's lover. Detective Jim Cypress was called in to his superior's office early that afternoon and the new case was laid out.

"Listen, Tonto, we got confusion here. The girl is dead, the guy is dead. Two different guns but they lived together. Two bodies. Think you can handle the case? It just grew."

Jim looked at his boss, a tall man named Hector Perez, a good cop who had worked his way up through the ranks. "No sweat, kemo sabe," he grunted. "So we got it wrong. Not a street gang. My investigation came to quite a few dead ends on that score anyway. No street banger's been talking about a hit. Elliot Barclay was probably killed by one of his own. I'll start interviewing people at his bank."

Jim looked uncomfortable at his own words. Big business made him nervous; he was more at home on the streets or in the Everglades.

"Can you do it?" his boss asked. "Deal with all these money types?"

"Absolutely. I'm on it, Hector. My possible witness looks good. A kid. I'm going slow with her because she says she didn't see anything. I think she did."

Jim could have said right then that he knew Leonie knew something, because of the pizza evidence, but he wasn't sure how to go about it, and he really had to talk to Leonie about how Red Baron pizza sauce got on Barclay's shirt before he told anyone at the station house. If it was ever going to become police knowledge. Jim Cypress always went slow and sure, and this was his case. The way he handled it was strictly up to him. That's the way police detectives worked. Cases were private fiefdoms, and that little girl was his. But time was running out on this one. Miami Beach didn't like double homicides. Murder was extremely bad for tourism.

"Keep at it," his boss said. "Anything else new?"

Jim nodded. "The report from the lab says Elliot Barclay had AIDS. I ran a check on the local clinics, hospitals, whatever, and came back with a positive. He'd definitely been tested. The victim knew he was sick. Chances are Nica Rabelais had it, too. There's a funny bend with the AIDS population around here: the haves and the have nots. Each side believes they got something on the other. It has me thinking maybe there's a connection."

"Interesting idea, Tonto." Hector slapped Jim on the back and chuckled. "What else?"

"I'm interviewing someone at the Royal Leaf Bank. All day tomorrow. Today, I have some leads to follow up."

Hector nodded. "Fine. Take a look at this, too." He handed Jim the file on Nica.

Jim left the office in a hurry, only stopping by his desk to take a quick look at Nica's file. He wanted to get to the school before Leonie got out. When he had picked up the lab report on Elliot's shirt from Henry Peoples late yesterday, he had been shocked by the AIDS discovery, but he had been terrified by the pizza sauce. He had to talk to Leonie.

His Mitsubishi was in the police officers' parking lot in the place usually reserved for Reggie Peele. Reggie wasn't there. He was having back trouble again. Officer Peoples had confirmed that fact. "Poor old shit, he could barely walk yesterday," Peoples had remarked. "He went out to the bone crusher, came back, and then he left again. The man was in serious pain."

Jim had refrained from remarking that Reggie generally was a serious pain. Reggie's offer to help him yesterday had seemed odd at the time. It still did. Jim knew Reggie better than most because he listened to the man's words and how they were said. He knew Reggie hated him and just about everyone else in town. Maybe the older man had changed, but it seemed unlikely. Hatred was a driving force. Jim wondered briefly what hatred like Reggie's could do to a man, then he shrugged and let the thought drift away.

20

LEONIE was walking her usual route home when Jim saw her. She looked up as he approached. "Well?" she asked.

"What's up?" He fell in step beside her.

"The sky." Leonie smiled.

Smart ass, Jim thought. "I've been worried about you," he said. "You could have drowned that day."

"It was nothing. Just water. I like water. I was talking to fish, looking for jellyfish. . . . whatever." Leonie sounded defensive.

"I gotta talk to you, Leonie. Serious stuff. Can you take some time right now and get an ice cream? We can talk on the way to the Frieze."

Leonie gave a very deep sigh. Too deep. It meant much more than ice cream deliberation. "That's too far."

"We can go in my cop car."

"Sister Cecile would have a fit."

"I asked her permission to talk to you."

"You did." Leonie made it a statement, as if she already knew.

Jim pulled out his badge and waved it at her. "On my honor as a cop."

"Honest Injun?"

Jim looked sideways at the twelve-year-old. She had a devastating tongue and a face that was going to sink ships. She was going to be a powerful woman. In some ways, she already was. "I am a most honest Injun," he said.

"Let's go." Leonie's words slid out softly.

The Frieze was a renowned ice cream shop just off Lincoln Road Mall. Who could resist, Jim thought as he led her to the car. Leonie had changed, he realized. The girl was much more familiar than the last time. He had the feeling he was being conned. Something was going on.

"What's this Miccosukee license plate?" Leonie asked.

"Comes with the face." He moved up and held the door open for her.

"That's cool, but this isn't a cop car. Where's the bubble gum machine?" She slid in and he went around, resuming talking when he got in and started the ignition.

"I'm a police detective. This is my own car and we Miccosukees get special license privileges. Look in the glove box, you'll see the light."

She opened it up and pulled out the magnetic light. Jim saw her hands shaking. He drove fast. He had a feeling Leonie would go up in smoke if he didn't get this over quickly.

"Cool light. Where's the siren?" she asked.

Jim pushed a button and the car let out a whoop. Traffic slowed around them.

"I have to know about that night, Leonie," he said after the whoop subsided. He was at Seventeenth Street and pulled into a No Parking zone. He flipped up a card that read Police Business and stuck it in the windshield.

Leonie hopped out of her side of the car and waited for Jim to come around. "What night?" she asked. They were walking. Jim knew she knew. And she knew he knew she knew. Leonie was almost grinning, hopping along. It was weird.

"The night Elliot Barclay died. On the beach. I know you were there. I know something happened." Jim was looking straight ahead as they walked up Lincoln Road and then across to where the Frieze was located. They went inside and joined a small group of people staring into a glassed-in freezer filled with canisters of ice cream.

"Me?" she asked. "I want the coconut, extra-large double scoop."

112

Jim ordered a large coconut ice-cream cone for her and a Key lime cheesecake ice-cream cone for himself. He paid, got the cones and handed Leonie hers. "Let's walk to one of those seats out along the mall."

Finally they sat down side by side on a stone bench. "So spill, kid. What went down on the beach?"

"Spill?" Leonie was obviously nervous now. The ice cream looked like it was going to topple.

Jim wished, suddenly, that he could shrink and just be a kid instead of a huge Indian. "Tell me all about it. The dead man had pizza sauce on his shirt. Red Baron pizza sauce."

Leonie's chin rose like she was listening extra hard. "No kidding. You could actually tell it was a particular kind of sauce?"

"Sure. Labs are very sophisticated these days."

"So, maybe we have the same taste in pizza," she said, sticking a finger into the ice cream and putting it in her mouth.

"Not likely."

"No." She nodded and licked around the edge of the cone. "Why don't you look at me when you talk?" She turned sideways, staring at him.

"Miccosukee are taught to listen." Deliberately, he looked at her with his big, tan face that wrinkled at the mouth when he smiled. She reached up and touched the soft skin of his cheeks with a sticky finger. A warm bolt of electricity jolted him, as though she had touched more than his skin.

"Maybe he really did have a pizza that night," she said. "Everybody eats pizza."

"His girlfriend was shot last night, Leonie. Dead. That's two people dead, and I'm worried about you. If you know something, you've got to tell me. You could be killed. I don't want that to happen." He kept looking at her now; she had blue eyes like Stephanie; she could be their daughter. The daughter they might have someday. And Barclay had AIDS. He stared at the girl, wondering.

"Two people dead?" Leonie looked legitimately shocked at

113

that. "His girlfriend? Who shot the girlfriend?" Leonie asked. "I mean, someone else did that, right?"

"Don't know yet. Maybe it was the same person who killed Elliot Barclay, and whoever it is will try to kill you if you know anything."

"It was not the same person," Leonie said positively.

"It probably was."

"No."

"He had AIDS. You know about that?"

"AIDS?" She looked instantly sick as though she were hit with a thick wad of fear in her stomach. The ice-cream cone slipped from her hands and dumped on the ground. "Shit," she whispered.

"I'll get you another one."

"No, please. Did the girlfriend have it, too?"

"We're waiting for the report on that."

Leonie closed her eyes. Jim stared at her, suddenly fearing the worst. Had she had sex with that man? Had he bled all over her? "You've got to tell me, kid."

"I told Cecile," she said finally. She was no longer relaxed. The words came out staccato. "She didn't say anything about AIDS. There was someone killed with the same gun? Well, now I know why. He did it. Elliot Barclay did that. I was wondering why he did it. AIDS is why he did it. AIDS. Damn AIDS."

Jim's shock was on his face. "He did what?"

"Yes, don't you see? Don't you know about people?" Leonie's mouth was set in a straight line and the words came out hard. "See, it all makes sense now. Elliot had AIDS. He was out killing bad girls, people he thought might have given it to him. Get it?"

"He was out killing bad girls. My God, Leonie. What were you doing?"

This time it was Leonie's turn to look away. Tears had stopped piling up in her eyes and were running down her cheeks. This time she was the one who didn't look, didn't

114

meet Jim's eyes. He stared at her, using all his senses. He could even smell her fear.

"He was going to kill you?" he asked.

Leonie's head went down, like the beginning of a nod. "Yeah," she managed. "That was the idea." Her shoulders shook. His huge arm traveled around her. She shook harder. "It was not my fault, though. Cecile told me. I know that."

"You killed him?" He pulled out a white handkerchief from his back pocket, using his free arm. A few people passing by paused to look at the big tan man hugging the crying girl, but they didn't stop. This was Miami Beach. "You killed Elliot Barclay?"

She couldn't answer for a moment. Finally she got the handkerchief in her hands and blew her nose. "You'd think I already cried enough about this. I thought I was done crying. I cried too much already. No. I didn't kill him. No, I never did that. I was going to. Maybe I'd feel better if I had. He had me down. I got ahold of his gun, all ready to shoot, but I couldn't. He grabbed it, I struggled and he pulled back on it somehow and he shot himself, like he was holding the gun for balance when I jerked under him. I didn't even have my hands on the gun. Cecile explained it all to me. It's my beach. I could be there. My face. I could wear lots of makeup if I wanted to. *He* attacked *me*. He tried to kill me."

Jim didn't say a word. He was reacting the same way Cecile had, one arm around the girl, unspent tears in his dark eyes. "Damn," he whispered. "Damn him."

"I told Cecile last night."

"Good for you."

They didn't talk for a moment. Leonie became limp against the big man. Jim just tried to think. It was hard to be a rational white-man cop sometimes. What the hell was he going to do with his murder case? It all boiled down to this little girl.

"Where's the gun?" he asked.

"Under a sea grape tree. What are you going to do? My fingerprints are all over it. See, he thought I was a prostitute out on the beach. Zoe and I had a lot of makeup on that night.

He even called me a hooker." Words spilled out. More words followed, explaining, tearful words until they were all there, spread out on the Lincoln Road Mall being mashed by scores of young men on Rollerblades and walkers, oblivious to a peculiar couple sitting on a stone bench.

Leonie sniffed and wiped her eyes. Then she sniffed again hard, and swallowed. Then she sat up straight. "I'm okay now. It wasn't my fault. I'm done crying. I cried last night, cried now. I guess this wraps it up." She gurgled a tiny sob. "I didn't kill him. I'm free. Cecile said."

"Sister Cecile told you exactly right. Not your fault. Not any of it. And here we are, all talked out. You didn't do anything wrong, but . . ." Jim removed his arm and sat back against the bench. "What should we do?"

"Do? I don't know what to do. Cecile and I were going to tell you, but we didn't yet. I mean, I did." Somehow she laughed. Jim wanted to kiss her for that. He was proud of her, like a father.

"Do I have to go to the police station?"

Jim Cypress was silent. Finally he spoke. "I'm thinking." Then he was silent again. Someone killed Nica. Did that put Leonie at risk if her name came out? It could. Could Leonie face the hours of police questioning, the publicity, the suspicion that she had indeed pulled the trigger even though she hadn't? It was too much for this kid. And the bottom line: it was dangerous. There was a real murderer out there. Jim knew he had complete control of the case. It was nobody's business how he handled it as long as justice was done and the guilty were caught. As far as Leonie was concerned, he was going to keep his mouth closed. Tight. For her safety, if for no other reason.

Leonie sighed like the sea breeze blowing off the beach, long and deep. "I didn't," she said.

"No," he said.

"It's almost funny, you know?" she said. "Cecile was trying to find me, sort of. Like, who killed that creep."

"Sister Cecile? Why?"

116

Leonie explained carefully about Sister Cecile's new case, ending with, "I shouldn't have told you, but see? It's complicated. Everything is crazy. She has to figure out what to do now, just like you do."

The hot Florida sun sparkled through exotic palm plantings, dappling the ground at their feet, turning the spilled ice-cream cone into a part of the sidewalk. A breeze moved by.

"Well, we just go one step at a time. First thing is replacement ice cream," Jim said when the silence had worn out. He was looking down at the milky puddle on the pavement. "About the AIDS. Was there any blood contact?"

Leonie shuddered. "I don't think so. Some on my shirt, but not my ear. He ripped at my earring."

"I'll speak to the nun. You should be tested, but I don't see any problem. Just a precaution. I'll give her a call right away, so you don't have to go through all the talk, telling her you talked to me. I'll save you some words."

"You're the one who doesn't like words."

"So, you tell her," Jim said.

"No. You. Mostly I should just get back soon. After the ice cream."

"Ice cream. And I'll think about what to do. It's a tough call, but I don't want to get your name out there. I think maybe I'll let the case slide and work on the Rabelais case. That's the girlfriend. So you don't have to worry about anything, kid. Except maybe what flavor for the next ice cream."

"Right," Leonie said. "I'm fine."

Jim listened to her words very carefully. Fine? Not yet. But she would be. He promised himself that.

21

LATE that same afternoon Amy Peele was pacing the floor in her office. She was usually miserable, today more than ever with her tweed suit stretched across her back, her pigtails unraveling slightly as she chewed mercilessly on the ends of her fraying hair. Few people ever saw her chew the pigtails, but she did, particularly on bad days. This was a very bad day. She had been cheated by life, now she was cheated by death. It wasn't fair.

She was glad she killed Nica Rabelais because of Elliot and the AIDS thing. But now what? What justice was in Nica's death? She had done Nica a favor by putting her out of her misery. No justice. The burning question still remained. Who had killed Elliot Barclay?

The rotten nun was on the case. The Miccosukee was on the case. Daddy would find justice, Amy thought as she spit out a pigtail and started on a fingernail. The cuticle showed blood. She wiped it with horror on the underside of her suit jacket. Blood. Infected blood. It was everywhere. But not hers! She was clean.

Death was so commonplace these days, one more here or there didn't matter. It was something to think about. She went over to her desk and sat down to dial a number. Moments later Reggie Peele answered.

"Daddy? What's new?" she asked.

"Things look good," Reggie said softly. Amy could hear the squeak of his chair as he tipped it back to talk better. Daddy was slightly indolent, she knew, and not really all that smart, but he was a bulldog on a case. She listened carefully to what he said.

"I came in late today, so I had to catch up a little, but it looks like Jim Cypress has a real lead. But he's not talking. The damn Injun kind of hummed a little, looked through the Barclay file, made some notes, and went over to the evidence room to look at something. I asked him if he had anything new, if the lab tests showed anything, and he just grunted. Damned Miccosukee don't give nothing away, don't even speak English, but I could tell."

"He can't put anything over on you, Daddy," Amy said.

"It's got to be the kid connection. We got to reach the kid, Amy. And that's going to be your job. I been following her all the hell over the place, but you know that doesn't set well, old man following a kid like that. On the other hand, a beautiful woman such as yourself, you can come right up to her and ask her right out flat. Talk to the kid. Kids love you."

Amy Peele was silent as she tried to recall the last time she had talked to a kid. She couldn't recall. But she did love children. She told everyone that. "Right, Daddy. How do I find her?"

"Tomorrow when she gets out of school you and me are going to be there. I'll point her out, and then it's up to you."

"Got it." Amy looked up to see her new supervisor coming into the office. "I'll check on that information, Mr. Cisneros," she said formally. It was the sign to her father that she wasn't alone. She hung up moments later.

Sister Cecile saw Leonie briefly after school. She beckoned the girl to come out to the pool area. There they sat under the shade of the extended roof where they stared at the sparkling water. "Jim called. He told me about an AIDS clinic that does safe, anonymous testing."

"You don't think . . . ," Leonie began.

"Not a chance, but the test will give you security. You'll never have to think about it again. Otherwise it will haunt you."

119

"It does already," Leonie admitted.

Cecile felt the chill in Leonie's words. "I know. We won't tell anyone here. Nobody. Tomorrow morning we'll take a run over. You'll like riding in the new car. And once you know for sure you don't have AIDS, you'll feel much better. Then you can forget about it." And test again in six months, Cecile thought. To be absolutely sure.

"Okay." Leonie looked almost cheerful. "Raphael got a new video game from her nephew. Can I use the computer? Like, right now?"

"One hour on that machine," Cecile advised. "One. Then homework, swim, or whatever. Use your brain, don't let it use you. I'm going to take a little nap, myself. I have a late-night appointment with someone about this case."

A strange thought hit Cecile. "The case, of course, is solved. I'm working on the Rabelais case now. I spoke with Jim about it earlier. We're both convinced there's a connection, that to reveal your involvement right now would be dangerous, not to mention a dreadful ordeal for you. So he and I are keeping it quiet. Easy for him, but I have to rationalize my continued involvement in the case. I'll figure out some reason."

"You're good at that," Leonie said.

"Am not." Cecile stared at her ward. Could Leonie be right? "Well, maybe so. I'll work this mess out. Don't worry. And, of course, you shouldn't talk about it either. It could be extremely dangerous if it comes out that you were there. There are two deaths connected with this man. One of them is clearly murder. We won't say a word. Good idea?"

"Very," Leonie said solemnly.

When Cecile leaned back on her bed to take a brief nap to get ready for a long night on Miami Beach, she knew she wouldn't really fall asleep. She was worried. Figure it out? Make everything work? It was going to take a lot of mental gymnastics to know what to do next much less what to say to the consortium. She tried to think, then she quit and prayed instead, dwelling on the meaning of her life, the consecrated life. "Fraternal communion is a God-enlightened space in which to experience the hidden presence of the risen Lord," she thought, reviewing words she had recently read. The meaning gave her a moment of peace.

Sister Cecile was asleep in less than five minutes. She had made plans to meet Barcus Dumplig for a late dinner at Pacific Time on Miami Beach. When she explained over the telephone that she wanted a tour of the Beach's nightlife, Barcus was willing. "Fun don't start till midnight or so. Let's meet at eleven."

Maybe those words crept into Cecile's subconscious, demanding she sleep to get ready for the ordeal, or maybe, she told herself sometime later, maybe she didn't quite know what to say to the consortium member and she was sleeping as an escape. Or, most likely, it was just the peace of Christ.

It was late when Sister Cecile peeked in to say good night to Leonie, but the girl was sound asleep, her ceiling fan humming softly overhead. It seemed cool, so Sister Cecile turned off the fan then tiptoed over to her ward and delivered a light kiss to the top of Leonie's head. Leonie had gone through some rough days. It was going to be very difficult to explain all this to her father. Plus, Leonie would need some serious nurturing. The child needed some quality time. Yes, that was what the child needed. Quality time.

Cecile tiptoed out and closed the door quietly.

Moments later Leonie was up, switching on her fan again.

Cecile decided to dress in contemporary beach style: blue jogging pants she had brought from Massachusetts, cut off at the knees. She took the matching top and pulled it on and down over the pants. It looked good, particularly with her gold cross dangling from her neck. Crosses were some kind of fashion statement these days, although she couldn't figure out exactly what they were supposed to be saying in that respect. She had her own motives. She put on some makeup, just a glossy pink lipstick. She looked sallow, she thought as she glanced in the mirror, just like a beach person.

She sighed, wishing she had more time for Leonie. For the first time she realized the dilemma of being a working mother. Then, like any working mother, she fluffed up her hair.

On the way out, she stopped in the chapel for ten minutes and prayed to make up for sleeping through compline. So many things to pray for, so little time, she thought on her way out to the community room. She called a cab.

Cecile's taxi arrived in five minutes, exactly. She slid in gingerly. The seat was ripped; the driver smelled of beer.

She had the cabby let her out on Seventeenth Street near Lincoln Road and walked into the large section of the mall that remains closed to cars. Palms, bamboo, fountains, huge sculptures, people on Rollerblades, bicycles, an occasional escaped infant running madly through the safe space; even at this time of night the mall was filled with people. Cecile strolled through, suddenly feeling like dancing because Miami Beach was that kind of place. Lights and people, even little kids were out late at night here. The air had diamonds in it. Everything looked new.

The urge to dance left as quickly as it came. Cecile felt a vague unease and forced herself to pause, to examine a palm closely, running a finger over the strange stuff that passed for bark. She had to think, be sharp. She looked for the man she was supposed to meet. Barcus had said he would be wearing a cowboy hat, standing outside, near the restaurant.

He was. A six-foot-tall, thick-bodied man with a leather face lingered near a growth of bamboo that tinkled in the light wind. The man sported a white cowboy hat. As she drew nearer Cecile could see his face clearly in the bright night lights.

The lines around Barcus Dumplig's mouth appeared to have been sewn on with brown thread. He had a mole, mid-cheek, and an inflated body; not really fat, just stuffed.

Barcus saw her coming and kept his eyes on her as she walked up. "Real pretty," he drawled. "How 'bout we meet later tonight? I got me some business first with a nun. May sound odd, but it's the damn truth. A honest to God nun."

122

"You have business first with me," Sister Cecile said and put out her hand. "I'm the nun. Nice to meet you, Mr. Dumplig."

"Sweet cheese, you're the nun?" Barcus shook her hand a little too diligently.

"Shall we find a table?" Cecile was anxious to settle down to business.

Pacific Time had chairs and tables spread over the sidewalk. They found a place beside one of the massive bamboo plantings and made small talk while they studied the menu. Cecile ordered a first course of Mongolian hot pie and a main dish of grilled Florida mutton snapper. Barcus called for tuna tartar, then barbecued breast of Long Island duckling with plum wine, huckleberries and Peking pancakes.

"About Nica . . . ," Cecile said.

"Try this bread. Gotta have some. Can't talk about her and eat at the same time. We need a good wine with all this."

She nibbled the bread, crusty with sesame seeds. "About the consortium . . . ," she tried again.

"Best damn food in town. Got to come here more often. How's the drink?"

"Fine, excellent. You're right about the food." Cecile settled down and enjoyed it as best she could. The food was admirable. She wasn't so sure about Barcus. He kept a running commentary about the incredible food to be found on Lincoln Road. "Got to get to Yucca. Albita sings there. Real sensation. Hell of a place," he said, dragging his rare duck through a purple sauce. "Can't beat this, though."

"You know about Nica," Cecile finally ventured.

"Damn it, not while I'm eating."

She waited until the coffee arrived, then let her words all out like a dam bursting, hoping to wash away Barcus's talk of food. "We really must discuss the case. We're dealing with death, two cases of AIDS, and a very high-class call girl who was murdered with the same gun that killed Elliot. That makes three dead. The killer is clearly having a field day. Nica may have died because she knew something. Another member of the consortium died, too. Cosima Benedict. That adds up to four dead. Do you think there's a connection? What do you think?"

With all the words, she was treading lightly, trying to shift the emphasis away from Barclay to anyone else. Dumplig could have killed Nica himself. He had as much a motive as anyone.

Barcus picked a front tooth before he spoke. "You're looking at Cosima, too? Interesting thought, and definitely in the Elliot Barclay circle, you know? She and him had a little thing. But very little. Cosima wasn't apt to become serious except with the business. Or with money."

He stopped and rubbed the tooth with a finger, then resumed talking. "Cosima's death was deemed accidental. Nica's was definitely not. And, of course, there's Elliot, so maybe we should forget Cosima for a minute. As for Nica, she knew everybody in every way. She got around. Now, I would suggest to you that a lot of us had cause to seek a little revenge on that girl. Elliot must have got the disease from her. And believe me, if that was how it happened, he would of done her in himself if he'd lasted that long. And done it in a most unkindly manner. Like hook her on this bamboo. Stuff grows a foot a day. See that sharp little new growth pushing up?"

Cecile looked over at the swinging green poles, then down at the base where spiky new shoots were emerging from the earth. "Yes."

"Used to be, tie a man on a bamboo plant. Tie him down hard, and guess what?"

Cecile stared at the sharp new growth. "A foot a day?" Her stomach lurched. The wine turned bitter in her mouth.

"Grows right through a man. Hurts like hell, they say."

Cecile swallowed hard. "Reality, Barcus. People don't kill people who give AIDS to them," she said firmly.

Barcus shrugged and grinned. "If that little girl gave me that bug, I'd feel real mean about her."

"But Elliot died first."

"True."

"I can't lay his death on the consortium as Manuel Beaumont seems to think I should," Cecile said firmly, mentally crossing her fingers, "particularly in the light of Nica's murder. There's a connection with Nica's death. I think I should include that in my investigation. I want to know his contacts on the Beach. Elliot Barclay was killed on Miami Beach, not in his office. Anything that ties Nica's death to Barclay will be helpful."

"Sure thing," Barcus agreed. He handed the waiter a credit card with the bill. "There ain't exactly that many Beach contacts that Elliot had. See, he didn't attach to people much. Not a real friendly sort, not gregarious. Just a few saw him now and then."

"But he did do business with you all. With the involvement of his girlfriend, we increase the possibilities. Right?"

"Yep. So we'll cover the Beach. We'll just make us a pilgrimage to all the usual places, like you nuns do. Pilgrimage. Get it?" He guffawed.

Sister Cecile forced a dim smile.

"We'll start at the Union Bar and Grill. That place is what I would call interesting. Elliot Barclay hung there now and then. With and without his baby doll." Barcus scratched a leathery cheek. "Soon as I pay this up we'll go check it out."

"I'm ready," Sister Cecile said.

"That you are." His eyes ran up and down her blue jogging outfit, stopping at her eyes. Then he looked down at the cross. "You're a nun," he said. "You sure?"

"Sure as shooting."

22

"WHAT I want, I guess, is a handle on who killed the first prostitute," Cecile said. "The one shot with the gun that shot Barclay. And then on to Nica. We'll do this circumspectly."

"Elena," Barcus scratched his chin. "She was popular. Not exactly a prostitute, but always ready. Maybe we can find something." Ten minutes later Cecile and Barcus Dumplig pulled up in front of a night spot on Washington Avenue. The cab let them out near a roped-off area guarded by bouncers who looked them over carefully until Barcus slipped one a twenty.

Cecile looked around at the mobs of people and had a fast moment of self-doubt. Life began after midnight here, she did know that, but it still felt very improbable. Nuns didn't operate like this. But she was more than a nun.

She knew it was early for the Beach scene, but there were still throngs of partially dressed, forever-young people all wearing various shades of black. Lots of skin showed, even on the men, who had hairy chests or shaved chests, cleverly revealed by peekaboo half-opened shirts.

Once inside, Barcus escorted Sister Cecile beyond a curtain and into a room that resembled an English club, replete with book-lined walls, comfortable chairs, and two bars selling drinks. The air-conditioning was on high. The place was a refrigerator. The noise level caused pain. Bodies writhed, if not to the beat then perhaps in agony from the volume.

Barcus paused at a bar and ordered himself a double martini. Cecile asked for seltzer water.

She looked around in the gloom as they waited for the drinks.

Beautiful people in the haze, but up close not all of them were really beautiful.

Finally Barcus scurried her on to another room where there was a dance floor filled with couples moving in pain to a booming sound. He dragged her past a huge bubble-shaped fish tank in a wall, filled with live fish and shrimp. "Okay," he muttered, "Gustavo Bestard's here," and pulled Cecile farther, to the other side of the floor. "He knows what's going on."

Barcus edged Cecile through a row of beefy bodyguard types. They approached a tall, black-haired man with wet lips. Ultraviolet light made the whites of his eyes glow. He looked ugly. Everybody, in fact, looked vaguely diabolical. But they were people, Cecile reminded herself, God's people, all loved by their creator.

Barcus talked rapidly to the man, Gustavo. He ended by pushing on Cecile's back, bumping her within inches of Gustavo Bestard's thick lips for a fast introduction.

"Gustavo, this little sweetheart is looking for anyone who knew Elena, the one who got killed the other night." He spoke loudly, the music made the words garble and clank until Cecile wasn't even quite sure what Barcus had said.

"That right?" Gustavo stared at Cecile. He looked down at her, way down. Gustavo was a big man. Possibly he was about her age, but he showed the effects of smoke and drink. His shirt was opened halfway down. She saw dark chest curls. He smelled thickly of money and strong cologne. Odor of tree rot, Cecile thought as the man looked at her with manic intensity. On the other hand, God loved him as much as he loved her. If not more. Their gazes met.

Apparently he liked what he saw. He spoke directly to Cecile in a soft voice. "We can meet later, I'll tell you what I know." He didn't smile; he'd been caught up in Cecile's eyes. She hadn't seen a look like that since junior high school.

"This is business," she said, "and I'm with Barcus."

Gustavo laughed. "Beat me to it, Dumplig?" He shrugged and half closed his eyes. "You want to know about Elena?"

"The night she died," Cecile put in.

127

Gustavo stared down at Cecile's gray eyes and a soft smile crossed his mouth. "For the lady. Hey, Jasper," he bellowed at a short, thick man wearing a brilliant green earring. "You know where she was that night? Elena? Night she bought the farm?"

Jasper nodded slowly. "Elena, that night? She was out early at the VIP Lounge, then to Xandro's. I saw her leave for some place with Barclay," he shrugged. "They was high, like usual." His eyes riveted on Cecile. "Then they was gone, probably to her place up the Marlin Towers. That's Elena's kind of night. Her place or someone else's."

Cecile knew that Elena's body had been discovered at her own place, but not until much later.

"Was Elliot acting odd that night?" Cecile asked him, raising her voice to be heard as the music moved up a notch.

"Elliot Barclay was always odd." Jasper flexed his massive shoulders back and forth. "Least whenever I saw him."

"Thanks, Jasper," she said, suddenly aware that there was a conversation going on over her head. A few critical words floated to her ears through the din, words with her name mixed in. Strange words. She tuned in.

"Twenty grand," Gustavo was saying above her. "Tell her that, just for one night. I like the eyes."

"Don't think it's a sale, not this one. Make your own offer," Barcus replied. Barcus winked at Cecile as he spoke, a half grin on his face.

The words sounded blurred to Cecile, barely audible through the music, but she didn't like what sense she made of them.

"You hear that, my precious?" Gustavo asked.

"Not exactly."

"You finish the night with me," Gustavo said to her. He leaned close, his thick breath closing in on her air space. He was straight-faced, dealing business. "Twenty thousand for tonight. You and me. We'll dance in the foam, go home and dry off."

Cecile blinked. Twenty thousand dollars to spend a night with Gustavo? Was it a joke? Did he just call her precious? "Me?"

"You. You come home with me. Twenty grand."

Not a joke. Cecile's imagination went wild briefly. They could retile the pool area, do all the floors, fix the last two rooms with new air-conditioning units. The Lord was teasing her again. She sighed audibly. Temptation run amuck was still temptation. "No thanks. I'm taken."

Gustavo pushed out his lips. "That right? Change your mind, give me a call. Barcus there, he's got my number. And I promise you, sweetheart, I'll be in touch with you. Something in the eyes," he said in a near whisper. "Something in the eyes. Can't let that get away. I *will* be in touch later."

"Really, I'm permanently busy," Cecile said to him, then looked pointedly at Barcus. "Let's go."

Barcus patted Gustavo on the arm. "Keep in touch." Moments later they were out through the overcool lounge, past the curtain, and into tropical air. Barcus asked the valet to find a cab.

They stood in the dense silence. Blessed silence. Cecile smelled the Florida beach scene, rotting fruit, salt water and car exhaust.

"Thanks," she said. The heat of still-warm pavement seeped through the soles of her shoes, giving her comfort after the icy air-conditioning inside. She needed that.

"You're taken," Barcus was saying. "That was mighty nice of you, darling. I will see to it that you don't regret those words."

"I rarely regret anything," Sister Cecile said. "What I do, I do with my eyes open, and Barcus, I really am taken." She flashed her left hand to show the small gold band on her ring finger, the sign of her commitment to her Lord. "I'm a nun. Remember?"

"Well now, ain't that the damnedest," Barcus said, grabbing her hand and bringing it up to his mouth for an expert, southern gentleman kiss. "I do remember, and I will guard you with my honor."

She retrieved her hand quickly, wanting to rub the kiss off somewhere. There didn't seem to be any place that would do.

"I would appreciate that, Barcus. Your friend Gustavo looks like he doesn't accept a 'no.' " She looked behind her as a group of noisy people exited the bar. Not Gustavo, thank the Good Lord.

"He don't normally have to. Want to try another bar or you want to dangle on home and be a nun somewhere? Maybe put in some praying time?"

Cecile wasn't sure. "We found out Elliot was with the prostitute the night she died. That he was weird, that he was always weird at night. Do you think he had something to do with the prostitute's death? Were they both friends with Nica?"

"One never knew with Elliot. Are you aware that Elliot had a family in Canada some place, wife filed for cruelty, got a few dollars off the man. Claimed our sweet man, Elliot Barclay, abused the daughter. Now, I don't know why I'm telling you all this, you being a nun and all. Shouldn't even hear the word divorce, much less all that other stuff. Right?"

"Everything's important," Cecile said. "I do know what goes on in the world."

He raised his eyebrows. "You sure?"

"Do you think there might be more to learn? Like where they went afterwards?" she asked. She forced herself to ignore his not-so-veiled patronizing and her own apprehensions. "Or maybe some other connections?"

"Hell, no. I think we hit the bottom of the info pit. What Gustavo don't know, nobody knows. If you think there might be more, I suggest you arrange some more time with Gustavo."

"Please, no. I don't want to see Gustavo again if I can help it."

"Then, I think what we do now is just go out and have a good time. Catch up on the drinks. Your buddy, Gustavo, he always ambles over to Liquid later, so maybe you want to head some place else? Maybe make an effort to avoid the man?"

"Exactly."

Barcus was being surprisingly agreeable, a true southern

gentleman. "You got any sisters somewhere?" he questioned hopefully. "Some that look just like you?"

"No sisters who aren't sisters," Cecile said dryly.

Barcus guffawed and slapped his thigh. "Now, if it ain't true you even got a sense of humor."

The valet finally produced a cab and helped them in. "I'll take you home to all them sisters, and I'll just string on back, check out the sights. You see those ladies?" He pointed to a group entering the bar. "New ones every night. That's the Beach."

"The Beach," Cecile murmured and yawned. It was one-thirty in the morning and people were just arriving. "Yes, I may as well go home. Thank you, Barcus. It was a very informative evening."

"Evening's just begun," he mused as he slid into the cab beside her. "Too bad your being a nun, like this. I could antici-pate some real good times."

As the cab drove away Cecile looked back just in time to see Gustavo and Jasper exiting the club. Gustavo was pointing at the cab, Jasper was nodding. But she was heading home. She had seen enough of SoBe nightlife.

23

THE next day it rained off and on all morning. By the time Leonie emerged from school there were massive puddles all over the edges of the streets, and dark clouds hanging in the sky. The rain had stopped. That didn't mean much. It could start and stop on a dime here and you could drown in a minute.

131

Miami rain was very heavy stuff that was warm enough to swim in.

Leonie stood with Zoe and chatted. They both stared at the low, black clouds edging the sky. The lightning seared the horizon like fire curtains. Overhead, the sun came out and suddenly it looked like any other warm summer day, except, of course, this was January. Leonie knew that in moments the sun could hide and the rain fall. "So, I gotta split," Leonie said. "This is definitely not Washington, DC. Weather rules."

"Power sky," Zoe agreed. "See you."

Leonie said good-bye to Zoe and turned toward home quickly, her book bag over her shoulder. She noticed the blue Taurus behind her. She had seen it before, and she was beginning to wonder about it. This time it turned off down a side street littered with a blowing pile of wet handbills. One handbill splattered across the car's windshield, causing the car to swerve momentarily. While the driver was distracted, Leonie squinted to make out who was behind the wheel. There was a dim blur through the tinted car window. She could make out a man's head, larger than normal, with a bush of white hair. She looked away just in time to avoid her scrutiny being detected as the car pulled over to the side of the road. Then, out of the corner of her eye she saw a woman emerge from the car carrying a huge red umbrella against the potential deluge.

Leonie kept on walking; the car was just a car with darkly tinted windows. Perhaps half of all cars in Miami were dark with dark windows, and the woman who had gotten out was just a woman.

The sun vanished. Rain fell again, and big drops hit her like a warm shower. Power sky. Leonie loved it. She sang, aiming for puddles. Getting her school shoes wet was like revenge on the old folks, revenge just for being old and never really understanding anything. She really did love water, and this was water. Lots of water.

"Come on under. I can help keep you dry!"

It was the woman with the red umbrella, slightly out of breath from racing across the street, a woman determinedly cheerful and flapping the big umbrella over them both. Maybe this woman wasn't so normal after all. She was about the same age as Sister Cecile, but dark-haired and ugly, at least in Leonie's quick eye. She was wearing pigtails, Leonie realized with a start. And a suit, dark green and droopy like someone would wear in an old Humphrey Bogart movie.

The rain came down heavily and Leonie found herself reluctantly herded along the main road, protected from being drenched by the woman's massive umbrella. In truth, she would rather be wet.

The woman squealed, "Oh, oh, oh," as though they were passing through some great adventure together. The rain danced madly on the umbrella. Leonie laughed in spite of herself. It was kind of crazy with the rain coming down cats and dogs, puddles two inches deep after only a minute of rain, and a lunatic lady with a red umbrella squealing like a nut case. Leonie deliberately sloshed through a huge puddle, forcing the woman to wade along in her high-heeled shoes.

They arrived under a juice bar's awning and the woman lowered the umbrella. "That," she gasped, "was terrible!"

"Rain," Leonie said, "is cool."

"Let's have a juice," the woman invited. "Until the rain lets up. Isn't it lucky we're right here!"

Leonie hesitated. This was a very strange woman, and Leonie didn't like her. Something was abnormal about her teeth, for one thing, and another was that she had emerged from that suspicious car. But Leonie was curious. It all must mean something, and she was going to find out. Everything meant something, Sister Cecile always said. And everything needed to be understood. Besides, she was perfectly safe in a juice bar.

"I don't have any money," Leonie replied, knowing what would come next.

"Oh, I do. No problem. My treat."

"Sure," Leonie said and stepped through the door and into the juice bar first.

This was a great place. It sold fruit salads, carrot juice, mango juice, vegetarian burgers, and things made from coconut. Leonie loved coconut. "Coconut shake and two macaroons," she said. It couldn't be poisoned if they made it in front of her. She would never, ever take anything from this woman otherwise. She shouldn't anyway, but it really was pouring out. She was trapped.

"I'll have the carrot juice," the woman said, then she turned to Leonie, showing her teeth. Leonie took a good look. It wasn't that the teeth were bad or anything, Leonie realized on close inspection. It was just that the teeth in the top row were rounded at the bottom. She couldn't see if the bottom teeth matched, but it gave Leonie something to look for.

"My name's Amy," the woman said. She tapped her folded umbrella on the tile floor. It dripped water, a small flood caused by the tapping.

"Hi, Amy," Leonie replied. She would never give her name to a stranger, especially this one.

"You live around here?" Amy asked.

Leonie nodded.

"You must know what goes on."

Leonie shrugged.

"I love the excitement on the beach," Amy said.

"Really?" The drinks appeared and Leonie took a long drink. It was great.

"Strange things happen," Amy said mysteriously.

"Sure. Like, it rains." The woman was making Leonie increasingly uncomfortable.

"I saw a man once wearing woman's clothes," Amy said, and she giggled, girl-like. Leonie saw at once the standard ploy the woman was pulling, trying to shock her with cool revelations about stupid things. Who cared.

"No kidding," Leonie said.

"What have you seen strange around here?" the woman asked.

"Strange?" You, she thought. "Oh, I saw a bunch of people on the beach wearing Indian costumes. That was neat."

"I saw a man singing opera on Ocean Drive," Amy said brightly.

She was trying to make a game of it, Leonie realized. Then the woman smiled so hard it looked painful. Leonie stared at her mouth. Round. The bottom teeth were rounded at the top.

They both sipped their drinks. Leonie kept an eye on the woman beside her. It all had to do with Elliot Barclay, she realized suddenly, because everything had to do with Elliot Barclay. This woman wanted something, knew somehow that she, Leonie Drail, knew something. Leonie didn't like it. Jim couldn't have squealed on her; this person couldn't be connected with the police, so who was she? She was odd enough to be dangerous, Leonie decided. The coconut drink began to taste like chalk juice.

"I saw a whole bunch of green parrots the other day. They were really fresh." Leonie made her voice cheerful, knowing Amy was going to lose patience soon.

"Parrots? How about people? What other stuff have you seen people do?"

Leonie was right. The woman wanted something. There was an edge to Amy's voice now.

"People? Sure. Old people with plastic skin and silly hats, people wearing shorts that hang funny. I saw a Ferrari at school the other day. Silver stretch limos all over the place. And a cool fifty-six Cadillac."

Amy's round teeth clenched together. "I mean, people, not cars. Like at night, doing things."

"I can't go out at night by myself. I'm too young." Leonie sighed.

"You must sneak out. Don't kids sneak out anymore?" Amy sounded like she had discovered a great truth. Her hands were clenching and unclenching, athletic, long hands that looked unusually strong for a woman's.

Leonie didn't know what to say. She was tired of the game. The woman was too strange for her and she felt out of her depth. Instead of answering she went to work on her coconut drink. It was gone in less than a minute. Leonie picked up the

135

two macaroons Amy had bought for her and stuffed them in her book bag. "I have to go. Thanks for the stuff."

Leonie hopped off the stool and walked out. Behind her she could hear the woman. "Wait, I have to pay. I'll walk you home with my umbrella. Wait!"

It was pouring rain. Leonie didn't care about getting wet at all, now. It was a warm rain, and anything was better than being with a woman who had sick blue eyes and a mouthful of round teeth.

Leonie ran, shooting through monster puddles, around the corner and down the next street. She ducked into a small alley between two buildings and went to the end, turned and came up to the back door of a small tobacco shop. She walked in, panting for breath.

A smell of sweet tobacco filled Leonie's nostrils. It smelled good. Safe. She stumbled and dripped her way through piles of aromatic boxes that had "Habana" printed on them in wavy red ink. She stopped halfway to the front of the shop. Through the dingy windows she saw Amy stalking by, her face a thundercloud under the red umbrella.

Two Hispanics were talking behind the counter, waving their arms. Apparently they didn't care about Leonie, who studied the glass case full of cigars while she caught her breath. Corona Corona, Hav-A-Tampa, some strange, long black things that looked like dog turds. They all looked like dog turds. Leonie wanted to leave, but Amy-The-Tooth was out there somewhere.

Leonie pulled open her schoolbag and dug out the macaroons. She looked from the rain outside to the men behind the counter and nodded. "It's raining," she said, and bit into a macaroon.

Ten minutes later she left the cigar shop and walked home. The rain was over and Amy was gone. The sidewalk was filled with steamy puddles and the air smelled like Palm Sunday. Leonie walked through water, remembering how she had done it as a child and come home with wet feet to a solicitous housekeeper, or maybe it had been her father. Darn, where was her dad? Why wasn't he here?

When Leonie arrived at the retirement community she was met by Sister Cecile who was skulking by the front door, obviously waiting for her.

"Almost dry out. That's good," Cecile said, staring at Leonie's wet shoes that made squashing noises when she walked. "You went to bed early, I was out late. Come and have a snack with me in the kitchen. We can catch up."

"I'm not really hungry," Leonie said. "But I'll watch you eat."

Cecile looked worried at that. "Did they have a big lunch at school?"

"Actually," Leonie said, thinking about the oversized coconut drink and the two macaroons she had just eaten, "I'll have some celery." Eat, eat, eat, she thought. Everyone always wants me to eat.

"Sounds good."

In the kitchen they settled down at the long center table with a huge pile of cleaned celery and munched, Leonie chewing very slowly. Her wet shoes ended up under the table for Sister Germaine to find later.

"I've missed you," Leonie said suddenly. "One late night and I miss you. Guess this thing is still bothering me."

"Well, it should. That's normal. It was terrible. A nightmare," Cecile said, patting Leonie's hand. "You know how much we love you, I love you. . . . We're your family, too. And speaking of family, we have to tell your dad. When he calls next time, okay?"

"I suppose. He's calling in a week, he gave me a list of dates to make sure I'm in when he calls. I'll tell him."

Cecile looked relieved. "Good. He might come home when he finds out."

"I'd like that," Leonie said. "I'd like it a lot."

"Let's hope, then. So, what else is new?" Cecile asked.

"Nothing. The usual. Actually, there was a crazy lady out there today asking me questions."

Cecile choked on some celery. "Crazy lady?"

"Well, everyone's a little nuts here. She had round teeth, let me share her umbrella in the rain, bought me some cookies."

"What did she say?"

"Nothing much, just started talking about how everybody was strange out here, and have I ever seen anything strange. I got the cookies and took off. She was creepy."

"Beach people," Cecile nodded. "You've got to be careful, Leonie. You shouldn't have talked to her."

"Well, I know. She trapped me under a huge umbrella, and it was really pouring, but there were lots of people around and I split, fast."

"Leonie, you can't talk to strangers! Promise me."

Leonie felt a little sick to her stomach. Cecile was absolutely right. "Okay."

"And we've got that blood test." Cecile looked at her watch. "We can go over now. Are you up to it?"

"Ugh. Do I have to?"

"What do you think?"

"I think yes." Leonie sighed.

"Good. I want to get it over with. By the way, tomorrow's Saturday, and we have a big surprise for you."

"We do? What? Metrozoo?"

"No, the Everglades. Jim Cypress and I figured it would be good to get out of here for a day. He called and suggested we all go down south and see some of the real stuff. He's a Miccosukee."

"I know." Leonie nodded thoughtfully. Jim had actually mentioned it to her while she was having her second ice-cream cone. "Cool. Tomorrow?"

"Yes. He and his wife, you and me. He said we could go in his Mitsubishi, but I offered my new old Jaguar. He liked that idea."

"His wife?" This was news to Leonie. Why would Jim want to bring his *wife* along?

"Stephanie is his wife. She's a chemist. She works at a lab in Miami."

138

Leonie frowned. "Why bring her?"

"I think he loves her. They only just got married a few months ago."

"I would think just the three of us could go. She's not an Indian?"

"I don't know. Anyway, tomorrow morning at eight, so set your alarm early. We can walk through the national park, go to the reservation, maybe canoe, whatever they do in the Everglades. A nice peaceful Saturday."

"I could use that," Leonie said. "Peace? There are probably a zillion mosquitoes, alligators, crocodiles, death everywhere. I know about the Everglades. I read."

Sister Cecile closed her eyes as though she were praying. By now Leonie knew what it meant: deep thoughts, very deep and a serious premonition of problems.

"No death," the nun said finally. "Maybe an apple snail, an air fern. I read, too."

"Sounds like tons of fun. Apple snails." Leonie giggled. "And bread sticks. Know what a bread stick is?"

"Fuzzy things that grow there underwater. It will be fun. Wait and see."

Leonie felt an odd spark in her chest. Was it her own premonition of problems or just a tickle of excitement, when everything else in her life had been too solid with pain? "I can't wait," she said. "I hope nothing goes wrong."

"Impossible," Cecile said. "How could anything go wrong in the Everglades?"

24

"How's the case coming?" Reggie Peele asked. "Them lab reports give you anything?"

Jim looked away. Reggie Peele had been very friendly lately. He wasn't sure how to take it. "Sure. They all have AIDS. Elliot, and now his girlfriend. Might not mean anything, might mean everything."

"AIDS all the hell over the place," Reggie agreed. "She probably gave it to him. Ain't nobody safe."

"Hard to say," Jim said. "Maybe he gave it to her. Maybe they both already had it."

Reggie's face grew a shade redder than normal as though he were repressing words that wanted to explode from him. "What's with the kid? Your source?"

"Nothing much."

"Panned out?"

The Miccosukee shrugged. "Nothing much there. She's a nice kid. We're going to the 'Glades tomorrow."

"What for?"

Jim turned slowly to look directly at Reggie. He couldn't figure out Reggie's sudden interest. Jim decided to tell him less than nothing, not because Jim was suspicious, just that he was contrary, particularly when it came to Reggie Peele, a man who had snubbed him for years. "Just look at the 'gators. Look for wood storks. Kid doesn't have much of a family right now."

"Injun land," Reggie muttered. "Like to see it. Got room?"

Jim didn't usually have to work at hiding how he felt, but

sometimes it was hard. Like right now. He knew Reggie hated Miccosukees and just about everyone else. He could even hear it in the rasping voice. What was with this man, anyway? Jim took a long breath and spoke slowly, very politely: "Sorry, Reggie, I'm not driving. The kid's guardian is, and she said it's a pretty small car. Old 1967 Jag, Mark II. I'll be going out again in the Mitsubishi sometime; you can come along then."

"Sure, some other time. Going out early?"

"Eight. Beat the heat. These are northern people."

"Bunch of Catholics," Reggie said.

Jim heard the undertone of hate in the old policeman's voice and wondered, not for the first time, if there was anyone whom Reggie Peele actually liked. The real puzzle was why the old man had been so friendly to him lately. Maybe Reggie Peele was mellowing in his old age, Jim thought. Maybe there was hope for the old bastard after all. Maybe pigs fly.

"Jim, you need to sit up front," Cecile directed. "The backseat is miniscule. So Leonie, you and Stephanie can sit in the back."

"*I* could drive," Leonie said. "Or Jim could drive and I could sit up front."

"No license," Cecile pointed out. "I need to drive. It's my car. I'm used to it."

"Sister Cecile, you drive. I'll stretch out my feet and give directions," Jim ordered when he saw the mutiny in Leonie's expression. It was pretty obvious the kid was jealous. He caught his wife's eye and Stephanie nodded and got in the backseat first, sitting behind Sister Cecile.

"In the back, Leonie. The boss speaks," Stephanie said. She was not a Miccosukee at all, but a very blond person from Minnesota.

"I thought women were liberated these days," Leonie muttered and climbed in back. "Do you really do what he says?" she asked Stephanie. She sat as far as possible from Jim's wife and turned her face to the window, apparently not really wanting an answer. Everyone else in the car could see that Leonie was jealous of Stephanie, who was pretty, a lanky blond who had married a Miccosukee. Leonie was the only one in the car who didn't see that she and Stephanie could pass for sisters.

"I do what makes sense," Stephanie said.

"Well, we're all set," Cecile said. "Buckle up, Leonie."

They were off Miami Beach and onto the newly landscaped Julia Tuttle Causeway by eight-fifteen. Conversation dropped to a minimum, limited to remarks about the hundreds of palms and gumbo limbos and flowering trees that had recently turned the causeway area into a modern-day rain forest all the way down the cut through Biscayne Bay.

"A lot of the biggest trees were sold to the city by ranchers from the middle of the state," Stephanie told Leonie as they passed by dozens of sable palms. "Very cheap sale and look what it's done."

"Fabulous," Leonie muttered. She kept her head averted, looking out, looking back.

Stephanie kept talking about trees. As they reached the Calle Ocho exit she was still chatting at Leonie and had produced a running commentary about the birds, the trees and the cloud patterns in January. "In the summer it thunderstorms almost every day and the mosquitoes in the Everglades cannot be imagined. I brought bug repellent. We should put it on now." She pulled a plastic bottle out of her bag and squirted some into her hand before passing it to Leonie. "Just in case, but today everything should be fine. It's been relatively dry and there's a good wind. It really is winter even though it's eighty degrees."

"I know," Leonie said. She didn't look at the insect repellent. She turned and looked back, one more time. That was when she spotted the dark Taurus with tinted windows just before it dipped behind a fish truck. She mouthed a very quiet "shit," and faced front. She opened the repellent and started putting it on.

Stephanie heard her. "What?"

"Nothing. Got a crick in my neck." Leonie squirted another pile of goo into her hand.

Jim had been listening to his wife and Leonie talk and had heard the whispered "shit." He knew there was more to it than annoyance at the seating pattern so he pulled down the visor and looked into the vanity mirror, adjusting it carefully so he could see Leonie and the tense expression on the girl's face. She was still having problems with this business. It was a wound that would take a long time to heal. Definitely troubled. Then he focused on the road behind them. The fish truck filled the mirror. As far as he could see, there was nothing unusual there except normal traffic. Maybe it was just Leonie with a crick in her neck, he thought. Maybe.

Neither of them had noticed a more visible omen, a dark green Mercedes that was rolling along the left lane; nor should they have seen it as anything suspicious or even remotely dangerous. Many Florida cars had their front windows tinted heavily and their side windows tinted almost black against the subtropical sun. There was nothing unusual about this particular massive Mercedes-Benz except the grin on the driver's face and the flash of a green earring. It was Jasper, Gustavo's gofer.

Jasper had his instructions, not detailed instructions, just vague enough so he had a lot of leeway.

"Get the woman. I want her." That had been enough. His boss had wanted this woman on sight and was willing to pay big. Jasper had already decided that this so-called Sister Cecile was just pretending to be a nun, because she damn sure didn't act like one, what with a kid, and now ripping along Calle Ocho, ducking red lights like a professional, and with a big hunk of a man beside her in a Mark II, no less.

Gustavo Bestard always got what he wanted. One way or another. It was Jasper's job to see that he did. Jasper was certain that Gustavo would be very pleased to see Sister Cecile wrapped and packaged for his pleasure.

The road rolled west through Little Havana, past rows of X-rated motels, past car dealerships and finally into the dry outer environs of Miami where white ibises roved along the roadside looking for bites of bread crust from discarded sandwiches, and strange lunch stands offered grilled alligator meat.

Stephanie continued to talk incessantly, directing the words at Leonie. "I met Jim when he was sixteen out at the Indian school. My mom came out here to teach the kids and she brought me along. I went to school with them. I was your age."

"I'm almost thirteen," Leonie said.

"I fell in love with Jim way back then," Stephanie said. "My mom didn't have a clue; there she was teaching the Miccosukee all about hygiene and mathematics and I was falling in love. He finally noticed me one day following him out to a hammock. He was going for a cigarette, and this huge alligator crawled out and I barreled up a mahogany tree, scared to death. Those things are nasty to climb, so I sort of screamed for help and he saved me. You should have seen him."

"No kidding," Leonie said. She was being drawn in. She turned and looked at Stephanie hard. "How did he save you?"

"I took out my knife and stabbed him between the eyes," Jim said from the front seat. "We had him for supper. I fell in love with Stephanie that night when she ate my mother's pounded alligator with Granny's pumpkin bread. Any white kid who could eat what she did had my utmost love and respect."

"You ate alligator?" Leonie looked a little green.

"Tastes like chicken," Sister Cecile said, her eyes firmly on the road. They had just passed a huge dead thing. It was bloated beyond recognition. Roadkill in Florida had a tendency to swell up big in the heat. Jim declined to tell everyone that it was really just a gas-filled dog.

"I think alligator tastes more like turtle," Stephanie said. "It's great."

"We'll have some for lunch, maybe," Jim said. He half turned in the seat, dark eyes scanning the road behind them. He saw the green Mercedes, but the Taurus was three cars back. He let his mind relax and listened to his wife trying to make friends with Leonie. She was succeeding.

144

They passed bean fields, migrant workers, crop dusters with huge, noisy engines. Finally they rolled along a flat, barren expanse of wavy grass and sky. Huge, Everglades sky. Jim felt himself relaxing. He was coming home. "Stop up ahead, Cecile. Take a right by all the signs."

Cecile pulled off where a sign tried unsuccessfully to fill up the sky with advertising. "Airboat Rides," Leonie read as the car stopped.

Everybody hopped out and stretched.

"This is one place where tourists support the tribe by taking rides out into the Everglades," Jim said quietly, waving his huge hand at small batches of tourists speaking German, a carload of laughing Hispanics, and a small busful of environmentalists discussing panthers and the mercury level. "People look real small here against our sky."

Jim looked with satisfaction at Stephanie, Cecile and Leonie. They stood against the whispering world like three figures on the moon. Curious, excited, beautiful. The Everglades stretched out around them on all sides. The air held odd, murmuring sounds, birds calling and the endless swaying of the river of grass. Peace cradled the elements, from the sky to the edge of darkness that was the horizon, light years away. Above were only soft clouds promising nothing but a soft winter day. It was very safe. Wonderfully safe.

Leonie glanced around. "I don't suppose much ever changes out here," she said. "It looks boring."

"You wait," Jim said. "Things always happen out here. It's a very exciting place."

"Sure," Leonie said. "Sure."

25

JASPER pulled in behind the small tour bus and sat, his air-conditioning system blasting, his mouth moving slowly to "Heartbreak Hotel." Through the tinted window, he kept an eye on Sister Cecile and her entourage. He was casing things with no specific strategy yet, but he was absolutely certain a plan would cross his mind because things always fell his way. All he had to do was wait for a perfect opportunity and the nun was his.

Jasper had ways of dealing with women. He was prepared.

Reggie drove in next. He parked beyond the crowded area, stopping his car down near a big banyan tree planted twenty years ago by an early white settler from Coral Gables. A fantastic tree to look at, its open-air root system hung down from the branches in a massive circumference of three hundred feet, creating a perfect breeding ground for thousands of tiny, black mosquitoes who fed on the tourists.

Reggie got out of the car and strolled under the banyan. He stood within the dangling roots, hidden from view. It was a flawless post from which to observe everything, but remain unseen. Reggie was dressed carefully as a tourist, his white hair covered with a large hat, eyes shaded by mirror sunglasses, knees protruding from beneath green Bermuda shorts. His pockets were stuffed with police-issue handcuffs and his gun. A baggy shirt hung out to hide the stuffed pockets.

He had forgotten mosquito repellent.

The mosquitoes homed in immediately. Defiant as ever, Reggie stood still and stared out at the grassy swampland; he was intent on pretending to see the great blue heron and several egrets posing, motionless against a gray-green backdrop of tall grass. His plan was to capture the kid, take her some place private, and question her. He had all the equipment he needed.

He didn't move except to scratch right above his left kneecap. Out of the corner of his eye, Reggie watched the nun, Leonie, Jim and Stephanie all go into the airboat area and start looking over the boats. Somehow he would have to get the kid away from the adults. Then it would be easy. He swatted his legs, five fast whacks, then walked closer to the dock, away from the tree.

"Airboats here run on old 1971 Caddy engines," Jim was saying as his eyes swept the area. "Five-hundred-cubic-inch GM V-8 four-barrel carburetor engine. Real stoic cast iron. Incredible horsepower."

The women barely heard him. They were staring wide-eyed at the huge propellers. The airboats resembled giant swamp mosquitoes, strange, dreamlike monsters. Everyone's thoughts went in different directions. Sister Cecile thought about a James Bond movie she had seen with airboats and bad guys. Stephanie recalled the time Jim had made his own airboat and almost cut a hand off. Leonie wondered if, given enough momentum, the things could fly.

Jim spotted a tall man wearing a red bandana, standing near the boats. "Jack," he called and walked over to the man. His words faded in the din of an incoming boat.

The women were left staring at airboats and into the glassy water of the Everglades where a little black snake was writhing under the surface of the water. Tough Cadillac engines didn't thrill them as much as the birds, the bugs, the reptiles, and their own dreams.

They couldn't hear Jim as he spoke. Only Stephanie picked out the low rumbling of words in the Mikasuki tongue.

He returned a few minutes later. "Okay. Everything's set.

We can get a canoe in a while and go out to my mom's place. Meanwhile we can take a tourist ride or hang out in the souvenir shop. Maybe you can buy some dead alligator skulls and chill out with the air-conditioning."

"Alligator skulls?" Sister Cecile asked.

"Boat ride?" Leonie said hopefully, beginning to rub on more lotion.

Stephanie nodded. "Boat ride," she agreed. "How about you, Cecile? We'll be going out later in a canoe. The airboat ride is tourist-oriented. The driver feeds the alligators marshmallows. It's a good show."

Sister Cecile pulled her eyes up from the snake in the water. She appeared to have entered the nature zone of her mind, not a world of huge propellers and noisy monster airboats, but of birds and bugs and beasts. "I think I'd like to stay here and look around. I want to get close to that big bird." She pointed to the heron outlined against some tall grass. "I'd love to just walk around here and enjoy the peace. Do you mind? I'll be all right alone. The airboats are so noisy."

Jim approved. "Good choice. You'll see a lot here. Just gotta look. Most people don't know how. I'll go with the other ladies on the airboat. The trip starts in five minutes, so let's get seats. We'll be back in a little less than an hour, Cecile."

"I'll be around here. Then we'll go to your mother's and eat alligator."

Sister Cecile watched everyone pile into one of the airboats. Under the engines and propellers were wide flat-bottomed skiffs, loaded with rows of tourist seats. Above and to the rear of the boats the massive engines were mounted and attached to airplane propellerlike fans that pushed them across the trembling meadows of the Everglades. Cecile watched the driver hand out wads of cotton for the passengers to stuff in their ears, then the engine was cranked up with a terrible roar. She saw Leonie's big grin, then watched the strange craft pulled out, sending grasses and water back in a blast of air from the high-mounted propeller.

148

Cecile watched the load of twenty-some people spread out on the flat bed, like passengers on a bus. Then they took off, skimming over the bending grasses on the way to alligator country. It looked wild. Maybe she should have gone.

On the other hand, it was quiet here. Much better.

Cecile wandered about the compound. She hiked to a large area where a thatch-roofed Indian hut stood, built there to demonstrate how the Miccosukee really live. Or lived. She saw Reggie Peele, who was meandering nearby, but he meant nothing to her. She had never seen him before. He could have been any red-faced tourist swatting mosquitoes.

The small canal that ran along the Tamiami Trail was a good place to look for wild creatures, Cecile decided, and she walked on the embankment. Waterbirds poked the surface with long bills. One caught a gar, then lifted its iridescent head to toss the long fish up and into the head-first position before swallowing. A giant water bug skirted by, four inches of deadly poison. God's more interesting creatures, Cecile thought with a shudder. The drone of a million insects filled the sultry, sun-drenched air. Peace and Mother Nature; it was a perfect place to do a little praying.

A large anhinga outlined against the saw grass distracted her, and then she heard a voice that seemed directed at her. She ignored the voice. She didn't want to talk to anyone. She stared at the big bird as it basked in the sun, dark wings spread to dry in the simmering heat. Maybe whoever was calling would think she didn't understand English and go away.

"Lady, you there. I need help."

She couldn't ignore the plea any longer and walked across the small footbridge to the parking area where the man stood beside a green Mercedes. The man looked vaguely familiar, but she couldn't quite place him. "What's the matter?" she asked.

"My kid. His foot is stuck in the seat belt."

"Oh." Cecile moved quickly at that. "Let's see."

She stuck her head into the backseat through the partially opened door. She smelled something strange, but after the glare of Florida sunshine, she could see nothing but shadows in the dark backseat. She didn't see any child, anywhere.

A bag of heavy cloth came down over her head. She gasped. The fumes were thick, compelling, nauseating. Cecile barely opened her mouth to cry out when she was sucked into some other world where deep breaths were easy. She breathed, relaxed and breathed again twice before slumping down on the seat.

Less than two minutes later the big green Mercedes pulled out onto the main road and was on the way back to Miami. The big Mercedes engine was almost as silent as the nun in the backseat.

"Seven alligators," Leonie said. "Wait until I tell Sister Cecile. She should have come." Leonie was grinning all over when the airboat drifted up to the dock. The motor's roar stopped with a thud. Everyone aboard removed the cotton from their ears.

"What?" Stephanie asked.

"It's very cool out there," Leonie said.

Jim Cypress had remained silent for the trip except to point out elusive alligators. "We'll be going on to my house in a little bit," he said. "Friend of mine is coming in at noon with the canoe." He addressed Leonie. "Let's find Sister Cecile."

They disembarked. "Cecile!" Leonie yelled.

No answer.

"She could be anywhere," Jim said. "She's probably in the building, where it's cool."

"Or out where it's hot," Leonie said. "She's always doing the opposite of what I expect."

Reggie Peele was lingering inside the weathered souvenir shop where the Indians sold quantities of artificial artifacts, beadwork, alligator skulls, nature books and herbal remedies. For fifteen dollars Reggie bought some all-natural Miccosukee Indian mosquito repellent and spread it on his exposed parts. It felt like honey on his skin, but no mosquitoes bit him as he stood on the badly screened porch watching the boat unload.

He moved behind a row of soft-drink machines as Jim, Stephanie, and Leonie came in. "Where could she be?" Leonie was saying.

"It's air-conditioned inside," Stephanie said. "She's probably found a book to read, or something to eat. They have frozen fruit bars."

"I want one of them," Leonie said as they passed inches from where Reggie stood with his back turned to them, his eyes blankly focused through the screen to the wet prairie beyond. Reggie had been wondering himself what happened to the nun. He had been aware of her presence when he had gone out for his foray among the mosquitoes, but that was the last he had seen of her. She wasn't inside, she wasn't on the porch. She must have gone for a long walk on one of the trails, he speculated. Meanwhile it didn't look as if the girl was ever going to wander off by herself. But there was still time. Reggie patted the handcuffs in his pocket. He had no compunction about grabbing the kid, attaching her to some tree out there and leaving her for the bugs and gators as soon as she told him the name of the killer. She must know. Why else would the damn Injun spend all this time buttering her up?

A few minutes later the small group emerged from the building and turned toward the fake Indian village set up nearby. "Where could she be?" Leonie worried.

"Walking," Stephanie said. "I bet she went on one of the trails. Does she like to walk?"

"Loves to," Leonie said. "She likes to go off and pray, I think. She never says what she does when she walks, she just smiles if I ask her. Besides, maybe she didn't really want to eat alligator. Maybe that's why."

"She got a watch?" Jim asked.

Leonie shook her head. "She hates time. Only wears one when she goes out on business."

"So she might be gone for hours. Maybe we can leave her a note at the office here. Think she'll check?" Jim asked.

"Sure," Leonie said. "She knew we were going to your mom's for lunch. It's her fault if she misses. It's gotta be she

151

saw an alligator and doesn't want to eat one now. I know her. She's somewhere praying for alligators."

"Maybe. I'm sure she'll be okay, though. And they have tuna sandwiches and drinks inside. Expensive, but not bad. She won't starve. Besides, Tommy is here now." Stephanie smiled at an approaching stranger who was dressed in authentic Seminole garb. The man wore a long tunic covered with vibrant patchwork done in the traditional pattern of the loggerhead turtle. He wore a red turban wrapped around his head.

"Tommy Tigertail," Jim said. "This is Leonie."

Leonie stared at his outfit. "Hi, Tommy. That looks neat. Isn't it hot? All that cloth?"

"Keeps off the mosquitoes. That's why the women wear the long dresses, too. Good medicine," Tommy said. "Keeps tourist money coming. Hey, I got your boat here, Jim."

"Thanks, Tommy. We'll have the canoe back this afternoon," Jim said, and then he instructed his friend to keep an eye out for Sister Cecile and gave him a complete description of the nun. "I'd wait but I told my mother we'd be along. She gets worried."

"Cecile's out someplace on a trail," Leonie added. "She might be gone for hours. Tell her to wait here."

"I'll tell Billy at the counter inside, too," Stephanie said and went back indoors.

Jim Cypress looked after his wife's slender figure, then he looked at Leonie. Neither of them seemed worried that the nun had vanished without a trace. And maybe they were right not to worry, but he knew the Everglades. Mosquitoes and alligators were simple to deal with, but there were people out there. People could be very dangerous.

26

Jᴵᴹ Cypress's mother owned one of the best canoes in the Everglades. She didn't use it much herself, but, like all the women of the tribe, she was the boss of her family and the canoe belonged to her to do with as she wished. She had loaned it to Jim's friend, Tommy, when her son had married out of the tribe. Jim had accepted the loan as a sign of her authority. But here it was. Tommy had brought it to them to use.

The canoe was a long wooden dugout with perfect balance, considerably slimmer than the average northern style canoe. Jim Cypress knew it like the back of his hand. He had grown up with it.

When Leonie first saw it she was not filled with confidence.

"I can't go out in that," she said. "It's too skinny."

"Sit in the middle. Steph and I will paddle." Jim tapped the side of the canoe with his paddle. It rocked against the reedy side of the channel. "I know you can swim. Get in, very gently."

"There?" Leonie looked from the canoe to the water. The water, in fact, was glass clear, but filled with weeds. "It might eat me."

"Get in," Stephanie advised. "It's fun."

Leonie finally got in, sitting carefully on the bottom of the canoe, legs outstretched on the dark wood. The canoe tilted and dipped as Jim hopped in, barely moved as Stephanie climbed aboard. One last look around for Sister Cecile and they left, heading into a silent, grassy world. Leonie's hesitancy evaporated when they glided by a frisbee-sized turtle that followed them for a few feet. "It thinks we're good to eat," Leonie whispered, then she looked up as Jim pointed to a huge bird.

"Wood stork. Not many left of them," he said softly. "But after a couple years of heavy rains, there's actually been a resurgence. A lot of the nesting habitat's gone to the sugarcane growers. People figured another five years, they'd be extinct. But maybe not. Mother Nature flooded this place. Made up for all our damming it up."

Leonie didn't respond, but she twisted her neck to feast her eyes on the huge bird standing like a sentinel of doom against a backdrop of mangrove roots. It was an odd-looking thing, an imaginary bird, living in an unreal world.

From a distance, Reggie Peele watched the little party leave. The dark wood canoe slipped gently into a clear channel through the reeds and the mangroves. His opportunity was going fast.

Reggie spotted an empty boat pulled up along the grassy edge of the water, a small green boat with a tiny one-horsepower motor and a pair of oars. Some fool had just left it there, he realized. Just for him.

This could be a perfect chance to get the kid, Reggie thought, particularly if the little group went to a hammock somewhere and went off wandering around the hardwoods. Reggie knew that in the middle of the Everglades there were countless raised ridges called hammocks where small hardwood forests and grasses grew, making homes for deer and the Miccosukee.

Kids always took off by themselves. It was a slim chance, but a possibility too good to ignore, that Leonie would wander off by herself once they got to a hammock.

Reggie lumbered down into the boat and first thing, got his feet wet. There was about a half inch of water in the boat. No problem, he thought. A little rain water.

He checked the motor. It had a shield to protect the small propeller from tangling in the weeds, a specially designed Evinrude just made for travel in this kind of swamp. It looked good. There was even a small red gas can beside the motor. A shake proved it was full.

Reggie pulled out the choke, then yanked on the starter cord. The motor buzzed to life, then sputtered. Carefully Reggie pushed the choke back in, out, and then in again until the motor finally purred. He knew these little babies. He'd been fishing on the canals in Dade County for years.

Moments later he was out in the water, the canoe just out of sight behind a bend in the open-water trail. He followed a trail cut through by countless airboat excursions. This was a piece of cake.

Reggie Peele put-putted along, feeling the warm heat of tropical sun on his back. The gentle breeze, stirred by his movement, cooled his face. The hum of bugs meant nothing to him now that he was coated with Miccosukee insect repellent. It had been a major rip-off at fifteen dollars, but essential. Damned if it didn't even work. Recently he had read a newspaper article explaining that in Dade County, the Mosquito Control department measures ferocity of infestation by counting the mosquito landings on a person in sixty seconds. At the worst times, on the southern tip of Everglades National Park, over two hundred may land on a person every minute. By that scale, today was a very good day. Even so, Reggie knew that without the insect repellent, he could be in bad shape.

Reggie even took a moment to gaze at a flutter of zebra butterflies that swooped above some swamp lilies. This was definitely the Elysian fields. Beautiful country. He should come out here more often. Maybe take Amy for an airboat ride sometime. Meanwhile, all he had to do was keep the other party in sight and grab his opportunity. He hadn't felt so good about anything in years.

Jim was conscious of the sound behind them. He knew exactly what it was; it was the familiar sputter of Marcus Huttle's little outboard motor. Marcus liked to fish in the Everglades and the Indians always left him alone. He was a harmless old codger who bummed around in that little green boat and caught just enough fish to feed his family. He had lived at peace with the natives for years. Marcus probably figured he was going fishing and was following Jim into some good grounds.

Jim pushed the sound of the motor to the back of his mind.

"Be at the hammock in ten, maybe fifteen minutes," Jim said quietly. He was looking straight ahead for the big gators. A gator could dump a little canoe like this with one big twitch of a tail.

"It's cool here," Leonie said. She sat, legs out in front of her, on the bottom of the canoe. "Are we really going to eat alligator? I mean, actually eat one of those things?"

"Probably," Stephanie said. "They cook it on a slow fire for a long time. It's good."

"Like chicken?" Leonie asked.

"No. It tastes like alligator," Jim said, paddling down hard against the rusty grass spikes pushing up from the water. This time of year the swamp grasses were brown and dry and tinkled like glass against the paddle on the return stroke. It had been dry this month, but there was a feeling of weather change in the air. They might get a little storm pretty soon. His face was impassive but he was smiling inside. He loved his Everglades. They were his and his tribe's for all eternity. He knew everything that grew and breathed here. After the rough cement and art deco of Miami Beach, he felt at home among the air plants living in the dancing mangroves, the rare bald eagle, the black vultures and the big sky.

That was the thing here, the sky. He looked up at the towering thunderheads moving in swiftly to his right and saw a heaven-splitting lightning bolt. The soft clouds vanished in a matter of minutes. Like the mosquitoes, lightning was less common in the winter, but there it was. Rain was coming. The big sun would hide, the rain would fall in buckets. They'd be safe at the chickee by then. And hopefully Sister Cecile would be in the Miccosukee souvenir shop. Everything was fine.

Jim paddled hard at the helm of the canoe, knowing Stephanie could keep the craft going straight from the rear. All she had to do was paddle.

Behind him he still heard the one-horse motor. It meant nothing to him.

His thoughts turned to his wife. He was still consciously delighted that Stephanie loved him, even now, ten years after they had met. Now he had everything that a man could ever want: Stephanie, the 'Glades, and his tribe, the only tribe that had never been defeated. In the sixties when the Miccosukee had demanded recognition from the United States government and been refused, they had gone to Cuba where Castro was prepared to give them the diplomatic recognition they craved. Since then the United States had caved in. Now the Miccosukees were a respected and powerful group of people with a homeland of their own, and bingo halls. A new four-million-dollar bingo hall had just gone up. Ironic that they should prey on the white man's weaknesses, Jim thought. Of course, as a policeman, he, too, lived on weakness.

Jim turned and looked back at the two women. They looked like sisters, two delicate white flowers in the back of his canoe.

"You'll like alligator," he said firmly.

Leonie mumbled a sound that could have been taken for "Sure thing," when a huge creature jumped out of a rare stretch of low hammock land that had been running alongside the canoe path. Leonie let out a shriek as the animal leaped into the boat, tipping it radically. The beast landed directly in front of Leonie and stared down at her with strange, liquid eyes, eyes of translucent ice blue color set deep in a lively face. A growl rose in the creature's throat.

A scream stuck in Leonie's throat.

"Oh! Speckles!" Stephanie spouted. "It's okay, Leonie, it's Speckles. Okay, boy, she's our friend," she said to the dog, whose strange eyes were still fixed on Leonie. The dog was no longer growling, though. He was whining. Suddenly he looked like an ordinary dog.

Speckles was as abruptly entranced with the girl as she was

157

with him. The two pairs of blue eyes met and something clicked.

Leonie whispered, "Hi, poochie," and ran a light hand down the dog's velvet head. Then she reached around him and gave him a hug. Speckles gave a delighted whine and settled down on top of Leonie's outstretched legs. He flopped his long, ropelike tail up and down on the canoe bottom. Instant love.

Jim watched silently. Speckles was his family's Catahoula Leopard dog; a prized beast who protected his mother, his sister and her family and helped with hunting in the 'Glades. "Catahoulas don't take to strangers, Leonie. He must think you're family," Jim said. "He's got instincts; he knows when someone's good or bad."

"He's cute," Leonie said and rubbed the dog's speckled head. "He's very funny looking. What is he? A Cata-what?"

"Catahoula Leopard dog. His ancestors came over with Hernando de Soto, kind of a bull mastiff-type dog that inbred with some of the local critters. The breed developed from that. It's been around a long time in the South. Great for hunting and protection," Jim continued as he watched the dog lolling in Leonie's lap. "They hunt by sound and scent. He must have sensed us coming. Strange, him taking to you like that so sudden."

"Good thing," Stephanie said.

Suddenly Speckles's ears pricked up and he jumped back out of the canoe, rocking it wildly as he leaped into the water and up a grassy line of the hammock. He let out a baying sound that sent chills up Jim's spine. The dog took off in a direction behind them, silent now, tracking something on the wind or something his ears had heard.

"Damn, he's going after Marcus Huttle, that old fellow who fishes out here. He's been behind us all along."

"Speckles just might encourage him to go back," Stephanie said. "Good thing, too. I think it's going to rain. He'd be smart to head back."

"Marcus would," Jim agreed.

Leonie looked up to the huge sky and saw the thunderheads. Bright sky behind them allowed the sun to shine brilliantly on the water, but ahead the lightning running along the underside of the clouds looked forbidding. She was relieved when Jim and Stephanie both paddled hard. It was really incredibly neat here. The most peaceful place she'd ever been. She grinned and trailed a hand in the warm water as they sped though the swamp. She pulled it back suddenly. Not a good idea, she thought as a splash from the side made her look hard at impenetrable weeds. It could have been a turtle, could have been an alligator. Only a ripple remained as they glided on.

Nobody was thinking about Sister Cecile.

27

SISTER Cecile woke up in the backseat of the green Mercedes just as it was crossing the causeway to Miami Beach. Jasper had drugged her lightly because he knew that Gustavo wouldn't want his beautiful woman to arrive puking her guts out. That had happened once before.

As it was, Cecile felt very much like doing just that. She lay absolutely still for a few moments. Then she tried an arm, moving it just a fraction of an inch. It worked. Gingerly she tried each body part. She discovered that her hands were unbound and free, legs were cramped but usable. She was not tied up, not bound, not gagged. The only gagging was what would happen if the rolling motion in her stomach got the upper hand. She thought cool blue thoughts, pictured still trees in a windless forest and took long, deep breaths of stale, air-conditioned car air. She would not get sick. She would control her body and figure out what was happening. No getting sick. Yet.

Her mind whirred into gear while her stomach churned. Where was she going, and with whom? She concentrated on the man who had abducted her. He had been familiar. Her mind reached back in time. Yesterday, the day before, where had she seen him?

Suddenly she remembered the green earring, the man at that place on the beach, the one with Gustavo. What was his name?

Jasper. Her stomach lurched as the name popped into her mind. Jasper, Gustavo Bestard, the twenty thousand dollars. He had wanted her and he was getting her. She was on her way to a date with the man.

Ha. Fat chance. Now if only she could keep from heaving while she figured this all out. Ideas and nausea each vied for ascendancy. Thoughts and perceptions spun through her mind, faster and faster.

Somehow she managed to quell the queasiness and form a plan. When the car finally rolled through a gate and into Gustavo's elegant but private home on Star Island, she was ready.

She played dead on the backseat, trying not to cringe as Jasper pulled her out, off the soft seat of the Mercedes. He propelled her ostensibly lifeless body from the car and into the simmering heat of a Florida day at high noon. Cecile drooped as though unconscious, feeling herself dragged and forced upright, then propped back against the broiling car door.

Jasper methodically slapped one side of her face, then the other. "Wake up, little lady. Gustavo wants you. Let's go, baby doll." Jasper spoke in a singsong voice as though he was bored with the entire operation.

In fact, Jasper was a little bored. Fortunately dragging doped women home was not a daily event in his life. The truth was, most women were more than willing to come along for the sheer thrill of being with Gustavo, who had such incredible amounts of money to spread around, and, in fact, was not such a bad-looking stud. Jasper couldn't understand why this one had turned down the money in the first place. His boss was too

160

generous. This was a lesson in reality. She should have taken the money up front. "Wake up, baby. We gonna meet the man."

Cecile gauged her movements carefully. The slaps weren't hard and she allowed her body to sway and her eyelids to flutter just enough to see where Jasper was. She made a small moaning sound to distract him. Then she struck.

Thunk. Her knee went up with a swift movement. She caught him, dead center in the groin. Chop. Her left hand moved like a knife and whacked him just below the chin. A little more power and she could have broken his neck. Chomp. Her foot smashed down on his instep. Mush. Right in the stomach with her thumb aimed out.

He was down and groaning before he knew what hit him. Cecile spotted his holster, a thick leather thing hanging on his belt. With a quick motion she leaned over and pulled out the gun. The gun handling lessons she had taken after her last case were actually proving useful. She was instantly armed and dangerous. Not that she would use a gun. She would never, ever use a gun. But she knew how to handle one.

"Get up, Jasper," she said evenly.

"Ohhhh, shit," Jasper managed between clenched teeth.

"Up."

He got up, swaying, holding himself slightly bent. He met her bloodshot eyes with his own. "What the hell you do that for?"

Cecile held back an appropriate answer. "Where are we?" she asked grimly.

"This here's Gustavo's. Star Island," Jasper said, gesturing slowly around him at the Spanish-style villa surrounded by a jungle of tropical plantings. Cecile stepped back from his movements. The man had huge arms, longer than some orangutans she had seen.

"You were supposed to bring me here?"

"Yeah, right. Sort of. My idea, actually. He wants you. I get what he wants."

"Why?"

Jasper shrugged. "He wants you."

"I don't want him. You tell him that for me."

"Hey, I'm doing my job."

"Don't do it on me. Understand. Next time you won't get up so fast. Got it?"

Jasper rubbed his crotch. "Yeah, got it."

"I need to be somewhere. Give me the keys to the car. I have to meet some people back at the airboats. You can pick the car up there." She pointed the gun at his chest.

Jasper just stood, slightly tilted, and stared at Sister Cecile. His jaw dropped.

"Give me the keys. Toss them. Gently."

He tossed.

"Now, tell me what you know about Elliot Barclay's death."

Jasper looked puzzled. "Who?"

"Elliot Barclay. How about Nica Rabelais. What do you know about her?"

"Her? She hung around. Everyone knew Nica." He grinned through his pain. "Everybody."

"Great."

"Why?"

"She was killed."

"She's dead?"

It was hopeless. From an apparent source, the man had degenerated into a nobody who knew nothing. Useless. Cecile was tempted to kick him, but it wouldn't have been the Christian thing to do now that she had the upper hand.

"I'll leave the keys under the front seat, along with this gun. The car will be out by the airboats, out where you picked me up," she informed him politely. "Please don't tell anyone about this or I will file charges of kidnapping and aggravated assault. Your car will be fine."

Sister Cecile left Star Island, driving carefully. After all, it wasn't her car. She didn't think Jasper would call the police and report that someone had stolen the green Mercedes. Not with a kidnapping charge in the air. She also still felt woozy

162

and wasn't sure she could handle fast speeds safely. In fact she felt an overriding urge to relieve herself of her breakfast.

"No. I won't," she said out loud and kept her eyes glued on the road ahead, a road teaming with hot, fast traffic. She got off the MacArthur Causeway by sheer willpower and kept going. Twenty minutes into the drive west, aiming for the Everglades, she knew the turmoil inside her stomach was getting the upper hand. Luckily she could make a right hand stop, but she didn't want to. Not yet. Another few miles went by and she knew it was now or never.

Sister Cecile pulled off the road, shuddered abruptly and blinked. She didn't have the strength to open the car door. Waves of nausea rolled over her. The light shimmering through the heavily tinted car windows seemed to turn a violent shade of green and her stomach did its thing. Breakfast came up on the leather seat beside her.

Sister Cecile wiped her mouth on her sleeve and took a slow breath. Much better. The car seat looked bad, though. It had even spread to the driver's side.

Good. It served them right. All of them.

Now she had the choice of efficient air-conditioning or wide-open windows. Sister Cecile decided she needed real air. The windows went down, and she drove as fast as she could toward the Everglades while the hot Florida air blew through the car, drying up the spill on the seat into a permanent dark stain on the soft hunter green leather. It would be a pungent and perpetual reminder to Jasper of his failure, and to Gustavo of the folly of his desires.

28

REGGIE Peele was careful to avoid the weeds so as not to tangle the little one-horse motor's propeller. It took some fancy doing and considerable skill, even with the weed shield. He alternated between lifting the motor up, and tilting it just enough to allow it to skim over the grassy water and keep up with the distant canoe, then dipping it in the water for a power push. He kept barely out of sight for the entire trip, pressing his luck. It didn't occur to him that there was a reason Jim Cypress hadn't stopped and checked who was following him. Reggie just figured Jim hadn't noticed.

Reggie was smiling to himself, contemplating the success of his venture, when a strange ice-eyed creature leaped out of the swamp and onto his boat. The beast stood facing him. A strange growling sound came from the animal's throat.

"Son of a bitch, a panther!" Reggie exhaled and reached for his gun.

Speckles was a hunting dog; he knew about guns, how they meant death to the one down the barrel. Even before that, he had known this guy was an enemy. It had been in the air itself, a scent of evil on the wind. A growl rose in the dog's throat. The hackles stood up on the back of his neck. He attacked.

Speckles jumped clear after he gave a ripping bite to Reggie's right arm. The dog's bite wasn't enough to make the policeman drop the gun; instead Reggie let off a wild shot. Speckles was out of the boat seconds after the shot, swimming like mad with his strangely webbed feet. But he couldn't move fast enough. Reggie got off a second shot that winged the dog in the leg. Speckles still didn't stop paddling. He vanished behind the high grasses, leaving a red stain in the swamp water.

"Got the bastard," Reggie muttered. His arm was bleeding from the tearing bite. Then he heard some thrashing in the water ahead. Jim Cypress coming back, or maybe the damn panther again, Reggie thought in panic. He had to get out of here! He revved up the little motor.

That was when the propeller jammed with weeds. The motor stalled out with a helpless sputter. Frustrated, Reggie lifted his gun and shot a round in the direction of the thrashing sound. It had to be the damn panther, he thought with satisfaction as the thrashing noise stopped. He heard a strange wailing sound.

"The panther," he muttered aloud. "I got the damn panther."

He didn't know he had hit Stephanie.

Reggie turned to the oars and painfully rowed the boat around to head back the way he had come. He paddled ferociously, moving fast in spite of his age and the state of his chewed arm. He aimed the boat at some tall reeds and kept rowing. He would wait there until things calmed down. Then he could pull the weeds out of the jammed motor and get the hell out of here.

Somewhere in the sky a huge rumble of thunder rolled, long, hollow, and ominous across the grass prairie. A lightning bolt flashed and hit a mahogany tree only a mile away.

Stephanie clutched her shoulder as blood oozed out. The bullet had entered her left shoulder just above the clavicle. It looked bad. Blood was running down her navy shirt in dark, spreading blotches. Speckles appeared, struggling through the water, his blood puddling out in the water behind him. A strangling howl came from deep in his throat.

It was a nightmare.

Jim Cypress stared at his wife, then at his dog. He didn't move, caught between two horrors. Leonie saw him, saw the fear, the indecision, strange emotions in a strong man's face. A killer was out there, Stephanie was hit, the dog bleeding in the water. Time had stopped.

Leonie saw everything in slow motion. The dog, Stephanie, Jim, all three barely moving. "Get Speckles!" she heard Jim yell.

Leonie jumped overboard.

The water was shallow; Leonie knew that, had been thinking all along how great it would be to jump in and cool off, barring alligators. The water only came up to her chest as she grabbed for Speckles. He was moving slowly, exhausted and bleeding, but he was still a large, slippery beast. After three attempts, Leonie finally wrapped her arms around the dog.

"Hokey, boy, you're gonna be fine. I have you," she murmured to the animal. She held his head up above the surface and dragged him though the chest-high water, back to the canoe. "I got him," she said, but Jim didn't even look her way. Alone, she managed to dump the dog over the side of the canoe. She saw Jim had already moved down to the end of the boat and was leaning over Stephanie.

Leonie hung limp on the edge of the canoe and caught her breath. The dog was safe in the canoe. Now she had to get in, too, somehow, without tipping everyone out, because on top of everything else, there were the alligators. She had seen them. Seven of them. And there was blood in the water.

"Lie flat," Jim commanded his wife. He tore off a piece of his shirt and made a quick pressure bandage. He ripped open her blouse and found the bullet entry site and applied hard pressure to stop the bleeding.

Leonie moved to the other end of the canoe and jumped up and down from the silty, soggy bottom, trying to get some momentum. Finally she took a leap and dove headfirst into the opposite gunwhale of the canoe, then flipped the lower half of her body over the side and in. With a final push she heaved herself up and ended flat on her back on the canoe bottom. She lay, blinking, catching her breath and staring at the darkening sky above her.

Black clouds swarmed in overhead. The world had turned upside down in the space of five minutes. Leonie's mind was a blank as she gasped for breath. Off to her left another massive lightning bolt split the sky.

"Speckles," she said suddenly and sat up. Jim was with Stephanie. She had to help the dog. *Everybody* was dying.

Reggie waited. He had managed to row the boat deep into the grasses where he sat and listened. He felt like an Indian, but better, much better. He felt proud because he was in control even while he was in pain from the animal bite. It was a power trip in a strange way, and it felt good for a man of his age to win a battle with nature and the elements.

Reggie listened to the hum of insects and the silence of water animals. Gators were everywhere out here but he was safe in the boat. Safe and smart. He looked down at his arm where the panther had taken a bite. Damn thing had ripped his skin halfway to the bone and it hurt like hell. Tetanus, he thought, maybe rabies. He'd have to go to the emergency room and get a shot. Damn, he would love to tell people how he faced down a real Florida panther. At least he could tell Amy, nobody else. She would tell him how great he was.

First he had to get back to Miami.

Lightning sliced through the sky. It finally occurred to Reggie that a storm might be coming. Another bolt split the blackening veil. It was definitely coming. He had to return to civilization before the rain let loose. No problem there, but to be on the safe side he should row for a while so as not to make any noise. This was not the time to start the motor, because he was sure Jim Cypress and his crew would head back and try to find the source of the shots.

He rowed for a good five minutes before he decided the motor wouldn't be heard. Drifting in the murky water, Reggie tilted up the little motor and pulled off weeds from the propeller, one strand at a time.

A few minutes later he had cleared it of all but one long strand of saw grass. He gave a pull and the propeller twisted backward somehow. Reggie heard a faint plop as a small piece of metal dropped in the water.

He kept pulling on the weed. Another plopping sound, but Reggie missed it as more lightning lit up the sky. Then the weed was off. Then the propeller dropped into the swamp.

Reggie was speechless.

Finally he cursed, a long string of words that would have been a credit to his grandfather, a London dockworker with a profane vocabulary second to none.

It was all downhill after that. More lightning bolts, huge crashes of thunder that rocked the quaking earth, then the rain fell. It was more than rain; the sky let loose. More than buckets, more than a drenching, it was like being under a waterfall. Reggie could barely breathe. Visibility dropped to zero.

Finally the deluge let up. Just when Reggie got his nerve up and was about to jump into the swamp to find the lost propeller, a grinning, eight-foot alligator drifted up beside the boat.

Reggie decided to row. No big deal.

Within five minutes the rain was history and the sun was out again, but his mosquito repellent had washed off and what was left of the bottle was safe in his car where he had tossed it after a hefty application.

By the time Reggie rowed up to the airboat settlement he was uncomfortable, to say the least. He itched, he burned, he hurt, and he was ready to kill. Lucky for him, he landed unseen. Tourists had just left in one of the huge airboats after a rain delay, and the deck was clear. The place was sparkling after the rain, quite beautiful, if Reggie had cared to notice. Lucky for him he still had his car keys. Lucky for him he didn't shoot the first Indian he saw, because that was what he wanted to do, but his arm hurt too much and he was thoroughly dehydrated from sweating and rowing in eighty-seven-degree heat, eighty-nine-percent humidity.

As a matter of fact, Reggie Peele was lucky to get home at all.

29

THE Cypress family was not a primitive group of Indians off in the steamy swamps. True, they eschewed air-conditioning and dwelled in a modern version of the chickee, the palmetto-leaf-covered buildings that their families had inhabited for generations. But modern conveniences had crept in; life was better than ever, taking in the good things of two worlds. The Cypress family's dwellings were of thick, block construction, heavily screened against the bugs. A garden grew nearby on solid, composted dirt. It was a hobby garden in the hardwood hammock. Tomatoes and squash and beans decorated the tilled land. A generator hummed quietly, providing electricity for a refrigerator and evening lights. A cellular telephone stood beside a campfire where pungent alligator tail was braising in a black pan set over the open flames. It seemed, here, that it had hardly rained at all. The only signs were a sparkle of rain-drops on low grasses and a steamy look to the air.

By the time the canoe pulled up, Speckles's bleeding was under control, and the big Catahoula dog rested quietly on the canoe floor. Leonie was as close to Stephanie as she could be, applying gentle pressure to the gunshot wound while Jim worked the paddle. Everyone's clothing had almost dried from the sun.

The canoe bumped to a stop and Jim jumped up onto the waiting earth, pulling the craft after him. "Wait here. I'll call," he ordered. "You, too, Speckles," he commanded the big dog who had begun to rise to follow his master in spite of the pain. "Stay."

Speckles settled back with a big, doggy sigh.

"I'll get the helicopter," Jim said. "You all wait here," he repeated. "No moving around, Steph."

"I'm okay, Jim. Leonie's here."

Leonie was scared but didn't show her fear. She had been through troubles before, too many for someone her age, and she knew she could handle this one. Somehow. But wasn't it time to lighten up? Enough, God, she thought ferociously. Give me some peace. And please help Stephanie be okay. Please!

Then she realized she was praying. She shook her head and she almost grinned. Praying? Her? This was not something she would ever admit to Sister Cecile. It was just another thing she would add to the list of things to keep private.

"Stephanie, does it hurt much?" she asked.

"It's just my shoulder, Leonie. I'm going to be fine. No big deal. It was probably just some crazy hunter . . . some nut with a gun. They're everywhere these days. The Everglades are full of people like that."

That made sense to Leonie. There *were* nuts with guns. This was probably a dumb hunter who had thought Speckles was a wild animal. She knew people shot cows all the time during deer season. "I wonder where Cecile is," Leonie said more to herself than to Stephanie. "I wish she were here."

"She'll be along," Stephanie managed. "Momma Cypress will take care of you here. And don't worry about me, Leonie. I'm fine."

Leonie took a deep breath. A good scent wafted through the shimmering air. Then Jim was there with two large men. Jim and one of the men hoisted Stephanie up like a big rag doll, the other man picked up Speckles. Leonie followed along, her eyes going from one of the strangers to the other. Both were short versions of Jim Cypress; they were his brothers, she was later to discover.

"Helicopter is coming from Dade County Fire Rescue," Jim said as they came up to the gray structures in a clearing ahead. "It will take us right to Jackson Memorial. I'll ride in with you, Stephy."

170

Stephanie grimaced as pain sparked through her shoulder. "I'm fine. Don't worry." Then she fainted.

A lightning bolt shot through the sky and the heavens opened up again. Just in time they entered the main chickee. Stephanie was lowered to the floor. Speckles was settled down beside her with a whimper, while Leonie stood back and waited, wondering if anyone had noticed she was even there.

Outside the rain fell again in torrents, creating a comforting racket with its drilling, splattering sound. Leonie stepped back farther. It was dark and warm in the corner of the big open room, and she tried to become invisible. Everything was wrong, somehow. And it was definitely her fault, although she couldn't explain why. She just knew it.

Jim saw her. He must have seen into her mind, too. He came up close and spoke in a low voice. "Leonie, I'm going to ask my brother to get you back to the airboats when the weather lets up. Cecile will be wondering what happened to us, otherwise. I'll have him call in with a message and tell her not to worry. Okay?" He patted Leonie on the shoulder. It was almost a hug. "You're doing great. I couldn't have got her here without you. You're the best. Have some lunch, okay?" He grinned. "Then you'll be on your way home."

"Fine." Leonie managed a smile and it felt real because, strangely enough, it was fine, very fine, and then everything happened just the way Jim said it would. The helicopter arrived within half an hour, not bad time considering the fact that visibility had been zero in the Everglades for the minutes of heavy rain. Then the sky cleared up magically, as it often did in South Florida. Blue sky, bright sun, the air was like a steam bath. Leonie watched it all from one place or another.

No one had remembered to call the airboat shop yet to tell Sister Cecile what was happening.

Leonie found herself a place beside Speckles where she sat and patted the dog and waited. It took a few minutes for peace to return to the hammock after the noisy departure of the helicopter. At last someone came over to her.

171

It was Jim's mother. She was tall for a Miccosukee, tall and slim as opposed to the usual thick women that typified the tribe. "Lunch is ready. Maybe you can help us eat? I've made enough for a lot of guests, and now we have just you and my sons."

Leonie didn't feel hungry. Another person telling her to eat. It happened all the time. But she sat down at the low table and ate.

With everything else that had happened she might just as well die eating alligator as getting shot in the Everglades. She took her first bite, chewed bravely and swallowed.

"Like it?" Jim's mother asked.

"Not bad," she murmured. She cleaned up her plate and slowly the world began to reshape into something she could handle. But where was Sister Cecile? She really should be here. And Jim, and Stephanie. "Did anyone call Cecile? We have to call Sister Cecile."

"Oh, the nun at the airboats. I'll call," one of Jim's brothers volunteered.

Sister Cecile parked the big car in a space by the canal and walked into the souvenir shop. At that exact moment she heard her name called out.

"Sister Cecile? Any Sister Cecile here?"

"That's me!"

"Sister Cecile? I have someone for you on the phone. Take it behind the counter, please."

"Hello?"

"Billy Cypress here. Jim's brother. Here's Leonie."

At the camp, Leonie took the telephone from Jim's brother and talked. It was hard to explain exactly what happened, because Leonie wasn't exactly sure how to make it sound right, and the last thing she wanted to do was to frighten the nun. She tried to downplay everything. "Anyway, someone was shooting. Maybe it was an accident, probably just a crazy hunter," Leonie said. "But they got Speckles, the dog, and Stephanie. She's okay, I guess, and Speckles is fine. He's here now and Jim's brothers both took care of him. But it was scary. Billy will be bringing me back right away."

"Billy?"

"Jim's youngest brother. Guess what, Cecile. We had alligator for lunch."

"Great."

"Yeah. It's cool out here. I wish you had come with us."

"Me, too."

Sister Cecile had been sick before, but now she was *really* sick. Her pallor was even whiter than before. She felt a wild rush of blood and her face turned purple, then again white. Stephanie was shot? A dog was shot? It didn't sound good at all. What if Leonie had been hit. She would die herself, if anything ever happened to that child.

Sister Cecile knew it wasn't an accident. In her world shootings weren't accidental, but who could it have been and why? This was crazy. Everything so far today was crazy. It had to stop. Enough, God, she prayed. It was a prayer, a very short prayer and one surprisingly similar to the one Leonie had recently sent up. Very probably, at that point, God smiled and contemplated the odd fact that people do begin to act like each other when they hang around together. God knew, long before humans ever noticed, that if you give a man a poodle, he will start to look just like a poodle.

It had happened again.

30

SISTER Cecile was pacing the wide yard by the water when she saw Billy Cypress and Leonie arrive at the main camp. They came in a miniature airboat, the kind Sister Cecile had seen once in a movie, and they pulled up at the airboat dock. Leonie was riding up high next to Billy and looking fine.

Cecile ran up as Leonie dismounted onto the dock. She gave Leonie a huge hug. "Leonie, are you all right? I've been so worried since you called. You don't know what I've been through." She spurted the words all out, gray eyes intense but bleary.

Leonie pulled back. "What on earth have *you* been through? You smell awful, Cecile. Did someone throw up all over you?" Leonie looked at Cecile carefully. "You have gunk on your shirt. Sister Cecile, are you all right?"

"I'm wonderful, just an upset stomach. But you? They shot at you. Leonie, I'll never forgive myself. You've had a terrible time! Tell me everything. Is Stephanie all right?"

Billy Cypress waited patiently while the two females blabbered, then he coughed gently.

Cecile looked up. "You're Jim's brother? The one I spoke with? Thank you so much. This has been such a day. I'm Sister Cecile."

Billy introduced himself quietly. "Jim said he'd check in with you tonight. Said to tell you." Billy kept his eyes on the water as he spoke.

Sister Cecile nodded. "Billy, thank you." She fought back

174

the urge to give Billy a hug. She felt like giving everybody a hug.

"I gotta be getting back. Okay? Jim said everything was going to be fine."

"Thanks, Billy," Leonie said. "Make sure Speckles is comfortable, okay?"

"Sure thing. See you." He turned and hopped into the boat. The motor caught with a deafening roar. Billy turned and gave a bashful wave before he revved up the huge engine and sped away.

Sister Cecile and Leonie stared at each other for a moment, checking each other out. They both smiled at the same time then walked over to a bench. It was afternoon, the sun was already at a winter angle against the horizon. It was beautiful. The air was thick, but there was a faint breeze and the bugs were temporarily washed out by the rain.

They sat on the bench and didn't say a word, both fighting to bring their minds back to where their bodies were. Finally they spoke of what had happened. Leonie went first and gave an accurate description of the shooting. "I don't know who shot at us. Jim thinks some crazy hunter. When Stephanie got hit, first he froze, then he went sort of nuts, like he was going to get him, whoever it was that shot her. I really feel sorry for the guy, if Jim ever catches him. Shooting Stephanie and the dog, too. Talk about rotten." Leonie paused, finally, and looked at Cecile. "What happened to you?"

"I, I got a little sick to my stomach," the nun said. "It's still a little queasy in there."

"You went for a long walk and got sick?"

"Something like that."

"I see."

"Well, I'm ready to go home. How about you?" Cecile asked.

"Sure. Maybe we should get some ginger ale first?" Leonie brushed her blond hair back as she spoke, her eyes fixed on Cecile's washed-out face. "If you think you can keep it down."

"I can," Sister Cecile said. "I hope."

Reggie did not go to Jackson Memorial Hospital with his panther bite. Instead, he stopped at the Deering Hospital emergency room on South West 152nd Street. Jackson Memorial was for the riffraff, the stabbing victims, the abused children and the homeless people suffering from scabies. He wouldn't be caught dead there.

"Looks like a dog bite," the emergency room specialist said as she checked out Reggie's arm. "Not too serious. Any chance we can bring the dog in and have it tested for rabies?"

"No," Reggie grunted. "It was wild." He had decided to keep the panther story to himself. Wouldn't do to have it get around at the police station that he was out in the Everglades the day Jim Cypress was there.

"I'll give you an antibiotic. And you'll need the rabies shots. Too bad, but I'd really recommend it."

"Yeah, okay. What do I do?"

The doctor explained the series of shots, then wrote two prescriptions. "Antibiotic, and an antihistamine. You have an incredible number of mosquito bites."

"Yeah, malaria, yellow fever, encephalitis. I know."

"You're not likely to get any of those. Just itch."

"Yeah, sure, thanks, ma'am."

"Doctor," she corrected mildly. "Dr. Milner."

An hour later Reggie arrived home at his small Miami Beach efficiency and crawled into bed. He hurt and itched everywhere. He blamed Jim Cypress.

At least he was right about one thing.

Sister Cecile and Leonie didn't talk much on the way back. They were both emotionally exhausted, and neither was hungry.

"I hope Stephanie will be okay," Leonie whispered.

"Billy said so. I'll pray," Cecile said. "I'll have all the sisters pray. Don't worry."

Leonie hid a smile. What would Cecile ever think if the nun knew she already had?

Compline was held very early in the retirement home for the benefit of the older nuns who lived there. It was group prayer and the nuns met in a room, formerly a small banquet hall, that had been turned into a chapel. Now the room had an old Spanish look; Mexican Saltillo tiles were on the floor, the altar for celebrating Mass was made of antique pine. There were soft kneelers for old knees. In one corner a statue of Our Lady of Guadeloupe, donated by a wealthy patron, looked down from a large niche. The thick wrought-iron bars on the window looked more stylish than protective although they managed to be both.

The several laypeople who rented rooms from the nuns were always welcome at evening prayer; some actually came, finding it a fitting ending to the day. Tonight there was an old couple along with the nuns. Sister Cecile had showered and changed and was there, and in the last pew, Leonie sat. It felt good to be there.

Sister Raphael was leading the prayers tonight, reading quietly from the Old Testament. "Who will bring back to me the months that have gone," she intoned from the Book of Job, "and the days when God was my guardian. . . ."

Leonie listened from the back of the chapel. The words made her think about her father. Everything was so crazy. If he were only here, she thought, he would figure it all out.

Her dad, Damien Drail, was an officer in the Central Intelligence Agency, who had worked with Sister Cecile on the nun's last case. Leonie went over it in her mind. They had both been great. Her father had been injured, but not enough to keep him from going back to work. Now he was off again in another part of the world, and Sister Cecile was temporarily in charge of Leonie. Again.

Not that the nun wasn't competent. Not that Leonie hadn't learned to love Cecile and all the rest of the nuns. A tear sprang to Leonie's eye. It had been a rough day. She sat and listened to the entire service. She wasn't a Catholic, but she had learned to enjoy the evening prayer. It was a good time to think about her dad.

Sister Cecile was totally aware that Leonie was in the back of the chapel. Poor Leonie had been through some bad times lately, and the ironic thing was, they had all occurred while she was here, living in a nuns' retirement home. It was really ridiculous. This was supposed to be a place of peace. Cecile knew it, and she prayed extra hard. Being a mother, she had come to realize, required a very active prayer life.

31

SISTER Cecile came up to Leonie after compline. "We need to talk. Want to go for a walk?"

"Now? It's dark out. Is it safe?"

"There are two of us. What do you think?"

Leonie frowned for a moment. "Let's go."

They decided not to go to the Frieze and get ice cream. Instead they walked to a small shop that sold natural fruit and vegetable juices. It was not the one where Leonie had gone with Amy, but a better one, where the coconut came right out of a coconut. As usual, Leonie bought a coconut drink. Cecile went for a mango-lime "froojie." They took their drinks and walked until they found a bench by a bus stop.

"I was hoping we could all talk in the Everglades," Cecile said.

"Yeah, that really blew up," Leonie said.

"The problem is," Cecile said after a sip, "I don't know what to do. I'm hired to solve a crime that isn't a crime. I know you understand all this. That's why I want to discuss it with you. Because you're the heart of it. It affects you, and I don't want to keep what I decide to do a secret from you."

"I don't want to go to court," Leonie said.

"You won't. Jim and I have discussed that."

"Still, my fingerprints were all over that gun."

"That's a fact."

"And, like Jim said, it's dangerous. There really is a killer out there. But, as a cop, doesn't he have to report all this stuff? I mean, couldn't this get him in big trouble?" Leonie sounded worried.

"I asked him just that, and the answer is 'no.' The reason being that he isn't suppressing evidence of a crime. He's suppressing evidence of *no* crime. Plus, detectives are responsible to nobody except the ultimate police boss. They are allowed to pursue their own thing in their cases. Jim explained this to me. So Jim's okay. He can just let the case stay in the unsolved box and find Nica's killer. That's real."

"I've been worried."

"I know."

"And what about you?" Leonie asked.

"No problem," the nun replied. "I'd never turn you in. You know that."

"Good. Maybe Jim's home now. Maybe we should call him. It's not too late," Leonie said.

"Let's. I want to find out how Stephanie is, anyway."

"Me, too."

They walked back to the convent, talking all the way. They covered the wild day in the Everglades, chalking it up to the solunar schedules. They discussed school. They even discussed zits. Cecile didn't mention her trip to Gustavo's house in the backseat of a Mercedes and neither of them mentioned praying.

Sister Raphael was wandering around, turning out lights as they came in. It was almost ten o'clock. "Where have you two been?" she asked.

Leonie and Cecile shrugged simultaneously. "Talking," they said in unison and both giggled.

"Well," Sister Raphael said, "there's a call for you; I took a message. From Detective Cypress. He left a number."

"I'll call him right away. From my office. Come with me, Leonie."

"Jim? It's Sister Cecile. How's Stephanie?"

"Excellent. She's spending the night at the hospital, I'll pick her up tomorrow morning. She's fine. How's the kid? I've been worried."

"It's been a day for that. Leonie's okay. She's had a lot to handle." Sister Cecile's eyes drifted over to her ward, who moved up beside her. Cecile wrapped her arm around the girl and gave her a hug.

"Today was just one of those days." Cecile smiled to herself. "So that leaves me. I'm the one with the problem. I feel like I'm cheating the people who hired me," Cecile said. "I've been hired to find the killer. Now I have an ethical dilemma."

"Maybe you can talk to these people who hired you and broaden the scope to cover Nica," Jim suggested. "Then you'll be investigating a legitimate murder for them. I'm moving in on it, too. We can just shift the emphasis from one death to another and still fulfill our contractual obligations."

"You sound like a Talmudic scholar."

"I'm one of the tribes," he said.

"Well, it's a good idea. I'll talk to the consortium on Monday. What about the gun? It's buried out there under a sea grape tree."

"What gun?"

"It wasn't a crime at all," Cecile said. She was watching Leonie as she spoke. The girl was listening carefully to Cecile's half of the conversation and seemed to relax at the words.

The only problem was that unresolved questions inevitably left a hole, a black hole. Cecile felt it, she knew it with her heart and soul. It was a little frightening, because black holes were dead suns, lots of mass and the gravitational field can pull everything into it, even light. No telling what it would pull in.

180

"Maybe you can share some information on Nica's murder with me?" Cecile asked. "Do you have anything you might like to share?"

"Hardly," Jim muttered. "I can't believe I'm having ethical problems with a nun. You'll look into the Rabelais case, then?"

"If Barcus is willing," Sister Cecile heard herself say.

"What?"

"Oh, a quote from *David Copperfield*. No, I mean, the consortium has to keep me on for this." She shook her head at the telephone.

"We're doing fine," Jim said. "Assuming the consortium wants you to go on, let's get together and I'll give you some help. Say, we meet for a snack around four on Monday. At Clock's on the beach."

Jim sounded patronizing. Like she needed his help, but he didn't need hers.

"It's the best we can do." Cecile kept her voice even. "But, if the people who hired me don't go for my looking into Nica's death, too, I'll resign from the case. I can't keep taking their money for nothing."

"We'll talk," Jim confirmed.

Sister Cecile finally hung up and turned to Leonie who was pretending to be asleep in the big leather chair.

"It's all over, Leonie. Did you hear what I said?"

"Sort of."

"We're both going to finesse the Barclay case, pretend to investigate, maybe, but basically forget about it. As far as you're concerned it was just a horrible accident. Which is nothing but the truth. And that man," Cecile said darkly, "that horrible Elliot Barclay probably got just what he deserved."

"He was nice looking at first," Leonie said softly. "He was just a person. A drunk, dying person. I've thought a lot about it. He had AIDS; he had nothing but money and death ahead of him."

Leonie's compassion frightened Cecile. She, herself, was the one who was supposed to be kind and forgiving, not this

181

little girl who barely knew God existed. What was the matter with her?

"Leonie, I'm sorry. You're right. I get so angry at the thought of your being hurt." Suddenly tears sprang to Cecile's eyes. "I couldn't bear to lose you."

Leonie's blue eyes sparkled. "I'm tough to kill," she said.

"Thank God," Cecile whispered. "It's late. Let's go to bed."

Sunday morning rolled around too soon. A visiting priest from Pennsylvania was renting a room for the week at the home and had agreed to say Sunday Mass for the community in their small chapel. It was one of the perks of running a retirement home with spare rooms. Cecile envisioned a steady round of priests in sunglasses and plaid shirts, coming to Miami for some R and R, a nice time on the sand and the golf courses, and a private chapel to say Mass in. All for a minimal fee. It was a cheap vacation.

Having an in-house Mass made it easy for the oldest nuns, who found it difficult to travel. This morning the small chapel was packed with the retired couples, the nuns and Father DeVainder from Erie, Pennsylvania saying the mass of the season. Sister Germaine had decorated the altar with drooping hibiscus, the candles were burning, the chapel was beautiful.

How lucky we are, Cecile decided as her mind moved to thoughts of thanksgiving.

Leonie wasn't in the chapel. No surprise. Her father had raised her as a nonfunctioning Methodist, and for the most part, she still was. Sometimes the girl would show up for Mass or a prayer service, like last night. But after their late-night conversation Cecile realized she had a few practical points to learn from her ward, church or not.

"It's tough, God," Cecile prayed. "I would have killed that Elliot Barclay myself. It's very tough to forgive him."

32

THERE was a message on the community answering machine, but nobody noticed it until after breakfast.

When Sister Cecile finally heard it, it was too late, he was already on the way.

"Gustavo is coming here," Cecile informed Sister Edna, who usually nunned the phone. "In five minutes!"

"Gustavo? Who's that?"

"A man. I'll wait for him by the front door. I don't want him in here."

Gustavo Bestard was prompt. At exactly ten o'clock he walked into the lobby of the retirement home, his dark eyes sweeping about. Today the place was full of nuns, most wearing habits, some dressed in secular clothes with veils and crosses. There were three nuns in habits, sitting at the glass-topped coffee table playing Old Maid. Sister Edna was about to join them, a portable phone in her hand, bringing her work to the game.

"Good morning, Gustavo," Sister Cecile said primly. She was at the door, determined not to let him in. No telling what this animal would do.

Gustavo stood in the doorway, a huge open-mouthed grin on his face. His mouth finally closed, and he looked hard at Cecile, dressed in white blouse and skirt, a small veil perched on her shiny curls. "You're the one," he said. "You took out Jasper. The man was sick when you got done with him."

Sister Cecile didn't even want to speak to this person. "Jasper was not a nice man. We really have no business together, Gustavo. This is a retirement community. Donations can be mailed."

"Just like that, you're a nun."

"I'm always a nun. Shall we move outside?"

He looked past her at the card game. He looked at the wicker chairs at the other end of the room, at the rough, unfinished edge of one wall. "There," he pointed to them. "We sit. We talk."

"We have nothing to say to each other."

"Nothing? I thought you just asked for a donation."

"That was my way of a joke. You can't be seriously considering such a thing."

They continued to stand, Cecile barricading the way in with her presence.

"I give a great deal to charity. Cubans for Independence, the United Way, stuff like that."

"The United Way? They fund abortions."

"Okay, say I give an equal amount to you guys. I'm a generous man. Save the kids. Do what you want with it."

"I feel you're just saying this as some kind of ploy."

Gustavo looked vaguely embarrassed. It was hard to believe he could look that way. It was probably just another ploy. "Listen, I feel bad. I want to make up for what happened. Can't a man feel bad?"

Cecile nodded very carefully, her mind working hard. She didn't believe a word of what he was saying, but she was a Christian, at least she tried to be one. Leonie's lesson of charity was still stuck in her mind. She had to forgive, to be kind. God asked a lot of his people. The forgiveness part was particularly tough, but if Leonie could do it, she certainly could give it a try.

"After what I went through, you should feel bad. We'll think of some kind of restitution. Come in and have a seat. We can talk."

He followed her into the home. The nun chatter at the card table ceased as pious eyes followed Gustavo to the other side of the room. He was a huge man dressed in close-fitting dungarees and a skintight T-shirt with gold studs decorating the front. His eyes were slightly red, dissipated; that only added to his aura of creeping worldliness. He was undeniably handsome. Even old nuns take note of such things.

"Sister Cecile's at it again," Sister Edna whispered.

"Hush, Edna; play cards."

The nuns returned to their game while Gustavo talked. "I should apologize," he said. "You didn't look like a nun the other night. I'm used to women."

"I am a woman."

He grinned. "Prove it."

"You owe me an apology." She did not smile.

"Sorry. Jasper did that on his own."

"Sure he did."

"My car smells. It was full of yak."

"I should apologize? I was drugged. Kidnapped. The drug made me sick. I could bring federal charges. I'm considering it."

He didn't answer that, but he looked around at the refurbished motel. It was nicely done except for the unfinished wall. Of course, the furniture had come from an old rectory in Hialeah, the floor tiles were still stained from years of use. The desk was pale, art deco style but slightly scratched. It was not a new desk.

"How about I could fix this place up a little? I got me some construction workers need some work time, can't lay 'em off. Got a truckload of new toilet fixtures. Need any toilets?"

"Our toilets were installed in 1970. Harvest gold. They're post art deco and don't function as well as they should. We could use something nice in our rental suites."

"How many?"

"Ten."

"No problem. Nice art deco toilets, showers and tubs to match. Your place will be the rage. I'll have my interior construction man give you a call. See, it's all deductible."

"Right." The ulterior motives were beginning to surface. There had to be more.

"So, you take care of old nuns here." He looked around. "Are they sick?"

"This is a home for retired but mobile sisters. Some of them still do volunteer work. Sister Edna rocks cocaine babies at Jackson Memorial Hospital. She spends hours rocking babies. Sister Paulette helps with Meals on Wheels. And so on. Gustavo, I don't think these toilets are free. What do you want from me?"

"You have rental suites?"

Sister Cecile didn't like that. Was he still looking for a night with a nun? Here? He was mad. "We rent on a permanent basis to several old couples. It gives us an income. We have a suite for visiting priests. We supply three meals, laundry service. I suppose we're comparable to some of the residential hotels, but we also have a chapel with prayer services, compline for the nuns, matins, and masses said here from time to time. We're a Catholic community."

Gustavo nodded. "I been thinking," he said. "I heard about this place before, see. Word spreads about anything new on the Beach. I been looking at it."

Sister Cecile remained silent.

"My mom. She hates my place. Don't like the noise at night. Hates the neighborhood. Likes going to church. This place," he looked around. "Don't even smell bad. You got a nice room for her?"

His mom? Gustavo had a mother? "Actually the yellow suite is empty. We just finished the floors. It does need a remodeled bathroom, but it's functional."

"How's the food?"

"Excellent. We have a French chef. She's learning local cuisine, so she cooks black beans and rice, collards, as well as coq au vin."

"I'll bring Mom by. Meanwhile I'll have the boys start on them toilets."

"Uh, Gustavo, I'm astounded. Just like that? You must be planning on sending a bill."

"I'll write up a contract, says it's all free."

"Why?"

"Hey, what the heck," he shrugged. "Jasper gave you a bad time. I owe you one, and I don't want kidnapping charges brought on my buddy. Besides, I like it here. Mom's gonna go for it. You're something else. How did you really get loose from Jasper?"

"He wasn't expecting it. I've been trained. I'm a nun, *and* I'm a private detective. I'm looking into the Nica Rabelais murder and its connection with Elena's death. That's what I was asking about when we first met. Remember?"

"Sure, I remember. Truth is, I heard something about Nica."

"You did?"

Cecile was suddenly conscious of the nuns playing cards at the other end of the room. They were being unusually quiet. When Sister Beatrix became the old maid there were no guffaws of laughter. They were listening. Cecile wondered what they could hear in Gustavo's deep baritone besides rumbling sounds rolling out like erotic waves on sand.

"I saw her, night before she died," he said. "She was out, just like ever, looking for a new man, she said, but kind of funny about it when I made an offer. 'Not you, Gussie,' she said. 'You got a big life to live.' "

"She had AIDS."

Gustavo shook his head. "Jeeze." He paused for a moment's mourning. "You know, there's a real thing out here. They get this look in the eye. The club members, we call them. She did have that look, now that I think of it. She told me she had become very important because Barclay had some information when he died and everyone thought she had it."

"Did she?"

"Beats me."

"She wouldn't say?"

He shook his head, then he stood up. "Makes me think she didn't know anything. That's all. She was innocent. Probably

187

died for no reason. Nica, innocent?" He chuckled. All the old nuns looked. It was an indecent sound.

"Got to get going, Sister." He stared at Cecile, looking down, his eyes boring into hers, making her feel very short. She stood up in order to be closer to his level.

"You are without doubt the most woman I've seen," he said, "for a nun."

"Thank you," she said dryly.

"I'll get the toilets going and bring Mom over sometime next week."

"That would be fine. We do have to charge her regular rates, you understand. Toilets or not."

"Business is business," he grinned. He reached into a back pocket and pulled out a card. "Hang on to this. Need anything, or maybe the workmen give you any hassle, just give me a call. Make sure they do a good job. Call me, you need anything at all. I mean, anything. Got it?"

"I do." She took the card. Then he was gone, leaving Sister Cecile wondering about art deco toilets, Gustavo's mom, and Nica, who had known nothing at all and was innocent.

Then she thought about the kidnapping. Federal charges just waiting to be made. Was Gustavo a creep with a kind heart or just a smart businessman?

She thought about the toilets again and decided it didn't really matter. The church was always receiving donations from people trying to buy their seats in heaven. In this case, they were toilet seats.

Later that afternoon Sister Cecile scheduled a meeting with Manuel Beaumont for Monday morning. She felt nervous and deceitful. Her words would need to be very carefully chosen.

She was treading on thin ice.

33

EARLY Monday morning Sister Cecile arrived at the small, downtown coffee shop where she and Manuel Beaumont had agreed to meet. She settled into a bright corner booth with a cup of coffee and a *Miami Herald*. Manuel arrived shortly after, walking fast.

"Ms. Buddenbrooks." He slid into the other side of the booth. "You have some news on the case?" His morning had been chaotic and he felt harassed. At the most, she represented a break in a hectic schedule. "You said we must speak."

"I brought you my report for the first week." She handed him a manila envelope just as a waitress appeared and took his order. "Things are going quite well, actually, Manuel. But I need your permission for something. In some ways the death of Nica Rabelais has widened the field, in other ways, narrowed it. I need your authorization to include the investigation of her death in my parameter. It appears to the police that Nica's death is related to the death of Elliot Barclay; some think it's possible her murder was committed by the same person. By including her death in my investigation, I think I will be that much closer to closing things down. Twice as many clues, twice as many opportunities for the murderer to have made a mistake. Twice as close to a solution."

Manuel narrowed his eyes. He was a very bright man and he detected something in Cecile's tone. He decided to push. "Nica could have been killed by anyone."

"True. But she was Elliot's live-in girlfriend. She knew what he was like."

"We all knew what he was like. We all knew Nica as well. He never told that woman anything. It could have been anyone who killed her. She had a past."

"So did Elliot Barclay."

He didn't have time to spar with the nun. Manuel looked at his watch, took a sip of the coffee that had arrived. He had meetings today. Endless meetings. "All right, include her in your work." He tapped the envelope she had given him. "Any news on the missing paper? The numbers? The deal with the members is getting close. We *need* the numbers."

Cecile shook her head. "Nothing. I went through the apartment. Nica knew a paper of importance existed. She did mention it, actually, but the person to whom she was speaking thinks she didn't know where it was."

"So, I was right. I told you, she knew nothing. She wasn't important."

"She's *key*," Sister Cecile said. "Her death is key."

"Perhaps." He looked at the coffee distastefully. He'd been trying to cut down. He pushed it away. "Anything else?"

"No. I included some information about lab tests on Barclay in the report. I was able to contact a policeman who was helpful. The police have nothing on the case, some still tend to blame it on a random street gang, others consider it related to Nica's death." She shrugged.

Manuel shook his head. "No chance it was a street gang. Have you finished conversing with the consortium? Any leads?"

"I have a few interviews to go. Things are sorting out."

"Fine." He glanced at his watch. "Sorry to rush. Meetings today. All day long." He rose, thrust out a hand to shake, then he was gone.

He turned at the door for one last look at the nun before he left. She was watching him leave, a rather self-satisfied look on her face. He gave a very tiny wave that she returned. An enigma, this woman, but one he didn't have time for. Too bad.

Sister Cecile lingered in the coffee shop for a few minutes, enjoying the sunny table, the clean decor; but the clinging thought that she should interview the remaining members of the consortium whom she had missed disturbed her peace. Maybe that would be a good idea, she mused. This was what she was supposed to be doing, after all. She had spent a lot of case time on Leonie. Of course Leonie was the case.

That was an understatement.

She would give Ross Olhm a call immediately. She pulled out her black notebook and studied her notes on the man. Olhm was vice president of Erste Gesamtdeutsche Bank. She had his private number and nothing else.

She found a telephone booth in the back of the shop near the ladies' room. From there she dialed the number.

"*Ja?*" The tone was curt, heavily Germanic. It reminded Sister Cecile of her father's voice. It was not an auspicious beginning.

"Mr. Olhm? Cecile Buddenbrooks. I wonder if we might get together to discuss the Barclay case."

"Barclay case." The words were bland, like he had never heard of the man. Then, "*Ja*, today? Now? I have time. Lunch at the Pigshit?"

"Uh, where?"

"P-i-g-e-t-t-e," he spelled carefully, then gave a downtown address. "French. Early lunch. Meet at half past noon?"

"Yes. I'll be there."

"Goot. Bye-bye."

Cecile hung up on a dead line. Goot, she thought. Lunch at the pigshit. No more guilt about a case she had functionally ignored.

Amy Peele had spent an uneventful few hours that morning reorganizing all of Barclay's office. Another bank officer was moving in that afternoon and Amy would have to begin working with him at once. A gentleman from Toronto named Dennis Rubenstein was flying in that morning and would be her new associate. She was not looking forward to the change. Nobody could ever replace Elliot.

191

Amy pounded her fist on Elliot's cleared desk. The picture of Nica and Barclay was long gone. There was nothing left. It didn't seem as though anything was ever going to justify her lost lover's death. Nica Rabelais's murder was a bomb, emotionally. And it got worse because of the AIDS.

But Amy still demanded to know Barclay's killer; she still felt something for the man, frustration at the idea of time wasted, perhaps, or maybe the humiliation of a lingering crush that ended badly. She consoled herself with the fact that her life resembled a Greek tragedy, and in that way she was intensely important in the metaphysical scheme of things.

And there was Daddy. Poor fool. He wasn't getting anywhere. He had to suffer the indignity and pain of rabies shots, shots at the site of the area, shots in the leg, another shot on the third day, one on the seventh day, and so on for twenty-eight days. Poor, silly Daddy. He blamed his suffering on the nun now, and he constantly complained about everything to Amy. He wanted to kill the nun, just because she was Catholic, or perhaps because it was all her fault that he was suffering.

Daddy, she decided, not for the first time, was just plain stupid. Amy had felt that way about her father when she was young, later had given him a few moments of grace, and once again had settled on the obvious fact that her old man was a dud. She closed Elliot's empty office and left. At least *she* knew what was important and how to solve this mess.

Amy Peele called Manuel Beaumont at noon. He was in the third meeting of the day, not counting the moments in the coffee shop with Sister Cecile.

"Yessss?" he hissed. Her call had been put through as urgent.

"Amy Peele here. I need to talk to you about the investigator. I need to know what's going on with Barclay's death."

"Nothing. The detective is broadening the scope, investigating Nica's, too. She assumes it was by the same person."

"Nothing else?"

"Amy, it is not your concern. I'm busy."

"Fine. Thank you, Manuel."

After that unsatisfactory conversation, Amy left work. Manuel was no help, but the nun might be. She would have to get to Sister Cecile before Daddy did something else dumb. She had to discover what Sister Cecile knew about the case, and if there were any loose clues surfacing on Nica's death. If the nun appeared to know anything about Nica, she would have to be eliminated immediately.

Amy decided the best way to find out what Sister Cecile knew was to go and see her. On the other hand, maybe it wasn't a good idea. She would drive out and think it over as she went.

Decisions, decisions.

Amy Peele retrieved her Acura from the parking garage and headed for Miami Beach. Traffic was light. She crossed the causeway in minutes, hit Alton Road and headed north. The retirement community was easy to find, on a main street in a slightly seedy side of town. The Beach still had its rough spots in spite of new money.

She parked the Acura in an empty space some fifty yards from the home. The nuns had a decent sign: MARIA CONCILIA RETIREMENT COMMUNITY done in the ubiquitous art deco style, this time a pink profile of the Virgin wearing a gold halo, set against the green silhouettes of palm trees, all painted on both sides of a large chunk of wood.

Amy considered herself an expert on the art deco style. This wasn't bad.

She walked right up to the front door of the building, which still resembled the motel it had once been. The door was clear glass. Through it she could see the jungle of potted plants and a few old people meandering about the lobby. She walked in.

Sister Edna rose from the flower-print chair beside the glass-topped table where she was knitting. The portable telephone was on the table. "May I help you?"

Amy stared at the old nun. Sister Edna was wearing a partial habit: white blouse and skirt, white veil and a Holy Spirit pin on her collar. She smelled faintly of old roses and candle wax.

Amy was vaguely Church of England and didn't understand nuns, much less anyone who pursued celibacy, although she had only slept with two men herself, one on her high school senior prom night, and the second when she was a junior at Florida State and had a romance for the spring semester. For her, making love really hadn't been much fun. Messy business designed to keep the men happy, she had thought at the time; it could be used as a perk someday for whatever she could get from a man. Recently she had been saving herself for Elliot Barclay. She was positive that he would have been a wonderful, considerate lover. Perhaps with him she would have learned to enjoy sex.

Such thoughts rolled through her mind as she stared at Sister Edna. Finally she spoke. "I know there is a Sister Cecile here. I'm interested in speaking with her. Is she in?"

Sister Edna slowly pursed her lips, turned, just as slowly, and stared at the huge clock over the front desk, then turned back to Amy. "She had business this morning. I expect she could be back at any time, although, perhaps she's gone for the day. Can I do anything to help you?"

"Do you know what she's doing right now? Her job, I mean."

"Her job? I believe she said something about a man coming by to redo the bathrooms. She's done a fine job. New toilets. I'm waiting for them. The toilets."

"New toilets. Well, I'll give her a call later."

"She'd love to hear from you." Sister Edna smiled.

"I'll be by again," Amy said and then succumbed to one of her major weaknesses, pride. She pulled out her gold-embossed card that read "Assistant Executive Director of the Royal Leaf Bank" and placed it in the old nun's quivering hand. "You can tell her I called."

Amy Peele turned swiftly and walked out, ignoring Sister Edna's final words of farewell.

Edna fingered the card and ran a wrinkled thumb over the letters. They were raised and felt very important. She loved gold-embossed letters. She would have to study it later when

194

she had her reading glasses on. She slipped the card into her pocket and promptly forgot about it.

Sister Edna carefully made a note on the message paper at the front desk that Sister Cecile had had a visitor who would be by again. She would mention it to Raphael the minute she saw her friend, just in case it was important. She would mention this at lunch, Edna decided. Then her mind returned to contemplating toilet possibilities. What could art deco toilets be like? Certainly anything would be better than the current ones, all a dull shade of mustard with oversized tanks that hissed and gurgled when flushed. The added possibilities of new sink fixtures and tubs entered her mind and sent a quiver of delight up her old spine. Life was *very* exciting here in Florida.

34

SISTER Cecile had an hour to kill before she was to meet Ross Olhm for lunch so she spent it walking on Flagler Street. She passed shoe stores, a fruit salad vendor who was chopping mangos into juicy, dripping bites, and countless clusters of Spanish-speaking people.

In actual fact, she didn't notice her surroundings at all. Her thoughts dominated her consciousness as she walked. She moved quickly, looking busy and purposeful as though she actually had something to do besides waste time before lunch. It was useful time for thinking. Not that her brain was working well. All she heard was her own words echoing in her mind.

"Nica is key," she repeated out loud. A homeless man stared

at her as though she had borrowed on his prerogative of talking to himself.

Why was Nica key? She was just dead, and dead for no reason. The consortium was supposed to be convinced that her death was related to Elliot Barclay's death. Well, it wasn't. Elliot had died by accident; Nica had been murdered. So, no connection.

Or was there? Why had Nica been killed, anyway? Cecile had liked Nica Rabelais. Now she had a personal stake in solving Nica's murder and she was being paid to do it. But there was more than a financial obligation to find a killer. She wanted to.

Why would Elliot Barclay's death cause Nica's death? That was the real question. Were the deaths, in fact, connected? And Cosima Benedict? Remember her? Had she, in fact, been murdered, and where did that fit in?

"Yes," Sister Cecile said and turned around. "There are *no* coincidences."

It was time for lunch at the Pigshit.

Ross Olhm wore faded dungarees and a black T-shirt with "Jamaica" splashed across it in red letters. He wore a Mickey Mouse watch and plastic-framed glasses. He had a thatch of blond hair, his eyes were deep blue and his cheeks craggy. His nose was too large for him to look like a classic German. All in all, he was an attractive older man.

"You're an anomaly," Sister Cecile said over her duck braised in sauerkraut.

"Anomaly, perhaps, but, you understand I'm not a Utilitarian, not a Benthamite. I'm not even a Unitarian. I do what I please, guided by a well-formed conscience. I feel the guilt my father didn't. I exercise in order to eat. I take my pleasures but I don't hurt anyone."

"I'm sure. Do you think Nica knew about the edge corporation you were setting up? Would she have taken the list Manuel is so anxious to find?"

"Ach, she wouldn't know shit about a list. Wouldn't have

196

cared if she did know." He took a huge bite of *veau Sylvie*, veal roasted with ham and cheese. The melted cheese dropped softly to his plate leaving a creamy puddle. He scooped it up with a fork and ate it. "I keep fit at a gym out on the beach. Good equipment. Bad company."

"Mr. Olhm, who would have killed Nica Rabelais? The poor woman had AIDS. There was no reason to kill her."

"You are correct. There was no reason to kill her. One of the walking dead." He shuddered visibly then pushed some rice onto his fork with his knife. He licked the knife. "Tell me, your last name is familiar. I recall a Jerry Buddenbrooks. Know him?"

"My father."

Ross squinted through his glasses, looked her up and down and frowned. "Jerry's kid? He died a few years back. What killed him? Terminal irritability?"

"Something like that. He became angry at a problem about a merger. It obsessed him at the end. He died throwing papers at the president of a corporation. Heart attack."

"Astute man. So you have all that money now? Yes?"

"Not exactly. I became a nun."

"I see." He picked up a piece of bread, methodically scooped out the soft insides and formed a small ball of dough that he placed on the side of his plate. Then he chewed on a crust. "And a private detective with a fine reputation. I saw Manuel's references for you. Sterling."

"Yes, well, I do my best. Did you know Nica, personally?"

Suddenly, as he spoke more quickly, his German accent burst forth. "Fortunately, no. I have a vife, Bruhna. She insists on coming here wit me. Loves the beach. Gets involved in saving manatees. I'm afraid I got to know Nica only troo small talk, however, that can be wery revealing. She talked to Bruhna, you understand. Vomen tell each other strange things, like their entire sex life to another voman they met only a minute before. It happens, and my vife tells me."

"Being a nun has its advantages. I don't hear things like that."

"You might find it amusing." He looked at her carefully. "Jerry's daughter. Yes, you would find it amusing."

"Perhaps. What did Nica say?"

"She was proud to be with Elliot, big rich banker, but Elliot was a cruel man with a voman. Nica wouldn't have stayed much longer. She told Bruhna that."

"I know. Did Elliot know she was going to leave?"

"Elliot? Didn't care shit. See, there was always vomen for Elliot. He told me about one, funny-looking lady, he thought she might be kinky. Crazy about him, called him at home all the time. She was next; he even told me that. But it never happened."

"Did he tell you it never happened, too?"

"Sure, he told me. And Nica told Bruhna about the same voman, Nica told my vife. They laughed together over it."

"But it never happened," Cecile repeated.

"Never that I know. So sorry I can't help you on that one. I don't know the name of the voman. I never listened to the vomen about that." He looked at his plate. While speaking he had cleaned it, scraping little bits of sauce with bread crusts, getting every last drop. All that was left was the round ball of bread insides on the side of his plate. "I will pay for the lunch, and must be back to the bank. Things are always vaiting for me there. Any more questions? A lead on this killer you got?"

"Maybe," Cecile mused. "I have a few ideas, a few facts." Her own plate was empty now, too. It had been good food. "I'll keep in touch with Manuel on all this. Of course you didn't do it, did you, Ross?" She smiled faintly, making a joke. She watched his face very carefully.

"Elliot? Nica? No reason to kill those two. No, neither of them, I killed." He returned her faint smile. "I am making a joke, you understand. I don't kill. A joke."

It sounded like a "yoke."

"Yes, a joke."

Ten minutes later Sister Cecile was out on the sidewalk walking rapidly in the direction of the parking garage where she

198

had left her car. Ideas were beginning to form in her mind. Ross had insights, even though they weren't exactly what he had tried to convey to her. It was interesting, she realized, that all the bankers considered her not quite as smart as they thought they were. They didn't really expect her to solve this case because she was a woman. Of course she already had solved it, at least Leonie had. Now the trick was to convince them that someone else had killed Elliot Barclay. There really was a killer out there. But not Elliot's.

She was no closer to an answer than before.

35

JIM Cypress pounded on his desk with a big fist. He was looking at mounds of paperwork. Nothing in it was relevant to the truth. He had already called his home twice to check on Stephanie. She was home from the hospital now and feeling fine. Another call to the Maria Concilia Retirement Community confirmed that Leonie was safely at school. He was afraid for Leonie after the abortive canoe trip. Dreadfully afraid. Meanwhile he had to fill in reports.

He was convinced that someone was after the kid. It didn't make sense, but someone had shot at the canoe. Stephanie had no enemies, no reason to be shot at. Leonie, on the other hand, was mixed up in something hard to finger. Maybe someone out there knew what had happened, or even thought the little girl had committed murder. The beach was rarely empty. Maybe someone thought Leonie had killed Barclay. She could have been seen with the gun in her hand.

No. It didn't make sense. Nobody had seen her. It was just a random shooting. A hunter gone mad. There were plenty of those in the Everglades.

Jim forced his mind back to his work. He finished reviewing Nica's last known connections. There was a statement from a woman Nica had worked with in a restaurant on Washington Avenue. A dead end. Then Jim read a transcript of an interview with a man Nica had dated prior to the time she had dated Elliot Barclay. Another dead end. There were two more interviews to review, then he had to write everything up in a coherent form. He had done the same thing with the Barclay investigation. Lots of paperwork. No conclusions.

His fingers started pecking away at the computer terminal. Twenty words a minute while his thoughts roamed back to Leonie and the shooting.

Reggie Peele hobbled into the big office where Jim was at work on the pile of papers. Jim's desk was one of several in the room. Reggie pulled up a chair beside Jim and sat down, favoring his right arm, grunting as he sat.

"What's up, Reggie?" Jim asked. Any excuse to stop typing. Even Reggie Peele. He looked across at the older policeman, his eyes questioning. Bum back, chewed arm, but Reggie was there. Reggie didn't look good; the red face still showed the effects of too many mosquitoes, his arm clearly caused him pain. Normally that would have kept Reggie home. It all added up to making Jim Cypress very curious, but he never connected it with his own Everglades caper. Mosquitoes were everywhere in Miami, and so were loose dogs.

"Not much. You know I got bit by a damn dog. Ought to shoot all the wild dogs in this county. Packs of 'em all over the damn place."

Jim nodded. "Yep." He waited for Reggie to continue.

"How's it doing?" Reggie asked.

"Fine. Everything's cool."

"I miss being on the street," Reggie said. "Like to keep my finger in." He gave a pathetic little smile.

"Sure," Jim agreed. He typed a single word and frowned at it.

"Maybe I can lend you a hand?" Reggie asked hopefully. He appeared thoroughly miserable as he spoke. Jim might have agreed with Amy Peele who, last night, had told her father he was a stupid shit. Actually she'd said, "conceptually disadvantaged," but Reggie had known what she meant.

Jim did see the strange look in Reggie's eye. But Reggie always looked malevolent, so it was not a new look.

"I'd like to help you with this Barclay case. What can I do?" Reggie asked.

Jim swiveled around in his chair and looked at the old policeman. "The Barclay case? Well," he said slowly, "I pretty much worked out what happened to Elliot Barclay. I'm putting the effort into the Nica Rabelais murder now. We need to find a seriously motivated killer here. Find one killer, we got both. All we need is to make the connection, and that's what I'm working on. Two for one."

"Damn sure," Reggie agreed. He winced. Jim thought it was from the pain in the man's arm. He didn't connect it with his mention of investigating the Rabelais case.

"What about the Barclay case? What you figure?" Reggie asked, his old hands clenching and unclenching.

Jim's eyes dropped to the floor. Miccosukee habit; he should have been looking at Reggie. As it was he missed the gleam in the man's watery blue gaze. Jim began to talk, skimming over the facts. "Well, I got some information from a nun. Nice lady. She helped me out. Pretty much has things settled for me, but I just need a few more facts. Some concrete things. Get those and work out the connection to the Rabelais case and we'll have it done. That's where I could use some help. Maybe you could recheck her known associates."

Reggie's mouth cracked into a quick smile, then the fists clenched again and the mouth straightened. "Funny you should ask about the Rabelais case," he said. "I got a good street connection on that one. I'll put out the word. You can count on me. And let me know what you find on the other one. I'm your man here. I'll sift papers, whatever you need doing."

"I really appreciate that, Reggie. Anything you can do would be a help."

"Glad to assist, Jim." Reggie pushed himself up from the chair and patted Jim on the back. Jim felt the reluctance in the touch, but he didn't suspect anything. It felt good to be included in the old Anglo's schemes. Reggie was a known mover. How else would he have pulled off that million-dollar desk job. Maybe the old man wasn't so bad after all.

"The case will give me something to think about while I sit at that desk," Reggie said. "Mind's still damn good even though the old back causes trouble."

"Must be tough, Reggie," Jim said. "I appreciate your help on this one."

Reggie sighed. "You're doing me a favor, Jim. I need something to get my mind into."

"Good," Jim nodded and turned back to his paperwork as Reggie walked away.

Reggie returned to his front desk with a skip of unsuppressed glee that sent his arm into a spasm of pain. But he was satisfied. Jim Cypress was convinced he was going to help on the case. Meanwhile he would find out the scoop on who killed Elliot Barclay. The nun knew. That was clear. Somehow he had to get the nun. Then maybe he would kill her like she deserved.

His mind began to turn. An hour later, fending calls at his desk, Reggie had devised a plan.

Jim stacked all his paperwork into a neat pile and turned off his computer. When he passed Reggie at the front desk he merely nodded, but Reggie seized the moment. "Going out on our case?" Reggie asked softly. "How's it going?"

"Great."

"You working on it now?"

Jim smiled faintly. "Yep."

"The nun?"

"We're meeting. She's a good connection."

"You'll get it, Jim. You think she actually knows who killed this Barclay?"

"More than that," Jim said.

Reggie's eyes never left Jim's face. It was obvious that Jim was flattered by Reggie's attention. Jim never gave out case information even to fellow cops. Reggie Peele, for all his hatreds, was a master of the art of flattery, and he knew it. He could use that sly, inclusive smile that made the recipient feel he was part of something big and important. Maybe, because he was usually so dour, a compliment felt twice as good as it should. Reggie had insights. Contrary to what Amy thought, Reggie was not a stupid man at all and he knew Jim Cypress like a book. The man was plagued by the uncertainties that follow many nonwhite males. It had to be tough for a Miccosukee in a white man's world, tough falling in love with a white woman and having all the doubts that she could actually love him. Jim Cypress basked in admiration and Reggie was astute enough to see it.

"Where you going?" Reggie asked, pushing it.

"Clock's."

"Good luck." Reggie turned both thumbs up and nodded. Jim was hooked.

Reggie waited a few minutes until he was sure Jim was well out of the building, then he picked up the telephone and began to dial a familiar number. He was going to blow that Indian out of the water. Internal Affairs was going to get an earful.

36

SISTER Cecile drove across the causeway with both windows of the black Jag rolled down. It was one of those perfect days with towering, golden clouds blowing across a huge sky. She had seen photographs of the Miami sky years ago and had thought it was a trick. Such a sky couldn't happen. Now she knew it was no trick, but sometimes even the reality didn't compensate for everything she had left behind. Today, for example, the air was almost crisp, vaguely reminiscent of an early fall day in New England. She felt a sudden catch in her throat at the thought. Memories of Boston superimposed themselves on the massive cruise ships anchored to her right out in the bay. The palms and the aqua water all faded out and she saw Boston's Commonwealth Avenue with its stately trees, the fresh green leaves drooping on a summer day. She saw the convent in Dorchester rise like a mist across the bay, smelled the dank corridors, remembered, suddenly, that this was January and the convent roof was probably leaking again and the furnace was groaning and wheezing just to keep the place bearable. The potatoes under the kitchen sink were probably frozen again. There were no green leaves on "Comm Ave." What was she thinking? It was winter in New England, the roads were icy, new potholes were forming in preparation for bouncing off hubcaps during the first spring thaw.

She looked out the car window again and saw the firm reality of South Florida, the colors of heaven meeting earth, a seaplane turning into the warm wind, then brushing the water of Biscayne Bay. Salty air blew through the car, a warm breeze.

Paradise. And she was in it. She was glad to be here, she told herself. Really.

Clock's was right off the causeway looking out over the water. A collection of boats was tied up at the small piers beside the restaurant, piers that splayed out like colorful spokes poking into the bay. Masts of white sailboats and yachts gathered like spires from a clutch of churches. A huge clock over the restaurant door looked out over the bay. TIME AND TIDE was inscribed under it in gold letters, giving a sense of the urgency of life.

They would have fish on the menu, Sister Cecile thought, and she could pay for it with her credit card. It was good to use some of that money the way she should, entertaining clients. She loved good fish and it was so expensive. They rarely had it at the community.

Cecile felt a moment of guilt as she pulled the black Jaguar into the parking area. Here she was surrounded by material things, Mercedez-Benzes, Cadillacs, other Jags, incredible boats, things that cost lots and lots of money. Maybe she wouldn't order fish after all, but something she didn't particularly care for. Yes, that would do. A small meal, something more in line with her vow of poverty.

Jim Cypress was waiting for her inside Clock's. He put out a hand and they exchanged greetings. A formally dressed waiter wearing a stiff face and a bow tie escorted them to a glass table, past a bar busy with an early happy hour. It was too soon to be noisy, words were soft, bare backs glowed in simmering dim light; the place exuded opulence.

The dining tables were about a third occupied with perfectly tanned beach people wearing casual clothes, sipping drinks, and pushing food about their plates. It was that kind of place where food was excellent and costly and everyone was thin.

"Stephanie's doing well?"

"Perfect. Enjoying some time off."

"I'm so glad. What an ordeal." Sister Cecile, full of resolve as a sister of poverty, barely glanced at the menu before ordering

205

grouper chowder and a salad. Nothing special. Maybe she wouldn't even enjoy it.

"It's time we figure this out, Jim. We've got to decide exactly what we're going to do," she finally said.

"Number one, we keep the kid out of it," Jim said. "No problem there. Nica's killer is priority. I'm putting in an honest day's work on that."

"I'm shifting my emphasis, too," Cecile said. "The consortium gave the okay. All we need is a game plan to catch Nica's killer. Any ideas?"

"Just paperwork, so far. Catch-up stuff. There hasn't been anything new. But, here's something. I've got one of the old boys at the station working on the case," Jim said. "Hard to believe, but Reggie Peele has offered to lend a hand. He's been on the Beach force thirty years and just stopped by and offered to help. Irritable man, but smart; he said he was bored. It's hard to believe he's so up on this case."

"Is that really so surprising?"

"Sir Reggie?" Jim laughed. "Far as I know he hates anyone who isn't as white as he is. He's going out of his way for this though. Maybe because Elliot Barclay was from a Commonwealth country. Reggie thinks he's an Englishman although I've heard his maternal grandparents were from Lithuania. Odd sort of guy. But he'll turn up something. He was a smart street cop."

"Admirable. We can use all the help we can get. As for me, I spent the afternoon interviewing another member of the consortium. A few things have turned up. . . ."

While Sister Cecile and Jim talked, Reggie Peele finally reached the head of Internal Affairs, Mark Cruz. He asked for an immediate conference and moments later was upstairs.

"I think we got a crooked cop," Reggie said, sitting uncomfortably in the straight wooden chair the head of Internal Affairs usually reserved for his private inquisitions.

"Reggie, do you have any proof? This is a serious allegation. We need something concrete before we make a move on an officer, especially a minority."

"I'll tell you the deal, and you tell me."

"Okay. Let's hear it."

Reggie thought a minute. He wanted to get this right the first time. "It's the Elliot Barclay case, Mark. I been watching how Cypress was handling it from the first, and it struck me bad. Now it turns out he's got a witness who knows who killed Elliot; some nun out here knows the entire story, and so does Jim Cypress. But he's doing squat. As we speak he's having late lunch with the nun at Clock's, pigging out, you can bet, laughing his head off that they got the case wrapped up and doing nothing. Now you tell me what he should be doing? Pulling in the killer, that's what."

Mark Cruz frowned. Reggie knew this was a tough sell because Mark liked the Indian. But he was counting on his own reputation as an astute cop. Everyone knew that Reggie Peele always got the goods.

"So, nothing irregular there." Mark sounded impatient. "Maybe he needs proof? More leads? It's easy to get people talking over a good meal."

"She spent the weekend with him." Reggie nodded firmly. "This is a nun? I think maybe there's more to this than lunch. A very expensive lunch at Clock's, by the way."

"An affair with a nun? Come on, Reggie."

"This nun drives a Jaguar. She's a looker. I've heard a lot of stories about nuns. They do anything, these days. World's gone to hell."

Mark Cruz nodded. He looked sad, like he didn't care for what he was hearing, but he was believing it. "An affair?" he repeated.

"Maybe. It looks bad." Reggie knew better than to say more without any proof. "Talk to Cypress and see. I think he's covering up because he's got the hots for her. It's that simple. I think there's a cover-up going on."

"You think maybe this nun killed Barclay?"

"Her or someone she knows."

"And Jim Cypress is covering up? It doesn't sound like Jim. He's straight."

"Everyone is straight." Reggie met Mark Cruz's skeptical look square in the eye, his blue orbs accusing, watering, but direct. "Until you look under the sheets."

Mark didn't respond to that. "I'll have a talk with Jim," Mark said. "And then we'll see."

"I hope you do. There's a killer out there, a vicious killer."

Reggie stood up from the chair with a painful lurch. "Thanks for hearing me out, Mark. I don't like to see a good cop go crooked, covering up for friends, or whatever. Maybe we can stop this before it starts, clean it up before anyone else gets hurt."

"Right, Reggie. Thanks. I'll take care of it."

Mark Cruz felt a real pain in his gut at Reggie's speculations. He watched the old policeman leave the office, Reggie limping and clearing his throat. Reggie didn't look well. Everyone had heard about the so-called rabid dog bite and Mark wondered seriously if it had gone to the older man's head. Whatever, he was going to have to call Jim Cypress in for an appearance immediately. This kind of accusation deserved a face-to-face interview, quick.

37

"WHERE are you off to now?" Jim asked Cecile. They walked out of Clock's and down to one of the docks. The cool blue bay looked glassy. A brown pelican posed at the end of the pier, perched on a tall piling.

"Not sure. I've got some thinking to do. Maybe I'll stop by Elliot's apartment and see if I can come up with anything on Nica. She was living there; that's where she was killed. It wouldn't hurt to have another look, maybe have a few words with the doorman. I've really got to start working on it. I'm being paid."

Jim chuckled. "Sure. Solve it for me, would you?"

"I guess I'll have to," Sister Cecile said.

"Right." Jim didn't sound quite sincere enough for Sister Cecile. As though she couldn't actually solve a real crime. People always felt that way about her. It was tough building a reputation. Even her wins tended to look like losses.

They spent a few minutes talking before going back up to the parking lot. Jim appeared to be optimistic. Sister Cecile had no clue to his thoughts about the shooting in the Everglades. She never guessed he might be trying to protect her from worrying.

Sister Cecile was worried anyway. Apparently Jim was taking this all very lightly now that Stephanie was on the mend, and Leonie was well out of the case. But there was something still wrong somewhere. Sister Cecile could feel it. And Jim was doing nothing.

"Keep in touch," she murmured as they turned and went to their respective cars.

"Will do," Jim said, and he was gone.

Sister Cecile drove directly to the big apartment complex that Elliot Barclay had called home. She still had the key she had received from Manuel Beaumont when she had first begun the case. Odd, she hadn't thought of the key before, hadn't thought much about Nica at all except for the tragedy that the woman had contracted AIDS. There had been so many things happening, irrelevant things, odd things. Nothing fit in this case. Nothing made any sense. But it was going to.

She found a reasonable parking place in a residential zone. The little Jaguar was so cute, maybe it wouldn't be ticketed.

Fat chance, she thought. Maybe she could deduct the ticket as an expense? She would have to ask her accountant.

The doorman was a short Hispanic who regarded the nun dolefully. Sister Cecile had been wearing her partial habit all day and it was wrinkled from the heat. The navy skirt showed creases where it should have been perfectly pressed; there was a spot of chowder on her white blouse. Only the small black veil perched on fluffy brown curls looked fresh. That and the gold cross around her neck could withstand almost anything. She looked like a nun, but a slightly rumpled nun.

"Hello, could I ask you some questions?" she asked the doorman.

He shrugged.

"I'm looking into the murder of a young woman. She was killed here a few days ago. Nica Rabelais. Did you know her?"

Silence. Cecile smiled hopefully. "Did you?"

"Okay, I know her."

"Do you remember the night she died? Were you here?"

"I be here ever night. Four to twelve. Ever night I here. *Aquí. Yo.*"

"You remember the night?"

"Sure. Polices come and talks to me."

"They asked you who came in the building. Do you remember what you told them?"

"Sure."

"Can you tell me?"

The man looked at Cecile. He was about her height, his dense brown eyes stared into her gray ones. His face was wooden, no expression at all. "There was polices here, *todo*. And the people lives here. I told them that."

Sister Cecile thought a moment. "There was police here, yes, but before the murder?"

"Yes, I tell them that. *Aquí, aquí.* They think I don't know police."

"Lots of police? Was there a crime here earlier that night?"

"Not here, like out on the beach somewhere, Mr. Barclay dead out there."

"So the police came before to check that out. A tall man, sort of dark, Officer Cypress?"

"*Sí*, like I tell them, they all *aquí*."

"He came with his partner?" Sister Cecile was almost lost in the man's Spanglish.

"No, the other policeman, smaller, old guy. You know the one? Red face. Girl policeman, too." His voice had become loud; he was talking as though Sister Cecile was stupid.

"He was here, too." Sister Cecile nodded. It must be the one Jim was telling her about, the one helping him with the case. Apparently this particular policeman had been in on the Barclay murder all along.

"Okay, sir, I'll go upstairs and take a look now. Maybe I can find something new this time." She dangled her apartment key. "I have authorization to use this. I have permission."

"What you have?"

"I was given this key to look in the apartment. Understand?"

"Of course I understan."

"I'm going to look now."

"I be here."

The doorman returned to staring out at the street as Sister Cecile walked into the lobby. She didn't realize he had told her something very important. She should have listened harder.

Sister Cecile took the elevator up, letting the doorman's words float around in her head. It had been hard to follow everything he had said, but the bottom line seemed to be that there had been no people going to the Barclay apartment except police. And, of course, Nica. Whoever had murdered Nica had come in some other way. But was there another way? That she would find out.

The apartment was hot and stuffy, filled with the appalling smell that comes out of garbage disposal units that haven't been used recently, and a lingering scent of death. Everything was damp. Cecile saw the wall switch and turned on the air-conditioning unit. She set it at eighty degrees.

211

She began to look around, going methodically from one room to another, from one drawer to the next. It was a slow job, particularly because she didn't want to leave any fingerprints anywhere. She covered her hands with toilet paper. No fingerprints would be left behind, even though she was sure the police had already finished with that.

Cecile lost track of time. She read letters, went through bills, mulled over ideas and numbers. There was no connection to a crime. There was no list for the Benthamite Consortium either. And that was why she was here, wasn't it? It was that group of men who were actually paying for her time and they wanted results. She owed them.

Nica had left a few things behind, but little of a personal nature. Odd letters from a friend in Kentucky, a pile of unpaid utility bills. Everything appeared to be exactly the same as it had been before except for the yellow police tape spread across the door to the bedroom. Cecile stared at it. The dark stain on the rug looked bad from a distance. It would look worse close-up.

She went into the kitchen and opened the refrigerator. She discovered sour milk, catsup, condiments, beer and diet soda. The side-by-side freezer was loaded with gourmet diet dinners.

She closed the door. What was she looking for anyway? There was nothing here. Nobody was here, nobody had apparently come here. But Nica had died. Murdered. Her death had been no accident.

Cecile paused for a moment and listened intently, as if the quiet air might still hold Nica's last words, or the name of the killer.

She heard only the soft hum of the central air conditioner.

Finally she decided to cross the tape and go into the bedroom. Cecile felt a strange fear wash over her. The scene of a murder holds ghosts, devils of vengeance, and a curious emptiness that some would call hell. Philosophically speaking, hell was the absence of good. Sister Cecile knew that. She also knew that there was no good in this place.

It took a real effort for Cecile to bring her mind back to where

212

it should be. First she said a prayer, blessed herself, and went to the plate glass window to look out at the sparkling water. Sometimes she just didn't understand God at all. Death was such a mystery. But the room smelled. The sour, dead smell of a body long gone, the scent of old blood.

The bedroom proved to be as unproductive as the rest of the house. Cecile went through the two closets, shuffled through countless drawers, looked under the huge bed, looked up at the huge mirror on the ceiling. There was nothing under the pillows, nothing but clothing in the closets, just beauty supplies and shaving toiletries in the bathroom.

She left the bedroom and stuck the yellow tape back the way it had been. The air was improving as the air-conditioning hummed. Maybe that explained the chilly breeze. There were no ghosts.

Cecile decided to call the community. Maybe there was some news, something that would give her a clue and tell her where to go next.

The phone was picked up after three rings. "Maria Concilia Retirement Community. May I help you?" Cecile heard Sister Raphael's voice, slightly out of breath.

"It's Cecile. What's happening?"

"Where are you? No, wait, don't say." The old nun was whispering, her old voice strangely raspy over the phone.

"What?"

"Shhhh. The phones may be tapped. I just received an urgent call from Jim Cypress. There's an APB out on you. That means 'all points bulletin.' Don't come home. I think the police are here now. Sister Edna's at the door, holding the gates."

"What! Why?"

"They think you killed him. The police claim that you know who killed Elliot Barclay and somehow they got the idea it was you. Jim's been temporarily suspended from the force for refusing to cooperate, but he gave me a call to warn you. That's how I know everything."

"Raphael, I don't believe this. What on earth happened? Tell me. And don't worry about telephone taps. It's too soon."

213

Raphael took a deep, audible breath. "This afternoon Jim was called into Internal Affairs and asked point blank if you knew who killed Elliot Barclay. Jim agreed that you did. They wanted to know who, and of course he said nothing. Apparently the man interviewing him got furious and started saying it was a cover-up. Jim got really stoic and refused to speak. I have a feeling he can be a very stubborn man. So, of course they got mad at Jim and suspended him. And they want you. But who was it, Cecile? Who *did* kill Elliot Barclay? Nobody ever told me. I've felt terrible, lately. You never talk to me anymore."

"Listen, Raphael, you know nothing. Nobody there does, and we left it that way on purpose. No spilling the beans if you don't have any to spill. Tell the police the truth. You just don't know."

"Well, I should know."

"I can just picture Jim Cypress," Sister Cecile mused. "I suspect he can be a very obstinate man. Where is he?"

"Home, I suppose. Who knows. You're taking this very calmly."

"It's interesting. It means something broke somewhere. Things are moving."

"Like what?" Raphael demanded.

"I don't know. I'll have to think about it. Has anything else happened there today? Anything to do with the case?"

"What are you going to do? Where will you go? The police are coming in now."

"Raphael, what else happened there today? Did anything happen? Think!"

"Nothing. Just that a woman stopped by. A woman with pigtails looking for you, said she was involved with the consortium. Sister Edna told me. And Edna told her you were out. She was weird, anyway, Sister told me, probably of no consequence. And shortly after that sixteen toilets arrived. They're out in the patio by the pool waiting for the workers. And right now there are some people measuring and checking pipes.

214

They're starting tomorrow on the bathrooms. Why didn't you tell me about the new toilets?"

"They're self-explanatory."

"Wait! Five policemen just walked into the lobby. Sister Edna is saying she will give them a tour of the community. I can't believe this."

"Wonderful. I hope they like toilets."

"Of course they have no idea who I'm talking to. Will you be all right?"

"Fine. I'm in a very safe place." Sister Cecile looked around the fabulously expensive room. The former inhabitants were both dead, nobody was going to be around. She could actually live here indefinitely eating frozen diet dinners warmed in the microwave. "There's food here, a bed, I'm fine. But I'd better hang up, Raphael," she said. "I'm sure nobody can tell who you're talking to, but one never knows. Now, don't worry about me at all. I'll figure things out, and when I do, I'll be fine. I'll go directly to the police once I have the answer to this mess."

"Wonderful. I don't feel happy about all this. I wish you could tell me."

"Don't worry. Make sure you tell Leonie that I'm all right. Tell her everything you know about the case. Absolutely everything. It's important. She might have some good ideas. She always does. Tell her to tell you everything. Tell her I said that."

"Yes. I'll do that." Sister Raphael was sounding cautious now. In the background Sister Cecile could hear the low rumble of male voices and one female, a high-pitched voice that was clearly not Sister Edna. They had probably brought a police-woman along to frisk the old nuns.

"I'll keep in touch," Cecile said. "Take care." She paused. "And pray."

38

"WHERE is Sister Cecile?" Leonie asked.

"I don't know. She wouldn't say. But she claims to be safe," Sister Raphael said. They had retreated to the kitchen where Sister Germaine was chopping up a tremendous pile of collard greens. They were all sitting at the long table that ran down the center of the room. The police were everywhere else, poking through the building, annoying everyone, but they had already been through the kitchen. One of the officers had even looked in a large oven, possibly expecting the nun in question to pop out like the old witch in *Hansel and Gretel*.

"I hope she doesn't starve," Sister Germaine said, pulling out the tough stems before chopping the greens some more. "I always worry about that."

"No. She said there was food." Raphael looked at the greens. "Collards? I cooked them once. They weren't very good."

"I talked to a woman in the market," Germaine said. "She told me exactly how to do them. In fact, I attracted quite a crowd trying to get the cooking time down. How long do you cook collards? Nobody knew. The woman said, just like this, 'Get them ham hocks cooking and start chopping up the greens. 'Bout the time the greens are cut up, put them in and then start your corn bread. By the time the corn bread is done, it should be done.' Then she said, 'Ummm um, you got something going.' I wasn't sure exactly what she meant, but it sounded good." Sister Germaine had slipped into a deep Afro-American accent. She sounded more at home in it than in the Boston-English-French she usually used.

"Ham hocks?" Leonie asked.

"Ham hocks are very good. But they're the least of our worries. We have to solve the case," Raphael said. "Leonie, Sister Cecile told me to talk to you. She thinks you may have some good ideas, some insights, maybe. She suggested you tell me everything. Now the problem is, the police think Sister Cecile killed Elliot Barclay. We know it's impossible but they're out there looking for her, for murder."

"That's silly," Leonie said. "I mean, that's absolutely dumb. Did she really say to tell you everything?"

"Yes. Apparently she knows who killed Barclay. And she hasn't told me anything." Raphael regarded the girl suspiciously.

Sister Germaine was back at the stove, stirring together the greens and ham hocks. She was pretending not to listen but Raphael knew she was.

Raphael lowered her voice. "Not only does Cecile know who did it, but Jim Cypress has been suspended for not telling what he knows. It's a very bad situation."

"Suspended from the police force? Jim? What's he going to do?" Leonie's face turned red and an odd look appeared in her eyes. "I can't believe they could be so dumb. Jim's off the force?"

"Suspended."

Leonie spoke softly. "They can't do that! Raphael, I want you to come with me for a minute. There's something I have to tell you privately." She looked over at Germaine and tilted her head in a gesture that indicated even Germaine shouldn't hear what was coming.

"Where? The police are everywhere."

"How about we try the pool area?" Leonie suggested.

"Yes."

Germaine didn't look up as they left. She would have been very surprised to hear what Leonie was about to confide to Raphael.

Outside, Leonie Drail perched on one of the sixteen art deco toilets spread out along the side of the pool deck. Sister Raphael, after some deliberation, took a seat on another toilet. The lawn chairs had all been stacked to one side while the new construction was under way.

"Well?" Raphael asked.

"It's like this. Are you ready?"

"Of course."

Leonie began gently, with the background. She told about the trip to the Everglades over the weekend, how Stephanie was shot, and how a strange woman had been trying to gain her confidence after school. "And she was wearing pigtails. Very weird. But that's just what happened Saturday. Now for the rest we have to go back a few days. . . ."

Leonie told the entire story.

Sister Raphael listened to the narrative, moving slowly toward a state of shock. In spite of her words, she had not been ready for this. Her old heart pounded painfully as she envisioned Leonie's near rape. Several tears squeezed out of her eyes and her old hands wove together and clenched at the picture. And, to think, she had been worried about sand fleas on the beach.

Raphael took a deep breath and listened harder, bringing her total concentration into the effort to appear calm.

Leonie, she noticed, appeared quite cool as she spoke about everything that had been happening. The girl had already talked about it enough; the terror was all gone.

Raphael didn't say a single word during the entire narration. She let Leonie finish. Such is the wisdom of age, Raphael thought as she bit her tongue to keep silent.

Leonie kept talking. "So Cecile is protecting me, and Jim Cypress is protecting me. Everyone is doing stupid things for me. I suppose I should go right to the police and tell them everything. I can handle it. This protecting stuff stinks."

Finally it was time to speak. Sister Raphael clamped down on all her fears and roiling emotions and let her words come out carefully, rationally. This was a time to run with the head, not the heart. "No, absolutely not. I think you should keep your mouth shut, firmly," Raphael said with the most assurance she could muster. "Because, as you said, your fingerprints will be all over that gun. They have ways of bringing up prints. I read about it. Even after years. And, believe me, you wouldn't like to be charged with accidental death. It's brutal, being involved with the police and the court system, no matter how the thing resolves itself. And there has been another murder, don't forget. There really is a killer out there. Jim was right. You might be in deadly danger. Danger to you is the bottom line."

"Jim did say that," Leonie agreed. "Cecile told me all about this Nica person. She was Elliot Barclay's girlfriend and she was shot to death in Elliot's apartment."

"Besides, Leonie, something's very strange about all this. Very strange. Who is this woman with the pigtails? She keeps appearing. She was here today."

"She was?" Leonie jumped up off the toilet and went over to stand by the pool. The water reflected patches of light off her pale hair and the edges of her rumpled white shirt, creating a chiaroscuro angel. "Was she looking for me?"

"No. For Cecile. She spoke with Sister Edna and Edna told me everything. The woman said she was part of the consortium, or connected to it somehow. That's the group that hired Cecile in the first place. She was vague on that. Something's going on here that I don't like. Why was Jim called into Internal Affairs, and why do they think Sister Cecile is a killer? Someone must have planted the idea. Who?"

"And that gross woman was following me." Leonie was thoughtful. "All right, what else is strange?"

Sister Raphael looked around. "Sixteen toilets in our pool area."

"Where did they come from?"

"Gustavo Bestard. He wants to plant his mother here in our best suite. At least Sister Cecile told me that much about the man. I don't know anything else about him except he had all the sisters in a twit. Apparently he looked like some late-night movie star, someone from the 1950s. Edna couldn't stop talking about him. I didn't even know where the toilets came from until I asked the man who delivered them. He just said, 'Gustavo.' "

219

Leonie shrugged. "Call Jim."

"I will, but we just spoke a few minutes ago. He's incredibly concerned about you, Leonie. He doesn't know how resourceful you can be. On the one hand, I can't think of anything that we can do just sitting here on toilets, avoiding the police. We certainly can't get into any trouble. But on the other hand we can't get Cecile out of trouble, either."

"Maybe we should do something very definite," Leonie suggested. "I mean, we really have to. Cecile is stuck somewhere, you say? She can't do anything."

"Don't underestimate Sister Cecile. Besides, you have school to attend, and I don't even have a car," Raphael said.

"I have the last three days off from school this week, so I'll be free to help you," Leonie said. "Maybe I should skip tomorrow."

"No, go to school tomorrow. We don't want to do anything unusual. It might attract attention. But we'll get to work on Wednesday."

"Wednesday is too late. We have to start now." Leonie began to walk, balancing along the edge of the pool.

"You're right. Wednesday is too late."

"We can think of something to do. Just about anything to find the real killer. I mean, this Nica's killer," Leonie mused, turning on one foot and walking back toward Raphael. "Like, we should be doing something this very minute. I want to figure out who that woman is. The pigtails. I'm suspicious."

"Maybe. She looked harmless though. I saw her leaving, myself."

"I saw her the other day, and she's creepola. I don't think she's harmless." Leonie was adamant. "Here comes Sister Germaine. She probably wants me to stir the collards or something."

Sister Germaine didn't want Leonie at all. There was a telephone call for Sister Raphael.

"Take it in the kitchen, Raphael. It's more private. The police are still all over the place." Sister Germaine's features were grim. She added in a whisper, "It's Cecile."

The kitchen phone was next to one of the two huge refrigerators. Raphael took the receiver with one hand while she opened a refrigerator door with the other. When she was nervous she did odd things like that. When her mind wrestled with problems, her hands liked to be busy elsewhere. "Sister Raphael speaking."

"It's me again," came a familiar voice. "I just realized that the Jaguar is parked right up the street from where I am. I want you to get the extra set of keys from my right dresser drawer, Raphael, and come get the car. It's a dead giveaway that I'm here."

"Dead giveaway," Raphael whispered. "I'll be right there." She was shaking slightly as her eyes focused on a half-eaten, cold chicken in the refrigerator. It looked much better than the ham hocks. "Don't worry. I'll call a cab. Bye-bye."

"Raphael, wait! I have to tell you where it is. You're panicking."

"I'm very cool," Raphael said and reached for a small shred of chicken. "Where is it?"

As she picked at the cold chicken with one hand, she listened to Sister Cecile's instructions. "Fine." Raphael nodded and chewed. "Yes, I'll get the car and drive it right back here. Nobody will be suspicious. . . . Good. Keep in touch, Cecile. I'll move your car out of there within a half hour. Don't worry about a thing."

Leonie had come in and eavesdropped on the entire conversation, shamelessly. As soon as Raphael had hung up and closed the refrigerator door, she spoke. "Now you have a car. A neat, black Jag."

Sister Raphael's blue eyes widened. "Why yes, I believe I do, Leonie. I should call a cab and go pick it up."

"Cool. Now we can get to work."

221

39

SISTER Cecile was trapped in a luxury apartment. The walls began to close in on her, the ceilings began to lower, the brilliant light that reflected off the ocean formed into a spotlight pinpointing her against the white wall. The police had an all points bulletin out on her? Why?

She began to pace, talking to herself out loud. "Well, it couldn't be Jim Cypress that pulled this. I mean, he's under suspension for protecting Leonie and me. But there's nobody else who even knows me at the police station. The only policeman Jim's ever mentioned is the one that wants to help him. A policeman with a bad back. An older man with a red face. Jim said it struck him odd because the man didn't like Indians. Was that what he said? And there was something else Jim said, something I should remember. Why would an old policeman want to help Jim? Jim said he didn't usually help anyone. There must be something there. And it's connected with the police. It has to be that. But why?"

She paused in her pacing, stopping in front of a small marble sculpture of a dewdrop. The sculpture was vague, pointless, saying nothing, but it reflected a translucence that hinted that all was not what it seemed. Still waters run deep, she thought, or maybe it's A stitch in time saves nine. One of those proverbs. Answers could be anywhere. She continued to talk out loud.

"Well, people's motives can be very deep. I'll ask Jim. I'll call him, but not yet. No way they would tap his telephone is there? No. Why should they? But they might. On second

222

thought, I won't call him. He was very condescending about my solving this case. I'll just go ahead and do it without him."

Meanwhile she would prepare to leave. Change out of her nun clothes into something of Nica's. She needed a serious disguise.

For the second time, Sister Cecile removed the police tape from the door frame and stepped into the dead lovers' bedroom. The huge bed, draped in a shimmery satin cover, looked obscene in its opulent luxury. Above it the mirror picked up light, making the room undulate with reflections. The couple who had used it was gone but their ghosts moved in the light. The bloodstain on the floor was the only dark spot in the room.

Cecile went to the closet and opened the door carefully, her hand wrapped with the material of her skirt. Fingerprints again. It was even more critical now, with the police after her, that she be careful and not leave any evidence that she had been here. Had she been careful enough? Could carelessly left fingerprints prove she had committed murder? Maybe she would have a prison ministry after all.

Nica had a lot of clothes, everything from beaded gowns to conservative suits. On the top shelf were several large, clear-plastic boxes. Wigs.

Sister Cecile pulled out a bright red dress with a form-fitting, knit top and a low-waisted filmy skirt. She undressed, changed into the red dress and hung her conservative nun clothes in the closet, mixing them in with Nica's huge wardrobe. She removed her veil, folded it and tucked it into a drawer. She put on a long, straight-haired blond wig.

The person in the mirror was no one she had ever seen before. This was definitely not her. A touch of Nica's bright pink lipstick, a pair of perfectly round, blue sunglasses, and Sister Cecile had vanished. Who this was, was yet to be seen.

As an afterthought Sister Cecile moved everything from her conservative black purse into a red bag of Nica's, including the borrowed sunglasses. Then she tossed in a spare wig: one that had straight, shoulder-length red hair. Just in case she wanted to be somebody else again. Nica wouldn't miss anything where she was, and of course the clothes would help her discover Nica's killer. Borrowing Nica's personal possessions was perfectly all right. In fact, it was a good thing to do. No ethical dilemma.

Another look in the mirror left Sister Cecile satisfied, although still slightly shocked with the image she presented. Nobody would take her for a nun. She gave a little twist and a wiggle to put herself in the right mood.

Now she could check and see if there was some way out of this building besides the front door. Maybe she could solve Nica's murder while she was in the building, and/or trying to get out.

Sister Cecile grabbed her new red purse and keys and walked out the door of the apartment and into the hall. Not a sound: the hall floor was covered with a long, plush carpet. To the right was another apartment door with a man and his dog disappearing into it, to the left was the elevator and the stairwell. She decided to try the stairs. Maybe they would lead down to a basement, maybe to a rear, emergency exit.

It was worth a try.

She heard the elevator door open, the hiss and swish of metal and air, just as she entered the stairwell, vanishing behind the steel fire door. That was when she heard a voice, low and muffled, but clear and close enough for her to distinguish every single syllable.

"I spotted that black Jaguar outside, so the damn nun's probably in here, right in Barclay's apartment. She probably killed the Rabelais girl, too. Scares the shit out of me, someone like that pretending to be a nun."

It was the police.

40

THE person speaking had a nasal twang that sent chills up and down Cecile's spine. She heard the first half of the words as the door swung shut with a soft click, the second half with her ear pressed up against the crack in the stairwell door. Did that voice just accuse her of pretending to be a nun? That was a laugh. She wasn't someone pretending to be a nun. She was someone pretending not to be a nun.

Obviously the police knew very little as far as facts went.

She kept listening but the words dwindled into murmurs as she heard the soft sound of a key in the lock. She heard a loud thud, then voices shouting: "Police! Freeze!"

She heard the stamping of feet as the police entered the Barclay apartment with firepower. They thought she was inside! It must have been the doorman who told them a strange woman had come up. A woman who looked just like she did. They knew she was here!

Cecile stood motionless against the stairway door, her insides ice.

Slowly Cecile forced herself to draw away from the door, flex her arms, her legs, take a series of long breaths. She began to move automatically down the stairs. One step, another, another. No sound. They hadn't heard the door click shut, hadn't seen the revealing crack of light before it closed.

She kept moving.

Gasping, she was at the turn in the stairs, then past and on down: a frantic run from a nightmare. Her pulses throbbed, sending shock waves of heat through her body. Any minute now she knew the police would send someone down the stairs. Above the clatter of her own feet she listened for the click of a door, rapid footsteps in pursuit, the shot of a gun.

Barclay's apartment was on the fourth floor. She was dizzy by the time she hit the level that read "Lobby," on the exit door. She listened over blood pounding in her ears, and she looked. The stairwell was empty. No police, no sound.

Her eyes searched frantically.

Yes, there was another way out, a back door. She could leave, simple as that. Maybe she was safe. Maybe there was nobody out there. Maybe there was a policeman out there. There probably was.

Of course the back door had a one-way lock. Once out of the building it was pretty clear there was no way back in but through the lobby and past the traitorous doorman. The rear, steel door was double locked with a series of alarms set to go off if anyone tried to break in from outside. A second glance told Cecile that Nica's murderer couldn't have come in this way. At least she had one question answered, for all the good it would do her. And once Sister Cecile left the building she wouldn't be able to get back in either. She tried to think.

Should she exit into the lobby and leave that way, casually as though she was a totally innocent blond in a red dress? Would the disguise work on the doorman? Or should she stay here and hope the police didn't check the stairs? Maybe she could return upstairs when they were done searching and live on frozen dinners for weeks, staying in hiding, letting Jim Cypress untangle this mess. Could Jim? Would he?

None of the above. She wanted out, and out she would go. They had no reason to post a guard outside the rear door. She hoped. Boldly Sister Cecile opened the exit door, pausing only for a quick prayer that nobody really was out there waiting for her.

It looked clear.

* * *

226

The policeman, Luis Correro, didn't see her at first either. He had been posted with a stiff admonition from Reggie Peele, "She's a probable killer. Be prepared to shoot."

Officer Correro was propped against a wall, the warm sun toasting him at a late-afternoon angle. He was dreaming of ground fishing, the hook, baited with fresh diced shrimp, rolling along the reef bottom waiting for a snapper to take hold. He could almost feel the pull on the line, see the pole bend. "Damn," he muttered to himself, what he wouldn't give to be out there right now with the warm sea air blowing in his face. His buddy just got a new boat, sixty horsepower. He was out there right now, cruising in paradise, fishing, drinking cold beer. Salt water, big fish, and dinner everywhere just begging to be caught. Correro pictured the awesome, billowing clouds, the endless blue sea, almost felt the line in his hands, pulling as it slipped through the water.

He jumped when he heard the door bump shut. He turned fast, gun out, ready to shoot.

"My, my, my, what are you doing, sir?" the woman asked. She was about five-feet-five, gorgeous long blond hair, face like an angel. But the red dress, the pouty lips, the shoulders moving under the red knit; all that didn't come from any angel. She looked just like all the beautiful women who inhabited Miami Beach. When Officer Correro wasn't dreaming about ground fishing he was dreaming about women just like this one.

"Uh, what are you doing here?" The gun shook in his hands. "Why the back door?" The officer relaxed suddenly as her cool gray eyes ran up and down what he considered to be a very manly physique. He was flattered by the woman's direct gaze, the eyes that wandered boldly over his body. Flattered, in fact, was not quite the word. The gun in his hand seemed to twitch of its own accord.

"I'm just going home. I was visiting a ..." Sister Cecile paused and forced her lips into a smile before she completed the sentence. "A friend. I don't like going by that doorman. He gives me bad looks. Don't trust him at all, to tell the truth."

227

"Oh, yeah," the policeman mouthed. "Has he ever bothered you?"

"Looks. Like he has no business doing it like that. He's supposed to be a doorman, you know? He's supposed to just stand there, keep the creeps out. The doorman makes me very nervous, so I always leave this way. Going by that man once, when I come in this place, is quite enough, thank you very much." She slid forward, undulating just enough to send her shoulders moving.

"I can understand that. Uh, you see any other woman around, sort of looks like a nun?" It didn't occur to Officer Correro that he didn't know what the quarry was supposed to look like. But everyone knew what a nun looked like.

"You mean old?" Cecile's laugh was tinkly and light.

"Yeah, old, like, dark clothes maybe?"

Sister Cecile looked thoughtful. "No. I saw someone with a dog."

"A woman?"

"Well," she giggled. "I think it was a man. Hard to tell sometimes. Not a nun, anyway."

"Not a nun. Okay." He nodded.

"Are you going to shoot me?" Sister Cecile looked at the gun, still pointed at her.

"No. I mean, no. Sorry." He turned the gun away. "We're looking for a killer. Sorry about that."

"A nun killer?" Sister Cecile sounded incredulous. "Someone's out killing nuns? That's terrible!"

"Something like that."

"Scary."

"People these days," the officer said. "You never know."

"Can't tell a book by its cover," Cecile added.

"That's right."

"Can I go? I mean, will I be safe? I won't be killed or anything?"

"Of course not," Luis Correro said. "I'll cover you from this side. There are more police around front. You'll be safe."

"Great. Thank you, Officer."

228

Officer Correro straightened his shoulders and cleared his mind as his eyes watched the woman in the red dress stroll gracefully down the back alley behind the building. He wondered whom she had been visiting, and then, why. His mind took a few leaps and pictured a love nest. That wasn't all he pictured.

Sister Cecile walked away slowly, walking, in fact, most unlike a nun. She had chosen the alley heading in the direction of her car. If she could keep going in this direction for about a block, she should come out near it. Maybe she could catch Sister Raphael and wave just to signal to the older nun that she was all right. "I will be safe," she told herself, and almost giggled again.

Sister Cecile found an alley that connected with the main street half a block down, quite close to the Jaguar, in fact.

She felt drained. The back of her dress clung to her skin, damp with sweat. It wasn't just from the warm weather. The conversation with Officer Correro had been very stressful, maligning the doorman, pretending to be someone she wasn't. Those kinds of things she had no trouble with, she'd done things like that before, but it was work. Her kind of work.

She paused at the head of the alley and stared out. Palms lined the street, cars were parked head to toe, a few people were walking by looking curiously at the police cars. Then she spotted a strange scene: thirty feet away Sister Raphael, in black veil and white skirt and blouse, waving her car keys at a uniformed policeman.

"My car," the old nun was saying. Sister Cecile could barely make out the words. "Yes, I know it was rented by my superior, but I have important business for the retirement community and it's my car at the moment. When you live in a community you use one another's things. That's just the way it is. You can't stop me from taking it."

"Where's the nun?" the policeman asked.

"What nun? We have a lot of nuns. Eight of us. I'm a nun."

"The nun that rented this car. Sister Cecile, her name is. Where is she?"

"Oh, that nun?" Sister Raphael looked puzzled, old, helpless. Cecile almost applauded. Raphael was a master of deceit without ever telling a lie.

"Well, I don't know, to tell you the truth. I believe she's doing some business for the convent. She didn't leave word as to her whereabouts. I need to go now. I have to go to the bathroom."

The officer eyed his gun, loose in the holster. He eyed Sister Raphael, old, wrinkled, fidgeting. She looked just like any of the hundreds of elderly people who inhabited his beat except she was in a nun's habit. And that made it even worse. He swallowed. "Where are you going?"

"Home. I have to go instantly."

"Your name and driver's license, please."

Sister Raphael fumbled a moment with her purse and drew out her driver's license. "See." She smiled crookedly. "It's me."

He glanced at it and handed it back. "Fine. Thank you very much. You can go."

Sister Raphael opened the door to the car, slid in and turned the ignition key. The car bucked as she pulled out and shifted into second gear too soon. Then the car glided into a smooth rumble and was gone.

41

SISTER Cecile used the moment of Raphael's departure to step boldly out into the street and walk away. She held her head high, the wispy skirt of the red dress blew lightly against her thighs. Her mind was busy, moving concisely from one plan to the next, even while her body swayed. She needed a telephone. She needed another car. She needed a center of operations.

The convent was unsafe. The police would be looking for her there. Jim Cypress wasn't safe. They would be keeping an eye on him. She thought of all the people she had met in Miami since her arrival some months ago. She drew a blank. Nothing in her mental Rolodex. No convent in the city was safe, so she couldn't visit her friend at the Little Sisters of the Poor. The consortium members wouldn't do. She felt sweat roll down her back. She walked faster, then forced herself to slow down. Be casual, she instructed her body. Be cool.

Her mind roamed on. Then it stopped with a sudden, blinding lurch. Gustavo Bestard, the toilet man, the man who had offered a vast sum of money for one night with her, the man who had seemed truly remorseful for what his follower, Jasper, had done. Gustavo was the man she could send to jail for kidnapping. Gustavo owed her more than a few toilets. He owed her big time.

Was this man safe from the police? Yes. But was he safe? Not at all. Maybe. Well, he certainly had wanted her to stay with him before, but that was an entirely different matter. Could she stay with Gustavo safely now? Morally speaking.

Maybe. Maybe not.

Everything from her black purse was now in Nica's red purse, including Gustavo's card. There was a block of telephones on the next street corner. Sister Cecile was only moments from Ocean Drive now. She kept walking until she was there, putting one foot ahead of the other carefully envisioning herself as a blond woman in a red dress and not a nun at all. She moved accordingly.

At the phone booths, she found one that worked, pulled out a quarter and dialed. Gustavo himself answered.

"Hello, Gustavo? This is Sister Cecile."

"Hey, how you doing? Yeah, my men tell me they dropped off the toilets. Whaddaya think?"

"Grand. I'm amazed, Gustavo. The toilets are beautiful. But I need another favor. I'm in a little trouble and I thought of you."

"You thought of me. That makes me feel real good. What's this trouble? I know about trouble. That's what this man's for." She could almost hear his chest swelling over the line.

"Well, first I need a ride. Could you pick me up? I mean, I could take a cab to your place, or somewhere safe. I need to go into hiding immediately. Or even better, I need a car."

"Pick you up? Where are you?"

She looked at the street sign in front of her and gave the address. "I'm at a pay phone," she added. "And I have long blond hair at the moment."

"Sure, yeah. See, I'm just done with a job, I'm in the truck myself, on the cellular, so I'll be along in maybe fifteen minutes. Can you hold on?"

Sister Cecile's eyes roamed behind her in the direction from which she had just come. Three police cars were still in front of the building. One had flashing lights. They didn't look as though they would be leaving for a while.

"I'll hold on right where I am. I'm in a red dress. You can't miss me. And the hair. Long and blond. I don't look like myself at all."

She heard Gustavo chuckle, a sound she had hoped never to hear again. How did she get herself into situations like this anyway? "I'll be right here," she said. "Please hurry."

Ten minutes later Sister Cecile had been approached by three men. Only one asked her for her rate. Mary Magdalene, Cecile thought, did this for a living, hung out on street corners in Jerusalem wearing red dresses waiting for strange men. Of course, there was more to Mary Magdalene than that; there was a lot more. And there was more to Jerusalem than Miami, or maybe they were very similar. Tall palms, diverse races, heat, dusty streets. Maybe Miami was the new Jerusalem.

An overweight, forty-year-old man slid up beside her.

She held the telephone to her ear and started talking. "Harry, I promise. . . . Yeah, I know I left you with the kids. Right. . . ."

The man sped up and walked on by. Where was Gustavo?

Finally a truck pulled up across the street from the telephones, a large white truck with a huge tank on the back. It looked vaguely familiar: "Sanitary Disposal Unit, Dade County Portable Toilet Corporation." The telephone number under the green writing looked familiar, too. It should have. Sister Cecile had just dialed it to reach Gustavo.

Sister Cecile looked up at the face leering at her from the cab. Gustavo himself, grinning, called from the driver's side. "Looking good, sweetheart. Climb aboard."

Sister Cecile crossed the street and went around to the passenger door, opened it and hauled herself up and into the seat. She sat for a moment, pulling the red skirt down as far as possible, breathing the air-conditioned air. She finally turned to meet Gustavo's heavy-lidded brown eyes.

"Well," she began, "I can't tell you how much I appreciate this. Is this what you do? I mean, sanitary units? Portable toilets?"

Gustavo kept on grinning. Cecile refused to think of it as a leer. He didn't answer, just pulled away from the curb. The truck was modern, big, air-conditioned, with soft music on the stereo. Sister Cecile felt a sloshing sensation as the products in the rear slapped and gurgled against the insides of the massive tank mounted on the back of the truck.

She didn't think about what was in the tank, but there was a faint smell of something earthy, very faint. It was a smell that she carefully ignored.

"Like I said," he answered finally, "I just finished a pickup. See, I could hire people, sit back in the office and rake in the bucks, but then I'd lose touch. Gotta keep your hand in this business, so to speak, or you lose the feel of things."

"Right," Sister Cecile said. She received a swift mental image from his words. "Hands-on is the only way to succeed."

"Lotta money in shit," Gustavo continued. "Lotta shit out there."

233

"Exactly," she agreed. "A valuable and necessary service industry."

Gustavo made a right on Ocean Drive. He glanced down at the red dress. "You're looking like a service industry yourself. I like the blond hair. What's up? Change your mind about me?"

"Absolutely not, Gustavo. I mean, I really appreciate what you're doing here, but I'm still a nun. On the other hand, I have this problem." She stopped, searching for words. "Well, there's an APB out on me."

"Cops after you? You?" Gustavo frowned. "I saw the cops there behind us. Whatcha do? Rob the collection basket?"

"I did absolutely nothing. But they're definitely looking for me. Remember when I first met you, I was after information about Elliot Barclay? And then Nica Rabelais? You knew they're both dead, and because I hid some information from the police, someone at the station thinks I killed them, or killed Nica, anyway. I mean, it's ridiculous. Of course I didn't kill anybody."

"You're sure?" He raised an eyebrow.

"Absolutely, Gustavo. I don't kill people."

"Then what's the information you have? What do the cops want? What won't you tell them?" Gustavo sounded sharp, too sharp. He was driving along Ocean Drive, slowly, the huge sanitation truck edging through traffic heavy with luxury vehicles. They all gave him a wide berth. He wasn't chuckling now, he was thinking, probing. He was suddenly a mind to be reckoned with. It occurred to Sister Cecile that she was dealing with a very acute businessman, not just a playboy.

"What do they want to know?" he repeated.

"Oh, nothing really."

"Tell me about it."

"I can't really. It's not important."

"I think it is."

"No, it's nothing."

"Wanna walk?" He pulled over in front of an open-air café.

"No. I mean, do you really want to know?"

234

"Information is my name. I want it all. I only play with a full deck. Or you can get off here."

"Well, it's a long story. It's about how Elliot Barclay died."

"Tell me about it."

"You have to promise not to tell anybody. I mean absolutely anybody."

"It might be worth money."

"Believe me, this information is not worth money. As a matter of fact, it has to do with a child."

"You having a baby?"

"No, no. It's a twelve-year-old. A girl, actually. I'm taking care of her at the moment while her dad's away."

"She's into drugs." He sounded positive. He pulled back into traffic, driving again.

"Much worse. But really she didn't do anything either."

"Go on."

Cecile did. It was that or forget all the help she hoped to get from this man. It wouldn't hurt to tell Gustavo, she figured. And he would understand about Leonie. He would have to.

She told the tale, starting with the accidental death of Elliot Barclay, continuing through the accidental shooting in the Everglades. "And I don't believe in accidents," she said.

Gustavo didn't say much, just a grunt, a nod, and, "Go on. What else?"

She told of Nica's clueless death, of her own questioning of the consortium members. "A dead end, I'm sure. The way things look Nica's death is something else entirely. The consortium is wasting money on me. I feel very guilty about the case. Where are we going?"

"Joe's. Keep talking."

"Oh." Satisfied with the destination, Sister Cecile spoke of the trouble at the station house and the all points bulletin.

"I don't get it," she said finally. "There's no motive for anything."

While Cecile talked, Gustavo had been heading south along the Beach. The Atlantic Ocean was to their left, rows of art deco hotels and hot spots to their right. They rounded the corner of Joe's Stone Crabs just as she finished the long tale.

Cecile had never been at Joe's, but she had heard of the place; one of those South Beach restaurants that everyone had to go to once in a lifetime. So far she had managed to avoid it. It didn't look too prepossessing. There were no long lines at this time of day. That would come a few hours later.

Gustavo pulled into the huge parking lot, gingerly edging up beside a silver Lexus. He turned off the ignition.

"Interesting story," Gustavo said and turned to look at Sister Cecile. "Very interesting," he repeated. "You see any pattern here?"

"I suppose. There are odd elements everywhere, but I don't know why. I can't find a motive. Why would anyone want to kill Nica?"

"AIDS? Or Elliot? Lust, love, what have you. Them things make people move in very strange ways. You know."

"I know."

"Let's get some stoners and think about it. Get our minds moving. You like stone crabs?"

Cecile had never had a stone crab. She looked down at the red dress, lifted a long strand of blond hair from her shoulder and decided that there was a time for everything. God wouldn't have made stone crabs if they didn't have some use in the world. Maybe this was it. "Maybe eating stone crabs will help," she said. "I'll try anything."

"Hop out. We'll go for the cure."

42

SISTER Raphael arrived back at the retirement community with a sense of having been in a movie. Miami Beach was a movie set any day of the week, but for the first time, Sister Raphael felt like one of the actors in a serious drama. She wished Sister Cecile was available to talk with about this new feeling. Plus the fact that she had some ideas. There was no one around except Leonie, though, and Leonie was only twelve years old. Still, she was a very intelligent child. Leonie would do. She would have to do. Besides, Cecile had explicitly told her to tell Leonie everything.

"Where's Leonie?" Raphael asked Sister Edna at the desk. "And why are you still at the desk? It's late."

"The police are still here," Edna whispered. "They've been all over the community, crawling around as though we're harboring a criminal. Imagine accusing Sister Cecile of a crime. She *wouldn't*. I told them that."

"No, she wouldn't," Raphael confirmed. "And the police still here. Why don't they just go."

"One's lingering around, down by the pool. I don't know what he's waiting for. And those men are putting in the toilets already. I thought I should stay here. It looks better. More professional, don't you think? Here, this is a card that woman left for Sister Cecile. I forgot all about it in the confusion."

Sister Edna pushed Amy Peele's card at Sister Raphael. "In case you see her. It was the one I told you about. I completely forgot about the card, and of course I don't remember if she ever did tell me her name. Anyway, it's on there. Sometimes I

237

really think I'm losing my brain, Raphael." Edna shook her old head slowly.

"Not true, Edna. It's been a rough day for all of us." Raphael looked at the card. "Amy Peele. I'll let Cecile know when I hear from her." Raphael pocketed the card. "Where's Leonie?"

"By the pool."

Raphael was only slightly worried when she realized that not only Leonie but also a policeman was by the pool. And they were talking. It meant nothing. Leonie was probably finding things out. The girl was good at that.

Sister Raphael stopped by one of the bathrooms to see what was happening with the toilets, then she headed out to the pool. She stood for a moment under the extended roof. As she had expected, there was Leonie perched on an unopened toilet carton, talking to a uniformed policeman. Leonie was grinning, talking, laughing, but mostly listening.

Maybe she should be left alone, Raphael thought. Leonie's dad was a CIA agent, and Leonie had definitely inherited a talent for finding things out. But when Leonie spotted the old nun, she beckoned for Sister Raphael to come over.

"This here's Officer Gumolta," Leonie said. "He's looking for Sister Cecile. This is my friend, Sister Raphael."

In odd moments Leonie exhibited good manners. It always surprised Raphael to see them sneak out from time to time.

"Glad to meet you, Officer. Although I think this chasing around after Sister Cecile is ridiculous. Taxpayers' money shouldn't be wasted."

The policeman shrugged. "I'll agree with that."

"Will you be here long?" Raphael asked.

" 'Nother hour. I'm just finishing up."

"Right. And then I suppose you'll leave someone to watch the convent. Maybe sitting in an unmarked car outside?"

Office Gumolta didn't answer the question. Instead he asked one. "You couldn't help us out, now? Tell us where this person is? I thought you people were on our side."

Raphael seemed to waver in the slanting sun. Not because of the words she was hearing from Office Gumolta, but because of the seriousness with which they were spoken. They really thought Sister Cecile was a killer. It hurt. She felt real pain. Tears came to her old blue eyes.

"I really don't know about all this," she said. The words came out in a whisper. "Leonie, when you come in, I want to talk with you. I'll be in the little garden."

Leonie nodded. "Okay, Raphael. I'll be there in a few minutes."

Sister Raphael managed a weak smile, her wrinkled cheeks quivering. Sometimes everything was just too difficult. It had been a long, hot day and it wasn't over yet. She felt utterly helpless. Maybe she was getting old, too. She and Sister Edna.

Slowly Sister Raphael nodded good-bye to the policeman, an ordinary, nice man just doing his job in a dangerous world, then she turned and walked back indoors, her pose suggesting defeat, or old age, or perhaps both. For once, it was not an act.

Sister Raphael loved Sister Cecile like a daughter. More, perhaps, because she had never had a daughter, and the need was even greater. She knew the younger nun's flaws, her impulsiveness, her blind spots. That's what worried Sister Raphael the most. Sister Cecile being out there in the real world was a frightening thought. There was no telling what she would do.

Raphael sat in the little garden and prayed for some time. Absentmindedly, she pulled a tall piece of grass growing up beside the stone bench and twisted it around her hand, making a link to bind herself to the still world of nature. Birds made trilling noises from the shiny-leafed trees nearby, and a dove cooed. She was going to cry. "No," she muttered, "I won't."

"Won't? Won't what?" Leonie appeared in the garden.

"Cry. I won't cry."

"Go ahead." Leonie settled down beside Raphael. "That cop is really nice, but they've got the highway patrol, the state cops, the Dade County cops, the Miami Beach cops, every single one of them out after her. Suspicion of murder. Sister Cecile really walked into it this time."

Sister Raphael blessed herself.

"But," Leonie continued, "I found out how it all came

about. Officer Gumolta, the cop I was talking to, told me that Jim Cypress just happened to mention to a cop that the nun knew something. Apparently he twisted it around and they brought Jim in and he refused to talk. Of course Jim wouldn't say a word except that Cecile did know about the crime. I mean the Barclay death, which we both know is not a crime. But Jim wouldn't tell anyone why. So of course they thought the worst."

Raphael nodded, knowing what was coming next.

"Because of *me*," Leonie said.

"It's dumb," Raphael muttered. "Very dumb."

"Major dumb," Leonie agreed. "Do you think I should turn myself in? I almost did, but you said not to. Jim said not to. Should I?"

"No. Cecile is the one they want now. They probably wouldn't even believe you. You know how people are about youngsters. The same way they look at old people. They think we're stupid."

"True," Leonie agreed. "But here's the thing. Cecile always says to look for the motive. My question is, who is this cop that got her in this trouble? And why? Does he want a promotion? What's the deal, here?"

Raphael pulled herself up straight. "Motive. That's a real problem. We'll have to talk to Jim. Maybe he knows something. Maybe."

"What else is going on? There must be other things happening around here that will lead us somewhere," Leonie mused.

"The someone who was looking for Sister Cecile," Raphael offered. "Now we have her name. The same one you said was so weird, the one with ponytails? Do you think that could be it?" She pulled out the card Sister Edna had given her and looked at it. "Her name is Amy Peele. She works at a Canadian bank."

"Lemme see that card," Leonie grabbed it from Raphael's hand. "Pigtails. Pigtails. Not ponytails. The woman that took me to the juice bar the other day. Amy. Got to be. She wanted to know about strange stuff here on the Beach, like Elliot Barclay. Maybe she knows something. But she really was not classy, Raphael. I mean, whatever she wanted from me, she was going about it very strangely."

"Maybe she was a friend of Elliot's?" Raphael asked.

Leonie shook her head. "I'm clueless. Let's go call Jim Cypress. Maybe he heard of this lady."

"I'm not sure that would be wise."

"Let me do it. I'm a kid. I can get away with it."

"True. Let's give it a try."

They walked back indoors together and decided to use the telephone in Leonie's room. Leonie had a separate number as a recognition of her independent status in the community. Leonie got Jim Cypress on the line at once.

"Hi," she began. "It's Leonie."

"Things okay there?"

"Yep. She's gone someplace. Nobody knows where."

"Good." Jim's voice was a deep rumble. "I don't have much to say," he said. "Not a clue. They don't trust me. They've been working on a court order to tap my line. It may be already on. I know how they work."

"Don't worry. I don't know anything, anyway. So I can't say anything."

"I figured."

"Listen, Jim. We gotta work this all out. I think it's someone at your end causing all the trouble."

"No. It's nobody's fault. Just things got mixed up. Don't worry about it, Leonie. I'll handle it."

Leonie didn't respond for a moment. She didn't think things were mixed up at all, but she'd better humor Jim. She was already aware of how men don't give females enough credit for thinking. "Okay. I'm cool," she finally said. "Listen, you know someone named Amy Peele? She was looking for Cecile today."

"Amy? Sure. That's Reggie's kid. I don't actually know her but he always talks about her. Everyone here's heard of Amy. Amy Peele's a big banker. He's very proud of her."

"Who's Reggie?"

"Reggie? He's a policeman, works here. He's been interested in the case. He even offered to help out."

"Oh. Okay." Leonie nodded and grinned at Raphael, making the victory sign with her fingers. "Listen, we gotta talk, Jim. Can you come by? I mean, in person?"

"Uh, wouldn't be prudent, Leonie."

"Prudent? No. Maybe not. Are you okay, Jim? I mean you won't lose your job, will you?"

"Not a chance," he replied, but he sounded worried to Leonie. She was good at seeing through adults. He was probably going to lose his job.

"Is Stephanie all right?"

"She's great."

"Okay. I gotta go. Tell her hello. Bye, Jim."

Leonie hung up the receiver thoughtfully. "Amy Peele is the daughter of a cop. The cop that's helping Jim. Helping? No. I think he's not helping at all. His name is Reggie Peele, and his daughter was that creepy lady. What do you think, Raphael? We have our connection. I wonder what it means."

"I wish we could talk to Cecile. I wish she'd call."

Leonie sighed. "Me, too."

They sat for a moment in silence, Leonie sprawled out on the bed, Sister Raphael sitting almost primly on Leonie's desk chair. It took a while for the next words to emerge, and they came from Sister Raphael.

"We have to do something," the old nun said. "We've saved Cecile before. We can do it again. We have to figure something out."

Leonie nodded thoughtfully. "You're absolutely right. The only thing is, Raphael, what are we supposed to be saving her from?"

"I'm not exactly sure. We'll have to figure that out, too."

43

"STONE crabs," Sister Cecile said, wiping her lips, "are not in season. This snapper is great."

"Next time, stone crabs," Gustavo affirmed. "A self-renewing resource. Fishermen catch a stone crab, remove one claw and toss the crab body back, still alive. Another claw regenerates."

Cecile set her napkin on the table. "How long do you suppose it takes? I mean, to grow another one."

"Don't know."

"What if a crabber took off all the claws and tossed the totally clawless bodies back? Would they live?"

"Don't know about that either." Gustavo took a long pull on his beer. He was staring at her intently, his mind apparently not on stone crabs. "About tonight," he said. "You should stay at my place. No cops there. Believe me. You'll be safe in my house."

Cecile looked at her rescuer through gray eyes that looked oddly pale surrounded by the platinum wig. She trusted him about as far as she could throw him. Did he actually think he could get the twenty-thousand-dollar night with a quick rescue and a meal at Joe's Stone Crabs? That was a man for you. On the other hand, he'd already begun fixing up the community bathrooms and had initiated plans for his mother to fill up the last remaining suite. God insisted we forgive our enemies, but it was hard to forget Jasper, hard to forgive. Still, she would. She just wouldn't trust Gustavo as far as spending the night. No reason to.

She tipped her beer and sipped. She had to keep in mind

that she was the one who asked him for help. It was restitution for him, or a way to keep her from bringing kidnapping charges. She looked again at his warm brown eyes. Complicated. What could his motives be now? He was being so nice. Maybe he just wanted to be her friend and was trying to make up for the kidnapping.

Not likely.

"I think I'd better go somewhere else."

"Why? Don't trust me?"

"Not a bit."

"I was brought up Catholic."

"So was Fidel Castro."

Gustavo tapped his fingers on the table. Sister Cecile could read the disappointment.

"Well, what would you suggest?" he asked.

"There are two priorities. I have to solve this case, and I need some transportation. My plan is to call the convent from a pay phone somewhere, then head to another pay phone, then another one, just in case they can trace the calls. We don't have caller ID at the community, but they may have put it on our number, somehow. I have a lot of calls to make."

"You want to move around."

"Precisely. Perhaps some of the consortium members have a lead. I've got to figure out who killed Nica and present the police with a legitimate suspect. I can't stay on the run for the rest of my life. I have to solve the murder of Nica Rabelais and do it quickly. That's got to be the key. There has to be a connection between that death and why the police are after me."

"Easier said than done, but possible." Gustavo nodded, then he waved a credit card at the waitress. "I'll make the first call to the convent for you. They need a court order for a telephone tap, but, like you say, you can't trust telephones."

"I don't."

"Yeah. My home phone is tapped," Gustavo said. "They think I'm connected with drugs."

"A nice Catholic boy like you? I thought you dealt with waste products."

244

"Same thing. People get confused."

"Do you have something for me to drive?" Cecile asked. "I need to have wheels for this."

"Right. You will. But first the call. Got to be methodical."

"Okay. You make the first call."

Gustavo called the convent from a pay phone in the restaurant, and at Cecile's instructions he asked for Sister Raphael. Moments later he heard a little girl's voice.

"Sister Raphael is busy. May I take a message?"

"Who's this?" Gustavo asked.

"Leonie."

"Loony?"

Sister Cecile grabbed the telephone, discounting all her fears of wire taps and police answering the call. Besides, she would be leaving this location immediately. "Leonie, what's happening there? It's me."

"Hi. Where are you?"

"Somewhere. What's happening there? Are you all right?"

"Yeah, fine. Cops been crawling all over the place here. Also, get this. I found out that someone named Amy Peele has been by the convent, snooping around. And the incredible fact is that she's Reggie Peele's daughter. He's the same cop that's been trying to help Jim. Does that make sense to you? It has to be the connection, doesn't it?"

"Reggie Peele? Amy Peele?" Sister Cecile took a strand of long blond wig hair and chewed on it. Her mind moved quickly, picturing Amy Peele and the demon in her eyes. The woman had loved Elliot. "Amy Peele. Thank you, Leonie. That's it. That's the answer. Okay. Where's Raphael?"

"Having a nap."

"Wake her up. Tell her that's it. That's the motive."

"What is?"

"Love. Passion."

"Whose?"

"Amy Peele, Elliot Barclay."

"Nobody could love her. She's the one who bought me a coconut thing last week. She's gross."

"Leonie, I can't believe it. That woman?"

"Believe it. She was very weird."

"I think she's the killer. Listen to this scenario: She loved Elliot Barclay, she probably killed Cosima, she had to have killed Nica. Watch out. Amy Peele is our killer."

"Her?" Leonie's voice squeaked, then, "Definitely the type. Who's Cosima? What are you going to do now, Cecile? Where are you?"

"I'm going to draw Amy Peele out. Listen, get Raphael. Now."

Moments later the old nun was on the line. "Are you awake?" Cecile asked.

"Absolutely." Sister Raphael's voice was hoarse, but she sounded alert enough. "What's happening?"

Sister Cecile quickly ran through her theory. "I think I can set up a plan but we don't have a lot of time. There are some things you have to do. Are you ready for this?"

"I can do anything."

"I hope. This is simple. I want you to have Jim Cypress do something for me in about two hours." Cecile glanced at her watch. "Now here's what I want you to do. Tell him this carefully so he gets it the first time. I don't want to call again."

Sister Cecile talked for five minutes, explaining every detail of what was to be done, working it out as she went. From time to time she paused to answer a question, then began talking again.

Joe's Stone Crabs was filling up rapidly as she outlined her scheme, lines of people were forming, anxious, hungry patrons waiting to be seated, and it became progressively more difficult to hear and be heard, but Gustavo stood his ground guarding the nun from the encroaching mob. He listened intently to one side of the conversation. His dusky face deepened into a concerned frown as Sister Cecile's plan unfolded. Then he chuckled. Then he frowned again. Finally Sister Cecile hung up.

"Well," Cecile said serenely. "It's all set."

Gustavo nodded glumly. "I say forget it. It's a risky idea. You say this woman's a killer? Stay away from her." He walked toward the door, grabbing Cecile by the elbow and urging her along.

"No. I have to end the case. I've been hired to solve the murder of Nica Rabelais as well as find the cause of Elliot Barclay's demise. This is what I do. One down. One to go. Nica's murderer has to be the policeman or his daughter, don't you think? I know you listened to everything."

They were out on the sidewalk now, passing clusters of people on their way into the restaurant. Gustavo looked around before he answered, speaking softly.

"Maybe. But, you tell me this kid was there when Elliot killed himself accidently, and you don't want to expose the kid to a lot of questioning."

"Right. There's no need."

"So, say you find Nica's killer. Say this woman is the killer you're looking for. Case is solved, right? Nica's case, but not Barclay's. What will you do about Barclay's death? Nobody killed him. You're back to square one with the kid."

"Well, I know. But God will have to take care of that problem. I can't figure it out. She'll be out of danger, anyway, if we get Amy Peele."

"So you think God will figure it out?" Gustavo sounded doubtful.

"Of course. No problem. Meanwhile, I have to get off the Beach. I feel like I'm in the hot seat here. Everyone is looking for me." She looked around as they walked across the parking lot. "You did say you have a car for me? I'm counting on it."

"I'm still thinking."

They were almost at the truck when Gustavo spoke again. "Tell you what, Cecile, I've got a little car problem. Someone puked all over the insides of my Mercedes the other day, and it's having new seats installed. Two genuine leather front seats don't come cheap. That's my main problem with the car question."

"Oh." Sister Cecile suddenly felt remorse. "I'm sorry."

"So I've been driving this truck. You wanna take the truck?"

Sister Cecile looked up at the large tank truck full of sloshing

247

waste from who knows how many portable toilets. But the cab was clean, she recalled, except for that very faint odor.

"Your truck? This truck? You've been more than generous, Gustavo. I mean, you did owe me one big one after your friend kidnapped me. It was a terrible experience. But you've really made up for it. I mean, what will you drive if I take your truck? Maybe I should hire a cab."

"No. I can grab the cab." He shrugged. "I was picking up a rental tomorrow anyway."

She looked at the truck. "Well. Nobody would recognize me in that, would they?"

"Not a chance. Hop up. I'll show you how it works."

He patted the back of the tank like a fond parent before he walked around to the driver's side. Cecile followed, listening to his instructions.

"There's a couple of things you don't wanna touch. Shakes the shit loose, you know? I mean, this baby's got a power hose that I fixed up myself with a little added compression. I gave it an added power boost, see. We had trouble clearing one of the tanks. Not something you want to mess with. Do it right and this thing can really shoot the poop."

"And I certainly wouldn't want to do that. Tell me what I need to know."

Sister Cecile hopped up in the driver's seat and made herself comfortable. Gustavo took the passenger side and pulled out his keys. He shifted uncomfortably, as though he hated to relinquish the power.

It didn't take long for Gustavo to explain the workings of the truck. "The control board on the right is strictly for the tank. See, you've got the pressure switch here. Takes a little oomph to get the stuff out sometimes so there's a minicompressor here. This baby will shoot twenty yards if you get the pressure up enough. Don't want the dial to get beyond the red line here or the thing will blow up a hose. Secret is not to start it. Start's the red button here. But you won't be messing with this stuff anyway.

"Just in case you push the wrong thing, though," he ges-

248

tured to a red button, "you gotta watch it. It shoots even if the ignition's off, as long as you got the pressure up. But the whole thing's nonoperational unless you turn it on outside, too. A nice system. Next to the hose there's a safety switch, clearly marked, so even if you mess up here, the thing won't pump the dump unless you hit the switch on the hose."

"I understand. And the truck drives with standard gears?"

"Regular gear pattern. But it's a big baby. You gotta take it slow starting up. It has a little speed on the highway once you get her rolling. Good Ford engine."

"I'm glad to know that." Sister Cecile could see how fond Gustavo was of his truck. Men loved their big machines, she knew, and Gustavo was certainly a man. He was patting the red pressure button as though he loved it. There was a faint grin of pride on his wide lips. To him, his machine was just a big toy.

"I'll take very good care of it for you," Cecile said confidently. "I've driven all kinds of things, so I won't have any trouble."

"Put on some of them coveralls in the back there, and you'll look like you work for me," he added, indicating a box behind the seat. "Just call me when it's all over. I might start getting worried this time tomorrow if I don't hear from you. Truck's got to be unloaded soon because this stuff starts to ripen, if you know what I mean, even with chemicals. We got a lot of heat here in Miami."

"I'll definitely be in touch."

It took him a minute to wrest the truck key from his key chain, then he inserted it into the ignition. "Okay. My baby is your baby." He chuckled. "See ya later." With that, he hopped out of the cab, slammed the door, and was gone.

From a disastrous start, they had become friends. There was good in everyone, she thought, not for the first time. It proved what forgiveness could accomplish. Now, if only there were something she could do for him. For one thing, she would be very careful with his truck. His baby.

249

The truck started with a roar that quickly subsided to a purr. Cecile slid the gear into first and made her way out of Joe's parking lot.

44

MIAMI Beach has street and sidewalk traffic at any hour of the day or night. Cecile knew that when she set up her plan. She needed strict privacy, and if all went as planned, she would have it. In fact, the nun needed more than privacy. She needed total control of her environment. She headed off the Beach to what she hoped would be the perfect place.

She drove down to the causeway, keeping the truck at a steady, legal speed. Her eyes lingered as she passed the cruise ships, docked and ready for trips to nowhere. Maybe she should just forget everything, and take a cruise. It was a very appealing possibility. With her credit card she could vanish forever and live the rest of her life on the high seas. Wanted for murder.

That was a troublesome thought. She forced her eyes back to the road, skimming the massive palms, compelling herself to drive at the maximum legal rate of speed. Fifty-five miles an hour felt out of control with this huge truck filled with noxious waste. It could be disconcerting barreling down Route 395 in any vehicle, but in this truck it was downright nightmarish. If she were hit by another truck, or even a car, the results would be worse than a molasses spill.

She shrugged off her fear and kept her foot hard on the gas. Keeping up with the flow, she raced through Miami proper. The lights of evening were on, the fluorescent neon edging the metrorail made the journey feel like a ride through an amusement park. In the spaces against the sky, buildings glowed with colored lights.

She didn't slow down until Route 395 became US 1, forcing its way down into Coral Gables, turning into a strip mall. If she kept going she could end up in Key West, another tempting way out.

But she was not going that far south. Instead she made a sudden turn into a Texaco station and pulled the truck off to one side, near a public telephone. She pulled out the red-haired wig stashed in her purse. Not that she suspected she had been seen, only because it was more conservative than the long blond one. Sister Cecile really didn't want to be noticed.

She struggled into the coveralls that were behind her seat in the box Gustavo had indicated. The coveralls went right over the red dress, a tan jumpsuit with a green label, "Country Sweet" stitched on the front. Classy. With the red wig, the coveralls and the truck, the Miami Beach floozy became a professional woman of another kind altogether. A septic sister.

She jumped down from the truck and swaggered over to the pay phone. From Nica's red bag, she pulled out her wallet, and from it, Amy Peele's card with her business and home telephone numbers, stashed there that long-ago day in Elliot Barclay's office. Cecile dialed the number. To her relief it was answered quickly with a dulcet hello.

"Amy Peele, please."

"This is she."

"Hi, this is Cecile Buddenbrooks, the investigator. I was at your office a while ago looking into Elliot Barclay's effects. Remember me?"

Silence.

"You don't remember me?" Cecile felt a first moment of doubt.

"Of course, certainly. It just took a minute. Uh, can I, uh, how are you?"

"Fine thanks. Just fine. You said to get in touch if you could be of help, so I'm taking you up on your offer. I hope this isn't a bad time."

251

"Oh, no. It's fine. What can I do?" Amy's voice rose a notch.

"I have some important information on the case and for some reason I haven't been able to reach any of the consortium members. I know you've worked with them. Manuel Beaumont mentioned you helped with the structuring, and I know you're concerned with the case. You seemed the obvious one to call for help."

Cecile paused, waiting. Her eyes roamed back to the truck she had arrived in. Truck. Hoses. Tank. Suddenly she had an idea.

Amy spoke carefully. "You did exactly the right thing in calling me. Now, what can I do for you?"

"Like I said, all the members seem to be out of town, or at dinner. The problem is, I believe I have the answer to the crime that resulted in Barclay's death, as well as the solution to the death of Nica Rabelais, Elliot Barclay's girlfriend. You probably don't know about that, but it's apparently a related death." Cecile couldn't stop herself from adding that part. After all, no one was perfect. Besides, it was part of the hook to draw Amy Peele out.

"That's wonderful. Tell me." Amy Peele's voice was shaking almost imperceptibly, barely enough for Cecile to hear the quiver. "Tell me everything."

"I think the police are connected. I'm very much afraid there's a dirty cop involved. I don't know exactly who, but it has to be someone at the Miami Beach station. I'm not sure where to go from here, because I have a serious problem. They seem to be after me. I mean, the police are actually after me. They think I'm connected with the murder for some reason. Believe me, I'm not." Cecile made her voice reflect self-righteous innocence.

"After you? How silly. And there's more? You actually know who did it?" The words were an urgent, whispered question from Amy.

"I don't want to say anything over the telephone. But, Amy,

here's what I need you to do for me. I want you to get a state policeman for me, not a local man. This is woman to woman. I know I can trust you, and this is very difficult for me. I'm actually hiding from the police. I don't know who to trust as far as the police are concerned. But I have to go to the law. I think a state policeman wouldn't be corrupt, at least in this matter." Cecile made her voice sound worried, uncertain.

The nun continued urgently: "We can meet. I don't want you to tell the local police you're coming to see me, but I need a policeman. It's a real dilemma. I'm terrified." She let her voice tremble.

"Don't be afraid," Amy's tone became confident. "I can handle everything."

"You can? I mean, nobody's going to believe me. That's why I wanted the consortium. I tried to reach Mr. Beaumont. Do you have another number for him?"

"No. I said I'd handle it." Firmly. "What do you have? I mean, what evidence that an uninvolved policeman will believe?"

"Evidence of police collusion in a crime. An officer who worked with Detective Cypress. He's a local policeman."

"Evidence?"

"I have hard evidence," Cecile didn't believe in crossing her fingers, and she didn't believe in lying, but she was dealing with a killer. She made vast mental reservations as she spoke. "I don't know the policeman's name and I don't dare call Detective Cypress because he's under observation, too. All I need is an honest policeman not connected with the local police."

"I'll find one and we can meet you." Amy's voice vibrated over the line. "We need a very private place, away from everyone."

"Yes," Cecile agreed. "How about Parrot Jungle? We can all meet in the parking lot. Parrot Jungle closes at six and I know for a fact it's an extremely isolated place at night. How about meeting in two hours at the back of the parking lot. We can talk. It will give me a chance to explain to the policeman what's happening."

"Wonderful. Don't you worry, Cecile. I'll handle this. We women have to stick together."

"Amy, you've saved my day. How can I thank you!"

Amy Peele laughed. It sent a chill down Cecile's spine. "No thanks are necessary. None at all."

"I'm grateful. See you soon." Cecile hung up and stood for a moment, just breathing. The trembling in her own voice hadn't needed any acting ability. It was real.

From her vantage point by the telephone booth, the gas station looked like a toy set with trucks, cars, and toy people coming and going. Hallucinatory. Her big truck waited like a part of the game. And she was a toy nun dressed like a sanitation lady. She took another gulp of air and joined the game.

Cecile was getting used to the truck and pulled out easily into traffic. She drove slowly into South Miami. She had time. Too much time.

She started to pray out loud. "Dear God, we have toilets all over the community pool, my ward is involved in an unexplained death, the police are after me, and I'm driving a sanitation truck on my way to meet a killer. This is not funny, God. You have to get me out of this. Help me, God. My trust is in you."

She felt much better. God would help. Sister Raphael and Leonie had their instructions. Jim would come, the criminals would be apprehended.

She saw the sign for Parrot Jungle and made a left on 112th Street, downshifting into second. The truck made an alarming liquid sound. She was ready.

45

CECILE drove through Pinecrest, the high-priced suburb of Miami where Parrot Jungle is found. Finally she arrived at the park itself, passing by the welcoming parrot sculpture with a feeling of relief. The entry was well lighted, but Cecile drove beyond the lights, heading for the back of the parking lot where shadows crept from every corner. Banyan trees dropped tendrils over tremendous spaces. The parking area was a mysterious place at the best of times. At night it was darkest Africa, mysterious India. It was, in actual fact, perfumed and privileged Pinecrest, a dark jungle surrounded by half-million-dollar estates.

That knowledge did not detract from the shadows nor the screams of parrots echoing from the interior.

Sister Cecile stopped the truck beside one of the banyans and turned off the ignition. She rolled down the window and listened to the noises. She could hear wild cats, parrots, perhaps the roar of the old silverback gorilla that lived in a rear cage. One sound could only be the bellowing of an alligator from the recesses of an ancient solution hole deep within the park. More than parrots dwelled in the interior.

Cecile thought carefully about the time she had been here before, when Leonie had ventured past the tropical trees and tangled vines, dragging Cecile this way and that, discovering, among other things, that the park could be entered or departed through a loose section in the high fence that surrounded it. Cecile stared at the chain-link fence and located the spot. A loose section covered by vines where her shoe had come off. The break in the fence was still there.

Cecile restarted the truck and backed up near the vanishing point. She parked carefully, then turned on the minicompressor and watched the dial rise. It wouldn't take long. Maybe three Hail Marys, and the pressure would be optimum.

She prayed, and the pressure gauge rose.

Then a small, black Jaguar, its lights off, rolled into the east side of the parking lot. It crept up beside a distant banyan tree and parked. Two silent figures erupted into the gloom and walked over to the truck.

"Cecile?" Raphael's voice wavered through the night air.

Cecile opened the door. "Leonie! Raphael! What on earth are you doing here?"

Raphael spoke, her old voice tight with emotion. "I called Jim Cypress to set things up, Cecile, but he wasn't home. So we came instead. We had to. There was no one else and we couldn't let you face this alone. We didn't dare call the police."

Cecile's heart dropped. "You'd better go back. There may be shooting. She's a killer, and she's bringing an accomplice. It isn't safe here. They're due any minute. You've got to leave."

"I left word with Stephanie where we'd be. Jim should come along any minute. Stephanie knows the entire story. She's going to reach Jim. He'll be here." Raphael's voice was strong now. "And I brought Leonie's camcorder with the one-twelve zoom feature, just like you asked Jim to do. We can do it ourselves. Leonie knows exactly how to operate it and it's all programmed to do night shooting. Everything is going to be just fine. When we're done recording, we can all just disappear into the jungle. Leonie told me how easy it is to disappear here. Nobody will even know we're shooting. It's going to be easy. You'll see."

"Easy? This woman's going to have a gun. You've got to leave. Now."

"No." Leonie spoke. "You may be able to order Raphael,

256

but I'm not going. Besides, Amy Peele won't know that we're filming it. You're the only one who will have to disappear."

Cecile closed her eyes. She couldn't believe this. How could Raphael even think of bringing the child here? What could she do?

Nothing, apparently. Leonie was strong-minded in the best of times and this was the worst. She would have to deal with it.

"Well then, set it up. Leonie, take Raphael through the secret entry. Get the camera in position behind the fence. I suppose I have no choice, so you might as well do it. But make it fast. Amy could be along any time now. Are you sure Jim's coming?"

"Absolutely," Raphael confirmed. "Any minute. Let's go, Leonie."

Cecile heard Leonie's words, fierce, quivering as she patted the camcorder she had been carrying. "Got it. Come on, Raphael."

They vanished, two darkly clad females on a mission. They would be safe behind the fence, Cecile hoped. And whatever happened to her, good, bad or disastrous, it would be recorded for posterity. Cecile thought about that for a moment. What if she blew it? The demise of Sister Cecile on a zoom lens. A new kind of snuff film. But at least there would be proof enough for a conviction. Leonie would be safe. And that was the point of this meeting.

Cecile could just hear Leonie whispering instructions to Raphael. Then there was silence except for Mother Nature's cacophony.

Time went by slowly. Cecile opened the truck windows and settled into the cab seat. Thoughts of disaster raced through her mind. She worried that her tan sanitation uniform was too visible. She should have had Raphael bring something black for her to wear. On the other hand, she hadn't known Raphael was coming. Maybe it would be better just to wear the red dress? Red looked black at night. But the dress was so skimpy. No, she would wear the tan jumpsuit. It made her feel like a James Bond character, except there should have been ten of her all carrying lethal weapons, all dressed identically.

Where were the other nine?

"Stop it," she murmured to herself and pulled off the red wig. Her own hair was wet with sweat, plastered to her head. Her mind was going wild. Well, she was scared, admit it. She had never been in such a spot with the police convinced she was the murderer, with the real murderer coming to get her with who knows what kind of backup. Death had developed the habit of looking over her shoulder, but tonight the Grim Reaper was sitting right there on that empty seat beside the wigs.

Suddenly overhead lights went on in the parking lot from an automatic timer. The low shadows were thrown into high relief. All the better for filming.

Not a sound came from behind the fence. Maybe Leonie and Sister Raphael had been eaten by an alligator. No, there would have been noise. Leonie would have yelled.

Cecile glanced at her watch. Five minutes had passed.

She checked the pressure gauge. It was still high. The needle wavered at the top against the red danger line. The pressure was holding. The tank was ready.

She blessed herself and climbed down out of the cab, closing the door behind her with a thud. She walked around the truck and looked at everything, making her few simple preparations. Everything was in order. This was going to be a piece of cake.

Silently, hose in hand, she stepped back behind the tank, out of sight, invisible.

She heard the first unnatural sound.

They were coming.

The sound of a faulty muffler grumbled across the parking lot. A small, dark car pulled up less than twenty feet away. The car stopped. Its lights went out. Someone turned off the ignition.

Cecile stood motionless, peering around behind a tangle of hoses. The car was a dark Taurus. She watched the passenger door open and a woman step out into the light from the parking lot lamps. Amy Peele.

Cecile remained hidden.

A moment later a short, pudgy man stepped out from the

258

driver's side. He moved up and planted himself beside the woman. He walked with a slight limp. Reggie Peele.

"Sister Cecile?" It was Amy's voice.

Cecile didn't speak. The sounds of the parrots and wild animals filled the air. Make Amy nervous, she told herself. Wait.

"She's not here," Amy whispered, then louder, "Cecile? Are you there?"

Cecile finally responded. "I'm back here behind the truck. It is you, Amy? Amy Peele? Who is that with you? Is everything all right? Did you do what I asked?"

"Yes, it's me. I brought a friend. Someone we can trust. A good policeman. Come out from behind the truck. We have to talk."

"Is it a state policeman with you? Sir," Sister Cecile called to the male figure. "Officer?"

"Yes, that's who I am," came a man's voice. "Come on out where we can see you."

"No. I'll talk from here. Step under that light a little bit, please. I want to see what you look like."

The man she assumed to be Reggie obliged; he moved closer to Amy. It was important that Leonie get him clearly on the videotape. Cecile was directing a scene that would have only one take. Maybe she should ask them to move a little to the left.

"Okay, we're all set to listen." Amy's voice sounded reasonable, but Cecile detected a note of excitement as the woman's voice came across the dark space.

"Tell us what's going on. Who killed Nica? Who killed Elliot?" Amy called softly.

"I can tell you about Nica," Cecile said, wondering, for the barest fraction of a second, if her hypothesis could be wrong. What if Amy were innocent?

It was time to find out.

"Nica's the one I know about," she continued. "Her killer was a woman, a person who knew her, someone Nica trusted, and would let up to her apartment. It was someone the doorman wouldn't even notice. I think a policeman is covering up for the killer."

"A policeman. You already said that. What's his name?" Amy asked. "Why would he cover?"

"Because the doorman said only police were up there that day. So that means a policeman was involved. And from what Jim Cypress told me, I've figured out that the policeman who's covering up is the one who works at the desk at the police station. It's the policeman who has a bad back that Jim Cypress told me about. He's the one. I know you can find out his name. Just call the station. You must have a cellular phone here. Call the station house right now. Call Jim Cypress."

"Fine. I'll do that. Now, what do you have on Nica's murderer?" Amy asked. "Why are you so sure it was a woman and not a policeman who killed her?"

"Because the woman has a motive. The policeman doesn't. It was someone who loved Barclay too much. The killer was in love with Elliot Barclay."

Cecile paused, looking for words that would break Amy into pieces. "No. That's not true," Cecile continued. "This woman didn't love Barclay. The murderer obsessed about him, she wanted him, but of course, Barclay didn't love this woman. I've got it all figured out. It was a crime of passion, unrequited passion. Barclay never loved her."

Cecile stopped again and waited, letting her words sink in, letting the night sounds fill in the empty space.

"Explain." Amy's voice cracked. "This makes no sense."

"Well, the only way it makes sense is that when Elliot died, for reasons I won't go into yet, the woman who thought she loved him went a little bit crazy and killed Nica. Not just because of jealousy, but because of AIDS. And ultimately because of insane frustration. Elliot was HIV positive, and our killer probably thought Nica had given the disease to him. The killer was getting even by killing Nica. So revenge was a motive, too. This woman's lover had been taken prematurely, although, in fact he was never her lover. That was the ultimate irony. Elliot Barclay had been given a deadly disease. AIDS makes people

260

do odd things. In some it brings out love, heroic behavior; in others, despair. Some people want to get even for AIDS in irrational ways."

"That's silly." Amy's voice sounded hollow.

"Yes, very silly. Especially considering the dormancy period of AIDS. Elliot could have contracted it years ago. Maybe he was a homosexual, bisexual, who knows. Everyone gets it. Anyone."

"Elliot was not gay." Amy's voice came out a whisper.

"How can you be sure?"

"He was not gay."

"Well, it doesn't matter, does it? We can't blame him, if he was. Or if he wasn't. Certainly not now. One is never sure. . . ." Cecile let her words dangle.

"No." Suddenly the man spoke up, the man who had to be Reggie Peele. He had been silent, but this was too much. His daughter was being tortured by this nun. "She wouldn't have loved him if he weren't straight. He loved her. Of course he loved her."

Cecile's words poured out relentlessly. "As far as we know, Barclay was with Nica until the night he died, except for that prostitute, whom he murdered. Apparently he didn't love anybody but himself." She used all the authority her nun-voice could muster.

"He relied on me. Me! He needed me." Amy finally broke through. It was what Cecile had been waiting for. She glanced at the dark fence to her left, hoping to see some indication that Leonie was taping all this.

She could see nothing. Not a flicker. Not the tiniest reflection of light off a lens.

"You loved him, Amy," Cecile said clearly. "You loved Elliot Barclay. He didn't love you, did he? He loved Cosima, but he never loved you. He loved Nica, but he never loved you."

"We loved each other. Cosima was a distraction. Nica was a foolish aberration. A nobody. She was nothing. Elliot was going to leave her. Everyone knew that. Nica was a slut, no good." Amy's voice was rising.

261

"Shut up," her father said.

"Nica gave him AIDS," Cecile taunted. "That's what you thought, didn't you."

"That bitch. It must have been her. He was married before Nica came into his life. And Cosima was clean." Amy was defensive. "Nica ruined Elliot. She killed him."

"And you killed her," Cecile said clearly. "I can prove it." She didn't cross her fingers, she just clutched the hose more tightly.

"I should have killed her earlier. I could have saved him."

"It was you, wasn't it, Amy?"

"Shut up, Amy!" Reggie Peele interrupted; his service automatic appeared in his hand.

"It doesn't matter, Daddy. She knows. I killed Nica. I killed Cosima, too. You didn't know that, did you, Daddy? I killed her, too. You know about Nica, I know it, and I'd like to tell the whole world. She was responsible! Nica was evil. She deserved to die. She made people sick. She killed people. And this damn nun has to die. We were going to kill her anyway, right, Daddy? Right? You said so. You even tried. You told me. Now you have to kill her, Daddy. Do it now! Kill her!"

Amy let out a gut wrenching sob. Then nothing.

There was a dead moment. Even the crickets and the parrots were silent. Reggie Peele gave a deep, audible sigh, the sound of a man who has been placed in an impossible position by a woman.

"Damn it, Amy, you're just like your mother." Reggie took a step, another step, then another. Amy was right behind him, her breathing raspy against the night sounds. He cocked his gun with a little click.

It was Cecile's first moment of real fear. Reggie had been forced into a box by his daughter. He had no choice but to kill her.

The nun's voice came from behind the truck, steady as a clam. "You don't have to do this, you know. We can end it all peacefully. Really, Mr. Peele, Amy. God forgives us. He'll forgive you."

262

"Too late," Reggie muttered. "Too late."

"Kill her, Daddy. Kill her." It was becoming a mantra.

Cecile swallowed her fear. It was time for the second part of the show. She would have to shoot the poop.

She looked at the dial on the hose. The switch was there, readable even in the poor lighting. All she had to do was move it, slide it just a half-inch.

"You don't know what you're doing," Cecile warned again. "Please. There's always hope."

Silence. Cecile couldn't see them, but she could imagine the Peeles nudging each other, gesturing, mouthing words. She heard a foot stumble on a piece of gravel.

They were coming.

She didn't really want to do this. Controlling the hose might be impossible. It could go anywhere.

Another step on gravel. Time had just run out.

Sister Cecile stepped boldly out from behind the truck, her hand on the pressure lever. One tiny movement, she hoped. It had better work.

"Kill her!" Amy shrieked.

Reggie brought the gun up; he aimed it. He paused. Sister Cecile's fingers pushed the switch. Nothing. She pushed again and it slid, slowly, then quicker, as though hundreds of pounds of pressure were behind it.

Everything let loose. A vast stream of brown shot forward, fast, furious. Revolting. The truck contents had begun to ripen.

Reggie let off one defensive round before the gun spun from his hand, caught in the heavy, effluvium stream. Cecile waved the hose in a back-and-forth motion, hitting them both, smacking one, then the other, with brown fluid shooting out from the extreme pressure. Momentarily, the stream wavered off target, then back to begin again. It was hard to control, like a fire hose gone mad, but Cecile stood firm, dousing her opponents.

"Stop!" Amy screamed. "Stop." The last came out sounding more like a blubber than a word. She should never have opened her mouth.

Nobody had noticed the cars pulling up, lights flashing,

men jumping out, not until Cecile pushed the switch into the off position and had the hose under control. She finally shut it down, holding the nozzle like a baby in her arms, pointed at the Peeles, dripping.

"Hands up, you're under arrest."

"Who, me?" Cecile asked.

"Them." Jim Cypress's voice was sharp. It sounded exactly like the voice of the Archangel Gabriel speaking for truth and righteousness. Cecile had never heard such a wonderful voice in her life.

Reggie and Amy Peele didn't say a word. They stood, silent, sick, smelly. Finally Amy spit on the ground, gagged, and spoke. "Get this shit off me."

46

THE unfortunate thing about the arrest of Amy and Reggie Peele was that not a single officer was willing to put the two suspects into the Miami Beach paddy wagon. Finally a maintenance worker appeared from the depths of Parrot Jungle and suggested he hose down the couple with the long hose used to clean the animal cages.

"See, first you spray, then add a little disinfectant to the hose device here, then spray again, then one more time with some clear water. We even used it on the turtle area once when old Mossback died. Dead for three days before we found him by the smell."

Not until the Peeles were satisfactorily cleaned and caged did Sister Cecile beckon to Sister Raphael and Leonie to come forth from the jungle and show the videotape to the arresting officer.

Jim Cypress watched from the side. He was silent now, having said his piece. The Internal Affairs man stepped forward as Raphael and Leonie emerged from the bushes.

"See, you can view the confession right here," Leonie pointed out to Chief Inspector Cruz, Internal Affairs. "I have the entire thing on tape. Push this switch."

"I know. You think adults don't know how to use this stuff?" Mark Cruz asked.

Leonie shrugged. Then she ran the tape.

"I'd like to declare this tape evidence," he said when it was over. "Will you sign a statement as to the time and place where it was taken?"

"Certainly, Officer," Leonie said politely. She was doing it again, being polite, confounding both nuns with her careful words and good posture.

Sister Cecile was suspicious of Leonie's demeanor. Too polite by far. She turned to Raphael with a whisper. "I think she's going to turn herself in to the police. This just isn't the time. We've got to get her out of here. Can you do it?"

Raphael pursed her lips. "Think of an excuse to get her in the Jaguar. Then I'll just take off for the Beach. She won't stand a chance. I'll kidnap her. She won't dare jump out of a moving car."

"Knowing Leonie, she might. First she's got to sign a statement about the videotape. Then I'll ask her to sit in the car a minute. I'll tell her I want to talk with her privately. But before I get there, you take off with her," Cecile murmured. Then Cecile put a smile on her face and turned to the policeman who was still talking to Leonie about the filming of the confession.

Cecile came close. "Where should Leonie sign, Officer? We can have Sister Raphael as witness, too, or will I be enough? Do you need paper?"

"I'll get some." The policeman headed for his car.

"Leonie, as soon as you do this, run over to the Jaguar. I want to ask you something," Sister Cecile said. "Privately."

Leonie looked puzzled, but she nodded.

Soon everything was in writing. Leonie carefully signed her name, Sister Raphael countersigned, and then Sister Cecile put her signature beneath them both. Finally two policemen witnessed the statement.

"Chain of evidence," a policeman muttered as he carefully wrapped the signed paper around the tape. "This will go right to the station-house evidence room and get locked up."

As he was speaking Cecile caught Leonie's eye and nodded at the car. Raphael headed over in the same direction as soon as she saw the gesture.

"Officer," Leonie said, looking at Cecile, then back at the policeman, "I'll have to talk to you. Later. Hang on."

Leonie skipped over to the car while Cecile deliberately asked Mark Cruz some pertinent questions. He was helpful, but somewhere along the line he realized that he was speaking with a woman for whom an all points bulletin had been recently put out. "I'm afraid I'll have to ask you to come to the station," he said politely. "We have to clear this up, although it's obvious from the tape that the charge is erroneous. At least as far as the murder of Nica Rabelais goes. Maybe you can clarify things, Sister."

"Absolutely, Officer Cruz. Would it be all right if I drive over in the truck? I borrowed it for the evening, and the owner was quite concerned that he get it back in good shape."

"We'll even give you a police escort for that truck," Cruz replied. He wrinkled his nose at the pervasive scent of the sprayed toilet contents. "If you promise not to use that hose again."

Sister Cecile tried to look angelic, and somehow, in spite of her being dressed in the tan coveralls, her hair mussed and flattened by a series of wigs, she did resemble a heavenly messenger. "I wouldn't touch that hose again for the world. I never imagined what awesome power it held."

Out of the corner of her eye she saw the black Jaguar pull out of the parking lot and tear off down Old Cutler Road. Yes!

Jim Cypress finally spoke.

"A discussion is definitely in order," Jim murmured. "I think it's time we explained our problem, Cecile. Now that she's safely out of the way." He nodded to the empty space where the Jag had been.

"Yes," Cecile agreed. "Amy's safely in custody." She winked at Jim. Of course he had been referring to Leonie. Hopefully Raphael would have hidden the child somewhere in anticipation of this development. They would do their best to keep Leonie out of this for now, but the truth would have to come out. "Shall we all go back?"

Forty-five minutes later Sister Cecile, Jim Cypress, and Officer Mark Cruz were sitting around a small, bleak table in the station house drinking thick, black coffee. A cold breeze was pouring down on them from the air-conditioning outlet above; clanging sounds came from somewhere. A tape recorder was in front of them, turned on.

"I was hired to discover the murderer of Elliot Barclay," Sister Cecile said. "And for a while I didn't know how it happened. I discovered the truth from Leonie Drail. Then Jim found out."

Jim Cypress looked down at the table.

"Go ahead." Officer Cruz looked at Jim.

The Indian's face showed nothing as he brought his eyes up, then he talked. "I suspected Leonie Drail knew something right away. I'm good at reading kids, and I could see she was in trouble. So I got to know her. Bought her an ice cream. After she told Cecile, she told me. Then we both knew all about Elliot Barclay's death."

"That kid killed Barclay?" Cruz was incredulous.

Jim spoke. "No, not like that. It was the other way around. Barclay tried to kill Leonie Drail. She's Sister Cecile's charge for the moment, until her dad gets back. He's a government official on assignment."

"No kidding." Mark Cruz was duly impressed. "Go on."

Jim began stringing words together. "Well, Leonie was

walking home from a friend's house that night. Elliot Barclay was out on the town. He'd killed a prostitute the night before. He was looking for another one and he thought Leonie was a hooker, a kid hooker, and tried to get her. He'd been on a binge, and he was still on it. He had AIDS, see, and apparently he blamed his having the disease on the working-girl population. So he was going to kill Leonie, thinking she was a kid prostitute. He grabbed her, pulled a gun and figured he might as well rape her before he shot her, just for kicks. He slapped her around a little, there was a struggle, Leonie got the gun and was going to kill him, she told me, then realized she couldn't pull the trigger. She just froze. Elliot Barclay grabbed the gun, yanked it out of her hands and it went off."

"Dear God," Cruz murmured.

"Elliot Barclay killed himself. She said his thumb was on the trigger. It was an accidental death."

It was a long speech for Jim Cypress and when he finished he wiped his brow, damp with sweat in spite of the cold air-conditioned breeze blowing from above. He looked exhausted.

Sister Cecile burst in then. "Jim was concerned that Leonie might be in danger, because by that time Nica Rabelais was dead. There definitely was a murderer out there. He was afraid if word got out how Barclay died, Leonie would be in serious danger. So he concentrated on Nica's murder instead. And there's the fact that Leonie's been through a hard time lately. Her father came near death a few months ago. Now he's out of the country. Jim and I didn't want to subject her to any harassment, even well-intentioned harassment.

"We were afraid for her." Cecile paused for breath, then continued. "Amy, of course, was in love with Elliot Barclay, and she killed Nica because . . . well, because of the AIDS, or maybe just jealousy, or something. You saw the tape. She's a woman obsessed. She roped her father into it somehow."

"Old Reggie. He would have retired next year," Cruz said. "Damn shame."

"Reggie didn't actually kill Nica, or anything," Cecile put in. "He just covered it up. It was his daughter. I suppose he had no choice. I don't believe he's really a bad man. He didn't want to kill me. He hesitated when he had the chance."

"Tough thing all around. So what should we do about Leonie?" Jim asked. "I still don't think she should go through hell for being a victim. You know how that is. Rape victims go on trial. That's why so many women don't press charges. It would be more of the same."

Mark Cruz was thoughtful. "What about the weapon? What happened to the gun that killed Barclay?"

"Leonie buried it somewhere. Maybe it's still there," Jim said.

"I think we'd better find out. Can you get her to look for it?" Cruz asked Cecile. "Like, right now?"

"Now?"

"It's time we wrapped this up."

"She's just a child. She's suffered enough. It's late."

"Cecile, we've got to end this. Leonie can take it," Jim said. "Can you get her now?"

Sister Cecile shook her head. It wasn't going the way she wanted. But few things ever did. "I think she's there. Maybe. I'll call the community," Cecile said reluctantly.

"We can meet wherever she says the gun is. I'll take a taped statement, and we can dispose of the case as what it was, accidental death. Providing, of course, there's some proof."

Sister Cecile's heart dropped. It was going to be hell for Leonie after all. Proof? What would the gun prove after all this time? But there was no choice. It never should have happened. "You don't believe it was an accident, do you?" she asked Cruz.

He shook his head. "Don't know."

"It was," Cecile said. "Really."

Jim and Mark Cruz looked at each other over the nun's head. "I think it was," Jim said. "But we've got to prove it, somehow. Barclay's fingerprints on the gun would do it. In the right places."

"Are you sure?" Cecile asked.

"Why not."

269

"Cecile, do you know a good lawyer in town?" Jim asked. "Just in case."

"Lawyer?" Cecile's mind raced. Was it coming to that? "I, I could find one. Not quickly, though. Maybe we won't need one."

"Here's hoping," Mark Cruz said. "I hate to go rough on her."

He didn't sound as though he meant it. Not at all.

A half hour later the black Jaguar pulled up in front of the police station. Sister Cecile was at the curb waiting for it in the dark, her face lit up by street lights and a fever of anxiety. It was late; too late, she felt, for any kind of an inquisition of this child. Should she have called a lawyer? Any lawyer at all? Maybe. Yes. She should have. It was too late. What a fool she was.

Leonie hopped out of the car and into Cecile's arms. "I'll take care of you," Cecile murmured.

Leonie didn't say anything. She just clung for a moment and let go. She turned her head away from Cecile and looked out into the night.

Sister Raphael was on her right, Sister Cecile was on her left.

"We should have called a lawyer in," she said to Leonie, "but if I interrupt you, just stop talking and we can postpone everything until we get one. Do you understand?" Cecile asked. "Promise me?"

Leonie nodded. She looked tired. Cecile suspected it wasn't normal exhaustion, but the exhaustion of bearing a heavy weight. It was about to be lifted. It had to be over.

They sat down together in the same chilly room. Leonie talked about the night of Elliot Barclay's death. Her voice wavered at first as she told what a beautiful night it had been, how Zoe had gotten stuck on the telephone with Raymond. Her words became precise. It appeared she had thought things out carefully. Sister Cecile was amazed. Mark Cruz appeared impressed. Jim Cypress smiled and met everyone's eyes, one person at a time. Sister Raphael merely prayed, her mind on things of the Holy Spirit, her old lips moving faintly as she lifted her heart and mind above the dingy, icy room and pleaded for divine inspiration for her darling.

Leonie paused when she reached the point of explaining how she didn't know what to do when it was over. How she felt blank, empty, devoid of reason. "All I could think was that they would accuse me of murder and I didn't do it. I couldn't even kill that man in self-defense. Even though he was not very nice." She shook her head in disbelief.

"So I picked up the gun again with the plastic bag, wrapped it up and buried it under a sea grape tree. After that, I must have cried for a while. I don't remember for how long, or anything. I remember standing under the sea grape, looking out at the ocean. Finally I went home.

"I cleaned myself up in the bathroom, then went out to say goodnight to Sister Cecile. I pretended everything was okay. I didn't want to worry her, you know? She worries and I hate that."

Cecile winced at her ward's words.

"I went to the kitchen. Sister Germaine had left me some cake, but I couldn't eat it. I almost puked. I mushed it around on the plate so Germaine would think I'd eaten it and then I dumped it. Then I went to bed."

Finally Leonie stopped. There was a sudden lift to her eyes when the words ended, like she had just remembered something. Cecile saw it. She would ask about it later. Meanwhile, there was this worry business. "You really must let us worry sometimes, Leonie," Cecile said. "We like to worry."

Leonie grimaced. "I've noticed."

"You say you wrapped the gun in a plastic bag. Why?" Mark Cruz asked.

"Well, I had the bag in my hand, and when I picked up the gun I just stuck it inside. Maybe so it wouldn't rust? I don't know, really. Dad always taught me to take care of things like that, like maybe someone would want it someday."

"Why would anyone want the gun?" Cruz persisted.

Leonie shrugged. "It was a funny-looking gun. It had killed a man. It was evidence."

"Shouldn't we have a lawyer?" Cecile put in. She was getting worried again, and it probably showed. She didn't even care. Let them all see her worry.

"All right, shall we go get the gun?" Cruz asked Leonie, changing gears. "Can you find it?"

"Sure."

"Let's go."

47

THE gun was buried under a foot of sand beside the sea grape tree, exactly where Leonie had said. It looked dry inside the bag. Dry and deadly. There was a brown stain on the barrel. It could have been blood.

Jim held Leonie's hand during the digging. "There'll be a heavy print on the trigger, maybe even one on the barrel the way he must have been pulling on the gun. I think that will wrap it up."

"You think?" Leonie asked.

"Most likely Jim's correct," Mark Cruz said as he dropped the gun into the evidence bag. "We'll have this through the lab early tomorrow morning. We already have Elliot Barclay's prints. We got yours before we left. A little checking and we'll be all set. Time for you to go home, Leonie. It's late. Get some sleep."

"Sure," Leonie murmured.

Sister Raphael yawned. She was still there, still hanging on, still praying, although it was way past her bedtime. "Come on, I'll drive."

"No, let me, Raphael," Cecile insisted. "You've had a long day."

"And you haven't?"

They got into the Jaguar, still arguing softly about who was more capable of driving, even after Cecile was behind the wheel.

"I have to call Gustavo," Cecile said, finally changing the subject. "Remind me when we get home, Raphael. His truck is safe in the police yard. Leonie, are you okay?"

"Fine. I feel just great. It's over. Some of it's over, anyway, at least until tomorrow." Leonie didn't look great. She was pale-faced and shaky.

"Don't worry. It's going to be fine," Cecile said.

Leonie shook her head as though she was totally resigned to her fate, whatever it was.

The rest of the ride home was silent. Sister Cecile didn't think to ask Leonie about the spark she had seen in the girl's eye at the police station. It had been nothing much, a mere flair of something. The thought had passed out of Cecile's mind as though it had never occurred.

Besides, Cecile was worrying again. What was wrong with her? Why couldn't she be like Sister Raphael and put everything in God's hands?

Cecile looked sideways at the old nun, wrinkled and peaceful. Raphael had so much faith, while she, herself, still struggled. Of course God let bad things happen, not, Cecile told herself, because he didn't care about mankind. Such things were the consequence of free will. Without freedom to choose evil, man was not free. Besides, she continued in her mind, God's son had died on the cross. Suffering had been ennobled for all time. But Leonie? Leonie?

Cecile continued her theological thoughts, her mind rambling this way and that as she drove slowly away from the area near the sea grape tree. They were close to home and in this part of town there were few people out. This was not South Beach. Here there were no people going from club to club looking for a life. No skin minimally covered by black clothing and high-heeled shoes. No pretty men with muscles. She saw no eighteen-year-olds kissing each other on the cheek European style. But it was no less wild.

Sister Cecile turned off Collins Avenue. All the way home her mind ran madly through her fears. Leonie would be off the hook tomorrow. Right? And of course the consortium wouldn't refuse to pay her. Should she tell the members she had known for some time about Barclay's death? What should she tell those people, anyway?

There were no answers.

Later, after a very long, soapy shower, as Cecile attempted to sleep, she pictured Leonie going to jail and her private investigator's fee flying away on wings. And when she finally drifted into an uneasy slumber, Sister Cecile dreamed of all the consortium members lined up, spraying her with the waste from Gustavo's truck, all chanting: "Whatever is useful is good."

Nobody slept much that night.

Leonie didn't even think about going to school the next morning. She got up at her usual time, went through the motions of eating breakfast and then settled herself down in Sister Cecile's room to wait. The nuns had all left for morning mass. They drove down the street to St Patrick's Church most mornings. Today should have been an exception, but it wasn't.

When the telephone rang, there was no one to answer it but Leonie.

"Maria Concilia Retirement Community," she said into Cecile's telephone.

"May I speak with Sister Cecile, please."

It sounded like Mark Cruz. It had to be. Leonie felt a moment of panic, then she firmed herself. "Is this Mark Cruz?"

"Yes, who's this?"

Should she lie and pretend she was Cecile? No. "Sister Cecile is out. This is Leonie. Is it all okay?" Darn, her voice was shaking.

"I should speak to Sister Cecile."

"Can't you tell me?" Leonie's voice squeaked. "Is everything all right?"

There was a long moment. Silence. Leonie felt her face flushing. She felt hot all over. Maybe she should run. No way they would charge her with murder. It hadn't happened that way. But it did happen that man had died, and she had been very much there.

"Leonie." He cleared his throat. "Well, okay, I can tell you, but have her call me, please. When will she be back?"

"Half an hour? Tell me what?"

"The fingerprints agreed with your story. No problem. Your prints are on the gun. They're partially covered by his on the trigger. Everything will be cleared up. We can list it officially as accidental death. Everything fits. We just need a finalizing statement."

"Oh, Lord."

It sounded like Leonie was praying.

When she hung up the telephone she wondered if maybe that was what she was doing. What in the world was going on in her life? This would have to stop.

Leonie cried when she told Sister Cecile what Cruz had said. It was one of those moments when they clung to each other, patted each other's backs and finally separated with two teary grins.

"So, it's all over," Leonie said.

"Yes." Cecile couldn't stop the smile that was splattered across her face. "It's all over. I'll call Inspector Cruz and then we can run down and finish anything that needs doing. Your side of this mess is going to be history in about fifteen minutes. I knew it would be all right. I just knew it." She paused and gave a rueful grin. "Then I've got to deal with the Benthamite Consortium. I'm not sure what to say. I deceived them, Leonie. Sort of."

"They were weird, weren't they?" Leonie asked. "I mean, did

they really care about that Elliot Barclay, or what? I mean, he wasn't very nice."

"Well, he had something they wanted. That was part of it. Something to do with business, an edge corporation, a list of people involved, some numbers. They assumed that the murderer had the list. That's what they really wanted. A list of names."

"List of names? Oh. That?" Leonie giggled. "No problem. Wait here a minute. I have this paper I was meaning to tell you about. I think it's a list of names."

DEAD SOUTH

Private eye Sister Cecile heads south to Miami, on special assignment for the CIA. Her job is to find a CIA agent who vanished shortly after he was seen drinking in a hotel bar. Sister Cecile's contacts in Miami's steamy underworld might fill her in on the agent's whereabouts—unless they decide to feed the nosy nun to the alligators. . . .

by WINONA SULLIVAN

Published by Ivy Books.
Available at your local bookstore.

WINONA SULLIVAN

The Sister Cecile Mysteries

Call toll free 1-800-793-BOOK (2665) to order by phone and use your major credit card. Or use this coupon to order by mail.

A SUDDEN DEATH AT THE NORFOLK CAFE

	8041-1213-4	$4.99
DEAD SOUTH	8041-1513-3	$5.99
DEATH'S A BEACH	8041-1568-0	$5.99

Name_____

Address_____

City_____State_____Zip_____

Please send me the IVY BOOKS I have checked above.

I am enclosing	$_____
plus	
Postage & handling*	$_____
Sales tax (where applicable)	$_____
Total amount enclosed	$_____

*Add $4 for the first book and $1 for each additional book.

Send check or money order (no cash or CODs) to:
Ivy Mail Sales, 400 Hahn Road, Westminster, MD 21157.

Prices and numbers subject to change without notice.
Valid in the U.S. only.
All orders subject to availability.   SULLIVAN

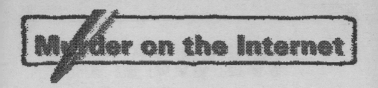